Pound Foolish

Neta Jackson
Dave Jackson

Evanston, Illinois 60202

Published in Evanston, Illinois. Castle Rock Creative.

ISBN: 978-0-9820544-9-9

Cover Design: Dave Jackson

Cover Photos: Beecham Street: Dave Jackson; Sky: Jake Hurst, www.designerfied.com; Money: Alex Slobodkin, iStock

Printed in the United States of America

Windy City Stories

by Dave and Neta Jackson

The Yada Yada Prayer Group Series

The Yada Yada Prayer Group, Neta Jackson (Thomas Nelson, 2003).
The Yada Yada Prayer Group Gets Down, Neta Jackson (Thomas Nelson, 2004).
The Yada Yada Prayer Group Gets Real, Neta Jackson (Thomas Nelson, 2005).
The Yada Yada Prayer Group Gets Tough, Neta Jackson (Thomas Nelson, 2005).
The Yada Yada Prayer Group Gets Caught, Neta Jackson (Thomas Nelson, 2006).
The Yada Yada Prayer Group Gets Rolling, Neta Jackson (Thomas Nelson, 2007).
The Yada Yada Prayer Group Gets Decked Out, Neta Jackson (Thomas Nelson, 2007).

Yada Yada House of Hope Series

Where Do I Go? Neta Jackson (Thomas Nelson, 2008).
Who Do I Talk To? Neta Jackson (Thomas Nelson, 2009).
Who Do I Lean On? Neta Jackson (Thomas Nelson, 2010).
Who Is My Shelter? Neta Jackson (Thomas Nelson, 2011).

Lucy Come Home, Dave and Neta Jackson (Castle Rock Creative, 2012).

Yada Yada Brothers Series

Harry Bentley's Second Chance, Dave Jackson (Castle Rock Creative, 2008).
Harry Bentley's Second Sight, Dave Jackson (Castle Rock Creative, 2010).

Souled Out Sisters Series

Stand by Me, Neta Jackson (Thomas Nelson, 2012).
Come to the Table, Neta Jackson (Thomas Nelson, 2012).

Windy City Neighbors

Grounded, Neta Jackson, Dave Jackson (Castle Rock Creative, 2013)
Derailed, Neta Jackson, Dave Jackson (Castle Rock Creative, 2013)
Pennywise, Neta Jackson, Dave Jackson (Castle Rock Creative, 2014)
Pound Foolish, Neta Jackson, Dave Jackson (Castle Rock Creative, 2014)

For a complete listing of
books by Dave and Neta Jackson visit

www.daveneta.com and www.trailblazerbooks.com

Chapter 1

FROM THE MOMENT NICOLE SINGER saw the long black Lincoln sliding toward her, she knew it was the same vehicle that had almost hit her and her two children a few minutes before as they'd dashed across Western Avenue in the rain. She gripped Nathan's and Becky's hands, lifted her head a little higher, and picked up the pace, ignoring the approaching limo and the large drops making their way through the branches of the overhanging elms.

The stretch Lincoln eased over to her side of the street—the wrong side, though there wasn't much traffic in this quiet neighborhood—and slowed to a stop as it came even with her. A dark rear window hummed down. "Excuse me," a man said.

Nicole kept walking, looking straight ahead to the far end of the sidewalk.

The car began backing up to keep pace with her. "Excuse me. Do you live on Beecham Street?"

Her six- and eight-year-olds were lagging, twisting to look at the speaker. "Mom, it's the McMansion man," Becky said in a stage whisper.

Nicole relented and looked.

The man in the limo chuckled, an easy smile spreading across his handsome features. "She's right, you know . . . big house across the end of the block? I suppose you could call it a McMansion, but to me it's just home. I'm Lincoln Paddock, by the way. And I'm really sorry my driver gave you a start back there on Western. I don't know why we were going so fast. I'm not in any kind of a hurry. Here . . ." He swung open the door to the plush limo. "I'm so sorry. The least I can do is offer you a ride and get you out of this rain."

Nicole hesitated. But Nathan tugged on her hand. "Can we, Mom? We've never ridden in a real stretch limo." At least her son knew what to call it. She hesitated, but Becky began to whimper. "Please, Mommy. I'm gettin' cold."

Nicole stepped across the parkway grass toward the curb. "I wouldn't want to put you out, Mr. Paddock."

"Please, just call me Lincoln. It's no problem giving you a ride. Please." He stepped out and held the door open like a gentleman ushering them into his coach. He was taller than Nicole and a real hunk under his black business suit. Nicole felt herself blush at taking note. How would she like it if that was his first impression of her?

Both kids had claimed the long side lounge seat, stretching out each way with their heads together in the middle. "Look, Mom. A TV in the car and a little kitchen with things to drink."

She could have walked all the way to the front and taken that seat, but it didn't seem dignified, all bent over from the waist, so she sat down on the far side of the back seat. "Kids, get your feet off the seats, now." They complied just as their neighbor closed the door and sat down beside her.

"Don't worry about it. The seats are leather and wipe right off with a damp cloth. Here, kids, let me find something for you to watch." He pressed buttons on the controller until a cartoon came up on the flat screen.

The car began to move, the driver proceeding without being told.

Paddock turned to her. "We've never met, but I've seen you in the neighborhood with your kids. So you are . . .?"

"Nicole Singer."

He extended his hand, and she shook it awkwardly. "Nicole. That's nice. Do they call you Nikki?"

She shrugged. Her husband was really the only one who used that pet name for her, but even then it'd been a while.

"After we almost ran you over, I thought I recognized you, so I told Robbie to go around the block until we found you. But," he chuckled, "what I want to know is, what you three are doing this far from home in the rain?"

Nicole was going to brush off his question by saying it wasn't that far and it hadn't been raining when they started out, but Nathan seemed to have two-track hearing. "We were at Indian Boundaries."

"Not *Boundaries*, dum-dum, Boundary! Indian Boundary Park," his sister corrected, proving she, too, was tuned in to more than the cartoon.

"Becky . . ." Nicole let her voice rise in warning.

"Okay, I know where that is." Paddock ignored the name-calling discipline. "No wonder you were rushing back across Western."

"Yes, we probably should've driven. Never can tell how fast rain'll come up in this spring weather." Nicole grabbed her damp blouse at the corners of the shoulders and lifted it away from clinging to her like a second skin, only to realize her actions drew Paddock's attention.

"Mom, can we have somethin' to drink?"

"Honey, we'll be home soon. You can wait."

Paddock chuckled again. "That's okay, but the bar's dry. We haven't restocked it for a while." He pushed a button. "Robbie, head up to Howard Street and swing by McDonald's to get these kids something to drink." He glanced out the back window. "There's another McDonald's back there a couple of blocks, but turning this thing around is like a battleship in a canal."

"But he"—Nicole let her eyes go wide—"he can get it through a McDonald's drive-thru?"

Paddock's chuckle was becoming characteristic. "Not a chance. We'll stop across the street, and he'll run our order over. I usually take one of our Town Cars. Robbie has to jockey this baby around in our cul-de-sac just to get it out of Beecham."

"Oh, please, don't go to any trouble on our account. The kids don't need anything, and you can drop us at the end of the block."

"It's no problem, Nikki. He was taking me home anyway." Lincoln Paddock looked at the children. "So why aren't a couple of bright kids like you in school today?"

His questions seemed far too personal, but when the kids didn't answer, she said, "We homeschool."

"Homeschool? That means you do your own lessons and, and . . ."

"And we get to go on field trips," Nathan offered, still staring at the cartoon.

"And your field trip today was . . .?"

"The zoo."

"Really? I didn't know there was a zoo in that park."

"Oh, it's not really a zoo anymore," Nicole said hastily. "Just a few goats and chickens." Then in case he got the idea that homeschoolers took field trips to nowhere, she added, "The kids have been studying hard, so this was more of a break than a real field trip."

"Yeah," Nathan said. "So when can we go to a real zoo, Mom?"

"Oh, you like zoos? Maybe one of these days, I could take you down to Lincoln Park Zoo, where they've got lots of animals. Would you kids like that?"

"Could we, Mom? Could we?" The cartoon had lost their attention.

Nicole's mouth fell open. What was with this guy? "Um . . . maybe someday, when Daddy's home." It seemed high time she brought her husband into the conversation. Though she had to admit, there was something enchanting about this ride in the back of a limo with a handsome stranger.

Chapter 2

GREG SINGER STOPPED THE JEEP CHEROKEE at the curb in front of his neat bungalow on Beecham Street and turned off the engine. "Okay kids, run on in and help Mommy with lunch. I'll be along in a minute. Just have to make one call."

"Oh, Greg. Not on Sunday." Nicole rolled her head back and gave him a sideways stare as the kids piled out of the car and ran up the walk. "You promised."

"It's not work." He grinned mischievously. When she didn't relent, he flicked his hand toward her as if sweeping her out the door. "Go on, now. I said it wasn't business. You'll see."

She sighed and stepped out, following six-year-old Nathan and eight-year-old Becky in her bright spring dress as they bounced up the walk. Greg gazed after them. Beautiful kids. Beautiful family. He was a lucky man . . . no, a *blessed* man, no question about that! The kids had their mother's blonde hair, blue eyes. Becky was already becoming tall and slim like . . . well, at least like Nicole had been when they'd first met. But the long winter had bleached the glow from her skin, and she'd become—how to say it?—more "full-figured." Had to be careful how he spoke of such things or he'd be in big trouble.

Not that the last eleven years hadn't affected him too. But he liked to think of himself as becoming "more solid," more like he'd played football than ran track. The wave in his dark hair allowed him to brush it casually forward to take a half-inch off his high forehead without it looking intentional. He was an executive in a sports industry and needed to look the part—trim suits, but open collars. He knew his hazel eyes and easy smile with just a hint of dimples caught the attention of most women, but he didn't flirt. Nicole was still the one to light his fire.

He punched in the number for Potawatomi Watercraft on his cell phone and waited. "Ah, Roger Wilmington, just the man I wanted to speak to. Sorry to bother you on a Sunday, but this is Greg Singer from Powersports Expos. I'm the guy who got you that prime location at the Chain o' Lakes Boat and Sport Show last February."

"Oh yeah, Singer. That was great. Best show in years. And they call this a recession! Can you believe that? Really appreciate what you did in positioning us."

"Uh . . ." Greg hesitated. Would Wilmington remember? "I'm calling about your cottage on Deep Lake. If the offer's still good, I'm wondering when it might be available?"

"Hmm. I'll have to check. My secretary keeps the schedule. When were you hoping to use it?"

"According to the weather report, the weather's supposed to be pretty good for the next few days. I know this is short notice, but, uh, now through Wednesday would be ideal, if that's possible."

"Ah, well, I know nothin's happening *this* week. Sure, it's all yours, Greg. My associate, Bob Kruger, went over there a few days ago and put the boat in. It's a brand-new sixteen-foot Crest-liner. You'll love it. Big Merc on the back and a Minn Kota trolling motor on the front. Crappie oughta be bitin' pretty good 'bout now too. Sure, you can have it. Listen, let me give you Bob's ad-dress. He lives just down the road from the cottage, less than a mile. You met him at the show. I'll give him a call, and you can drop by his place and pick up the keys. He'll check you out on everything. Okay, man? We owe you, and I wouldn't want you to think we don't pay up. After all, I'm lookin' forward to next year's show."

Greg took down the information, thanked Wilmington, and ran for the house, taking the porch steps in two bounds. This oughta satisfy Nicole!

"Hey, you haven't started lunch yet, have you?" he called as he burst through the front door.

Nicole appeared from the bedroom, buttoning a casual shirt as she headed for the kitchen. "How could I? I just now got out of my church clothes."

He followed her into the kitchen. "That's good! Forget cookin'. Let's go to Red Lobster." He grabbed his wife by the waist and swung her around a little.

"Oh Greg! We don't have to do that. I was planning on—"

"Come to think of it, forget Red Lobster. That'd take too long. We can catch some fast food on the way."

"On the way." Nicole pushed him away and stared at him. "On the way *where*?"

He'd wanted to keep the whole plan a secret until they pulled up to the cottage on Deep Lake, but he realized that'd never work. There was too much getting ready to do. They needed to pack—food, clothes, swimsuits, and beach toys—if the weather held.

Greg grinned at Nicole, imagining the joy a little getaway would bring. "Remember what you said the other night when I got home, how I'm never around to do anything with you and the kids? Well, like the pastor said this morning: 'This is your season. Reach out and grab it!'" That's what he liked about Victorious Living Center, even if it meant driving thirty minutes to the 'burbs. No doom-and-gloom from Pastor Hanson. "So I heard ya, Nicole. You've been working too hard. We both have. We need a few days away. The pastor promised we'd receive back tenfold what we seed into the ministry. Now I don't know if this is tenfold or not, but spring is in full bloom, and it's supposed to be great weather for the next few days—"

"Greg, stop! Just stop." His wife pawed at his arm. "You're not making any sense. *Seeding . . . spring*? What are you talking about?"

"A vacation!"

Her eyes lit up. "Really?"

"Yes. I realized this morning that even though the indoor season for Powersports has been over for a couple of months, I haven't taken a break. And now we're about to begin our in-water shows, which means I'll be totally busy until July. So now's the time—this afternoon. I've got a cottage reserved for us up on Deep Lake for three days. The weather's supposed to be beautiful."

A frown clouded her eyes. "But today? I don't know, Greg. It's so sudden. How far is Deep Lake? We'd have to pack, shop for food to take, and the kids have lessons to do. We can't just . . ."

"Run off?" He chuckled. "Of course we can. That's why you homeschool them, isn't it?"

"Well, yeah . . . I mean, no! We homeschool because it's best for our kids, but—"

"What's the matter, honey? I thought you wanted to do more things as a family."

"I did, but . . ." Nicole clasped her hands to the sides of her face as if to stop her head from spinning. "I do want us to be able to do more things together, but I wasn't talking about a vacation the other night. I meant I need you more on a day-to-day basis. And to cover for me sometimes. I . . . I just need a break." Tears were pooling in her eyes.

"A break, that's what a vacation is." Greg sighed. She wasn't reacting like he'd hoped. He'd always been more spontaneous than Nicole, but she usually came around.

Nathan wandered into the kitchen and looked back and forth at his parents. "Mommy, what's the matter?"

"It's nothin', snookums," Greg tousled his hair. "It's a big secret."

"A secret, a secret, a secret!" Nathan began hopping around.

"Greg, don't get 'em all revved up." Nicole wiped her eyes with the backs of her hands. "Wish you'd given me more warning. I'm not sure we can just take off like that."

"Why not? We haven't done anything like this for a long time, but that doesn't mean we can't start now. As the pastor always says, 'We're blessed and highly favored. We're the King's kids.' This is just one of the blessings. Of course we can take off!"

She let out a huge sigh. "I mean, we should've planned this *together*. I can't just drop everything at a moment's notice. I have the whole week planned, things that can't be put off."

Greg's shoulders fell, and he looked down at Nathan. "Guess we can't have any surprises in this family!" He knew he shouldn't have "used" him to make his point to Nicole, but he was exasperated. He looked back at his wife. "The kids like surprises, and so might you, if you'd only—"

A whine started deep in Nathan's throat.

"Ah, forget it." The whine grew. "No, not you," Greg told his son. "We'll do the surprise." He gave Nicole a glare as his youngest began bouncing again, quickly switching the whine to "Yes, yes, yes!" as Nathan scurried out of the room to tell his sister.

Greg leaned back against a counter, arms folded. "Point is, Nicole, this is a one-time opportunity. End of February we did a show up near Grayslake, remember? I had to stay over the whole weekend, and you never like it when I do that. But that weekend Potawatomi Watercraft, one of our biggest exhibitors, paid for a Class-A space in the fairground building. We had six Class-A spots laid out, but they felt the position by the main entrance was far superior to any of the others." He knew he was rehearsing details that wouldn't matter to her, but he was making his case. "Head guy said if I made sure they got the entrance space, he'd give me use of the company cottage for a nice getaway. And that's what we're doing!"

Nicole's eyes narrowed. "Sounds like some kind of a bribe."

"Not a bribe. A perk, Nicole, a perk! Their way of saying thanks!" Why did she always put a negative spin on things? Maybe it was her time of the month or maybe she was getting back at him for dragging Nathan into their fight. He clenched his teeth and drew a deep breath. Yeah, it had become a fight. He had to dial it down if he wanted to salvage this trip. This was no time to argue over things that would probably evaporate once they both got a little rest.

After staring at each other for a few moments, Nicole shrugged and turned away, then started to make coffee. "Why right now? Why couldn't we talk about this, plan for it, put it on the calendar?"

Greg sighed, intending to count to ten, but he only got to three. "'Cause I wanted it to be a surprise. Look, it's May. Spring's here. Weather guy said it's gonna be nice for the next few days, maybe even up in the seventies with some sun. I thought you'd like it, thought it was what you were asking for. Look, you can get some rest, catch a few rays lounging on the dock to get some color back in your skin."

A grimace flitted across her face. Oops, he shouldn't have said that. "What I mean, honey, is you deserve a break. *You* need a blessing. Didn't you listen to the pastor this morning?"

"Oh, don't go there, Greg. That's not fair." Nicole shook her head and then took a deep breath and turned back to him. "Okay. Let me get this straight. You want us to pack up right now—before we've even had anything to eat—and head off to this Deep Lake, wherever it is, for the next few days. The lessons I have planned for the kids require a computer to—"

"Look, they need a break too. Public schools have spring breaks, don't they?"

"They already had it back in April."

"But you didn't take time off, did you?"

"Well, not really, a day here and there. But . . ."

"There you go. The kids need a spring break. And the good thing about homeschooling is, we're flexible. We can schedule *our* spring break according to warmer weather." He could see she was running out of excuses, but he had to be careful. Try to close the deal too soon and it could backfire in a swirl of hurt feelings. "Look, if you really don't want to go, we don't have to. I might be able to get the cottage for some other time. It's just that it's available now, and I'm free till Wednesday, so think about it, please?"

Nicole threw her hands up. "Oh, I guess so. But you really don't understand what I was talking about the other night." She closed her eyes. "How much do we have to pack? Do we have to bring bedding and food and everything?"

He hadn't thought that through. He'd only envisioned taking personal clothes. "Okay. I hear you now." He held out his hands to calm her. "The place is supposed to be fully furnished, outfitted kitchen, cable TV, boat, everything, so I'm sure they have bedding. They use it for hosting manufacturer reps and big customers. But if it'd make you more comfortable, we can bring sleeping bags just in case. As for food, Lake Villa's real close. We can zip into town for food."

"Greg, that's okay for groceries, but what about things like salt and pepper, coffee, sugar—stuff I could bring from home so we wouldn't have to spend the—"

"Maybe it's already there."

She rolled her eyes.

Greg knew he needed to compromise. "All right. What if we all calm down and go to Red Lobster for now. Then we'll come home and pack—on the minimal side—and head up there first thing tomorrow morning?"

Relief flooded over Nicole's face, and Greg knew they had a plan.

The cottage was far more beautiful than Greg had imagined—high cathedral ceilings, open beams, floor-to-ceiling stone fireplace, and the lakeside was all windows. And it was fully equipped with everything but fresh groceries. They didn't have to use their sleeping bags or even bring in the box of condiments and assorted staples Nicole had packed. In fact, when Greg went by Bob Kruger's to pick up the key, Bob told him that when they left all they had to do was strip the beds they'd used and the maid service would take care of everything, including cleaning the cottage.

A few clouds gathered Monday morning after they arrived, but the temperature still reached 70 degrees before noon. The kids couldn't wait to run down to the lake to wade in the cold water, but Nicole remained unusually quiet.

"You okay?" Greg asked as he helped her put away the groceries.

"Yeah, I'm fine." She sighed and started making sandwiches for lunch.

Greg didn't believe her. He'd hoped that by the time they got to the cottage the tension from the day before would evaporate. Maybe he needed to give her more time. "Uh . . . well, as soon as lunch is over, you think it'd be okay for me to drive around to the east side of the lake to pick up some bait?" Wait a minute! What was he doing *asking* if he could go buy worms? Still . . . "What I mean is, Bob said there's a resort over there where I can get some bait. Thought we could take the boat out when I get back and let the kids catch some fish."

"They'd probably like that."

"How 'bout you? You wanna come along?"

She wrinkled her nose and poured glasses of juice. "Think I'll just sit on the dock and read. Catch a few rays, like you suggested."

"Sure, that sounds good. Though you could read on the boat, and we could all be together."

Nicole shook her head. "I just need some alone time. Besides," she glanced toward the big windows, "if it clouds over, I don't want to be stuck out there on the lake."

"Suit yourself, but you'd better bring a jacket or . . . ah, forget it." Greg wrapped a sandwich in a paper towel, picked up his Pro Bass cap from the table, and headed for the door. "The place I'm headed is called Jack and Lydia's. Be back soon."

Greg slammed the door of the Cherokee and took the narrow road a little faster than he intended. *Women*. Why were they so hard to figure out?

Chapter 3

GREG EASED UP ON THE GAS as he drove along the narrow road around to the east side of Deep Lake taking bites of his sandwich without noticing what kind it was. What was going on with Nicole? Why wasn't she enjoying this mini-vacation? Wasn't that what she wanted? He was the kind of guy who couldn't abide tension. He had to figure it out. Her happiness was his responsibility, after all.

Distracted by his thoughts, he nearly missed the sign announcing Jack and Lydia's Resort. He turned in and found a parking place between the scattered buildings. The older ones looked like converted barns and sheds, the newer ones like a cheap motel. He got out and headed for the end of the main building that had a sign over the door announcing Office.

Greg stopped on the steps and gazed down the hill where a four-wheeler, piled high with fishing gear, oars, and life jackets, chugged its way down the steep path to the lakefront. The ATV was so old and dirty Greg couldn't even recognize the model even though Yamahas, Hondas, John Deeres, and every other brand were on exhibit at the sport shows he organized. He watched the driver, who was wearing a "Jack and Lydia's Resort" T-shirt, roll the ATV out on the dock that extended into the lake and come to a stop beside the rowboats tied up along the leeward side. A man and boy, who'd been walking along behind, began unloading their gear and putting it in an aluminum boat.

Back on the grassy shore under towering cottonwoods, Greg noticed folks gathered around picnic tables or tending their smoking grills. A real family place. Maybe he'd bring Nicole and the kids over for a picnic in the next day or so.

He stepped into the office. Empty. "Hello, anybody here?" No answer, and no bell button on the counter to call for help. A refrigerator and a Coke machine lined the left wall while racks of life jackets and oars hung on the other. The wall behind the counter was covered with snapshots of bass and northern pike that guests had caught from the lake. In the middle of the display hung a mounted largemouth bass with a kaput clock embedded in its side. At least it told the correct time twice a day.

"Hello!"

The door in the corner opened and a short, stout woman with a haggard face entered the office. "Thought I heard someone out here." She spoke with a faintly European accent, perhaps Polish? "How can I help ya?"

"How's the fishing?" Greg had worked in outdoor sports long enough to know this wasn't like a drugstore where the clerk didn't know or care what you wanted so long as your money was green. He'd shoot the bull with her for a few minutes first, then get around to buying his bait.

"Crappie been bitin' pretty good, and the bluegills are workin' their beds. But we haven't seen much bass action this spring. Not sure why."

"Hmm. And the northern? This lake got any?"

"Oh yeah. There's a few. Fellow pulled in a twenty-eight-incher the other day. Fat as can be. Full of roe, I 'spect." She raised her eyebrows. "You want a boat?"

"No. Just some crawlers and wax worms if you got 'em."

"Right there in the fridge. Help yourself." She turned aside as though talking had wasted her time. Maybe this was more like a drugstore than he realized.

Nicole recognized the sound of the Cherokee's engine stopping outside the cottage. Greg was back. She sighed, expecting him to come in and ask her again to go out in the boat, like he hadn't heard her answer the first time. But she didn't want to bob around out there for the next three hours. In fact, she hadn't asked to come on this "vacation" where she had to continue making meals and doing housework but without the conveniences of home. It'd taken the whole time Greg was off getting bait for her to feed the kids and clean up the kitchen. Only now had she been able to sit down and gaze out the window on the lake.

The view was mesmerizing—a few clouds scuttling across the blue sky, the lake even bluer, birds flitting from lush bushes into the overarching trees—but she was going to enjoy it from the comfort of the leather couch where she could curl up to read her romance novel. Otherwise, she'd end up putting worms on hooks.

She watched him climb out of the Jeep. She didn't really know what was going on with Greg these days. He worked hard. He loved the kids, and she thought he still loved her, but . . . it was like they lived in parallel universes, filling the same space but not really connecting. Wasn't always like this. His every action used to be related to her if not focused on her. Those were the dream days, but lately she felt . . . what? Ignored? Not exactly. But unappreciated. Taken for granted. As for intimacy, well, it certainly wasn't what it used to be. She hoped he wasn't having an affair like the scuzzball in her novel. *No, no*. She shook that thought off. As good-looking as he was, she'd never seen her husband flirting with other women.

"Nicole, you still in here?" Greg stuck his head in the door. "Changed your mind about coming on the boat with us?"

She rolled her eyes. Her predictions had been accurate. "Thanks anyway. I'm staying right here. The kids are already down at the beach, but I told them to stay out of the water and off the dock until you got there."

"Okay. Guess we'll see you later."

His head disappeared and he was gone.

A gusty breeze out of the west kicked up a chop on the lake, but by motoring around the point to the north end of the lake Greg and the kids found some flat water. And it wasn't long before the red and white bobber on Nathan's line went under and stayed.

Greg scooted close to his youngest, eager to share the experience. "Hey, Nate," he said in a low voice, "I think you better wind in your line."

The boy lifted his pole.

"No, no. Don't lift it like that. Just give it a quick jerk, then start turning the crank nice and steady."

But they were interrupted by a squeal from Becky. "I got a fish! I think I got one!"

Greg hadn't even been watching Becky's line. "Then wind him in, just like Nate's doing." He looked back at his son. "Are you cranking?"

"I can't, Daddy. It won't come," Nathan whined.

Greg put his arms around him and helped, realizing he'd either hooked something pretty big or it had entangled itself in the weeds, but by this time Becky had a flapping bluegill on the surface beside the boat. "Swing your pole over this way so I can grab the line."

Nathan's fish was a bluegill too. And when they finally landed it, it proved to be the largest Greg had ever seen, almost like two hands sandwiched together. His son was so excited, he was trembling.

The hour that followed was not like those first few minutes of excitement, but by the time they headed back toward the cottage, they had enough fish for a good meal. More importantly, he'd provided his kids with an outing they'd remember. But Greg knew better than to ask Nicole to clean the fish.

"You forgot your phone," Nicole said when he'd finally put everything away and brought a pan of nice fillets up to the cottage.

"Sorry. Were you trying to reach me out on the lake?"

"No, your boss called. Something about your Waukegan show. Seemed real upset. Said you should phone him first thing."

The call from Chuck Hastings at Powersports Expos sent Greg and his family home from their vacation a day early. Two major exhibitors had pulled out of the upcoming in-water show at Waukegan

Harbor. Though it only ran Tuesday through Friday of the next week and had been small from the beginning, the deposits the departing exhibitors forfeited weren't enough to cushion the financial hit to Powersports' bottom line. Their large indoor shows in January and February had done well in earlier years but were floundering with the recession. To stay afloat, Greg's boss had begun experimenting by adding smaller in-water shows scheduled for May and June. ATVs and snowmobiles were out, of course, but most large marinas were happy for Powersports to bring in a slate of exhibitors and vendors for a few days that could attract a couple thousand visitors and perhaps a few new boat owners. But the profit margins on those shows were so slim, Hastings couldn't weather any cancelations.

"They're all blaming the economy," Chuck had groused when Greg called him back, as though it was news. The Midwest had been hit hard. "So get your butt back in the office, Singer. I need you to bring in some last-minute exhibitors. Empty slips and empty docks make the whole show look bad. Waukegan's a big sailing harbor, but get Lund and Tracker back in there. They did okay at the Chain o' Lakes show, didn't they? And we don't have any dealers representing them, so there shouldn't be any conflict. And how 'bout Ski-Doo and Sea-Doo? I don't see them listed. We've been cuttin' it far too close to the bone lately. We've gotta start erasing some of our red ink."

The kids raised a royal fuss about going home early, but Nicole didn't say much. At least he'd tried to do something nice with the family, hadn't he?

Back in the office on Wednesday morning, Greg could feel the tension in the air. Obviously, Hastings had communicated his anxiety to the other employees. Everyone knew the year hadn't started on a strong financial trajectory, but how could one bad show throw the whole company into a panic? Greg made the calls his boss had suggested, but most of the manufacturers cut his pitch short, said it was too late to manage logistics and do advance publicity, didn't make good marketing sense. A few said they might've managed to come if the show was closer to home, though Sea-Doo was built in southern Illinois, which didn't seem that far.

But the distance excuse gave Greg an idea. He started calling closer boat manufacturers. Starcraft and Thunderbird were in Indiana, but Starcraft reminded him one of their dealers was already exhibiting at Waukegan, and Thunderbird said they'd finalized their show schedule and budget six months ago and couldn't change it.

By late afternoon, Greg headed for Hastings' office. After explaining why his initial suggestions fell through, Greg reported on his own efforts. "The good news is, I came up with a couple other possible exhibitors, Rinker and Fluid Fun. Fluid Fun's out of Bristol, Indiana."

"*Fluid Fun*?" Hastings' face clouded. "Don't they sell kayaks? We're *Power*sports Expos, Greg! Don't mess with my brand."

"I know, I know, but you said we had to do something . . . how 'bout Rinker? They have some hot boats, and they might come." He paused until he saw interest kindle in his boss's eyes. "Only thing is, they want us to get them a fifty percent discount on the exhibit slip. Like I said, it's a slow—"

"Yeah, yeah, a slow year. Problem is, it's a slow year for us, too, so slow I feel like hiding every time Ethel comes in here to discuss the financials."

Hastings dropped his head, shaking it slowly as he stared at his desk. After a moment, he looked up. "Well, don't just stand there. Go sign 'em up for whatever they'll pay—but not Fluid Fun. We need to fill those other vacancies with boat people—anybody. It's bad for the spirit of the show if slips are empty."

By Thursday afternoon, Greg had signed up two more exhibitors, Extreme Cycles, a motorcycle dealership from Milwaukee, and Slingshot, manufacturers of kiteboards and wakeboards.

"What?" his boss roared. "This is May, not January. Besides, we don't do motorcycles. I learned a long time ago that cars and motorcycles are a different ballgame. And what's with these boards? They're not *power* boats!"

"Neither are sailboats, but they're exhibiting. And actual wakeboards require a powerboat to pull them. But that's not why I signed Slingshot. Kiteboarding has become a very popular extreme sport, especially along the beach just north of Waukegan

Harbor. Slingshot's willing to put on an exhibition right outside the breakwater."

"But we're not selling surfboards and parasails for a few hundred dollars. We want people who'll buy boats for twenty, thirty, a hundred thousand dollars."

"But their exhibition will attract hundreds of people."

"I don't know, Greg." Hastings shook his head. "And why motorcycles?"

"Because there are a lot of clubs up that way. They'll set up in the parking lot. It'll keep things happening. And they are *power* machines. Make a lot of noise."

"Oh yeah, just what sailors want, a lot of noise."

Greg pushed on. "And I've got one other idea. Now don't laugh, but what about ultralights?"

Hastings' eyes bugged. "Ultralight what? We don't do *light* anything!"

"No, I mean ultralight aircraft."

"Man, Singer, I think you're losing it. This isn't an air show . . . wait, you mean those things that are like a hang glider with a motor attached?"

"Yeah, and some of them use the same two-stroke engines that are in the ATVs and snowmobiles we exhibit in our winter shows. It's a pretty extreme sport."

Hastings frowned and chewed on his lip for a few moments. "But what are they gonna do, fly over?"

"Better than that. Get a load of this. You know the jetty that extends out into the lake just south of the marina? Basically serves as a breakwater, but it has a paved road along the top of it. Anyway, if the weather cooperates, they'll land and take off from that strip."

"What? It's not long enough, is it?"

"It's over four hundred feet, and these people claim the model they're bringing can take off and land in less than a hundred."

Chuck Hastings nodded. "Okay, okay. If they'll pay full price as an exhibitor." He stared off at nothing for a few moments, as though trying to imagine what it might look like to have a plane take off as part of his show. Then . . . "How about vendors? Make sure everything's covered. I want you to head up to Waukegan in the morning and see that this event has some pizzazz. Make sure the media's lined up. Don't rely on any secondhand promises. I want TV cameras and reporters and live radio onsite. See if you can get one of the local stations to broadcast from the show all day, like that talk radio we got in Milwaukee. Better yet, see if they'll come down and do this show. Whatever, but don't get any political kooks."

"Tomorrow? But I—"

"I know, you weren't supposed to go up there till Monday. But don't worry, I'll come on Tuesday for the opening. If everything's going smoothly, maybe you can come home early, soon as the show's over. I'll use some of the other people to wrap it up."

It was all Greg could do to not slam the door. No use arguing. Greg knew he had to do it or get busted. But now he had to go home and face Nicole.

When Greg told Nicole he had to go out of town over the weekend, her face melted like a candle in a hot oven. "Sunday's Mother's Day, Greg! We're supposed to take my mom out to dinner!"

"I know, honey, but this just can't be helped." How many times had he told her that lately? "But hey, I can't spend it with my mother either."

"Of course not. Your parents live in California, so they aren't expecting it. But we'd already arranged this with my mom. I made a reservation at Maggiano's and everything."

Greg felt a claw in his stomach. The truth was, Mother's Day hadn't even crossed his mind, which meant he'd also forgotten to send his mother a card and didn't have anything for Nicole either. He'd have to think of something for her, but right now, work took precedence. "Look, I'm sorry. I've gotta drive up to Waukegan early tomorrow morning, but Hastings said maybe I wouldn't have to stay the whole week."

"Greg . . ." Her voice turned pleading. "What am I supposed to do? Call Mom and cancel? She's looking forward to it." Nicole's mouth tightened and she suddenly straightened. "No. You know what? I'm still gonna take her out to dinner! So I get the Cherokee. You'll just have to rent a car."

The idea pulled him up short. With Powersports short on cash, he'd been imagining the brownie points he'd earn with his boss if he drove his own vehicle to Waukegan. And it kind of needled him that Nicole wasn't asking if he'd leave the car—more like a declaration. After all, who wore the pants around here? Still, Greg hated having to choose between his wife and his work. For the sake of peace . . .

"You're right, honey. I'm really sorry to miss Mother's Day—for your mom, and for you too. The least I can do is leave the car like you suggested. I'll rent a car for the weekend at least. You can have the Cherokee." There. Hopefully that would restore some peace to the ol' *hacienda*.

"Thanks." Her voice was flat as she turned away and headed for the basement with a laundry basket.

"Tell you what," he called after her, "if things fall into place over the weekend, I'll come home Sunday night to see you and the kids before going back on Monday. Sound good?" No answer. Huh. If this was peace, it was a grudging peace at best.

When he crawled into bed that night, Nicole turned her back to him even though they would be separated for the next few days. He sighed silently. How different things had become from when they were first married.

Chapter 4

FRIDA LILLQUIST WAS SITTING on the bottom step of her six-flat apartment building Sunday morning when Nicole parked the Cherokee out front. That seemed strange to Nicole, especially since her mother looked dressed for church.

"We're running a little late, so stay in the car," Nicole said to the kids as she got out. "Mom?"

"Oh, good. I was worried you might have run into traffic."

"Not traffic. Just getting the kids out the door by myself."

"Where's Greg?" Mrs. Lillquist still hadn't stood up as Nicole approached.

"Oh, he's up in Waukegan. Had to work this whole week. Mom . . . are you okay?" She reached a hand out to her mother.

"I'm all right, I think. I just turned my ankle and plopped right down here on the steps." She pulled herself up with Nicole's help. "Uh! I sat down kind of hard on my tailbone, and it dazed me for a few minutes, but I think I'm okay."

"You sure?"

"Yes, yes. Let's go or we'll be late."

Nicole slipped one arm around her mother's waist and held on to her other hand as they walked toward the Cherokee. Her mom was definitely experiencing enough discomfort to make walking difficult.

"You sure you still want to go to church? Maybe we should go back in the house and let you rest."

"Oh, no. This is Mother's Day. I wouldn't dream of missing."

With difficulty she managed the high step up into the Cherokee. But by the time they arrived at Hope Evangelical Covenant Church, her mother was able to walk in unaided.

It was the church Nicole had grown up in, and there were still members who recognized her and made a to-do over Becky and

Nathan and how much they'd grown since the last time they'd attended. Everyone was given a carnation when they came into the service.

"I want a white one like Grammy," whispered Becky.

"No. White is if your mother has died." Nicole hid a little smile. "The red ones are for everyone whose mother is still living." She winked at Becky. "Guess what, I'm still here."

Most of the service honored motherhood, including the hymn, "Faith of Our Mothers," which Nicole knew was just a knockoff of "Faith of Our Fathers." Why didn't mothers get a hymn of their own?

Maggiano's was crowded with Mother's Day celebrants, and even with reservations they had to wait a while to be served. Once the food arrived, Nicole's mother took her sweet time enjoying her salad and pasta, but the kids were antsy, so Nicole was relieved when they finally got back to her mother's house and sent the kids outside to play in the yard. Nicole insisted her mother sit down and rest her ankle.

"It's all right, Nicole. It hardly even hurts anymore. Want some coffee?"

"No, I'm fine. Please, I want you to sit down because I . . . I need to talk to you."

Frida Lillquist gave her a look, but obediently settled into her threadbare wingback rocker. "So, what's on your mind, sweetheart?"

"Well . . ." Nicole wasn't really sure how to begin, but she was already committed. "It's . . . well, I never really understood why you and Daddy separated."

Her mother's eyes widened in surprise. "Hmm . . ." She chewed her lip thoughtfully. "We never really talked about it, I suppose, because your daddy and I promised each other we wouldn't badmouth the other one to you. And we didn't, at least as far as I know."

"But Daddy's been dead for years, and I still don't know."

Her mother was quiet for a while, then finally spoke in a voice so soft Nicole could hardly hear. "Turned out there was another woman. I didn't know about it for years, though I sensed something had changed between us. One day when your father was supposed to be on a business trip in Toledo, he had a car accident right here in Oak Park at two in the morning. His secretary was with him. They were both injured, though not seriously, but bad enough to be taken to the hospital, and I got a call from the police."

Nicole's heart was pounding, aghast at the story. "But maybe it wasn't what it looked like."

"That's what I hoped, too, all the way to the hospital." Her mother's voice sounded distant, as though she were retracing steps down an old path. "But he was supposed to be in Toledo, and when the nurse mentioned the woman they'd brought in with him, I peeked into her room and saw for sure who she was. I was devastated, of course. Still didn't want to believe it, but when Eric came home the next day, I confronted him, and he admitted it."

Nicole felt as if someone had kicked her in the stomach. Gulping air, she asked, "So did you kick him out? Were you the one who divorced him?"

"Not exactly, but when he said he couldn't promise to break it off and not see her again, I said I couldn't cover for him. We finally compromised . . . for your sake—you were a teenager by then—and he left with the understanding that we wouldn't tell you until you were older." She shrugged. "You loved him so much, I just never had the heart to tell you even when you were grown."

Nicole sagged in her chair. "I . . . I can hardly believe it."

"I know, dear." Wincing, her mother got up stiffly from the rocker and came over to Nicole. Arms around each other, tears flowed for both of them.

A thousand questions tumbled in Nicole's mind, but she couldn't verbalize even one of them.

By the time Greg had arrived at Waukegan Harbor midmorning on Friday, advance people for some of the dealers and exhibitors were already there, checking out facilities and locations, making sure there were no permits still pending. Their enthusiasm always got

Greg's blood pumping. This was his world, and troubles on the home front would just have to sort themselves out.

The ultralight people had not only come, they'd already contacted the Zion Nuclear Power Station to confirm they had plenty of space for their little flights without approaching the two-mile, no-fly zone. Things were falling into place, but he still had a thousand details to attend to before heading home Sunday.

By the end of the weekend when he'd finally returned the rental car and Enterprise dropped him off at the house, it was almost time for the kids to be in bed. Nicole took the flowers he'd picked up in the floral section at the grocery store and arranged them in a vase. "Thanks, Greg. They're nice," she murmured. "Yeah, we had a nice time," she added simply, when he asked about her Mother's Day lunch with Mom Lillquist. She didn't bring up his Mother's Day truancy.

He left early the next morning, taking the Cherokee this time, to make sure he was on site before Hastings arrived.

When the boss climbed out of his Lexus at noon, he stood with his feet planted apart, hands on hips, gazing at the flatbed truck with the ultralight on it. "Aren't they gonna set it up?" he groused when Greg hustled over.

"Oh yeah, sure. The woman who drove the truck said it'll take them only a couple hours to have it ready to fly. They'll set it up early in the morning."

Hastings looked up at the overcast sky and frowned. "Hope this weather doesn't put a damper on our show."

Greg tried to keep his voice upbeat. "Yeah, might be some scattered showers tomorrow morning, but it's supposed to warm up later this week."

By Tuesday afternoon, the drizzle had stopped and the wind calmed down enough for the ultralight to take several flights, which kept many visitors interested. Greg started to feel relieved—he'd pulled the show out of the drink. That evening when he called home, Nicole asked how the show was going, no edge in her voice. Maybe absence did make the heart grow fonder. But he could tell she still wasn't her usual bubbly self. As the week progressed, he made sure he called each evening, and when the conversation started to lag, he asked to speak to the kids.

Those conversations were always fun, both kids competing to tell him what they'd been doing in school that day. "Hey, Dad! I'm doin' a project 'bout polar bears! Mom says we can go to the zoo so I can take pictures of a real polar bear!" . . . "Yeah, but polar bears eat baby seals. When we go to the zoo, I'm gonna take pictures of the seals."

But on Thursday evening, Becky asked, "Are you coming home tomorrow, Daddy? Mommy said you might."

"Hope so, sweet pea. The show's over tomorrow afternoon. Boss said I might be able to leave and let some of the other guys break it down and do the cleanup."

"Well, okay. 'Cause that means you'll be here for Saturday. We're having a party."

"A party! What kind of a party?"

"A welcome home party—"

"For me?"

His daughter giggled. "Well, yeah, we can do that first. But we got invited to a neighborhood party. It's for the old lady who used to live across the street."

"Not 'old lady,'" Greg heard Nicole say in the background. "Her name's Mrs. Krakowski."

"Yeah, Mrs. Krow'ski. Everybody's coming. I want you to come too."

Greg had no idea what Becky was talking about, but he said, "Becky, you can be sure, if I'm home, I'll go with you to the party." But he'd no sooner hung up than he wished he'd added, "If Mommy says it's okay." Should've checked with Nicole to find out what her plans were. Didn't want any more conflicts. He faced enough fence mending as it was.

He really did want to get home as soon as possible, but he had no idea what else he could or should say about Mother's Day. On the other hand, he'd learned the hard way that remaining silent about unfinished business seldom worked with Nicole. Maybe it didn't work with any woman, though it's what he would've done if he'd had a tiff with his brother or his dad back in the day. With guys, if they both left it alone, things usually blew over and got back to normal.

It was late by the time he fell into bed in his cheap hotel room, but he had a hard time falling asleep. Greg could understand Nicole being upset at his being away over Mother's Day, but there seemed to be more to it than that. Why hadn't their mini-vacation done more to calm the waters? He thought it was what she'd been asking for, but somehow, they were still missing each other lately, and he couldn't figure out why.

Two Powersports people got sick Friday afternoon—Greg suspected food poisoning from the taco vendor next to their management booth—and Hastings told Greg he needed him to help shut down. When Greg protested, his boss snorted. "Hey, man, whaddaya got to complain about. I probably won't get home till Sunday night."

Hastings finally let him go Saturday afternoon.

Greg had no idea when the party Becky wanted him to attend that evening was supposed to start, but an accident on I-94 turned the southbound lanes into a parking lot.

As a result, the sun was nearly setting by the time he got home, and he was met at the door by two bouncing kids screaming, "Daddy, Daddy, Daddy!" while their puffy eyes and red noses betrayed that they'd been crying. He pushed his way into the house and dropped his bag as both kids pulled on his arms.

Nicole came out of the kitchen with The Look hardening her features. "They thought you'd forgotten." Before he could think what to say, she added, "Well, did you?"

"Of course not. Didn't get away till nearly four and hit bad traffic—probably an accident." He gritted his teeth. What else could he say? She obviously thought he was responsible for these recent disappointments. But not wanting to make matters worse, he smiled to cheer things up. "But I made it." He dropped to one knee and gave both kids a big hug and smooch, launching them into the "wiggle giggles," as he called them.

Becky tugged on his arm. "Come on, Daddy. The party's about to start."

He looked up at Nicole. "Can you fill me in on this? What's it about?"

She shrugged. "Something to do with Mrs. Krakowski, you know, the elderly lady who used to live in the two-flat up the street. Mrs. Bentley—the people who bought her house—came by and invited us the other day. Said Mrs. Krakowski was returning to live in their first-floor apartment, and they thought it would be nice if everyone turned out for a yard party to welcome her home."

He decided not to say he barely knew the woman. "What time?"

"She said eight o'clock."

Greg looked at the clock on the fireplace mantel across the living room. "Guess we better get goin', eh, kids?" He eyed Nicole. "You coming?"

She waved dismissively. "Go ahead. I'm not quite ready."

"You look okay."

"I still need a few minutes, but I'll be along in a bit. Oh, we saved some supper for you. You can have it when you get back."

Food. He was suddenly famished. "We supposed to bring anything?"

She shrugged. "Didn't say. Bentleys are the ones who brought around those cinnamon rolls when they first moved in. She'll probably provide some snacks."

Greg wished Nicole was coming now. He didn't know that many of the neighbors. Maybe she did, could introduce him if he forgot a name. Wasn't like her to miss something like this. "Uh, kids. Give me a minute to change into some jeans and a T-shirt." But Nicole still wasn't ready by the time he and the kids headed out the door.

Across the street and a couple of doors north, twenty or more people milled around on the front lawn of the graystone two-flat. Homemade luminaries—tea candles inside paper bags weighted down with sand—lined the walk up to the door, giving the yard a festive atmosphere. As he joined the group, Greg recognized most of the neighbors, though he couldn't name many. He nodded at the guy who drove the big pickup with "Farid's Lawn Service" painted on the door. His wife was with him, head and shoulders shrouded in a pale headscarf. Muslims probably. Estelle Bentley, dressed in a loose African-print caftan, was trying to keep the kids from kicking over the luminaries as they chased one other across the yards in some game of tag.

Greg took in the sight with a smug feeling of satisfaction. It really was a great neighborhood, pretty safe for kids to run and play since Beecham dead-ended. And it was like a mini-United Nations—black, white, mixed, Hispanic, Middle Eastern, even an Orthodox Jewish family on his end of the block. He looked around but didn't see them—the father definitely stood out with his black hat and side curls. But the two gay guys from the north end of the block were there. He didn't see their boy, Danny, around this evening, but he was about Becky's age, and Greg had been dreading the awkward conversation that was bound to come up sooner or later when his kids asked why Danny had two daddies.

Greg recognized the father and teenage son of the black family on his side of the street. They'd sometimes waved to each other on Sunday mornings as both families headed out dressed for church. At least he presumed they were going to church. So with his kids in tow, he wended his way through the knot of people and extended his hand. "Hey, neighbors! Name's Greg Singer. We live on the other end of the block from you." He thumbed the direction over his shoulder. "Next-to-the-last house. And these two munchkins are Becky and Nathan." The kids nodded, but seemed antsy, so he nodded his permission for them to run off and play.

The man gave him a firm handshake. "Jared Jasper. This is my wife, Michelle, and our son, Destin." The man was a bit taller than Greg, solidly built, hair cut close, wore wire-rim glasses. Mrs. Jasper nodded toward the Bentley's two-flat. "Did you know Mrs. Krakowski when she lived here, Mr. Singer?"

"Hey, just call me Greg. No, didn't really know the old lady. I'm gone a lot with my job. But according to my wife, the new people who bought her house invited us to come tonight. Friendly folks, aren't they?"

"Uh-huh. You travel a lot?" Jared asked. "What kind of work do you do?"

"Event coordinator for Powersports Expos. You've probably heard—"

"Powersports?" The man's teenage son spoke up. "What's that?"

Greg smiled. What a job! It was as good a conversation starter as if he'd been a pro-basketball player—a dream that had died when he stopped growing at five-eight. "We do shows featuring sports vehicles all around the Midwest, though this time of year it's mostly boat shows. Say, you two got any interest in fishing boats, jet skis, stuff like that? Maybe you'd like to come to our next event. Gonna be down at Burnham Harbor, June 3 through 6." He winked at the son. "It'll be our biggest show this season. I might be able to get you and your dad a ride on a cigarette boat. What would you think of—"

Before either of them could answer, someone shouted, "Here they come!" and almost everyone turned to watch a pair of headlights cruising slowly up the street.

But it was the comment of a man behind Greg that got *his* attention.

"If you ask me, I think she could bring a great lawsuit against the city for what happened. You do *pro bono*, don't you, Mr. Paddock?"

Chapter 5

As the old Chevy passed the gathering of neighbors and turned around in the cul-de-sac at the north end of the block, Greg glanced over his shoulder to see who'd been talking about a lawsuit against the city. It was one of "Danny's dads" talking to the businessman who'd built "Housezilla" at the end of the street, making Beecham Street look like an English lane leading up to the great manor house. Greg chuckled. By comparison, his small brick bungalow and the others on the block seemed like peasant housing. How did that guy get three lots across the end of the street for his estate?

He casually joined the two men. "You an attorney?" he asked the tall man in the trim black suit, white shirt casually open at the neck. Greg reflected that he could've looked just as sharp if he hadn't changed. "Thought you ran a limo company. I see your Town Cars from time to time."

The man gave him a bland smile. "That's right. Lincoln Limo, but it's just for pickin' up the babes." He grinned wryly as he extended his hand. "I'm an attorney most of the time. Lincoln Paddock." He turned to introduce the other man. "And this is . . . sorry, but your name slips me."

"Tim Mercer. We live next door." He jerked a thumb at Paddock.

Greg shook hands with both men. "I'm Greg Singer. We're at the other end of the block." He turned to include Jared Jasper in the conversation, but by then Jared and his son had stepped away, greeting other people.

The Chevy pulled up to the curb and stopped. A lanky man came around to help old Mattie Krakowski out of the passenger side. As soon as he stabilized her with his offered arm, she gazed up at the two-flat, windows ablaze with light in the fading twilight, as though recalling a lifetime of memories. Greg wanted to ask what Mercer had meant about a lawsuit, but just then a lovely soprano voice began singing, "Should old acquaintance be forgot and never brought to mind? . . ."

"Here." Tim Mercer thrust a sheet of paper between Greg and Lincoln. "The words."

As the old lady advanced up the candlelit walk, she stopped every few steps and peered around at the chorus of neighbors as if she couldn't believe her rheumy eyes. When the song finally ended, several people shouted, "Welcome home, Mrs. Krakowski!" as Harry and Estelle Bentley escorted their new renter up the steps to the newly remodeled first floor apartment.

Once she'd gone inside, everyone stood in silence as if they didn't want to break the spell. Across the small gathering, Greg sighted Nicole. At least she'd made it in time, and like several others in the group, she was wiping a tear from her eyes.

"Now that was nice," said Tim Mercer, breaking the silence. "Good on her." He seemed genuinely moved.

"Oh yeah." Greg turned. "Hey, what were you were saying about the old lady having a good case against the city? What for?"

"Well, I'm no attorney." Tim glanced self-consciously at Paddock. "But it seemed to me the city might have incurred some liability when they failed to clear our street that day after the big snow. And when the city ambulance people couldn't make it in here, they just gave up and drove away. Mrs. Krakowski could've died in that basement when she fell."

"They left her there?" Greg couldn't recall the incident. Maybe he'd been out of town.

"Yeah. And nobody could get 'em to come back until later when Farid over there plowed a lane down the sidewalk with his pickup."

"Wow. I see what you mean. What do you think, Lincoln?"

The man shrugged. "Well, she might have a case, but it's usually not that simple." He stopped as if not wanting to offer any more of an opinion.

Greg arched his eyebrows. "Why not? I knew this man who went to Cook County Hospital with blood clots in his leg. For some reason he got overlooked and lay on a gurney in the hallway for three hours without any care. One of the blood clots broke loose and caused a stroke before anyone responded to him. He has some permanent impairment—not bad—but he won a three-million-dollar lawsuit over it."

"Oh, it happens, but it could take several years of litigation." Paddock gestured toward the two-flat. "Think she wants to spend the end of her life going to court over and over? And there are no guarantees."

"Maybe not," Greg said. "But shouldn't that be her choice?"

Tim lifted a hand. "Well, gotta go. Danny's home with a nasty chest cold. But I agree with Greg here. Just think about it, Lincoln."

Greg looked around, trying to keep an eye on the kids in the deepening dusk, and saw Nicole talking to an attractive black woman as the crowd started to disperse. "Oh, there's my wife." He raised his voice and beckoned. "Nicole! Over here!"

Nicole glanced at him and then went back to talking to the woman and Jared Jasper, who'd joined them.

"Oh. So Nikki's your wife?" Lincoln said.

Greg gave him a puzzled look. "You know her?"

"Not really. We just met the other day."

Really, and already calling her *Nikki*? The little crowd was breaking up and Greg beckoned to his wife again. "Nicole?" She finally broke away from the Jaspers and came toward them. "I was going to introduce you to Lincoln Paddock here, but he says you two already met."

Nicole nodded and seemed somewhat embarrassed. "Yeah, a couple of weeks ago." She gave him a shy smile. "Hello again."

Paddock smiled appreciatively. "You're all dressed up. You two going out or something tonight?"

For the first time, Greg realized Paddock was right. Nicole had changed into her white dress slacks, a pretty turquoise sweater, and sling-back heels—heels that made her two inches taller than him. She had fresh makeup on too.

"Uh, no, don't have any plans that I know about." He laughed self-consciously. "I just got home from one of our expos about half an hour ago, so if we are, ha ha, guess I'm the one who's not dressed right."

"I dunno, Singer." Paddock gave him a man-to-man wink. "If I were you, I'd take this pretty lady dancing somewhere tonight."

The whole conversation felt awkward and Greg tried to steer it away. "Yeah, well, guess we better collect the kids and get on home . . . oh, there they are. Becky! Nate! Time to go!"

The kids reluctantly stopped a game of chase that had them running all over the Bentleys' front lawn and bounced up to him. "Aw, Dad, do we have to? We're having fun."

"Yep, time to go."

As they started off, Becky turned back and waved. "Hi, Mr. Paddock!"

"Hi, yourselves!" he called after them and headed for his big house at the end of the street.

Once out of earshot, Greg asked Becky, "How do you know Mr. Paddock?"

"He gave us a ride in his big black car the other day, didn't he, Mommy?"

Greg looked at Nicole, waiting for an explanation, but all she said was, "That's right, honey."

What was *that* all about?

They walked on in silence until Greg's curiosity got the best of him. "So, why'd he give you a ride in his limo?"

"'Cause it was raining," Becky said matter-of-factly.

Nathan bounced around in front of them and skipped backwards. "An' he was gonna take us to the zoo yesterday, but he had to go to jail."

"Not jail," corrected Becky. "He had to go to court."

"Same thing."

"No it's not."

"Yes it is. I saw it on TV. You go to court and then they put you in jail."

Court? Greg frowned. Paddock had said he'd only met Nicole the other day, but she had worked as a paralegal for several years before the kids came along. "So, Nicole, did you know Paddock was a lawyer?"

"No, really? Hmm." Her voice sounded unconcerned. "I just thought he ran that limo company."

Lincoln Paddock was an attorney? The thought distracted Nicole all the way to church the next morning. When he'd called her to apologize for not taking the kids to the zoo because he had to go to court, it hadn't crossed her mind he might be an attorney. Someone with a limo company would undoubtedly have legal business from time to time or maybe it was a traffic violation, so she'd just dismissed the comment as one of those things.

But Greg said he was an attorney. That was intriguing. Did he practice as part of a firm? Or was the limo company his primary business?

What if she'd continued down that track? Would she be an attorney by now? It had always been a glamorous world to her, something she'd enjoyed from the day she got her first job as a legal assistant just out of college. That job had been with a commercial real estate attorney's office—no litigation, no courtroom drama. But she'd still liked it and within a year became a paralegal with plans to go to law school and study for the bar. However, once the kids came along Greg had felt strongly she should focus on parenting.

And she'd agreed. In fact, it had been her choice to do homeschooling. She was organized and disciplined. She could do it well. But there'd always been that *what-if* in the back of her mind. What if she'd become an attorney?

She didn't know that much about Lincoln Paddock, but the allure that surrounded him was how she'd imagined being an attorney—successful, suave, big house. The tingle of riding with him in the back of his stretch limo came back to her as Greg pulled the Cherokee into the church parking lot. The way he'd smiled at her and paid such focused attention.

The fact that he'd remembered his promise to take the kids to the zoo showed how thoughtful he was. And then when he couldn't make it, he'd taken the trouble to call and apologize beforehand, not afterward. Greg used to be considerate like that, but lately he'd blown through her expectations as though she ought to just understand the pressures of his job without him having to say anything.

Was this the kind of change in behavior her mother had noticed before discovering her father was being unfaithful? Hopefully that wasn't what was going on with Greg! She had no reason to think there was someone else. On the other hand, they'd been married for over ten years; and the fire in their relationship that had once crackled and snapped now smoldered like a dimly burning wick drowning in a puddle of melted wax.

Surely the fire wouldn't grow cold with someone like Lincoln.

Nicole almost stumbled on the steps going up to the balcony of Victorious Living Center. What was she *thinking*? The mystery of how her father had fallen for another woman washed over her. Was this what had happened to him? Had it all started by following a *what-if* muse? It'd been one of the questions she hadn't been able to ask her mother. Perhaps her mother wouldn't have known the answer. But it shouldn't matter. Nicole shook herself. She wasn't her father! She wouldn't follow in his steps.

From their seats high in the stadium-like auditorium of the Victorious Living Center, it was easier for Greg and Nicole to watch Pastor Hanson on one of the huge overhead screens than to squint at him way down on the stage. He was a large man, not necessarily overweight but, at fifty-five, a little soft looking, Greg had to admit. Still, his wardrobe was impeccable, and he never sported a five o'clock shadow or the need for a haircut. Squeaky-clean.

He stepped up to the clear plastic pulpit and plopped his open Bible on it with a thud. "Continuing our series, 'God's Blessings for You Today,' turn with me this morning to Galatians three, beginning with verse thirteen."

Since the Scripture passages were always projected on the screen, Greg rarely opened his Bible, sometimes wondering why he even bothered to bring it to church. But Nicole always looked up the verses, explaining, "I like to see them in context. Sometimes it matters."

As soon as the words were on the screen, Pastor Hanson began reading. "Christ has redeemed us from the curse of the law, having become a curse for us . . . that the blessing of Abraham might come upon the Gentiles in Christ Jesus . . . through faith . . . Now to Abraham and his Seed were the promises made . . . For if the inheritance is of the law, it is no longer of promise; but God gave it to Abraham by promise."

"Wait," Nicole whispered as she pushed over close to Greg. "He skipped some parts."

"Of course," Greg pointed toward the screen. "That's what those dots are for, those ellipses. He's just trying to make it clear."

Pastor Hanson continued, "Now there are three questions before us today: One, what did God promise Abraham? Two, who is Abraham's seed? That is, who's in line to inherit the blessing? And three, how is it received?"

The pastor had Greg's full attention. He'd missed last Sunday by being up in Waukegan, but this series was so exciting.

"Stay with me, now. I'm gonna be moving kinda fast, but in Genesis chapter twelve we find God calling Abraham and making promises to him. Verse two: 'I will make you a great nation; I will bless you and make your name great.' Verse seven: 'To your descendants I will give this land.' In Genesis thirteen-fifteen He promises, 'for all the land which you see I give to you and your descendants forever.' God is promising unimaginable material wealth here, brothers and sisters." Every verse the pastor quoted flashed on the screen. "And He can deliver. Don'tcha know that He owns 'the cattle on a thousand hills.' '"The silver is Mine, and the gold is Mine," says the Lord of hosts.' This is the promise God made to Abraham, and we've got a big God! He can deliver!"

Most of the congregation was cheering and clapping.

"And did God deliver, brothers and sisters? Perhaps you haven't noticed when you've read the Word, but in that ancient culture, Abraham became a wealthy man, a filthy rich man. We're talkin' Donald-Trump rich! And that's for you too."

Greg stood up and joined in the clapping.

"Anybody here have 318 male servants in your household? According to Genesis fourteen and fourteen, that's how many Abraham had. When Abraham sent his most trusted servant to find a wife for his son Isaac, the servant described Abraham this way in Genesis twenty-four, verse thirty-five: 'The Lord has blessed my master greatly, and he has become great; and He has given him flocks and herds, silver and gold, male and female servants, and camels and donkeys.' You gettin' the picture, folks? You gettin' the picture?" A swell of laughter filled the auditorium.

Having established that God had promised Abraham great material wealth and delivered on that blessing beyond anyone's imagination, Pastor Hanson proceeded to answer the other two questions he'd pulled from the morning's primary text: Who's in line to inherit the blessing? And how is it received?

"We're a Bible-believing church," Pastor Hanson often said. "That's why I always preach from the Word." And he did, too, floating every point of his sermon on a verse like individual snowflakes swirling in a Chicago blizzard.

"Don't you know we are the 'Gentiles in Christ Jesus'? Galatians three-fourteen says, 'the blessing of Abraham [would] come upon the Gentiles in Christ Jesus.'" Pastor Hanson zeroed in on his point: this promise of prosperity was for believers today. "We are Abraham's seed, in line to inherit the promise, and God never breaks a promise. Psalm eighty-nine, thirty-four says, 'My covenant I will not break, nor alter the word that has gone out of my lips.'"

Greg noticed that Nicole had her Bible open and seemed to be reading the whole Genesis chapter.

"That brings us to the third question," Hanson bellowed. "How is the promise received? Again, the answer's in the Word. We receive it just like Abraham did—by faith! Verse fourteen couldn't be more clear: 'We . . . receive the promise . . . through faith.' Simple as that! Do you want it?"

"Yes," half the audience murmured.

"Really? Doesn't sound like it. Do you really want it?"

"Yes!"

"Really?"

"Yes! Yes! Yes!" All hesitation gone.

"You want it today?"

That brought the house down as people again rose to their feet, clapping, dancing, raising their hands, and crying, "Yes! Hallelujah! Thank you, Jesus!"

Greg's eyes were closed and his hands were raised as the praise band began playing and a powerful soprano launched into, "It's a new season . . . of power and prosperity." The singer's voice was so like the woman who'd led them in welcoming Mrs. Krakowski back to the neighborhood, Greg had to open his eyes to check. Nope. Somebody else. But still . . .

"Do you believe it? Do you believe it?"

The singer's words brought Greg back to the present. But that connection to Beecham Street caused him to wonder what Pastor Hanson's message meant for him? He had a good job, and they were doing all right financially, but perhaps God had more in store for him. Maybe he and Nicole ought to start a new business. She could run it from home while she was homeschooling the kids. Yes, yes. What a teachable moment that would provide for the kids, to see an example of real entrepreneurship right in their own home! They might even be able to help out, depending on what the business was.

Ah, this was great! *Thank you, Jesus!* The education of children today had become so divorced from the family's livelihood. Used to be the whole family was involved together on the farm or in the shop, making shoes or selling produce in the marketplace. But now . . .

He felt as if God was giving him a vision.

Pastor Hanson's voice interrupted. "Be with us next Sunday as we explore 'The Law of Sowing and Reaping,' God's divine plan for exercising *your* faith to receive *your* blessing!" The pastor was talking directly to a camera that had zoomed in close. How did he know which one to look at? "And especially for you friends out there worshiping with us through television. You're as much a part of this family as those who are able to make it here to the Victorious Living Center, and so we want to provide a means for you to easily seed into our ministry."

Greg felt he was already seeding, and generously too. The next step for him was to receive the promise by faith so he could seed even more. He grinned to himself. Who knew where this would end? With a new lightness in his step, he headed for the Exit sign leading to the stairway. He would explain the whole thing to Nicole as they drove home.

Nicole had watched Greg's enthusiastic response to the pastor's message. He'd been on his feet, clapping and singing and raising his hands. It amazed her and made her realize she really was a lucky woman. Glancing around at the audience in the Victorious Living Center, she saw many women were there without husbands, probably single moms or wives whose husbands weren't interested in spiritual things.

At least Greg was interested, more interested than ever.

As they made their way out of the balcony and down to the lobby, Greg turned back to her. "If you'll pick up the kids, I'll get the coffee and cocoa and meet you at one of the booths."

Nicole nodded and headed toward the children's church.

If only she could feel more comfortable about the focus of Greg's passion. She wanted to trust him as the spiritual head of their family, but the more enthusiastic he became over this new direction Pastor Hanson's teaching had taken, the more she struggled to respect his spirituality. It seemed so . . . so self-centered, and she found herself comparing it to what she'd been taught in the church she'd grown up in. Sure, they'd had pledge Sundays and took special offerings for visiting missionaries. And there'd been the big capital drive to remodel the church basement into new classrooms, but no one ever offered an incentive. And yet there was that verse in Malachi that seemed to promise overflowing blessings to those who tithed faithfully.

She'd have to think about that, but she wasn't ready to swallow all Pastor Hanson had been saying.

Now where were the kids? They were supposed meet her right inside the door.

Chapter 6

GREG HAD TO WAIT IN LINE to get out of the church parking lot, but as soon they were driving east on Touhy Avenue toward home, he said, "Got an idea." When Nicole didn't say anything, he glanced over to see if she was listening. "Nikki?"

"Yes. What idea?"

"Actually, it wasn't so much *my* idea as a vision from the Lord, I think. Came to me during church." When she didn't ask what it was, he glanced her way again. She was still staring straight ahead, a small frown on her face. "Pastor Hanson's message inspired it. Wasn't it powerful? So clear how we're heirs of God's promise to Abraham!"

"Yes, but . . ."

"But what?"

"I don't know. Pastor Hanson applied that promise to our material prosperity, but to me, it didn't seem like that was what the apostle Paul was talking about."

"What? God made Abraham a very wealthy man, didn't he? I mean . . ." Did he have to preach the message all over again?

"Well, you're right. Abraham became rich. No question about that, but . . ." She sighed deeply. "Pastor Hanson read that verse in Galatians, but it actually seems to be talking about receiving the promise of the Holy Spirit. And he skipped over some verses in the same chapter that talked about Christ being Abraham's true heir." She opened her Bible and flipped through the pages. "Here, he skipped this verse entirely. 'The Scripture does not say "and to seeds," meaning many people, but "and to your seed," meaning one person, who is Christ.' That seems pretty clear to me."

Irritation tightened Greg's throat. Why did Nicole have to disagree with everything? "Maybe it's the translation. Your Bible's the NIV, and the pastor was reading from the New King James. Besides, doesn't the Bible also say somewhere that we're 'joint heirs with Christ'?"

Nicole was quiet. He gave her a sideways glance. Had he convinced her or just shut her down? Either way, he felt frustrated. If God had given him a vision this morning, why wasn't she eager to hear about it rather than debate details from the pastor's sermon? "Well, *I'm* for cashing in on whatever God has for us even if you're not."

She sighed deeply. "It's not that, Greg. It's just . . ."

He waited, drumming his fingers on the steering wheel as they sat at a stoplight. "Just what?"

"I don't know, it's this emphasis the pastor's been on for the last few weeks, it seems so self-centered. Like it's all about me. What's in it for me? Me, me, me. That doesn't sound like Jesus."

The light turned green. "Maybe we've got some wrong ideas about the life Jesus has for us. Maybe we've been thinking too small. I know I sure have. I grew up, you know, just plodding along, doing whatever was right even if it made me miserable. In college, when I transferred to the U of I, my roommate played baseball for the Illini. I didn't have any friends, but my roomie frequently invited me to go out for pizza with him and the other guys on the team after a game. I always said no because I knew they'd order beer by the pitcher, and I didn't know how to handle that. How miserable is that?"

Nicole remained quiet. Greg glanced in the rearview mirror. Becky was sitting behind her mom with her head down, hands folded in her lap as though she was about to cry. Why? Were the kids scared because they were arguing? If so, it wasn't his fault. He hadn't wanted to start an argument, just wanted to share his new vision with his wife, for pity's sake. But he had to admit the tension over the last few weeks had wound him tighter than an old guitar string.

"Hey, kids. What should we do this afternoon?" No answer. "Huh? Whaddaya say, Becky?"

"I dunno." Her voice was soft and muffled.

Greg looked out the window. "The clouds are breakin' up. We could go down to the lake. You wanna do that?"

"Maybe."

Not much enthusiasm.

Later, after a subdued Sunday dinner in the dining room, the kids ran upstairs to their rooms without mentioning the lake, something they usually responded to with glee. Knowing Nicole was still upset, Greg tried to make a gesture by helping clear the table rather than heading right down to the family room to watch the Chicago Cubs' game on TV.

She finally broke the silence as they carried dirty dishes into the kitchen. "Greg, I'm sorry. It wasn't right for me to shut you down like I did. If you feel God gave you a vision this morning, I ought to be the first one to invite you to share it."

"Thanks. I appreciate that, 'cause I didn't know what I'd done wrong. I mean—"

"It wasn't you, and I'm sorry. Why don't you tell me about your vision?"

Was it really safe to get into it now? She'd been touchy for weeks. Was there something else that needed attention first? Something he couldn't put his finger on. But she seemed open to listening. "Okay. See, I've been thinkin' . . . if God has more for us, it probably won't be a sudden inheritance from some long-forgotten relative, but it might come from something we do, you know, perhaps starting a little business, like a home industry." Greg set the last of the dirty dishes on the counter as Nicole started loading the dishwasher. "The kids are getting old enough that they could be involved. You're always looking for teachable moments with the kids. What could be better than providing them with an example of real entrepreneurship right in our own home?"

Nicole straightened, dirty dish in hand. "What are you talking about? You want *me* to start a home business?"

"Well, yeah, maybe. Of course, it'd have to be the right kind, something the kids could be involved in. Not anything that'd take you outside the home like selling real estate or anything. I mean, the kids couldn't be a part of showing houses to people, and besides you'd have to get a license for that. I'm talkin' about something you're good at, like . . . like cooking. You're a great cook! Maybe you could do specialty baking like cupcakes for birthday parties. The kids could help cook and take orders and keep records, and . . . and . . ."

Nicole gave a short laugh. "So you think I'm that good of a cook, do you?"

"Well, sure. You could do it." Though perhaps the idea of her baking cupcakes all day wasn't so good. "Or maybe you could offer a pet walking service."

"Dogs? What if they got in fights? I don't know how people do that, getting all tangled up in their leashes. We don't even have a dog ourselves."

He shrugged. "I'm just brainstorming. Maybe you could do some kind of a craft with the kids, like making jewelry. You know, custom-designed jewelry. People could use their cell phones to send you photos of them in their favorite outfits, and then you could design jewelry to match their outfits. How 'bout that?"

She finally put the dirty dish in the dishwasher and turned all the way around to face him as she leaned back against the counter, wiping her hands on a towel. "Slow down a minute, okay? Starting a home business is, um, certainly creative, but if we're talking about me adding to the family income, I'm a paralegal, Greg. I *chose* that field. I loved it, I studied, might even become an attorney someday, but . . ." She held her hands out in bewilderment. "I . . . I don't know anything about making jewelry or walking dogs or selling cupcakes. What exactly do you want from me?"

Greg put up his hands. "That's not it, Nicole. I'm not trying to put anything on you. It's just that . . ." How could he communicate his vision? Maybe he needed to wait until God gave her the same vision, in His own time.

Nicole blew out a large breath. "Greg, I'm not sure why you think I've got time for something else, anyway. Do you have any idea how long it takes to prepare the kids' lessons? When you're a teacher, it's the same amount of work whether you're teaching two kids or twenty. While they're working on one lesson, I'm busy preparing the next one. All day long. I don't see how I could take on anything else even if it was a good idea."

Greg sighed. "I'm not trying to make life harder for you, honey. I was just thinking, if we found the right thing, it'd fit right in with their education. Children used to be involved in the family business—farming, shopkeeping, weaving, you name it."

Nicole flipped the dishtowel over her shoulder and turned back to loading the dishwasher. "I know. But this is a different world we're living in. No more sweatshops."

"Nicole!" He knew he should drop it, but he couldn't let go. "You know that's not what I'm talking about. I'm trying to come up with something good for them *and* for you. Just think what it'd be like—"

"That's the problem, Greg. We've got enough on our plate the way things are. And right now I've got a load of laundry still sitting in the washing machine from yesterday." Nicole started the dishwasher and headed for the basement.

Greg watched her go. Was that it? The end? But maybe she just needed time to think about it.

Once he'd wiped the kitchen counters, Greg followed his wife downstairs. He could hear her transferring laundry from the washing machine into the dryer, but he went into the family room that doubled as the kids' classroom, using a long, low counter he'd installed along one wall for desks. The flat-screen TV was at the other end of the room, the old sofa positioned in front of it. TV and school lessons sometimes conflicted, but not too often. Today the Cubs were playing the Pirates, but when he flipped on the TV, he got caught up in watching coverage of British Petroleum's efforts to cap their Deepwater Horizon oil spill. A robot was trying to insert a siphon tube into the "top hat" dome to contain the leak. After attempting the same maneuver several times, it finally backed away, and all that could be seen was the wellhead with oil and bubbles spewing from it. A voiceover by a news broadcaster said, "We've just received word from BP officials that they think the metal frame on the tube has changed position, so they will have to bring the siphon tube back to the surface for refitting."

One more failure. For three weeks, oil had spewed into the pristine Gulf, yet everything they'd tried had failed to stop it.

Greg knew how that felt.

The commentator said BP had now spent several hundred million dollars attempting to stanch the flow and clean up the mess.

The program broke for a commercial. Greg frowned. So, what did that mean? Was BP telegraphing their intentions to quit? They couldn't do that. They had to keep trying no matter what the cost. Someone had to stop the spill!

He clicked off the TV. "Nicole?" When she didn't answer, he stepped into the unfinished portion of the basement. "Nicole?"

"In here."

He found her in their storage locker sitting cross-legged on their old steamer trunk, looking at a family photo album. She closed it as Greg approached, but not before he caught a glimpse of the page she'd been studying. He recognized it—snapshots from their fourth anniversary. They'd stayed at the Drake Hotel that weekend, ate fabulous food, and went out each evening. What was the play they'd seen? Oh, yeah—*Gem of the Ocean,* at the Goodman Theatre.

But it'd been on the Chicago River Cruise Sunday afternoon that he'd taken most of the snapshots now saved in the album. They'd supposedly been learning about the city's architecture while the guide chattered on as the boat slid beneath drawbridges and skirted glistening skyscrapers. But it'd been Nicole's "architecture" that held his eye. She sat in the back of the boat wearing a sleeveless pink top, sporting her long tanned legs in white shorts, the wind blowing her flaxen hair. She'd been so beautiful that day. In fact, as nearly as they'd been able to calculate, Nathan had been conceived that weekend. Thank goodness for the generosity of Mom Lillquist in keeping baby Becky for the weekend.

The dryer beeped and Nicole stood up, putting the photo album back on the shelf. "Laundry's finally done."

"Great." He followed her into the laundry room. "Hey, whaddaya say we call your mom and see if she's busy this evening? We could run down and see her, maybe take her out to eat at one of those Andersonville restaurants she likes so much?" Greg didn't much care for Swedish food, but . . . "I'd like to make up for being gone Mother's Day, for both of you."

Nicole busied herself pulling the warm clothes out of the dryer, then handed him the laundry basket. "Guess we could ask her, if she's not busy."

Quick thinking, Greg. Maybe this would calm the waters.

Chapter 7

CHUCK HASTINGS WASN'T IN THE OFFICE when Greg got to work Monday morning, and Ethel Newhouse, the office secretary, had no idea where their boss had gone. It wasn't an issue to Greg. He had plenty to do checking the invoices and writing letters to the exhibitors and manufacturers that had taken part in the Waukegan Harbor show. He needed to tie up all those loose ends and get a leg up on the final arrangements for the Chicago show at Burnham Harbor. He looked at his calendar and realized he was already behind on several critical details.

But by noon, his boss still hadn't come in or phoned. "I even called his home," Ethel said. "Thought he might be sick. But Mrs. Hastings said he left the house this morning before seven for some meetings . . . 'like a bat outta Gotham,' was what she said. I don't get it. I thought it was a 'bat outta—'"

"That's Delores, all right. To her, everything's Batman." Greg laughed. "Back when they were filming *The Dark Knight* here in the city, Chuck called in some favors so she could be an extra on the set, and she's never gotten over it."

"*Batman*?"

"Yeah, Batman lives in Gotham City, so *bat outta Gotham*."

"Oh!" Her eyes mimicked the oval of her mouth as she thought about it. "Well . . . anyway, she had no idea who Chuck was meeting, and I don't either. There's nothing on his schedule."

Greg shrugged and returned to his office. He had plenty to do, and his boss could certainly manage his day without anyone else checking up on him. But it was unusual. If anything, Chuck Hastings tended to micromanage his staff but in turn was unusually forthcoming, keeping everyone informed about what he was doing, new projects, and the company's direction as if he were accountable to his employees.

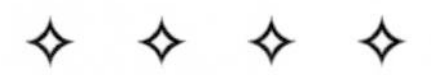

The next morning when Greg arrived at work fifteen minutes early, Hastings was already in his glass-walled office, sitting at his desk, talking on the phone. As Greg walked by, Hastings glanced up at him but looked quickly away without his usual wave.

Must have a lot on his mind, Greg thought as he entered his own office and tossed his brown-bag lunch into the cabinet. His office did not have glass walls to the interior, only floor-to-ceiling glass out onto the parking lot and a small window in his door. He had just turned on his computer when his desk phone buzzed. It was the boss. "Can you come to my office?"

Hastings was busily shuffling papers on his desk when Greg entered. "Have a seat."

Greg sat. "What's up?"

Hastings looked up, but his features sagged as he leaned back in his leather chair. "I spent all day yesterday having meetings with the bank, a couple of major investors in Powersports, and some of our creditors. Things aren't looking good."

"But I thought nearly all the exhibitors we wanted for the Chicago show were booked—"

Hastings held his hand up. "It's not just Burnham Harbor. It's the bleeping economy. And that stormy weather at Waukegan didn't help any." He sighed. "I dunno . . . Maybe we scheduled these in-water shows too early in the year, but I wanted to get a jump on the competition. In any case, attendance was way down, down by 38 percent over last year's show, even with your hang glider and kites." The pudgy man shook his head. "Once exhibitors get wind of such low attendance, some are likely to bail. I've seen it happen before. They'd rather lose their deposit and risk a breach-of-contract suit than mount a display, which of course has all kinds of other costs. We've only got one other show after Burnham Harbor, and I've already received three client cancelations."

"You have?" Greg frowned. "How come I didn't hear?"

"You probably would've, but when I realized we were in trouble, I started checking our key accounts. Like I said, three canceled and some of the others are so soft, I don't think we have a show."

Greg's jaw tightened. "Not good." He turned to gaze through Hastings' glass wall as Ethel and a couple of the other employees came into the office.

Hastings noticed, too, and got up to draw the drapes. "None of them know yet."

Know? Know what? Greg watched his boss return to his seat.

"I gotta pull the plug, Greg. Hate to break it to you this way, but I'm gonna let everyone go . . . except Ethel. I've already told the building landlord that we won't be renewing the office lease. Current lease is up June first, so I had to pay a premium just to get a one-week extension to take us through the Burnham Harbor show, after which we'll have one day to move out." The man slumped in his chair and raised both hands. "I may try to keep somethin' goin' out of my basement, but only to remain in position in case this recession eases up next year. Ethel can help me with that. But even if I go out of business completely, I'll need her to help shut things down."

Greg's mind was spinning. *Wait . . . Pulling the plug? Letting everyone go?* "But everybody?" Greg's index finger tapped his own chest. "You mean me too?" His boss nodded. "How soon?" It didn't make sense. He'd known things were tight, but Hastings had been spurring on everyone to lock in more accounts, line up more exhibitors.

"Sorry, Greg." Hastings shook his head. "I really feel bad about it, but I can't pay anyone beyond the Burnham Harbor gig. I've gotta close the doors the next day." He shrugged. "Of course, anybody who'll want to go sooner, can. But I can't pay anyone past June 7. And as much as I'd like to, I can't even offer anyone a severance package."

Whoa! Greg had to get his boss to back up on this thing. "Hang on a minute, Chuck. I thought the Waukegan show went pretty well. Didn't you?"

Hastings shrugged. "Depends on how you look at it. The slips were full, we had enough vendors, but attendance was . . ." He wobbled his hand back and forth. "And as you know, it's not the number of people who come through the gate; it's how many buy boats. And from what I've gathered from the exhibitors, only three sales were made during the whole show."

"But that's not our fault! We brought 'em in, so that's on the sales rep—the product, the pricing, whatever—but not us!"

Hastings snorted. "But we pay nonetheless. If the exhibitors don't sell, they don't sign up for the next show. That's what I'm trying to tell you! Huh. Maybe people brought their kids to see your motorized hang glider or whatever it was, but they didn't come to buy boats. They had no intention of buying anything larger than a hot dog—and they didn't."

Greg could feel his jaw working, pulsing the muscles at the side of his face. This couldn't be happening! He swallowed. "Look, Chuck, what if we hold off on this decision, do some strategizing? I mean, you've put together a strong team here. Let's work the brain trust and generate some viable alternatives." Hastings was shaking his head, but Greg pressed on. "I mean, everyone works hard here, but if they knew Powersports was on the line"—he jerked a thumb in the direction of the inner offices—"I'm sure we could all dig deeper and give that extra effort that would make it go."

"It's not you, Greg, and it's not the other people. You're all good employees. Give a hundred percent. I've got no reason to complain or put this decision back on any of you. But the bottom line is this . . ." Hastings' finger stabbed the papers on his desk. "When the investors saw the financials for last quarter, they pulled their money, every one of the big ones. And when the others learn sales have tanked and exhibitors are bailing, they're bound to pull the rest of our funding. It's out of our hands. I don't want to go into bankruptcy. This recession's gotta end someday, and when it does, I don't want a bankruptcy hanging over my ability to attract new investors. It's better to pull the plug now and avoid more debt. As it is, we're all gonna get the short shrift here. Even me!"

Greg frowned. "What do you mean? How?"

Hastings threw up his hands. "I'll be talking to our creditors, but I've got nearly half a million in debt hanging out there. I might be able to negotiate some of it down, but I'm personally gonna be eating most of it."

Unbelievable! "And the rest of us?"

"Huh, if gettin' laid off isn't bad enough . . . like I said, I can't afford to give anyone severance pay."

Greg sucked in a long breath, then blew it out. June 7 . . . not even three weeks away. How could the boss do this? He leaned forward, his mind scrambling. "Look, Chuck, if you're gonna cut that last show, the one after Burnham Harbor, there won't be that much for us to do. Why don't we all focus on recruiting new investors? If the old money's dried up, let's find new money!"

Hastings again shook his head. "I appreciate the sentiment, Greg. I really do. But it's a bird without wings. We don't have anything to sell right now! So who's gonna invest? I've been in business a long time, and I know what it takes to attract investors. Everybody's hangin' onto their money right now. All we have to offer is wishful thinking."

The man hefted himself out of his chair and stood in front of his office windows, hands jammed into his pants pockets, his back to Greg. "I've made my decision, and it includes stopping the bleeding, as soon as possible. All of it—the offices, the utilities, the phones, travel—everything. Monday the seventh is the last day, except for Ethel. Now . . ." He sighed deeply and turned back. "As you can imagine, I've gotta have some very unpleasant conversations with my other people. Could call a staff meeting, but I'd rather do it one-on-one. All I ask is that you not mention this news, and I mean not to *anyone*. Let me do it myself." Hastings came around his desk and headed for the door, indicating Greg's meeting was over.

Greg wanted to protest. There was no way Hastings would be able to call everyone in one-by-one without the others sensing something terrible was happening. He felt like yelling himself, and there was a good chance someone would. At least, there'd be tears. The others would figure it out pretty quickly. But—he shrugged—it was Hastings' call. *How* he told everyone was a minor detail, compared to *what* he had to tell them.

He stood up and met his boss at the door. Hastings' hand was extended, and for a moment, Greg was tempted not to take it.

"I'm really sorry, Greg. You're a good man, and you don't deserve this. Believe me, if and when I get back on my feet, I'll look you up."

Greg shook Chuck's hand briefly and then disengaged. "So what am I supposed to do with my exhibitors between now and the end of the Burnham Harbor show?"

"Good question. I want to tell the gold-star exhibitors myself, as a courtesy. But I could use your help notifying some of the smaller exhibitors and vendors. I'll let you know when to start. Just don't leak any of this to our major players, okay?"

"Right." Most of them were Greg's contacts anyway. Hastings hadn't ever spoken to some of them. But Greg knew why he wanted to do so now: It would put him in the best position should he decide to revive the business in the future. Made sense, but it galled Greg. Nevertheless, he said, "I'll be glad to help in whatever way you want." He nodded and went out the door.

A couple of people waved a good-morning greeting as he walked to his office. Poor suckers. None of them had any idea what the day would bring.

His office—half the size of Hastings'—for the first time felt cramped. What had he been doing here for the last seven years? Where had it gotten him? He sat down at his desk, head in his hands, and tried to review what had happened in the last thirty minutes.

His whole world had turned upside down, that's what.

His degree from Florida State had been in public relations with a specialty in meetings and event planning. Landing a position with Powersports Expos had been his dream job, combining his career training with his love for outdoor sports. He'd loved it so much he'd never given thought to a job in any other field. Hastings had been a good boss. And while he'd occasionally thought about starting his own business doing much the same thing, it would've meant a move to some other part of the country so he wouldn't go toe-to-toe with Chuck Hastings.

But now he was adrift—no job, no plan, no solid foundation from which to jump. However, he did have contacts, lots of contacts, prime contacts.

Lifting his head, Greg dug through the desk drawer until he found a box of blank CDs. Suddenly focused, he spent the next half hour downloading his email list, business contacts, and all the important correspondence from the last couple of years. If Hastings was right, sport shows might be cold right now, but shows weren't the only way manufacturers sold boats, snowmobiles, and ATVs. Greg knew the industry. He knew the market. He had contacts. All of those contacts and all of his experience in the industry had to be worth *something* that could land him a new job.

Greg leaned back in his desk chair, brow furrowed. Hastings said he wanted to call the major clients himself. But that hardly seemed fair. If he waited until after Hastings told them about the demise of Powersports Expos, Greg would have to approach them from a position of weakness, calling for help from a sinking ship. He'd be a lot better off talking to them *before* they heard from Chuck Hastings.

He gritted his teeth. This was a rotten deal. Why didn't the boss fight harder and let the staff help him salvage his business? It wasn't fair, because the staff was going to pay. On the other hand, if the boss was determined to close Powersports, Greg couldn't stop him, and he needed to look out for himself. He wouldn't spill the beans—doing so would be to his disadvantage—but he had to get to those clients before Hastings did.

Why not start calling now?

Chapter 8

Nicole turned sideways in front of the full-length mirror in their bedroom. She finally fit into her favorite white jeans she hadn't been able to wear for the last couple of years. And the little rolls at her waistline weren't so obvious either. Three weeks, only three weeks, but already her dieting efforts were beginning to pay off—smaller helpings at mealtimes with no seconds and no soft drinks during the day, and she'd been able to maintain a simple exercise routine each morning while the kids did their forty minutes of silent reading. Well, Nathan often needed help, which interrupted her, but still, she'd worked up a sweat on most days.

Would Greg notice? Just last Saturday at Mattie Krakowski's welcome home gathering, Lincoln Paddock had noticed. She smiled as she recalled him chiding Greg: *"I don't know, Singer. If I were you, I'd take this pretty lady dancing somewhere tonight."*

But he hadn't.

She stepped into the bathroom and freshened her makeup, not enough to be obvious but maybe enough to catch Greg's eye when he got home from work in a half hour or so.

Somehow things had to change.

As Greg walked the mile from the Metra stop to Beecham Street that evening, his mind jumped back and forth between strategies for presenting himself to prospective employers and how he was going to tell Nicole that Powersports was going under. Overcast skies had kept the day cool, but beads of sweat dotted Greg's forehead and pasted his shirt to his back. He slipped off his sport jacket and flipped it over his shoulder, two fingers hooked in the collar.

Just that morning, he'd felt so settled, but now . . . now they might have to move to some other city. He liked Chicago, and Nicole wouldn't want to leave her mother. He sighed deeply, glad that he'd suggested taking Mom Lillquist out to dinner the other night. At least that demonstrated he cared about her. And she adored the kids so much. She'd be lost if they moved away. Necessity could be such a cruel master. If they had to move, he and Nicole would have to be sure to plan frequent visits.

So far, he'd only called contacts at two companies that afternoon to feel out job opportunities. "Greg," said Tony Barns at the Sea-Doo plant in Brenton, Illinois, "I don't think you wanna be lookin' down in this neck of the woods right now."

"Whaddaya mean?"

"Well, rumors come and go like the seasons, you know, but this time I think Bombardier Recreational Products is getting serious about closing our plant. Might not be right away, but I'm pretty sure it's gonna happen. I just hope I can retire first, or I'll be calling you for job openings up there in Chicago. Ha, ha, ha."

"You serious?"

"Oh yeah. I'm serious." Tony's voice dropped to a whisper. "But don't tell anyone I said so, or I might have to track you down and gag you. Get my drift?" His voice returned to normal. "Seriously, I'm only tellin' you as a friend. *Comprende, amigo*?"

"Gotcha."

"Good. So, why are you lookin' around? Thought you liked it at Powersports."

"Oh, I do, it's just that . . . well, you know, for career growth a guy's gotta consider greener pastures sometimes. Know what I'm sayin'?"

"Maybe, but they're not greener down here, and with this recession, you better stay put. A job's a job, ya know. Hey, wait a minute. Is that what's goin' on up there? Is Powersports in trouble?"

"Oh, Tony, now you know if that were true, I couldn't tell ya." Greg laughed expansively to make a joke of the whole idea.

"You just did."

"No, no, no. I didn't say a thing."

His friend laughed with him, and in a few minutes the call was over, but it shook Greg. If BRP was thinking of closing the Brenton plant, maybe the whole industry was on harder times than he'd realized. Maybe Hastings was right.

The second person he talked to was Carl Montgomery, a major distributor of several ATV brands. Greg didn't know Carl nearly so well, and the conversation was much shorter. But business didn't sound any brighter for personal off-road vehicles.

Greg was so deep in thought reviewing these phone calls that he stepped off the curb at Touhy and Ridge against the light, and a driver laid on his horn like Gabriel trying to wake the dead.

He jumped back, heart pounding as he muttered, "Thank You, God. Whew!" God must be looking out for him, but did that mean He had his back in this job situation too? Sunday he'd been so confident God had given him a vision of coming prosperity, but now he was losing his job, and a replacement wasn't materializing.

Wait a minute. Wait a minute, Singer, he told himself as the light turned green and he crossed the street safely. *I made two phone calls, only two, and I'm already starting to panic.* A couple of weeks back Pastor Hanson had pointed out that the Chinese word for "crisis" was composed of two characters meaning *danger* and *opportunity,* so we shouldn't panic when we face a crisis. A situation might be dangerous, but it also provided a chance to develop something better. Maybe . . .

Greg's pace picked up. Could this situation coincide with the vision God had given him? He'd thought it involved Nicole beginning some kind of home industry with the kids to make a little more money, but perhaps God was shaking things up in a far bigger way, moving him out of Powersports to give him a more prosperous job.

As he turned up Beecham Street, Greg decided he wasn't ready to tell Nicole about Powersports yet. Why worry her? He still had two and a half weeks in the office and lots of contacts to follow up on. The conversation with Nicole was bound to go much easier if he could point to some attractive alternatives. Even the possibility of moving out of the city would go down easier if it involved a major upgrade in their lifestyle. Maybe a new car for Nicole, family trips built around educational experience for the kids, a bigger house. Who could know the great things God had in store for them?

Greg took a deep breath as he crossed Chase and headed up his block. Everything was going to be okay. He should relax. On the other side of the street from his modest bungalow he noticed his Jewish neighbor—Isaac Horowitz, if he remembered correctly—on his front porch weaving lush green boughs through the railings. Out of curiosity, Greg crossed the street to ask him what holy day it was. The Jewish family always seemed to be celebrating something.

"Shavuot," the man said as he stood up and adjusted his large black hat, sitting atop the small ringlet curls hanging down on either side of his face just in front of his ears. "The Festival of Weeks, sometimes called Festival of First Fruits." He waved his hand at the greenery. "Tomorrow the children will add flowers."

Still standing out on the sidewalk, Greg nodded. "So, it's like thanking God for the beginning of harvest?"

"Suppose you could say that, but it's more . . . how do I say it? You know anything about the Torah?"

Greg nodded. "Yeah, the Old Testament. Right?"

Horowitz raised both hands in a helpless gesture. "If you say so . . . part of it, anyway." He leaned back down and picked up another green bough as though he'd finished explaining.

"And . . .?" Greg prompted.

His neighbor straightened and gazed at him a long moment. "Well, maybe you remember Passover, when God freed the people of Israel from enslavement to Pharaoh."

Greg nodded vigorously, wanting to make sure his neighbor didn't think him entirely ignorant.

"Well, seven weeks later, Shavuot commemorates God giving us the Torah, the Books of the Law, so we could become a nation committed to serving Him." The man turned his attention back to the bough he was weaving into the railing.

Greg took the cue that Mr. Horowitz felt he'd revealed enough to this curious *goyim*. "Interesting. Thanks for telling me about it."

"Don't mention it," Horowitz said without even looking up over the banister.

But as Greg went back across the street to his own home, the idea of First Fruits intrigued him. Perhaps the end of Powersports was more like the beginning of a great harvest? Should he thank

God for it with some kind of sacrifice—a special offering on Sunday maybe? Of course, he wasn't under the Law, so it wasn't required, but wouldn't it express his faith and be a way to give thanks for what he wanted to believe God was doing on his behalf?

He tried to recall the words of the song about a new season they'd been singing at church lately. As he climbed his porch steps and hummed the tune, the words came back to him: *"It's a new season . . . of power and prosperity . . . coming to me."*

The employees of Powersports Expos were subdued on Wednesday, keeping busy in their individual offices or cubicles, perhaps hoping the bad news would go away if no one mentioned it. Greg was just as glad. As one of the senior staff, he didn't want to have to deal with people's disappointment or questions or insinuations that things would be different if he or anyone else had acted differently.

He didn't agree with Hastings' decision to shut down the company, and he certainly didn't want to have to answer for it. He had work to do, but he also took every opportunity when he was on the phone with one of their clients to ask how business was doing and to subtly inquire whether there were any senior marketing openings. Again, he was sobered by the responses. Opportunities seemed to be drying up, so it was good he was getting a jump on his search. But he had to be careful to keep his inquiries casual and vague enough to not reveal that he'd soon be out of work.

Last-minute details for the Burnham Harbor show were coming together, but it was hard for Greg to keep his mind on his work, and it wasn't until Thursday afternoon that he listened to an earlier voice message from the Chicago Park District saying they had denied permission to use Northerly Island as a landing and takeoff strip for ultralights. The "island," actually a peninsula east of the harbor, had once been Meigs Field, a small airport until Mayor Daley ordered bulldozers to destroy the runways in the middle of the night so he could turn it into a park.

Feelings among some citizens were still too raw to be reminded of the fact the land had once been an airport. To Greg, it didn't matter. He thought the ultralight demonstration had been a good draw for the Waukegan show, but Hastings no longer seemed so enamored by it.

Greg almost punched the button to advance to the next message when he realized there was more from the Park District. "Please be informed, construction begins June first on Waldron Drive east of the Museum Campus Drive, so the only way vehicles will be able to reach that side of the harbor will be through the McCormick Place north parking lot."

What? Why was he just now hearing about this? This would surely curtail casual visitors to the show and inconvenience the determined. And for the two days before the show, there would be vendors and even exhibitors who needed to get their trucks in there. Frustrated, he had to spend the rest of the day sending out emails and making phone calls to let everyone know about the change in directions.

Friday morning, Greg arrived at work to find a yellow Post-it stuck to the center of his desk with a cryptic message from his boss: "See me *now*!"

What was that about? Couldn't be much worse than the bomb Hastings had already dropped on everyone. He headed toward his boss's office. Maybe Hastings had changed his mind and was going to keep Powersports alive. On the other hand, the drapes were still pulled. He knocked.

"Enter."

"You wanted to see me?"

His boss looked up and watched as Greg closed the door behind himself. "No need to sit down. You won't be in here that long." His voice was as cold as his stare. "I asked you to let *me* notify our clients about Powersports. You understood that, didn't you?"

Greg's eyebrows went up. "Yeah, I heard you."

"But you couldn't wait for the green light before trolling for another job . . . and letting the cat outta the bag, could you?"

Greg felt his heart pump a little faster. "I didn't tell anybody you were closing."

Hastings snorted. "I've had three people tell me they already knew . . . from *your* phone calls!"

"What? But I didn't tell anybody." His skin prickled under his boss's glare. "I might've casually asked about other professional opportunities for myself. You can't blame me for that. But I didn't say anything about Powersports."

"You think these people are that stupid, not able to read through the lines?"

"Hey, if anyone figured out you were shutting down from one of my calls, it was a wild guess." But even as he said it, a hot patch crept up Greg's back and neck. Tony Barns down in Brenton *had* guessed, and right while they'd been talking. But he couldn't be held accountable for that.

Chuck Hastings raised both hands. "I'm not gonna get in a chicken fight with you, Singer, about how much or how little you said. Whatever it was, it was too much, and it was directly against my instructions. I don't feel good today. I don't feel like takin' any crap. You're finished. Pack your personal belongings and be out of the office by noon."

"What?"

"You heard me."

They stared at each other for a few moments before Greg turned toward the door.

"One more thing. If there're any more details for the Chicago show, pass 'em on to Marvin."

Greg stopped with his hand on the door handle, his back to his boss. He'd just been fired on the spot without just cause, and now his boss wanted him to do the favor of helping one of the other employees pick up the work he should be doing—*his* work. It was tempting to flip off his boss and walk out the door. By sheer willpower, Greg restrained himself. *Never burn your bridges. You might need to recross 'em sooner than you think!*

He turned around slowly. "Chuck, I'm sorry if I let any information slip, unintentional as it was, and I'll be glad to bring Marvin up to speed. But can I ask a favor of you? If I need it, will you give me a solid reference?"

His boss stared at him a moment, and then shrugged. "Sure. Why not?" He broke eye contact and shuffled some papers on his desk as though moving on to other tasks.

Greg nodded. "Thanks . . . and how about my check? Will you pay me through the seventh, like the others?"

"For two weeks of work you won't be doing? Whadda you think—"

"Hey, I'll stay and do it if you want."

"Nah, nah. I'll pay you." Chuck waved his hand dismissively but shook a finger at Greg. "At a time like this, I have to trust my people to do *exactly* what I ask. So just give Marvin what he needs."

Greg gritted his teeth as he turned and left his boss's office. At least he'd controlled himself enough to negotiate a reference and two weeks of pay.

Chapter 9

RIDING HOME ON THE COMMUTER TRAIN in the early afternoon, Greg felt certain everyone must know why he was carrying a large cardboard box on his lap, the box that held his personal items from the office. The picture of Nicole and the kids that sat on his desk, several framed prints from his wall of fishing trips, snowmobiling, an ATV trek into the jungle-bound hills of Jamaica, waterskiing on Cumberland Lake—all adventures he'd enjoyed while representing Powersports Expos.

The box also held pens, pencils, his small travel Bible, a clean shirt and tie—just in case—and the CD with all his contacts and recent correspondence.

But anyone who looked twice could tell that he was not bringing home the bacon in that box on his lap, not dressed like a businessman at this time of day.

He'd been fired!

How was he going to tell Nicole? He should've told her on Tuesday when his boss first announced the closing of Powersports Expos. Then it wouldn't be such a shock that it was all ending two weeks ahead of schedule. In fact, he could've explained his early release as a gift, a paid two-week jump on finding a new job.

He ought to look at it that way himself. This was a blessing. Why waste two weeks sitting around while Powersports ground to a halt when he could be looking for his new "dangerous opportunity"? Yes, he needed to come up out of his pity pit and see this as a blessing. He lifted his head a little higher and looked around the train car.

But no one was paying any attention to him one way or the other.

Thirty minutes later when he got home, he was glad to find the front door locked. The neighborhood was fairly safe, but he still encouraged Nicole to keep the doors locked when he wasn't home, especially if she and the kids were downstairs and might not see someone coming to the door. She often didn't do it, with the kids running in and out, but today she'd remembered. He let himself in. "Hello! Anybody here? I'm home early." He closed the door and went to the head of the basement stairs.

"Hello! You guys down there?"

No answer. That was strange. He went to the second floor stairs and called louder, still without any answer. He walked through the kitchen and looked out into the backyard. No one there. Hands on his hips, he stood in the middle of the kitchen, rejecting the tiny glitch of concern that grabbed him. They had to be around somewhere. He went upstairs to the kids' rooms and worked his way methodically down to the basement looking for any clues as to where his family might've gone. Books were open on their school desk. Becky's half-finished paragraph showed she'd been working on her cursive.

Today wasn't Nicole's usual shopping day, but perhaps she went out for something at the store. Yeah, that had to be the explanation. But just to make sure, he went out to the garage to make sure she'd taken the Jeep.

The Cherokee was still there.

He returned to the house and sat down in the kitchen breakfast nook. So far they'd managed with just his cell phone and a landline for the house, but he really ought to get Nicole a cell of her own. That way when she was out like this, he could keep in contact. It'd be a safety feature too. What if she needed help or one of the kids got hurt?

Greg sat in the breakfast nook for five minutes thinking about what he ought to do before he concluded there was nothing he could do right then and nothing to be alarmed about. They'd be back when they were done with whatever they were doing—playing in the park, visiting friends, going to the lake. Or maybe they'd walked to the corner of Howard and Western for ice cream at Baskin-Robbins. Yeah, that was probably it. The kids were always pestering Nicole for ice cream.

Might as well spend the afternoon setting himself up with a desk where he could do his job search. Greg wandered into the front hallway, visualizing each room. Their bedroom was too small, and it wouldn't work to make calls from the family room while the kids were doing their lessons. But he'd need to use one of the computers. They had two desktop computers, both set up in the basement family room. Nicole paid bills and did correspondence and homeschool research on one, while Becky made use of the other one. Nathan rarely needed one yet. But it was a "new season." Nicole and the kids could share one while he brought the newer one up to his new "office."

Greg surveyed the living room. It was really the only place. He could use that small table out in the garage. They'd meant to get it refinished, but it'd have to do for now. An hour later he'd commandeered a corner of the living room. He brought in the table, set up the computer on it, plugged in a lamp, found a paper stacker, and set up the picture of Nicole and the kids from his office box. Everything was plugged in and ready to check.

Nicole might not like it when she saw what he'd done, but it'd have to do for now, and he wouldn't need it for long. He borrowed a dining room chair, sat down at his "desk," and turned on the computer. It booted up just fine, and the Wi-Fi worked. He smiled, happy with himself that they hadn't relied on hard wires. Who wanted wires running all over the house?

He was checking email when he heard the kids scamper up on the porch. Glancing through the front room windows, he saw a fancy black sedan pull away. Looked like one of Lincoln Paddock's Town Cars. Had they come home in that?

Squeals of delight erupted when the kids saw him. Nathan and Becky galloped across the living room and hugged his legs as though there was not enough of him to share. "Daddy, Daddy, Daddy, you're already home! Mommy said you wouldn't be here till later."

"Well then, surprise." He looked up at Nicole coming through the door with a couple of bags slung over her shoulder.

"Hey," she said casually. "What brings you home so early?"

"A new job." Why not put the best spin on it from the very start?

"New job? What new job?"

Greg untangled himself from the kids' hugs. "Well, it seems Chuck Hastings got himself in some financial trouble with Powersports, and he's gonna shut it down."

"Shut it down? Why?" Her face seemed to pale as she stood in the archway into the living room. "Greg, what're we gonna do?"

"Now calm down, honey. Everything's gonna work out. Hastings is keeping some people on until after the Burnham Harbor show, but I got released early—with pay too. So we've got a little cushion while I land a new job."

"But . . . what? Where?"

"Well, I don't know yet. But I've got lots of contacts, and the Lord's gonna provide. Remember my vision? I think this may be part of its fulfillment."

"But—"

"Hey, come on in here and check this out. I set myself up with a little office."

Following his gesture, she turned toward the corner. "What? In here? Greg!"

"Don't worry, it's only temporary. Soon as I find something, I'll clear it all out."

Nicole stood in the middle of the living room, her hand over her mouth, staring at Greg's new "office." "But what are we gonna do when people come over? I mean—"

"Oh, come on, Nicole. When was the last time we had anyone over . . . other than your mother?"

Nicole dumped her bags on the closest chair. "That's not the point, Greg. I've been wanting to have some people from church over, but now this is gonna look like . . . like an office."

Irritation tightened Greg's shoulders. He'd just lost his job and she was worried about a corner of the living room looking like an office? But he kept his voice upbeat. "Hey, if it helps, I promise to keep the area neat, just like it is now. A lot of people have a household desk in their living area. It's no big deal."

The kids had drifted into the kitchen, and he heard them rummaging in the refrigerator. Nicole sank down on the couch, took a deep breath, and blew it out slowly. "So . . . when did this all happen with Powersports?"

He shrugged. "Hastings told us Tuesday, and I've been scrambling ever since. I wanted to make sure I'm in the best position to find another job. I've got all my contacts, so it's just a matter of choosing the best ones and deciding where we should go."

"Go? What d'you mean, go?"

Uh-oh, big mistake. He hadn't wanted to mention the possibility of moving until he could list all the benefits of the new location. "Well, with every career advancement, there's always the possibility of relocation, but of course we'd make that decision together if it truly benefits the whole family . . . including the kids."

Nicole closed her eyes and shook her head slowly, as if this was all too much to take in at one time.

Greg sat down across from her and leaned forward. "Look, Nikki, this could be a real opportunity for us. I'm not eager to move either. Trust me, that'll be the last option on my list and only if it really serves us. I'm looking at this on the bright side, glass half full, you know. In fact, better than that, I think this may be the fulfillment of that vision the Lord gave me."

"Yeah, you already said that."

"But really, I was thinking He had in mind a little side business for you and the kids, but I think He may be opening up a major career opportunity for me."

Greg stopped, gauging whether he was getting anywhere with her. She looked a little teary. Moving over beside her on the couch, he pulled her close. "Look, hon. Let's celebrate. Let's take the kids out to dinner this evening. It's Friday, and you've had a full week. I bet you could use a break. And if we look at this opportunity right, it's gonna turn out right."

She pulled back a little bit and wiped her eyes, but Greg could tell she was starting to accept the situation. "What do you mean, *look at it right*?"

"You know, with faith. Yeah, we need to have faith. Our faith will bring God's blessing, just like it did to Abraham."

He felt her stiffen ever so slightly before she dropped her head and nodded. She sniffed. "All right. Where's a tissue? I need to blow my nose."

"Does that mean we can go out and celebrate?"

"If you want. Doesn't exactly *feel* like time to celebrate yet."

"Don't worry. It will."

As Nicole got up to go to the bedroom and blow her nose, the kids sidled back into the living room, sucking on juice box straws, ever alert to family drama. "Is Mommy okay?" Becky asked, watching her mother disappear.

"Sure, sure . . . So where were you guys this afternoon?" he asked.

"We went to the zoo."

"But there weren't any elephants. They all died," added Nathan.

"Oh, I'm sorry to hear that. Who—"

Just then, Nicole returned from their bedroom, and Greg decided it wasn't the right time to ask who'd brought them home from the zoo in that black car.

Chapter 10

GREG WOULD HAVE TAKEN HIS WIFE AND KIDS anywhere for dinner—anywhere within reason, that is—but when he asked, Nicole just shrugged and said, "You choose." The kids voted for McDonald's, but Greg vetoed that and finally took the family to the Olive Garden in the Lincolnwood Town Center.

Nicole never said the words, but her demeanor throughout the meal kept asking, *What's to celebrate?* If he let his feelings catch up to him, he knew he had the same question, but he refused to give in to it. He kept telling himself he was exercising faith . . . but what was the difference between faith and human optimism? He had to remain upbeat. If he let himself get depressed or anxious, he wouldn't make a good impression when he talked to prospective employers. Still, uncertainty danced at the edges of what he hoped was faith. Was this the fulfillment of God's plan for him? Was God going to prosper him or not?

Nicole's mood irritated him. It wasn't fair. He needed her now, especially now, but she felt like a rubber crutch. Worse than that, she was . . . she was . . . The memory of that black Town Car easing on up the street came back unbidden. What was she doing riding in Lincoln Paddock's sleek Town Car this afternoon? Had Paddock taken his wife and kids to the zoo? That wasn't right. He'd have to get to the bottom of this.

He waited until the children were tucked in bed and Nicole was in their bathroom brushing her teeth before bringing it up. "The kids said you went to the zoo this afternoon. How'd that go?"

Nicole spit out a mouthful of suds and glanced in the mirror at him leaning against the doorjamb. "It was okay. I think they liked it."

"So which zoo did you go to?"

"Lincoln Park." She turned on the hot water.

"Of course, Lincoln Park. That's why Lincoln Paddock drove you home." He knew as he spoke that his words were swathed in sarcasm.

Nicole didn't respond but held a steaming washcloth up to her face.

Her silence goaded him. "So, did he take you down there too?"

She removed the washcloth and stared at him in the mirror, her face red from the steam . . . or was it from being found out? "Yes, he did. He promised the kids last week," she said matter-of-factly. "He dropped by today to see if we could go. Nathan's been wanting to take a picture of the polar bears for his nature project, you know. Seemed like the perfect opportunity." She put the reheated washcloth back over her face and began scrubbing away any remaining makeup.

Greg backed away from the bathroom, sat down on the edge of the bed, and took off his shoes. Something didn't feel right about another man—someone they barely knew—taking his family on an afternoon outing. And he might not have found out about it if he'd come home at his usual time. Nicole hadn't coached the kids to not tell, but they might've forgotten. And she hadn't phoned to ask him about the trip . . . or even tell him.

"So, you find this playboy Paddock to be an interesting fellow?"

Nicole grimaced from the bathroom. "Oh, stop it, Greg. If you only knew what it's like to come up with truly educational experiences for the kids all the time, you'd realize this was a blessing, nothing more."

"But you could've driven the kids down there yourself, couldn't you? I leave the Cherokee here for you so you can do errands and stuff. In fact, you took them to the zoo last fall, didn't you?"

"Yeah, that was when Nate got lost and nearly scared me to death for thirty minutes before I found him. Ya know, it really helps to have another adult along."

"Another adult. Who just happens to be a good-looking—"

"No!" she snapped. "A neighbor who just happened to offer *our* kids an outing. Come on, Greg, give it a rest. I don't want to talk about this anymore."

He said no more, and they both crawled into bed a few minutes later, back-to-back, but Greg could tell by Nicole's frequent sighs and movements that she didn't go to sleep any sooner than he did.

Nicole stared at the red numbers of the digital clock on her bedside table. In a blink, they went from 11:14 to 11:15 to 11:16, and before she knew it, to 11:37.

She flopped onto her back and closed her eyes tightly, causing a kaleidoscope of color wheels until the image of Nathan standing at the thick window into the big cat habitat materialized. A full-maned lion lay on the other side of the glass and pawed at the window, inches from Nathan's face, like a kitten wanting to play with a mouse. Fearlessly, her son had called for her to watch. It was both exhilarating and terrifying.

The whole afternoon had been that way—exhilarating and terrifying. But why? Why had it been scary? Because she'd enjoyed every moment of Lincoln Paddock's attention . . . and knew she shouldn't.

"You want a bag of popcorn?" "Let's let the kids ride the carousel." "Hey, I'll get on the unicorn if you ride the ostrich next to me." And he'd helped her up.

He'd taken her elbow when they stepped over a rough section on the path to the polar bear exhibit and when they went down the ramp of the great ape house. Nicole told herself he was just being a gentleman, but she thought his hand lingered a little longer than necessary . . . and she liked it.

When Nathan got tired of walking, Lincoln had picked him up and carried him on his broad shoulders without a complaint until the boy was rested and wanted to get down and run again.

There had been no "Robbie" to chauffeur them to the zoo and back in a stretch limo. Lincoln had driven a standard-sized limo, but the shiny black Town Car had seemed all the more luxurious with him behind the wheel.

"So what'd you do before you became a . . . what do you call it, a teaching mom?"

Nicole had felt herself blush as he glanced over at her on their way home. But why was she blushing? It was a simple, straightforward question any two people might ask as they got acquainted.

"I was a paralegal for a law firm."

"Get outta here! Really?"

"Yeah. I started as a legal assistant with Whitney, Young, and Gould right after college."

"Real estate law, right?"

"Uh-huh. On the near Northside, but then the kids came, and we decided I'd homeschool them."

Paddock had glanced into the rearview mirror at the two children in the backseat who were too tired to even talk. "Well, I think you're doing a great job." He was silent while he changed lanes. "Have you ever thought about getting back into the legal field?"

Her heart sped up a few beats. "Well, sure, sometimes. In fact, I wanted to get my law degree and become a lawyer, but . . ."

"Hey, don't give up that dream. You'd make a great lawyer. In fact, even if you want a part-time job, let me know. We're always needing help." He reached up and pulled a business card out of a packet in the visor and handed to her.

A part-time job? Nicole's mind spun as she studied the card. What an opportunity. Perhaps her legal career wasn't over. *Maybe . . .*

Her imagination had taken off.

And then she'd come home to Greg telling her he'd been fired and talking glibly about the possibility of moving to some other city, away from Beecham Street, away from her mom, and away from such an unbelievable opportunity.

The executives Greg needed to talk to in his job search wouldn't be in their offices on Saturday, so he spent most of the day prioritizing those contacts according to the companies that interested him most, personnel he'd met and liked, and location. He didn't really want to leave Chicago, so boat dealerships in the area headed his list. He'd go for something like Vice President of Sales or maybe Marketing Director, at the VP level, of course.

Sunday was Pentecost—fourth Sunday in May—and Greg took his family to church, eager for some encouragement about his job situation. He was not disappointed. Pastor Hanson directed his listeners to Acts 2.

"The Day of Pentecost is about giving!" he declared in a booming voice and then paused behind his Plexiglas pulpit while he surveyed the congregation as if waiting to see whether his pronouncement generated the surprise he intended. Finally, he continued. "It's not just our giving to God, but God giving to us. The gift of His Holy Spirit, the gifts given by the Holy Spirit, and the power and abundance to use them for His glory."

Greg leaned forward, listening intently.

"Now, do you think God is glorified by some miserly little token? No! He's a generous God who pours out His blessings in abundance in response to our own generosity. It was Jesus who said in Luke six, thirty-eight, 'Give, and it will be given to you: good measure, pressed down, shaken together, and running over will be put into your bosom. For with the same measure that you use, it will be measured back to you.' That's God's principle of sowing and reaping. And you can be sure He follows that principle in what He gives in return to what we sow in faith. Now, let's look at our passage in Acts two."

The pastor pointed out how amazed the onlookers were by the events surrounding God's gift of His Holy Spirit. These were sophisticated skeptics who had traveled from many countries and had seen the wonders of the ancient world, but they were utterly astonished with what they saw that day in Jerusalem. "And the church grew by leaps and bounds every day," Pastor Hanson boomed. "God was blessing their giving!"

This message was just what Greg needed to lift him out of the pit and chase away the doubts and fears that had nibbled at the fringe of his faith over the last couple of days. God was going to bless him. This was his time of opportunity.

Nicole leaned over. "Somehow Pastor turns every Bible passage into a sermon on prosperity, but it's really a message about the Holy Spirit," she whispered.

Greg gritted his teeth and gave her a cold stare. What was wrong with her? Of course, this teaching took a new slant, but that's because in all their years in church, no one had taught them about God's desire to bless them financially. All she had to do was look around. Other people were prospering. Look at the clothes they wore, the cars they drove. Why not them?

When the music began to play—the offering always followed the sermon at the Victorious Living Center—Greg pulled out his checkbook. In the back of his mind he knew he was acting in spite of Nicole's reservations, but he told himself he was just exercising faith . . . boldly. "Give and it will be given to you!" He whispered the promise to himself as he wrote the check for twice their normal tithe.

That afternoon as Greg was reviewing some of his contacts, getting ready for the next day, the doorbell rang. He let Nicole answer it.

"Nicole?" said a woman's voice. "We met last weekend when Mrs. Krakowski came back to the neighborhood."

"Sure, I remember . . . Michelle Jasper, right?"

"And I'm Jared." Man's voice. "Is your husband home? I actually came down to see him, and my wife wanted to come along to say hi."

Now Greg knew who was at the door. He'd spoken with the man and his son that evening. African American family. Lived at the other end of Beecham.

"You want to come in?" Nicole said. "Greg?" His wife stepped to the living room archway. "Someone to see you."

Greg saved the file he was working on and rose to meet his guest. "Hey, Jared, come on in and have a seat. I was just doing a little catch-up." He gestured toward his computer.

As they shook hands, the women wandered into the kitchen.

"So, to what do we owe this pleasure?"

"Well . . ." The man appeared a little self-conscious. "The other evening when the Bentleys had that welcome party for Mrs. Krakowski, you mentioned the possibility of going to a boat show you're putting on—down at Burnham Harbor, I think you said it was."

Greg nodded. Oh yes, and he'd magnanimously offered to arrange a ride in a cigarette boat. What had he been thinking?

"Anyway," Jared continued, "I have to miss an important family trip Memorial Day weekend—got a conflict, you know—so I'm hoping to make it up to the kids by doing something special with them. I remembered the boat show you mentioned. My oldest son seemed especially interested."

"Oh, I'm sure they'd enjoy it. It starts June third at Burnham Harbor, goes through the weekend. But, uh . . ." Greg leaned forward, elbows on knees, and rubbed his hands together. How was he gonna say this? "Unfortunately, I'm not with Powersports any longer. I'm in the middle of a job change, lookin' at some new possibilities." He sat up and raised both hands over his head like a referee signaling goal or a man who'd just been freed, not fired.

"Oh, I'm sorry to hear that."

"No, no. Don't be sorry. I'm movin' on to better things. I'd been at Powersports too long as it was."

"Well, I guess that's good, then. You got something specific lined up?"

"Let's put it this way, I've got plenty of solid connections. The only thing is, my connections probably wouldn't get me free passes for *this* show. But hey, tickets aren't too expensive, ten bucks online if you buy them ahead. Just put in 'Burnham Harbor In-Water Show.' There'll be all kinds of activities, a lot of really cool boats to see, demonstrations of every extreme watersport you can imagine. And . . ." He thought about his earlier offer. "You might be able to talk your way into a boat ride, though probably not in that cigarette boat I mentioned unless you're serious about buying one."

Jared laughed. "Not hardly. How much do those things cost, anyway?"

"Oh, you can spend over a hundred grand on them real quick."

"Yeah, well, we're not ready for the life of the rich and famous just yet, if you know what I mean."

Both men laughed to ease the awkwardness.

Jared stood up. "Well, listen, I won't keep you any longer. But I appreciate you thinking of us earlier. And I'll be praying that you get the right new job."

"That'd be great. I appreciate that."

After the couple left, Greg realized he'd never asked Jared what kind of work he did. Not good. He'd make a point next time they met. Would've been one way to get the conversation off his own "job issues" too.

Monday brought warm weather and blue skies with scattered, cottony clouds. Greg met it with the eagerness of a racehorse at the starting gate.

There was, of course, still the question of how much he should reveal to those he called about Powersports' situation. But having been "fired"—yeah, his self-image was strong enough to use that word—he didn't feel the same obligation to keep Chuck Hastings' secret. Apparently, the news was already out there, though he wasn't ready to accept the full blame. And by now, Hastings would've spoken to several other exhibitors, any of which could've passed the word.

In fact, it could be online by now. Greg typed "Trade Show Executive Magazine" into the Google search on his computer. As soon as the page came up, he scanned the "Breaking News" column. Hmm. No mention of Powersports Expos yet, but it could flash up there at any time. Okay. He wouldn't explicitly announce Powersports' demise to anyone, but he wouldn't worry if someone else figured it out. Besides, with all that Hastings was dealing with at this point, it was unlikely he'd remember to call Greg and release him to say whatever he wanted to those gold-star exhibitors he prized so highly. They were Greg's top candidates for a job too.

From his contact list, Greg made sure he remembered the person he was calling, how to pronounce his name, exactly what he did in the company, as well as reviewing the last emails or letters they'd exchanged. He also went online to refresh himself with the company's latest news, product promotions, and other features. He wanted to be completely informed and prepared.

Nicole and the kids were in the lower family room getting started on the day's lessons. He could hear Nicole's gentle voice as she helped Nate sound out new words in the story he was trying to read. Nathan had been slower to begin reading than Becky, who was reading chapter books by this age, but it sounded like Nate was finally getting it.

At five minutes to ten Greg started calling, late enough for his contact to have cleared away any urgent business that had collected over the weekend but hopefully before he got mired in the day's work.

Not many boat manufacturers were in the Chicago area. There was a company that built high-performance propellers, another that specialized in custom conversions, and a couple of racing boat builders who worked mostly on a project-by-project basis for the super rich. But there *were* a lot of boat dealers.

The first dealer Greg called was Roger Wilmington at Potawatomi Watercraft up on the Chain o' Lakes, the guy who'd let Greg use their cottage on Deep Lake. It would be a long commute, but a lot of people did that.

"Are you telling me you're actually looking for a position?" Roger asked once Greg had plowed the ground, so to speak.

"As a matter of fact, yes. I'm ready to move into a more commercial role."

"Well, you'd be the man for it. How'd that in-water show go you did a couple of weeks ago in Waukegan? Sorry we couldn't make it, but we had too much going on here."

"It was a good show." Greg took heart. Didn't sound like Potawatomi was in the kind of financial trouble he'd picked up in other quarters of the industry.

"Any boats sell?"

"Not as many as we would've liked, that's for sure." Greg knew Roger would find out the facts sooner or later. "But I think it would've made a big difference if Potawatomi had been there. Sometimes it comes down to chemistry. Know what I'm saying?"

"Oh, yeah. Oh, yeah. That's the key." There was a lull in the conversation. Finally, Roger picked it up. "So you're thinkin' about a move. When might you be available?"

"I actually could spring real soon. Chuck and I have had a good working relationship, and I think he understands what I'm looking for."

"So he already knows?"

"Oh yeah. No secret there. And he's glad to give me a good recommendation, if you need one. But then we actually know each other pretty well."

"That's good. Listen, Greg, let me get back to you on this. We're due for some reorganization around here, and you just might fit into our future. How 'bout if I get back to you next week, uh . . ." He paused, probably checking a calendar. "Oh man, can you believe it? Next Monday's Memorial Day. I'll call you Tuesday, a week from tomorrow. In the meantime, send over your résumé so I can have some talking points when I bring this up to the others."

"Will do. Thanks, Roger." He started to take the phone away from his ear. "Oh, and Roger . . .?"

"Yeah."

"Just thought I'd let you know. You're the first person I called . . . today."

"All right. I'll get back to you."

Roger had been the first person he'd called *today*. He almost hadn't added that qualifier. But then there'd been those calls from the office that had gotten him in trouble. Though he'd counted those more as "feelers" than actual job hunting.

He laid down the phone and leaned back in his chair for a big stretch. God was going to come through. He could feel it already. Blessing upon blessing.

Chapter 11

Greg knew he couldn't count on the job with Potawatomi Watercraft until it was actually offered, but Roger Wilmington had been so encouraging—almost like it was a sure thing—that Greg found it hard to keep looking. There really weren't any boat manufacturers in the Chicago area that interested him, but he kept himself on task, calling all the large boat dealers, ATV dealers, and snowmobile people within commuting distance.

Tuesday midmorning he overheard Nicole whisper loudly to Nate as he came up the basement stairs to get their snacks. "Don't go in the living room. You mustn't bother Daddy. He's very busy."

"But why?"

"Because he's working at home today. So that's his office, and you're not to go in there and bother him."

"But I use'ta phone him at his other office."

"Well, this is different, and you can't bother him today. What he's doing is very important."

Nate stomped into the kitchen, and Greg could imagine the big frown on his face, but he didn't come into the living room.

Nicole's support eased Greg's mind. That's what he needed, for them to be together in this quest. And it crossed his mind he ought to give Nicole that kind of support as well. He should probably drop that thing about Lincoln Paddock. After all, like she said, he was probably just being a good neighbor. They needed more neighbors like that on Beecham Street. He could remember when he was a kid how every parent on the block took charge of the kids. And during the summers a couple of moms would round up all the kids, load them in a van, and take them to the pool for the day. That's what neighbors were for. Of course, back in the day they were all moms, not some playboy hitting on his wife—

Stop it, Greg! he told himself. If he wanted Nicole to trust him, he needed to trust her. He had to put those suspicions out of his mind. What was it "The Love Chapter" in First Corinthians said? "Love . . . thinks no evil . . . believes all things, hopes all things." That's where his head needed to be, especially at a time like this.

As the week advanced, his job search proved a sobering process. There simply weren't a lot of opportunities out there. Tony Barns with Sea-Doo down in southern Illinois had been right—in a job market like this, he'd be smart to stay put. Only that was no longer an option. So he kept working the phone, sending out résumés, searching the web for other opportunities. As perfect as Potawatomi sounded, it seemed smart to develop alternatives. In fact, maybe he should be prepared to accept a slightly lower salary than he'd hoped for if it allowed them to stay in Chicago—and he would, too, if necessary. Though he pushed aside the nagging question of how that would fit with his vision for greater prosperity.

To find alternatives, he stepped outside the field of sports to see what might be open at the Department of Cultural Affairs and Special Events for the City of Chicago. The city sponsored huge events all summer long. Unfortunately, the mayor's office had hired a new "Relationship Manager"—the position that might have interested Greg—earlier that year, and by all accounts she was doing very well.

Next, Greg contacted McCormick Place, the Allstate Arena, the United Center, the Bears, the Bulls, the White Sox, the Cubs, the Blackhawks—any facility or organization that might need someone with his skills. Theaters, museums, even big hotels required someone capable of organizing and promoting major events. And he was their man.

Only he wasn't. After five days, Greg turned up only three open positions, and none of them attracted him. FarMor Marketing wanted an events coordinator and described itself as "a company committed to our consumers and results for our clients. Our goal is to expand through cross-training the appropriate individuals in all aspects of business and marketing, to build strong managers to take on additional campaigns . . . *blah, blah, blah.*" So much jargon Greg couldn't even figure out what FarMor did. A couple of universities needed events coordinators, but the salaries they posted didn't come close to Greg's vision of new—or old—prosperity.

Nevertheless, by Friday afternoon, he felt like he'd done his due diligence in looking for local alternatives. If Potawatomi didn't offer him a job next Tuesday, he'd have to look outside the Chicago area.

In spite of Monday being Memorial Day, Greg went to work refining his "outside-Chicago" call list. Should he start calling those contacts first thing Tuesday morning? Or wait until he heard from Roger Wilmington? What was the balance between faith and wisdom? The old song Pastor Hanson always quoted said, "Take your burden to the Lord and leave it there. If you trust and never doubt, He will surely bring you out." But that seemed kind of passive, perhaps even irresponsible when he could use his time to get a jump on exploring alternatives.

The fact was, he'd spent the preceding week exploring local alternatives without assuming that was a faithless exercise. Now that those options had proved fruitless, why not go national?

He wanted to get his plan together before the afternoon barbecue with the Bentleys, the older black couple from the two-flat up the street. Aside from that welcome home event for the old lady and waving to him a couple of times on the street, Greg barely knew the man, but Harry had come knocking last evening while he was out walking his black Lab.

"No, no." Bentley had waved him off when Greg invited him in. "Corky's been chasing her KONG toy up and down the alley. Don't want to bring her muddy paws into your nice house. But Estelle and I are inviting a few neighbors over for a Memorial Day picnic, and wondered if you and your family would join us."

"Nicole!" Greg had called.

Harry said they didn't need to bring anything, but when Nicole joined them at the door she insisted on contributing something—her mother's Jell-O salad recipe, full of whipped cream and fruit, not Greg's favorite, but Nicole liked to make it, and kids always loved it—so Harry had finally conceded.

"You, however," he'd smirked, pointing a finger at Greg's chest, "you could show up early and help me with the ribs. Say about three o'clock?"

Light rain showers driven by distant thunder rumbled through the area midday, but by three when Greg had finished his call plan and done all the background research he could think to do, the clouds were breaking up and the sun peeking through. Looked like a nice evening was in store after all.

He stepped to the doorway of the kitchen where Nicole was mopping the floor. "Anything you need me to do before I head on over to the Bentleys?"

"No, not unless you want to take the kids with you." She stood and pushed her hair out of her face with the back of her hand.

"Oh." He wasn't sure if it was an offhand idea or a request. "Kids downstairs?"

"Nate might be. Becky just went up to her room. Said she was bored."

"Not sure what they'd do over at the Bentleys. There's no one for them to play with." He waited in case Nicole had a better plan.

"That's okay. Forget it." She shrugged and went back to mopping.

The wistful tone in her voice didn't sound like it was really *okay*. He listened for kid sounds. Nothing. "Sounds like they're doing okay for now."

"Yeah. I'll bring them with me later."

"About five, then?"

She nodded and Greg left, grabbing his Cubs cap from the peg in the coat closet.

Nicole watched him go, feeling irritated. She'd frequently wished Greg could spend more time at home, especially with the kids. But over the last couple of years, his travel schedule had taken him away all too often. Now, however, she was having second thoughts. His presence in the house did not mean he picked up more of the housework or took more responsibility with the kids. It simply meant she had more things to coordinate.

The simple lunches that had been adequate for her and the kids weren't satisfying to Greg, so she had to fix larger meals, which inevitably meant she ate more as well . . . and had put back on a couple of pounds. Also, somehow she didn't feel so free to do her exercises while Greg was upstairs working on the computer.

Last Thursday while the kids were doing their reading, she'd been doing her exercises when he came down to the schoolroom. He stared as if he couldn't understand what was going on. Finally he'd said, "Did you wash my blue Van Heusen shirt yet?"

"No. Monday's my wash day."

"Oh. Well, if you get a chance . . ." And then he'd drifted back up the stairs.

But the steam had gone out of her exercises. He obviously had expectations. Flouncing into the laundry room, she'd started a load of laundry, including his Van Heusen shirt.

And now today, supposedly a holiday. She could've used a break, but no. *He* was the one getting a break. Sure, he'd been working most of the day, but so had she, typical wash-day-Monday stuff, but now he'd gone over to the Bentleys early and left the kids with her, even though she'd tried to hint that he take them with him.

Nicole gave the floor one more angry swipe with the mop. She knew single moms who had more free time than she did, especially when the kids were with their ex.

Turning in at the Bentleys, Greg followed the sidewalk around to the backyard. At first he didn't think anyone was there and that he'd come too soon, but then he heard some rummaging going on in the garage and realized the side door was ajar.

"Hello? Anyone in there?"

"That you, Singer? Just getting some chairs."

A black paw caught the door and swung it open as Bentley's black Lab trotted out and give a halfhearted *woof*, tail wagging.

Greg reached down so the dog could sniff the back of his hand. "It's okay, girl." The kids probably would've liked to play with the dog.

The older man stepped out into the sunshine, lugging several folding chairs. "Ah, you're right on time, but I'm a little late gettin' started. Didn't want everything to get wet with the rain earlier. Here, take these chairs, and I'll grab the bag of charcoal."

In a few minutes, Harry Bentley had his chimney starter filled with charcoal and lit. "There, that won't take long. Come on up and help me bring down a few things."

It took a few trips up to the second floor and back down, but it wasn't long before the coals were burning evenly, four racks of ribs were on the grill, and the two men finally sat down under the shade of the spreading sycamore tree while the Cubs versus Pirates game murmured quietly from the boom box hanging from the fence.

Harry flipped open the lid of a large cooler beside him. "Want somethin' to drink? Got Pepsi, some bottles of water, maybe some lemonade in here."

"Water. Thanks."

Harry handed him a bottle of water. "So, how you doin'?"

"Oh, good. Real good."

Harry lifted an eyebrow. "Is that good as in copacetic or good as in you don't want to talk about it?"

Greg didn't know what to say. He didn't know for sure what the word *copacetic* meant.

Harry chuckled. "What I mean, is, you ask somebody how they're doin' and they'll usually say, 'Good' as long they're this side of death's door. But I was actually askin' how you're really doing. I'm interested."

"Well, I'm, uh . . ." Greg looked at the older man for a moment, a slight sheen of sweat beading his shaved head and an easy smile crinkling his eyes. "To tell the truth, things are a little rocky right now."

"You don't say. What's up?"

Did he really want to tell this man about his personal life? Weren't guys supposed to do small talk first? But the man actually seemed interested. And the truth was, Greg didn't have anyone else to talk to.

Greg shrugged. "The company I've been working for the last seven years is going under. Recession, I guess, though I think the boss could've managed things better and survived. Anyway, I was the assistant Midwest coordinator—pretty much the VP level, though we weren't organized that way. I was depending on it thriving. Still think it could. I mean, this recession can't last forever. But the boss pulled the plug, so I'm out in the cold." Wait a minute, he'd never used those words before. Crisis meant "dangerous opportunity" and all that, but not *out in the cold*.

"You get a decent severance package?"

"Not really. Two weeks was all. But at least I don't have to stay on the job during that time like the rest of the staff. They got two weeks' notice but will only get paid if they work to the bitter end."

Harry Bentley nodded and frowned deeply. "Sorry to hear that. Got laid off myself once, though the circumstances were different. Had to take early retirement from the Chicago Police Department—"

Bentley, a cop? That was interesting.

The older man continued, "Involved a big legal case where I blew the whistle on some corruption." He waved his hand dismissively as though that was another story. "But bottom line, bein' without a job can be pretty scary, 'specially when you got family to support. I know."

Greg took a deep breath. "Yeah, well, didn't think it would bother me at first. But the last few days, the options seem slimmer and slimmer. I have all kinds of business contacts, but . . ." What was he saying? He hadn't even expressed those fears to himself. But this older guy was looking at him as though he really understood. "Anyway, I've got one good lead in the Chicago area. Supposed to hear tomorrow, but if it doesn't pan out, we're probably gonna have to relocate."

"Oh, that's big time."

"You're tellin' me. My wife will have a fit if we have to move, and I don't want to move either. I just don't know what we'll do."

"What kind of business you in?"

Greg explained the kind of events Powersports put on as Harry got up and checked the grill. When he returned to his seat, Greg told about his hopes for a job with Potawatomi.

"That sounds like somethin' to pray about. You a prayin' man?"

That took Greg by surprise. "Well, yes . . . yes, I am." Bentley's question reminded him of the faith he'd been nurturing, faith that God would prosper him and his family, faith that he was about to become rich! It was what he wanted to believe, but somehow in the last few minutes, the bottom had dropped out of that bucket. Why? What had happened?

It must have leaked away as he became honest with himself. He needed help. "Yeah, prayer would be good."

Harry reached his hand out toward Greg's shoulder, hesitating a few inches away. "Okay to pray for you right now?"

Right now? Greg was a little startled. "Sure, I guess so."

"Good. I always say there's no time like the present."

He let his hand rest gently on Greg's shoulder and began to pray.

Chapter 12

BEFORE THE RIBS WERE READY, the Cubs had lost to the Pirates—broadcast by Bentley's boom box hanging on the fence—and Greg and Harry had set up the chairs under the tree and the card tables.

"Catch these plastic tablecloths," Harry's wife called down from the second-floor deck. "And put them on the card tables so they'll look nice."

Harry caught them, and the two men finished setting up everything while the teenage boy Greg had seen with the Bentleys and three other lanky kids—at least one of them the Jasper boy from across the street—traipsed through the yard with a basketball. Must be a hoop out in back of the garage. Sure enough, the *thump thump* of the ball against concrete and youthful chatter played in the background as he talked with Harry. Turned out that Bentley was again working as a cop, though now for the Amtrak police, and he seemed to be a sincere Christian.

"You mentioned you go to church," Harry said. "That's good. Real good. You got any brothers to hang with?"

"Brothers?" Greg was an only child and hadn't mentioned anything about his family.

"Yeah," Bentley said. "You know, some guys to pray with and study the Bible. Some of us get together every Tuesday evening. Couldn't get along without 'em. You'd be welcome to visit some time, if you want."

The back gate creaked and swung open before Greg could respond, and an elderly couple came in.

"Ah, Mr. and Mrs. Molander." Harry got up to go greet them and Greg followed. "Come right on in. You're nearly the first ones."

"Sorry if we're early. We were trying to take a nap, but the *thump, thump, thump.*" He rolled his eyes toward the alley.

"Sorry about that. You know Greg Singer from across the street, don't you?"

The woman stared hard. "I don't t'ink so. Ve don't get out much anymore." Her accent sounded Swedish.

Harry turned to Greg. "This is Karl and Eva Molander. They live next door. Oh, let me take that for you." Harry reached for a dish covered with a tea towel that Mrs. Molander was carrying.

"Tuna casserole, a favorite at the church picnics, don't you know. We used to have years ago, but the new preacher doesn't do them anymore."

Karl grimaced. "He's been here ten years already, Eva."

"Maybe so, but he's not like Rev. Johanson."

Karl Molander sat down heavily in one of the lawn chairs, panting deeply. Harry eyed him carefully. "You okay, Mr. Molander?"

Molander waved his hand. "It'll pass." He took a deep breath as Greg glanced between him and Harry to see if Harry remained concerned.

The Molanders' house was a bungalow like Greg's, so it wasn't as if the man had descended three flights of stairs or walked a mile. Yet a gray and haggard pallor had fallen over his face. Finally, his labored breathing calmed and he looked around the yard. "Looks like you're expecting a crowd."

"Not really. Just you and a few other folks." Harry turned to Mrs. Molander. "Miz Eva, why don't I take you in to chat with Miz Mattie for a bit? Then I'll run this casserole up so Estelle can pop it in the oven to keep warm."

With Harry Bentley gone, Greg tried to think of something to say. "Uh, guess you folks and Mrs. Krakowski are the true old-timers on the block."

"Oh, yeah. We were here before any of the rest. Neighborhood used to be all Swedish and German, except for the Krakowskis. She's Polish, ya know."

"And you're Swedish, right?"

"Oh yeah. Like I said, about the only ones left in the neighborhood."

"My wife's Swedish, at least her mother is. She lives down in the Andersonville neighborhood."

"You don't say."

The conversation seemed to die again. After a few moments, Greg made another try. "So, are you retired?"

"Oh yeah. I was a machinist at Klein Tools. Twenty-six years. But I retired—been ten years ago now."

"Klein . . . that's over on Touhy and McCormick, isn't it?"

"That's the headquarters, but I was mostly at the Skokie facility."

"Twenty-six years. That's quite a stint. I bet you—"

"Greg? Oh, there you are." Nicole came around the corner of the house. "Could you watch the kids? I forgot my Jell-O."

As Greg's kids came bouncing across the yard, Harry Bentley's Lab, who hadn't moved a muscle when the Molanders arrived, gave a little woof and trotted toward Becky and Nate. Greg was pretty sure she was totally friendly, but just to be sure, he got up and stepped between them. "Sorry about that," he called back to Karl Molander. "Maybe we can pick it up again later."

But he needn't have worried. The dog and his kids immediately became a mutual admiration club—the kids loving on the dog, and the dog eating up all the attention.

"What's her name?" Becky asked, her arms around the dog's neck.

"Corky." Harry Bentley had arrived at the bottom of the steps, his arms piled high with paper plates, napkins, cups, and plasticware. "And if you'll toss that tennis ball for her, she'll bring it back to you all afternoon."

Becky started tossing the ball for Harry's dog, but Nate tugged on Harry's shirt as he put all the paper goods on the table. "Mr. Bentley, why did your dog have to go to jail?"

"To jail? What makes you ask that?"

"My mom said you were a policeman, and I saw you putting Corky in the back of your police van like they do with bad guys—you know, with bars and everything."

What in the world was his son talking about?

Harry Bentley laughed. "No, no, young man. Corky's my partner, and that's where she rides." He closed the grill lid over the ribs. "Here, come with me for a minute."

Beckoning the Singers to follow him into the garage—the *thump, thump* from the alley and thuds on the garage door were louder in here—Harry showed them the dog carrier in the back of his SUV. As soon as he opened the side door, Corky jumped right in, and Greg realized what Nate was talking about. The specially designed transporter filled what would've been the backseat and rear compartment. Bars separated the space from the front seats and covered the tinted windows. The walls were covered with metal. No wonder Nate mistook it for a police van.

"Corky loves it." Harry grinned. "Look here. See the fan? And the air conditioner even blows back here too. Go on—you can get inside."

Finally extracting the kids and the dog from Harry's SUV, Greg herded his kids back to the picnic. Estelle Bentley had come down and was introducing everyone. Eva Molander and Mrs. Krakowski had joined the group and Michelle Jasper from across the street had arrived. "Jared sends his regrets. He had to work today. I think all three of my kids are already here." She nodded toward the alley.

"We invited Farid and Lily too"—Estelle pointed to the house just north of them—"but they had somethin' else goin' on. And Grace Meredith across the street is out of town, has a couple concerts this weekend. But Rodney should be here any time—that's Harry's son." She added, "DaShawn's daddy."

Okay, so the boy shooting hoops out back was Harry Bentley's *grandson*. Greg hadn't known for sure.

"We gonna eat soon? Don't wanna miss my TV program," Mattie Krakowski groused. "*Dancing with the Stars* comes on at seven."

Estelle and Michelle went upstairs and brought down a couple of trays of appetizers—chilled deviled eggs and hot pizza rolls. The moment food appeared, the basketball stopped bouncing in the alley as if by magic, and the teenagers joined them. On closer look, Greg realized one of them was a girl. Must be one of the Jaspers—the mom had said three of hers were out back.

By this time, Karl Molander was on his feet and moving with everyone toward the tables. "Aren't we going to bless the food first?"

Greg saw Estelle give Harry a look. Harry grinned back at her as though they shared a private secret. "You bet." Harry winked at his wife. "We'd planned to pray before the main meal, but now would be fine." And he launched right in.

"O Lord, we thank you on this Memorial Day for the freedoms you've granted us, and we want to express our gratitude for the men and women who've served our country in defending those freedoms. Comfort families who've lost loved ones in conflicts near and far, and bring healing to those who were wounded. And . . . and bless this food we are about to receive. We thank you for it and ask you to protect us from all impurities, in the name of Jesus, amen."

Protect us from all impurities? What was that about? Greg disguised an explosive laugh as a cough. Maybe Harry was thinking about the Molanders' tuna casserole.

Estelle quickly stepped in to direct traffic by telling the teenagers they needed to wait until other people had served themselves. Greg noticed that Becky and Nate gravitated to the Jaspers' daughter—"Tabby," her brother called her. The young black girl seemed very patient with them. *Nice*. Too bad the father couldn't be here, someone more his age. What was it Nicole said the man did—air traffic controller out at O'Hare? He never would've guessed. Maybe they should get to know the family better.

Well, he could think about that when his job question got settled.

Greg awoke with the sun on June first, eager to hear from Potawatomi Watercraft about his position. He lay staring at the ceiling while Nicole continued to sleep peacefully. He sure hoped he could settle this job thing soon. His marriage needed some maintenance.

But he needed to focus on the job first, right? After all, he was like a farmer: Plant the crops before you build the house. A new house would be of no value if you were starving.

It sounded like proverbial wisdom, but Greg knew it didn't quite apply. They weren't facing imminent starvation, but his relationship with Nicole felt rocky. Not that it was an either/or situation. Still, it felt as if he could focus on her so much better if he knew what he'd be doing jobwise.

He slipped out of bed and went into the kitchen to make coffee. While it brewed, he sat in the breakfast nook and thought about Harry Bentley's prayer for him the day before. Harry prayed differently than Pastor Hanson—not that he'd ever had Pastor Hanson pray for him personally—but the pastor prayed such bold prayers, almost like he was commanding God to do this or that "in the name of Jesus." It really instilled confidence in the power of your own prayer.

Harry had also prayed in Jesus' name, but he hadn't prayed for a specific job. He'd prayed that God would be with the Singers during this time of transition, make his presence known, and protect them from anxiety and fear. Greg didn't think he was anxious or fearful, but the lack of opportunities had stirred some worries—though he knew how God could fix that real quick. Just give him the Potawatomi job with a great big raise.

After praying for Greg, Bentley had told him he'd just come through a period when he had a hard time figuring out what God was doing. He'd thought God was leading him in a certain direction, and then things kept changing. And every change that came along felt like all his plans got derailed, but now he was beginning to see God's hand in more and more of the journey.

Harry's words replayed in his mind: *I'm just sayin', it's like that verse in Isaiah where God says, "As the heavens are higher than the earth, so are my ways higher than your ways and my thoughts than your thoughts."* The older man had slapped him on the shoulder, and they'd dropped the subject as he got up to check the ribs again.

Greg didn't know if he went along with that. Pastor Hanson certainly seemed to grasp God's ways well enough. And that kind of confidence was what he needed today: "Believe it and you'll receive it!"

Thuds from the ceiling above told him the kids were getting up. He poured his coffee and took the cup onto the back porch. He wasn't quite ready to face the day with the family. But Becky and Nate found him, and soon it was breakfast and showers and hustle and bustle until Nicole herded them down to the schoolroom to begin their lessons.

"Uh, Nicole, wait a sec."

She paused halfway down the stairs.

"I'm expecting an important phone call anytime this morning, so I'd appreciate it if you'd make sure the kids don't bother me or make too much noise."

"Is this the dealership that owns the cottage we stayed in?"

"That's the one, probably the best option in the Chicago area, so—"

"Don't worry. I won't let them bother you. But let me know when you get the word."

Greg nodded.

It was business hours. He went to Potawatomi's website and reviewed every page—the products, the special offers, the executives, the company history page. He wanted to be ready to step onboard as soon as he got the call.

But minutes, then hours ticked by. No call.

He surfed the websites of boat manufacturers for which Potawatomi was a dealer to get background on each model, though he already knew most of them.

But by noon, when the call hadn't yet come, he began strategizing how he could call Roger Wilmington without appearing too desperate. Maybe he'd say he'd been out for the morning and wasn't sure his voice mail was working properly, wanted to make sure he hadn't missed the call. But that wasn't the truth.

By two o'clock he'd exhausted his patience. His insides felt wound up like a rubber-band airplane. He had to know. He punched in Roger's number.

The phone rang and rang and rang. Finally . . . "Potawatomi. Wilmington here."

"Hey, Roger. Greg Singer. I wanted to get back to you about the sales position we talked about last week. I think you said today you could—"

"Oh, yeah, Greg. Listen, I'm right in the middle of something here. Can I call you back a little later?"

Chapter 13

A little later didn't happen Tuesday afternoon, and by dinnertime, Greg's stomach was so tied up in knots he couldn't eat more than a couple of bites of the teriyaki chicken Nicole had fixed.

"You sick?" Nicole asked. "You usually love this."

"I know. It tastes great, but . . . no, I'm not sick."

She shrugged and forked another thigh for herself.

By Wednesday morning, Greg's anxiety had turned to anger. Why hadn't Roger called? Even if the answer was no, Roger owed him the courtesy of a call—and a timely call too. But if Potawatomi was so thoughtless, he wasn't sure he'd want to work for them even if they offered.

Wait a minute! Twenty-four hours ago he thought it was the ideal company, the only place in the Chicago area for him, and now he wouldn't work for them even if they offered? Whew! He needed to calm down. With effort, he made himself interact civilly with Nicole and the kids as they ate breakfast and finally headed down to the basement for school.

Once the first floor was quiet, Greg took his seat at his desk in the living room and turned on the computer, then called up his email.

There, third one down, a message from Roger Wilmington at Potawatomi Watercraft. He clicked, knowing before it opened what it would say.

Hey Greg,

Sorry not to get back to you by phone this afternoon, but can you believe it? Our phone system went down. I was going to call you from home, but I left your number at work. Fortunately, you're in my email contact list, so I hope this reaches you.

When we discussed the possibility of you joining us last week, everyone agreed you'd be a great asset to the company, but unfortunately we simply cannot afford someone at your salary level. And it wouldn't be fair to try to talk you down. So I'm afraid we're going to have to take a pass.

But I'm sure you'll land someplace great. Let's keep in touch, buddy. There are bound to be times in the future when we can work together.

Sincerely,

Roger Wilmington
Potawatomi Watercraft

Greg sat for a long moment staring at the email on his screen, anger smoldering. So, that was that. But he wasn't ready to accept what he'd just read. It wasn't just that Roger hadn't called him yesterday. Maybe his techno-excuse was legit, or maybe it wasn't. Didn't matter. The only thing that mattered was that Potawatomi didn't want him. And what was that crap about it not being fair to offer him a lower salary? Huh. Just Roger putting a spin on it to placate him, that's what. If they'd been sincere, they would've made him an offer and let *him* decide whether or not he was willing to accept it.

Greg got up from his desk and stomped out of the house, slamming the back door. He paced around the small yard, shaking his fists in the air and growling. On the fourth lap he crashed the palm of his hand into the gate, breaking the simple latch as it swung open. In the alley, he started north toward the cemetery, only to see Harry Bentley at the far end walking his dog. Before Harry looked back at him, Greg spun around on his heel and headed south. This was no time to face Bentley.

He walked down to Chase Avenue and turned left toward the lake. At Rogers Avenue, he angled northeast and continued walking with no plan in mind. Within a block he came to a park on his left and stepped through the gate into a colorful playground—

empty, probably because Chicago schools weren't out yet. He'd been by this park on other occasions, but had never paid much attention to how nice it looked. That was the thing about Chicago: it had parks in most neighborhoods. In fact there were two in this part of the Rogers Park neighborhood, both within easy walking distance of his house. Greg gritted his teeth as he passed a sprinkler pad, thinking of his own kids playing in the water on hot days. He didn't want to get pushed out of Chicago no matter how good a job he might find elsewhere. This was his city, and he loved it.

The park was larger than he recalled. Beyond the cluster of trees he saw tennis courts, baseball diamonds, fields marked out for soccer, a couple of outdoor basketball courts, and a large field house. But having left home with no plan and no destination, Greg suddenly realized he needed to find a restroom and had to go all the way around to the other end of the field house to find open doors.

When he came out of the restroom, he stopped by the front desk. Above it hung a bulletin board listing upcoming activities but topped with the words, "Welcome to Pottawattomie Park." *Pottawattomie*? He knew there was a Pottawattomie Park somewhere, but . . .

"Is this Pottawattomie?" he asked the attendant.

"That's right, *señor*. Can I help you?"

"No, no. It's okay. Guess I never knew that was the name of this park."

"*Sí*. It's named after the Native Americans who used to live around here."

"Oh yeah. Thanks." Greg turned and wandered out of the front door in a daze. Sure enough, on the fence by the street a much larger sign read, "Pottawattomie Park, Chicago Park District." The spelling was slightly different than Potawatomi Watercraft, but . . . Greg's head spun. The coincidence seemed too powerful to ignore.

If he'd happened by this park before receiving the email this morning, he would've taken it as a sure sign that God was giving him the job, but what was the point now?

He headed slowly for home, trying to make sense of it.

Could he have read the email incorrectly? Should he call Roger back to see if they'd had a change of mind, force Roger to speak to him directly? Maybe he ought to take the initiative and offer to work for them for lower pay. He could negotiate. Maybe work on straight commission. That wouldn't strain their budget, but it wouldn't compensate him for all he'd be contributing either. He was a promoter, an event organizer, not just a salesman.

"There you are." Nicole looked relieved when he came in the house. "We couldn't find you, so I went ahead and made some tomato soup and grilled cheese sandwiches for lunch. Is that okay for you?"

"Sure." He checked his watch—twenty past twelve. He had no idea he'd been out so long. "We got any sour cream to put in the soup?"

"Sorry, all out. Where've you been, anyway?"

"Uh . . . I just went for a walk." He probably ought to tell Nicole. He ought to admit how he was feeling. This seemed like a crisis, and they ought to be praying together, but . . . "Hey Nikki, you ever take the kids over to Pottawattomie Park?"

"Sometimes. We've been over there a time or two, but not yet this year. Kids seem to like that wooden playground with the frontier theme at Indian Boundary better. But Pottawattomie has more organized recreation. I'll probably sign them up for one of their sports programs when they get a little older."

"Yeah. Walked by there today. Looked pretty nice." He'd been ready to suggest praying, but somehow he couldn't steer the small talk around to asking . . . or even to telling her about the devastating email. "Uh, Nicole, would you mind if I put this food on a tray and took it to my desk? I . . . I gotta do some things."

She gave him a strange look but shrugged. "Sure."

Seated at his desk a few moments later, Greg woke up his computer and reread Roger's email. He hadn't misread it. It said exactly what he remembered with the same disappointing conclusion. No job from Potawatomi Watercraft.

An annoying pop-up ad filled a third of Greg's screen. He clicked the X in the corner to dismiss it. Thirty seconds later, the same ad returned. He was about to dismiss it again when the headline caught his attention: "Earn twice your current salary while working from home."

Huh. Greg didn't want to work from home, and it wouldn't take much to earn more than he was making at the moment, but he clicked on the ad and was taken to a classy-looking website for "SlowBurn, the Time-Release Energy Drink that won't let you down!" A video began, showing a parade of attractive young people advancing down a city street toward the camera, each drinking a can of something and then tossing the empty can into a recycle bin. "Cash in today on the fastest-growing segment of the soft drink market, and pocket your share of this nine-billion-dollar industry! Yes, you can earn fifty, seventy, a hundred-and-twenty thousand dollars a year or more and be your own boss while doing so."

Be your own boss . . .

It was that last phrase that kept Greg engaged. After the betrayal by Chuck Hastings for allowing Powersports Expos to collapse and the recent runaround from Roger Wilmington at Potawatomi, he wasn't much inclined to work for another boss. Why *not* work for himself—especially if there was that much money in it?

When the video was over, he read on, intrigued by SlowBurn's interest in sports. The company had already sponsored several marathon and triathlon champions. Leaning back in his chair, Greg rubbed his chin thoughtfully. If they were really going after the sport market, perhaps he would have something to offer.

When Greg clicked on "Build for the future with a breakout franchise," he was asked to type in his name—just his first name, "no obligation." He did so, and the next page describing SlowBurn's pay structure was personalized.

Greg, *you* can get paid in four ways:

1. *Direct profit*. As a SlowBurn rep, you can purchase this amazing product at an incredibly low wholesale price and sell it at whatever markup your market can sustain. It's up to you, the business owner—50 percent, 100 percent or more. Some representatives are able to move substantial quantities with a 200 percent markup. Imagine

getting back three dollars for every dollar you invest!

2. *Team royalties*. By recruiting a team of other reps to work under you, Greg, you can get a percentage of every sale they make. If each of them recruits teams under them, you would get a percentage of their sales as well. And you could build as many tiers as you choose. Unfortunately, there is a cap of $58,000 per week on this compensation. But it is the only pay feature of the program that is capped.

Greg's head jerked back, incredulous. If they had to put a cap on this feature, there must be some people who earned that much! He was a competitor and knew he'd soon be a contestant among the upper echelons, but even if he never reached $58,000 per week, just imagine what he could do with even half that much. A quick calculation in his head rang up a million and a half per year, just in team royalties.

And there was more.

3. *Instant bonuses*. The larger the wholesale quantities your team members purchase, Greg, the lower their price. And you'll be credited with instant bonuses for each order. These bonuses are available down through five team tiers below you. Your wealth and lifestyle is up to you, not the whim of some boss.
4. *Training premiums*. SlowBurn is interested in training its representatives and promoting you up the leadership ladder. For every level completed at one of our quarterly training conferences—held regionally—you will be eligible for an array of premiums.

The website pictured people enjoying a cruise, a yacht, even a Mercedes SLS sports car. "All of this," the webpage noted, "is possible from a business you own and can run from your home, on your terms."

Greg pushed his chair back from the desk. These people weren't talking about chump change. He could hardly imagine how his lifestyle would change. A hundred or two hundred thousand a *month*? What would they do? Where would they live? The possibilities were endless. Wow!

If this were possible, it represented the kind of prosperity Pastor Hanson had been preaching about. Pastor Hanson hadn't been talking about scrimping day to day the way most people lived. He'd been urging his flock to cash in on God's unfathomable wealth, telling them they were kings and the children of the King, so why not live like it?

This just might be the way to do it.

But what exactly would he be selling? Could he get behind the product? It had always been important to him to believe in what he was doing. Was SlowBurn really better than all the other energy drinks people bought at the supermarket?

Greg could hear the kids' chatter in the kitchen as they finished their lunch in the breakfast nook. Nicole . . . What would *she* think about going into business for himself and working from home? Would she just feel like he was underfoot?

He skimmed over the information on the computer screen again. If he did as well as the website testimonial, he could rent an office. Or buy a bigger house with office space. They could even get something grander than the McMansion at the end of the block.

Ha! That would be a sweet role reversal after how presumptuously that guy had behaved toward "Nikki."

Chapter 14

GREG NOTICED HIS LUNCH, still untouched. Absently taking a few bites of the cold toasted cheese, he continued to scroll through the web pages. He knew most energy drinks simply delivered a jolt of caffeine sufficient to make the user feel a surge of energy. But on every page, SlowBurn claimed to be something different. "A product you can sell without apology! A product like no other!"

Ah! A link to the ingredients. He clicked. Now he'd discover the disappointing truth that the whole scheme was nothing more than smoke and mirrors, a product he could duplicate with cans of several brands available at the local 7-Eleven.

A page popped up with a white box at the top listing all the ingredients, similar to what one would find on the side of a cake mix. He scanned through the list, and there it was: caffeine. But it was the next to last ingredient, certainly not the predominant item. SlowBurn contained triple-filtered carbonated spring water, electrolytes, stevia, quinoa, Ganoderma mushrooms, citric acid, natural flavors, taurine, sodium citrate, caffeine, color added.

Below this list, SlowBurn boldly described the ingredients that set it apart from all other energy drinks: quinoa and Ganoderma mushrooms.

Greg made a wry face as he stared at his computer. He'd eaten quinoa. It tasted good enough, but SlowBurn called it a superfood, far more than merely a nutritious substitute for rice, which was how Greg had eaten it. They claimed the extract they distilled from quinoa enhanced the body's ability to absorb oxygen.

Greg stopped. Could that be true?

He opened another window in his browser and searched the web for "quinoa" and "oxygen." A couple of hits would have sent him back to SlowBurn, but then he found an article that pointed out that quinoa had been cultivated for thousand of years by Native

Indians in the Andes of Peru and Bolivia at altitudes between ten- and twenty-thousand feet elevation. The article suggested it was the quinoa that allowed these hardy people to thrive at those altitudes by increasing the body's ability to absorb oxygen. In addition to extending physical endurance, more oxygen to the brain meant heightened alertness. All this made sense to Greg, even though the article didn't include scientific research in support of the theory.

SlowBurn's other special ingredient was an extract from the Ganoderma mushrooms, "an herb used in traditional Asian medicines to purge the body of pollutants." The product description claimed it had an anticancer, antibacterial, antiviral, antifungal effect, able to reduce cholesterol and protect the liver.

Wow! Either this was nothing more than snake oil or SlowBurn was really onto something. Greg was fascinated. He looked up the strange mushroom online and found much the same description SlowBurn gave it.

Every information page was accompanied by a popup box saying: "Click here to build your future, Greg, with a breakout franchise," and "Greg, the timing couldn't be better for your SlowBurn start. Click here." "When was the last time you were paid every time someone drank a soft drink? Click here, Greg, and start your income flowing."

Finally he clicked, and he wasn't surprised when he had to fill out his full name, address, phone number, and email address.

"You will be contacted shortly," was the only response on his screen when he completed the form.

Okay. He needed a stretch. Greg got up and paced around the living room to clear his head. This couldn't really be happening. He'd probably just been suckered into being added to a bunch of promotion lists that would feed him spam for weeks to come. He headed for the kitchen to make some coffee.

The coffeemaker had barely begun to gurgle when his cell phone rang. It was a Chicago exchange, but he didn't recognize the caller ID. "Hello."

"Greg Singer? This is Arlo Fulbright. I'm the Chicago area director for SlowBurn. Do I understand correctly that you recently indicated your interest in becoming a SlowBurn representative?"

Greg stood in the middle of the kitchen as the smell of fresh coffee filled the kitchen. "Yes, yeah. I'm Greg Singer. You caught me by surprise. I didn't expect such a quick response." For that matter, he hadn't expected any kind of a personal response. "How'd you get my num—oh, right, I filled it in, didn't I?"

"You sure did, which tells me you're serious about this. And we want to demonstrate our enthusiasm for anyone who is a viable SlowBurn representative. Now, because you responded online, you were referred to me as the director for the Chicago area. But if you join us, you'll be able to recruit team members who'll report directly to you. Only you would report to me. So tell me a little about yourself, Greg, and why you're interested in SlowBurn."

Greg glanced at the coffee. The carafe was only half full, so he drifted back into the living room, phone to his ear. Too excited to sit at his desk, he walked around the room telling Arlo about the position he'd held with Powersports Expos. Arlo asked all the right questions to allow him to highlight his achievements without seeming to brag.

"Well, I can certainly say that you're the kind of person who would be well suited for SlowBurn. So are you wanting to do this on the side, or are you looking to make a career change?"

Greg hesitated. "Well, to be completely upfront with you, Powersports is folding. So I'm looking for a new job. There aren't many options in my field in the Chicago area, but we don't want to move. So . . ."

"So you're checking us out. That's great, because I think you'll like what you find. Greg, I see that you live up on the Northside. I'm pretty tied up for the next couple of days, but any chance you'd have time Friday afternoon to come down to Hyde Park, where I'm located? I'd like us to meet face to face, make sure the chemistry is right. And of course, you need to sample SlowBurn and see how we're set up. Usually product is shipped from our Pennsylvania headquarters direct to the U.S. reps, but I've got a small regional warehouse here with the various packages. Sometimes there's a run on product and a rep can't wait for overnight delivery. Think you could make it?"

Greg hesitated only a moment. Free on Friday? He was free right now! But he said, "Sure, I could do that. Friday at . . .?"

"Three o'clock good for you?" Arlo gave his address, and the call was over.

Greg took a deep breath. Could this really be the answer to his prayers?

"Nicole? Nicole!" he called from the top of the basement stairs. His wife came to the bottom of the steps and looked up at him.

"Good news, honey. I've got a job lead down in Hyde Park. Got an interview Friday afternoon. I'm gonna take the Cherokee. That's not your shopping day, is it?"

"No." A smile warmed her face. "That's great, Greg. I knew the Lord would provide."

Greg grinned. "Yeah, well, you have no idea how huge this might be. But I want to check it out in person before I get too excited about it. Think I'll go for a run, work off some of the tension I've been under."

"Good idea." Nicole gave him one of her sunshine smiles. She really was a gorgeous woman. And, though he hardly dared mention it, he thought she might've lost a few of those extra pounds lately.

Changing into his running clothes, he felt lightheaded. If he was his own boss, he might be able to get back to running like he used to do. And a job like this might fix all the tension that'd been building between him and Nicole for the last few weeks. Probably his fault mostly. Even before Powersports let him go, he'd been uptight. And since then he'd worried far more than he'd acknowledged. When he got this job pinned down, he'd make it up to her.

Good heavens, he'd be able to do more than make it up. He'd turn her into a queen. They'd be moving on up.

Greg had no sooner left for his interview on Friday than Nicole dismissed "school" early. The kids had worked hard all week and completed all the assignments she had planned for them. Should she have prepared more? No. It'd been more than enough. She might be tired, but the kids were doing great. She told Becky and Nathan to run outside and play while she cleaned up the basement classroom and turned off the computer and lights.

When she got upstairs thirty minutes later, Nicole went out on the porch to check on them. They were fine, racing their bikes up the sidewalk on the other side of the street. "No riding in the street!" she called. "Sidewalk only!"

Nate waved one hand in the air while he concentrated on going even faster to stay ahead of Becky. This dead-end block of Beecham Street was fairly safe as far as traffic was concerned, seldom any cars other than those that belonged to neighbors. But occasionally a car drove too fast, like right now!

A black limo accelerated down the street from Lincoln Paddock's place. The rear sunroof was open, and just as it passed, two women stood up through the opening and yelled something. One was dressed in a well-filled halter-top and waved at Nicole like she was riding in a speedboat. The other was untangling a pink boa wrapped around her neck. They certainly seemed to be celebrating something.

Nicole had often seen people coming and going from the big house at the end of the street and had accepted the rumor that Paddock threw wild parties. In the past, she'd never cared. But today . . .

She watched the limo brake at the end of the block and turn west. Was Lincoln inside with those girls? Couldn't tell from the tinted windows. Seemed a little early in the afternoon to be partying. The Lincoln Paddock she'd come to know didn't seem like a playboy. He was certainly good looking—knock-'em-dead handsome, in fact. But he'd always acted like a gentleman, casual but refined.

Shaking her head, she turned back inside. The situation bothered her. But why? *Good grief, Nicole.* If the man wanted to throw parties, that was his business. She shouldn't care. No, she was only concerned about the safety of their street.

Still . . . what were those girls doing at his place? Were they friends of his? He'd seemed to enjoy having someone to talk to—like they'd done at the zoo—but if that was the case, why hadn't he just come down to her house? They could've sat on the porch and had a glass of iced tea. Or if that felt awkward to him, he could've invited her to come up to his place.

Nicole knocked her shin on one of the dining room chairs as she passed through the room. *What am I thinking?* She was a married woman, mother of two. She had no business thinking about a handsome bachelor inviting her up to his "pad." No. If he had asked her, she definitely would have said no. Maybe they could talk on her porch, but she wouldn't have gone to his place.

Traffic was light going down Lakeshore Drive until Greg got to Soldier Field, then it clogged with early rush-hour drivers. Greg calmed himself and flipped on the radio. Maybe some worship music on Moody Radio would help him avoid yelling at the jerks sneaking up along the right shoulder trying to pass everyone else.

Arlo's place faced west on the fourteenth floor of a modern building adjacent to Harold Washington Park. As Greg rapped on the door, he wondered why a multimillionaire wouldn't have insisted on an expansive eastside vista of Lake Michigan.

"Hey, man, right on time," Arlo said as he ushered Greg into what was obviously the apartment where he lived, not an office suite.

Arlo was about forty, with dark hair and a week-old beard, the kind some guys cultivated to appear too casual to shave but not countercultural enough to grow a real beard. He was dressed in jeans and an open-necked white shirt under a tan corduroy jacket. But Greg noticed that his black loafers looked like top-of-the-line Italian.

The apartment was pretty basic—nice, but nothing special, with the usual casual mess of a single guy. Apologizing for how things looked, Arlo said, "I'm focusing on my place in Florida. Now that's a domicile you gotta see to believe—sweet. But hey, first things first. Have you ever tried SlowBurn? You gotta try it, because I'm tellin' you, once you sample it, there'll be no turning back."

Greg followed him into the kitchen, only slightly troubled at how Arlo's description of the product sounded like a pitch for street drugs. But obviously this stuff was legal or they couldn't be promoting it all over the web.

The eight-ounce cans Arlo pulled from his refrigerator were a smoky brown with a yellow-tipped blue flame on the side. He poured each into a wine glass and handed one to Greg. It looked like a creamy iced coffee with a slight head on it. The taste was light, refreshing, and something like a cream soda.

"So, how do you like it? Think you can sell this stuff?"

Greg shrugged. "Yeah, it's good."

"But good's not what sells it. I'll ask you in ten minutes how you feel, whether you're more alert, are thinking faster, more in tune with your surroundings, without the jittery feeling of too much caffeine. Then you tell me what you think."

Greg nodded as they left the kitchen, not oblivious to the fact that Arlo had just described how he *ought* to feel in a few minutes. There was a lot to the power of suggestion, but Greg believed he could be just as good a salesman as Arlo was.

"Come on into my office, and we can get started."

Arlo's office occupied the smaller of the two bedrooms in the apartment, but it served adequately as a home office. Better than what Greg had at the moment. Arlo took him through a slick booklet reviewing most of the information Greg had already studied on the web.

"You'll get one of these promo booklets at your first training session, then you can use it to bring the teammates you recruit up to speed. By the way, we've got a Chicago-area training coming up in a couple of weeks, June 22 through 25, out at the Hyatt Regency in Schaumburg. You'll want to register soon. The training's only six-ninety-five, and we get a group discount on the rooms. It'll put you right on track with your first level Training Premium."

The idea of a local training program focused a question that had been in the back of Greg's mind ever since Arlo said he was the Chicago-area director. "How many franchises or reps are in Chicago? I mean, are we going to be competing for customers and territory?"

"Ha, you don't have to worry about that. There are over five million people in Cook County alone. And this training will be bringing in reps from all the collar counties, even Milwaukee, Rockford, and northern Indiana. We may be getting big, but you're in on the ground floor. I can tell you that right now, no one's covering that whole north end of the city, let alone Evanston or Skokie. But you're asking the right questions. See what SlowBurn will do for your mind? You'll be the man, Greg." He slapped him on the shoulder. "You're the man!"

Greg had a few more questions, but Arlo said, "Let me take you over to our warehouse. I want you to see the actual product packages we offer so you can get a better idea what you're dealing with."

The product was in a stall the size of a one-car garage in a nearby public storage facility—not what Greg had imagined as a *warehouse,* but it was clean and bright and certainly seemed to hold enough product.

"Here we go. As you can see from the boxes, you can choose from platinum, gold, silver, bronze, and starter packs. The starter packs are for team members you recruit, but I'd recommend you begin with a platinum supply because you're gonna sell a lot of this stuff, so there's no reason why you shouldn't earn the largest Instant Bonus from the outset."

"You mean there's no reason *you* shouldn't earn the largest Instant Bonus from the start."

"Ha, ha. There you go. I told you SlowBurn sharpens your mind. But really, we both benefit from the bonuses. That's the thing about this company: We're family, share and share alike. You know what I'm saying."

Greg frowned. "I've got just one other question. This whole thing sounds an awful lot like a pyramid scheme, and I thought those were illegal."

"Oh, they are. But a pyramid scheme, or a Ponzi scheme, as it's sometimes called, doesn't involve any product. In those schemes, a person pays money to join, and then the next level of people to participate begin to pay them off while passing on a portion of the money up to the next level, and so on. But when no one else joins, everybody but those at the top lose what they've invested. You can see why it's illegal—no product, no real wealth generated, just the top people collecting everyone else's money."

Greg waited to hear the difference.

"This is multilevel marketing with real product, and a very valuable product at that. Look, every marketing network in the country works on the same basis. There are the owners, the producers, the wholesalers, the retailers, and finally the consumers. All the way up the line, people are taking risks, investing their time and money to deliver the product to the consumer. Each one gets a little slice of the profit, but there's a real product, a warehouse like this, and satisfied consumers, or it wouldn't exist."

Greg nodded his head slowly.

"Hey, don't take my word for it. You can go to the library or online and check it out. This is as legit as snow in a Chicago winter."

They both laughed.

By five thirty that afternoon, Greg closed the tailgate on his Cherokee loaded with a platinum supply of SlowBurn plus two starter packs. He was an authorized representative of SlowBurn, with papers to prove it and a bank account that was $1,385.46 lighter.

He had something good to report to Nicole when he got home, but by the time he got to the Outer Drive, all lanes were backing up with rush-hour traffic. And then the radio reported a bad accident just north of Navy Pier was blocking three lanes of traffic. "Anyone who can avoid this area should choose a different route."

Greg checked his rearview mirror. Should he gut it out on the Drive or exit west on Roosevelt Road and find another way home? Glancing to his right out over the lake, he saw a green and black ultralight plane floating gently down for a landing on Northerly Island where Meigs Field used to be.

That's right! The Burnham Harbor Boat Show was in progress—the event he'd worked so hard to plan. The exit for Burnham Harbor was just ahead. He sure wasn't going anywhere fast creeping along on the Outer Drive. He flipped on his turn signal. Why not?

Chapter 15

FINALLY TURNING ONTO EAST 18TH DRIVE, Greg headed out to the harbor just as the ultralight took off again, clawing its way up into the broken clouds out over the lake. He watched it go with a sense of satisfaction. Before today, he wouldn't have dared show his face at Powersports' last in-water event. But now that he had a job—no, now that he was in business for himself—it'd be a pleasure to answer if someone asked him, "Hey, Greg, how's it going?"

He parked the Jeep and phoned Nicole. It rang five times and went to voice mail. Oh, well. "Hi, Nikki, I've got some great news. Everything's gonna be okay. I'll tell you all about it when I get home. But there's a huge accident on the Drive, so I'm stopping by the boat show for a little while until it clears up. Don't expect me before seven. Okay? Love ya."

The woman on the gate didn't know Greg, which was understandable since ticket sales, crowd control, and other such details were all subcontracted. But when he said he'd been the event coordinator for Powersports who'd negotiated the deal with *her* boss, she let him in for free.

As he headed toward the docks, he wondered if he'd see Chuck Hastings or any of the other people from Powersports. He'd be glad to see them . . . or not. It didn't really matter, but there was an ache in his chest as he walked around and saw the various boats on display and sensed everyone's enthusiasm. He'd loved his job, but now he passed through the show as if he were a ghost who no longer belonged there.

It was only slightly after seven when Greg finally got home, but the dining room table was still fully set for four. "Nikki, what's up?

When I said I'd be late, I didn't mean you had to hold dinner for me. The kids must be starving."

His wife waved her hand. "I gave 'em a snack, but I could tell you were pretty excited, so I thought we should all eat together." She grinned at him. "And besides, they helped me cook."

"Hmm, thanks." He pulled her to him and gave her a quick peck on the lips. "So what have you master chefs prepared?"

"Stroganoff and noodles," Becky boasted.

"But Mommy had to cut the onion because we were crying."

"There you go." Greg grabbed his son in a headlock and gave him a teasing Dutch rub. "Now you know that even superheroes like you cry sometimes."

"Ouch. But it wasn't me," Nathan protested. "The onion made me do it."

"Well, it's always something. C'mon, Mom wants us to come to the table."

They held hands as Greg said a blessing. "Lord, I want to thank you for my family and for providing for us. And especially for this good food. Amen."

As Nicole heaped noodles and stroganoff onto their plates, she smiled at him hopefully. "So what did you find out today?"

Greg chewed thoughtfully, making sure the kids knew he appreciated the meal. "The surprising thing is, this job isn't in event management, at least not big events with hundreds of people like I've been doing. Though come to think of it, those big venues might provide some great opportunities . . ."

"Opportunities for what?"

"Sorry, I'm getting ahead of myself. Still processing all the possibilities. Okay, so here's the thing: We're going into business. Well, actually, I'm going into business for myself. But it'll involve us all."

"You're what? You're going to compete with Chuck?"

"No, no. Powersports is a has-been. And I'm not doin' sports shows. I'm the new area rep for SlowBurn." He paused, waiting for her to respond. Nicole looked confused. "Okay, you probably haven't heard of it. It's too new. But you know what energy drinks are, don't you? You can get 'em in any store. SlowBurn's an energy drink, but it doesn't load you with a lot of caffeine, and it's not sold in stores. It's different. As their motto says, 'It's the Time-Release Energy Drink that won't let you down!'"

"And you're gonna, what . . . sell this stuff?"

He launched into an enthusiastic explanation of his new business. "First I have to create a warm list, actually two warm lists." Seeing the question in her face, he explained. "A warm list is people you know personally—family, friends, people at church, people I know. One list will be potential customers. And that could be just about anybody because the stuff is so great. The other list is people who have ambition to better themselves, to get ahead. Arlo—he's the area director for Chicago—said they don't need to be skilled salespeople because the product will sell itself. They simply need to be people who want a better lifestyle and are willing to put in the effort to get there. They'll become my associates, and—"

"Mom, I'm done," Nathan interrupted. "Can we go watch a video?"

"You haven't finished your salad."

"Aw, Mom, I don't want any more."

"Finish your salad. Then you and Becky can watch for half an hour."

"Aw, Mom, one video won't even be over by then, please?"

Greg caught Nicole's eye and gave her a *let-'em-do-it* shrug. He figured bringing Nicole up to speed might take more than half an hour.

She sighed. "Just eat your salad and go."

As soon as the kids left the table, Greg tried to continue his explanation, but Nicole peppered him with questions: Had he checked out the company with the Better Business Bureau? How would Greg get paid? Would there be any base salary they could count on? What about benefits?

"No, no, not in the traditional sense. Health insurance and retirement plans are things employees want but can hardly get these days. But this is a business, *our* business. We build it. We get the profits. And we're gonna earn so much that things like insurance and pensions will seem like mere perks."

She frowned. "Then what does the company provide, this guy you went to see?"

"The company backs us up, provides product, training, and support. Of course, in exchange for all that they get a small cut of our profits, but most of that'll come back in the form of the bonuses they offer. You can't imagine all the opportunities." Greg breathed in patience. Answering Nicole's questions was good practice for recruiting associates. "Remember I told you I believed God was going to prosper us? Well, this is it. I just gotta reach out and claim it."

Nicole nodded slowly. "Wel, maybe so." She put a hand on his arm. "Really, I'm glad if you've found something you're excited about. I never doubted God would take care of us. It's just . . . well, we'll see what God does."

"That's right, honey, and I can't wait."

"There's just one thing, though." The frown was back. "I always feel, you know, uncomfortable when friends or family use our relationship as . . . as leverage to get me to do something. I mean, even if it's a good thing, I still don't like feeling manipulated." She grimaced.

Greg threw out his hands. "You wouldn't say that about evangelism, would you? I mean, isn't it our responsibility to tell a friend about Jesus' love or . . . or even warn 'em about the consequences of rejecting salvation? You know, friends don't let friends go to hell, to put it in crass terms."

"Yes, but there are ways of sharing the gospel that don't manipulate. But when you talked about creating a warm list . . . I don't know. It seemed . . ."

"Hey, I'm not going to be manipulating anyone. It all depends on the product. If the product's really great, then sharing it is not only easier, it's like doing the other person a favor." He stopped, a shocked look on his face, and held up his hand. "Wait a minute! I forgot the most important thing. I'll be right back."

He returned from the kitchen with a clean glass, half filled with ice, in one hand and a can of SlowBurn in the other. "I forgot I had this in my briefcase. Here . . ." He sat down, popped the top, and poured. "Try it."

She hesitated to pick up the glass. "It won't keep me up all night, will it?"

"No. There's very little caffeine in it. Maybe like a cup of green tea. Go ahead, try it."

Nicole took a sip and then a larger swallow.

"Whaddaya think?"

Nicole's eyebrows went up as she licked her lips. "It's good. Kinda reminds me of a root beer float with enough ice cream to make it creamy." She took another swallow. "You sure it won't keep me awake?"

He grinned. "The idea of starting our new business might, but not the drink. And that's what I was trying to tell you. What kind of a friend would I be if I had the key to a six-figure salary and *didn't* share that secret with my best friends? What if the only people I offered it to were complete strangers, people I contacted through cold calls? It might be great for those strangers, but avoiding my friends and family because I was afraid they'd misunderstand and think I was manipulating them? No way. It's just like with the good news of salvation."

"But . . ."

"But what?" This was becoming frustrating. If Nicole were a potential associate, would he continue recruiting her? Would he even keep her on his warm list? He closed his eyes and exhaled. "So, what's your problem?"

"I just . . . guess I feel uncomfortable comparing an energy drink to the gospel. I mean, we know the gospel is true. Its rewards are obvious in the lives of millions of people, including our own, and we believe God's Word brings eternal life. But this SlowBurn is just a product—I mean, it tastes good, and it might be good for you, I'm not doubting that, and maybe you'll do well and make a lot of money, but . . ."

This wasn't going like Greg expected. He had to turn it around. "Honey, I'm not comparing an energy drink to the gospel. But it's all about believing in what you're doing. It's whether you know that you know that you know. Arlo kept hammering that into me today. You gotta believe in your product. And I do! I really believe this stuff is all it's cracked up to be, and there's a market out there for it—just like there was for the boats and ATVs that Powersports used to help sell. Or anything, for that matter. So I don't think I'll be manipulative."

Nicole's shoulders sagged as she sat back in her chair. "I'm sure you won't, Greg, and I don't mean to be challenging you on this.

I guess . . . I didn't realize how anxious about this job thing *I'd* become." She reached out and took another sip of the SlowBurn. That seemed like a good sign.

Greg got up and walked around behind her, leaning over and nuzzling her behind her ear. "It's okay, hon. God came through. More than that, he's stacked the deck for us to win. This is it. I can feel it in my bones. We're coming into our blessing, just like the pastor said."

"Oh, Greg, I hope so, but I just don't know if that's the right way to think about it."

"Trust me. It's happening whether we understand it or not."

They cleared the table in silence. His course was clear to him. What had seemed like a test would become his testimony. Maybe he needed to exert his headship of the family more strongly, focusing on the vision he felt God had given him even if his wife couldn't see it. He thought of other metaphors: a strong and steady hand on the helm, a tight rein on a narrow trail, determination in a sea of doubt. He could tell she really wanted to follow his lead. He just needed to stay in control in order to bring her along.

That night, after the kids were asleep upstairs, he reached out to Nicole in bed and drew her close. It had been a long time since they were intimate. Not good. But tonight she surrendered to him willingly enough and for a while seemed to respond with passion . . . but then it slipped away as though something had distracted her while Greg charged on until he lay spent and panting. Well, he couldn't help that.

As his wife's breathing slowed into sleep, he stared into the darkness reviewing the people he planned to talk to the next day about SlowBurn. His warm lists grew—prospective consumers on one and people who had ambition to better themselves on the other. They would be the most valuable because every sale they made would mean more profit for him. He finally fell asleep as the lists got too long for him to remember all the names.

Saturday—Greg got up eagerly and hurried through breakfast so he could unload the Jeep Cherokee, stacking the SlowBurn boxes in the garage, though they barely left enough room for the car. He warned the kids not to mess with the product, that it was Daddy's new business and would be very expensive if any of the boxes got damaged.

Nicole came out to the garage and leaned against the doorframe, surveying the stacks of SlowBurn cases. "Did you have to pay for all that stuff?"

"Yep, and it's all paid for. Which means everything we receive when we sell it goes into our pocket."

"How much?"

"Every penny."

"No, I mean, how much did it cost you?"

"Oh, that. A little over thirteen . . . almost fourteen hundred. But I gotta have product for my associates. Plus I get a larger profit margin when I buy in quantity. It's like any business."

Nicole just stared at the boxes, then abruptly turned and went back to the house.

Greg squared his shoulders. He couldn't let his wife's reservations slow down the launch of his new business. He had to get out there and make some sales. His warm list included family, friends, and former business associates—all those people he'd worked with at Powersports. He might not be in the powerboat and off-road vehicle business any longer, but he had wisely preserved all his contacts.

But first he needed some practice. He needed to make his pitch to several people who had good potential but weren't likely to become high-volume sales reps. People in his church and even those right here in the neighborhood might be good candidates—people like Harry Bentley and Jared Jasper, who Bentley said worked out at O'Hare Airport as an air traffic controller. Now that was a job where you had to keep alert. Greg grinned. Everybody in the tower needs "the Time-Release Energy Drink that won't let you down!" That ought to be an easy sell.

But first he'd start with Harry Bentley. They'd gotten to know each other pretty well at the Memorial Day barbecue. Going back into the house, Greg grabbed a six-pack of SlowBurn from the refrigerator, put a few brochures in his pocket, and headed over to Bentley's.

He rang the bell to the second floor unit three times with no response and was debating whether it was better to introduce SlowBurn casually—like he'd planned—or set up formal appointments with people, when the old lady from the first floor apartment came to the door.

"Oh." She took a step back. "I didn't know someone was here. I was just going to post this card to my son in Elgin. It's his birthday next week."

"Sorry to have startled you. I'm Greg Singer. We live across the street. You're Mrs. Krakowski, aren't you?" When she nodded, he went on. "Do you know if the Bentleys are home? I wanted to see Harry for a bit."

"Haven't heard them all morning." The old woman shuffled outside and clipped the card to her mailbox. "But sometimes I don't hear a thing unless they're playing that music with all that *boom, boom, boom.*"

"Oh, well, thanks anyway." Greg turned and stepped down the first step. "I hope your son has a happy birthday."

"Thank you. That's kind of you. We're going to have a big picnic with all the family a week from Sunday, but I wanted to get my card there on his actual birthday."

A big picnic with all the family . . .

Greg turned back. "Uh, would you have a few minutes to talk, Mrs. Krakowski? I've got something I'd like to show you."

Chapter 16

Greg didn't really see old Mrs. Krakowski as a blue-ribbon member of his team, but she was his first sale and, in fact, his first associate. Her check for forty-nine dollars was in his pocket, and he would take her SlowBurn starter kit over to her as soon as the rain stopped so she could sell it at her family picnic.

The thunderstorm had come up while they'd been talking, but it would pass quickly. Back home, he sat down at his computer and registered Mattie Krakowski's name and information under his own. At least it was a start, and who knew where it might lead?

By noon there were only a few drops still falling from the trees when he delivered her product and assured her she could earn fifty dollars or more, all depending on how much she sold the cans for. "But the best thing for you is to get some of your relatives to sell it too. Then you'll really make money."

She squinted at him, then shrugged and shut the door.

Before he left, he tried Bentley's doorbell one more time and was surprised when Harry's voice came over the intercom.

"Hey Harry, it's Greg Singer from down the street. Will you be home for the next few minutes? I've got something I want to show you, but I've got to run home and get it."

Selling Harry Bentley on SlowBurn wasn't as easy as Mrs. Krakowski. Not that his neighbor didn't listen courteously, but Greg could see in Harry's eyes when his interest switched off. Nevertheless, Greg hoped he might score a reversal.

"So, what do you think? You like how it tastes?"

"Oh yeah. Tastes okay, but I just like my coffee. Estelle too."

"Coffee's good, especially in the morning or when it's cold. But in the summer, people want something refreshing, and—"

"Then I grab a Pepsi. Used to be I'd reach for a brewsky, but I had to cut that out 'cause they seemed to, uh, multiply, if you know what I mean."

Greg chuckled and nodded. "But how about your grandson?"

"Oh, he might like one of these drinks from time to time."

"And that would be a good choice for you to encourage. You know, kids are always drinking something. What could be better than providing a healthy alternative, an energy drink that's not loaded with sugar and caffeine."

Harry shrugged. "Well, you can ask him. If that's what he wants to spend his allowance on, that's up to him."

"What about you? Even if you're not into energy drinks yourself, a franchise like this could provide a welcome income stream on the side. If you're anything like me, we all can use a few extra bucks. Right?"

"You're wanting me to sell this stuff?"

Greg raised his index finger as though asking to make one final point. "As your neighbor—as your *friend*—I just want to be sure you have a chance to get in on the ground floor of a serious business opportunity. I mean, working for Amtrak, you encounter thousands of people a week, and what better way—"

"Hey, I don't have anything to do with the food service or the concessions, either on the trains or in the station. That's a completely different department, probably managed out of D.C. In fact, I don't even have a clue who to talk to about that sort of thing."

"Oh, I wasn't meaning the official food service, but on the side."

"Not a chance." There was exasperation in Harry's voice. "There're regulations, against that kind of thing, ya know. But even if there weren't, that's not me. I'm just not into the entrepreneurial thing. Hear what I'm sayin'?"

"Yeah." Greg was tempted to press on, but Harry had made himself clear. "I hear ya. But, hey . . ." Greg stood up from the dining room table where they'd been talking. "If you ever change your mind, I'm your man. Okay?"

"You'll be the first to know." Harry reached out a restraining hand. "Before you go, though, sit back down for another hot minute."

Greg lowered himself back onto the chair.

"I didn't mean to put down what you're doin'. In fact, I'm interested in how it turns out for you. So, is this energy drink thing what you're doin' full time now, or is it more like what you said—you know, a side income?"

Greg looked down. Somehow the high he'd been riding was headed for a landing. But he pushed the throttle forward and looked up. "I think this is it, Harry. I think this is my big opportunity. I'm believing God for this. He has a big blessing for me—huge, beyond anything I can imagine. I really believe it."

With his eyebrows arched and his mouth in a *maybe-so* frown, Harry nodded. "Well, I hope it works out for you. But to be honest, if *I* was going after that, it'd be 'penny wise and pound foolish' for me."

"What? Oh, believe me, Harry, I'm not focusing on the small stuff. I'm going after the gold ring here. Know what I mean? And you could too." Greg slapped him on the shoulder. "Come on. Join me."

"Nope." Harry shook his head, his face sober. "But I will pray for you, Greg. Let me know how it turns out."

"I will. And hey, speaking of prayer, the last time we talked, you invited me to your men's Bible study. Any chance I could take you up on that?"

Harry's eyebrows went up. "Sure thing. Every Tuesday at seven. Want me to pick you up?"

"That'd be great. I'd like to get to know some of those other men." Greg stood up again. "Guess I'd better get goin', though. Nicole's gonna think I got lost."

A few moments later, as he was going down the stairs, Greg pressed his lips together and pumped his fist, "Yes!" Connections to more people would surely turn into sales sooner or later.

But outside the Bentleys' two-flat he hesitated, then crossed the street to the Jaspers' house. As he recalled, Jared worked a strange schedule, so he wasn't surprised when no one answered the door. However tomorrow was Sunday, and he knew the Jaspers usually went to church, so hopefully he could snag Jared some time in the afternoon.

But when he got home, he was surprised to find Jared's daughter at his house.

"Daddy, Daddy," Becky crowed as he came in, "Tabby's here. She's Mommy's helper, and we're gonna show her our school."

"Uh, that's nice." Greg had no idea why Nicole needed a helper, and he was starting to feel some concern about their money. But he'd talk to her about that later. "Hi, Tabby, it's good to see you. But don't let these rascals work you too hard down there or you'll have to join the Chicago Teacher's Union."

"Oh, I won't, Mr. Singer." The young teen grinned and followed the kids down to the basement.

Greg sat down at his computer to work on his warm list. He wanted to create a sublist of the eight or ten people he might see at church the next day. Some he only knew by first names—though Nicole might know their last names—but his intuition told him not to drag her into it just yet. A few of the people usually sat in the same section where he and Nicole sat, then there were the workers in the children's church they interacted with when they dropped off the kids, a particularly friendly usher, and a couple of people who worked the coffee bar where Greg always stopped after the second service. He knew the names of most of the pastoral staff—or could look them up—but he doubted if any of them knew him. And again, his intuition told him to hold off approaching the church staff.

After working the phone and Facebook for the next couple of hours, he had enough information to approach most of the people the next day and try to set up a meeting with them. He was proud of his sleuthing. But as he stared at the names on his list, he realized his church contacts were certainly different than the kind of relationships Harry Bentley talked about when describing his Bible study brothers. Sounded like those guys knew each other well enough to have each other's backs during the week. Huh. He could count on two hands all the people he knew at church, but didn't have a clue where most of them lived and hadn't been inside even one of their homes.

Must be the difference between a big church and a small group. At least now he'd get to know a few of the people from church—another benefit of SlowBurn.

That evening at supper, Greg eyed Nicole casually. "So tell me about this mother's helper bit. How'd it go?"

"I think it went pretty well. What'd you kids think . . . Nate?"

Nate shrugged. "Tabby's okay, but she didn't want to play any video games with me. All she did was look at Becky's school lessons."

Nicole frowned. "Hmm. Maybe she didn't play video games with you because you didn't have permission to play games this afternoon. At least you didn't ask me."

"But you said she was a mommy's helper, so I thought I could ask her."

"That's true, but next time we should talk about it ahead of time."

Greg forked a bite of pork chop. "So, was this just a one-time thing?"

"Not sure. I wanted to see how it'd go."

"You pay her? You know, hon, until SlowBurn takes off, we might need to watch our money a little."

"I paid her, but it wasn't much. More like a tip."

They ate in silence a few moments. Then Nicole laid down her fork. "Greg, I really asked Tabby to come as kind of a test. I was thinking, with you out of work, maybe I should step up. I don't think making jewelry or some kind of a home industry with the kids would make much money. But if I could get some reliable help with the kids over the summer, I might be able to pick up some part-time legal work."

"Legal work, part-time?" He tried not to snort. "That seems rather unlikely."

"Not really." Nicole lifted her chin. "Most of what paralegals do is pretty straightforward—drafting documents and contracts and other administrative duties. And with the Internet, you don't need a five-thousand-volume legal library, so I could help research relevant cases, court decisions, and all kinds of legal articles online."

"But the chances of actually finding a firm that would hire you—"

"Mo-om!" Nathan whined. "I can't cut my meat."

Nicole cut Nathan's pork chop for him. "Maybe. But Lincoln Paddock told me they're always needing help at his firm. He even said they have another paralegal who's part-time and sometimes works at home."

Greg's jaw dropped as he stared at his wife. "Paddock, the guy in that megahouse down the block?"

"That's right. He didn't actually offer me a job, but he gave me his card. I think it's a real possibility."

"Okay, now wait a minute. I don't really think that'll be necessary. SlowBurn's gonna take off, Nicole. I just know it. I mean, saying we need to be careful of our spending right now doesn't mean I need to send my wife out to moonlight." This whole conversation was making him upset. "By the way, when did Paddock talk to you about needing a paralegal, anyway?"

"When he took the kids down to the zoo."

"Huh. You mean the day he spent with *you* down at the zoo? Did you tell him I was out of work? Because I'm not. I'm starting my own business."

"Greg, that was the day—the afternoon—*before* you came home and said you'd been laid off. So, no, I didn't tell him you were out of work. I didn't even know it myself at the time."

"I wasn't laid off. Powersports closed. There's a difference."

Nicole gave him a look, then picked up her fork again. "Whatever."

Greg couldn't get Lincoln Paddock out of his mind as he sat through church the next morning. The man was hitting on his wife and she didn't even realize it. Or maybe she did, but there was no way he was going to let her work for him. In fact, there was no way he was going to let her become the breadwinner for their family. How would that make him feel? Some men might not care, but he did. And he was going to make a success out of SlowBurn to prove he could support his family with his own business.

But the response of the people Greg talked to after the service was mixed. Several said, "Sure, let's find a time." But more than half were hesitant, almost scared was the way Greg read them when he mentioned he had a business opportunity he wanted to share. Okay, that was understandable. Most people didn't think of themselves as businesspeople, even though they might have great presentation skills.

"Don't approach people like you're testing them," Arlo had said. *"Affirm them for who they are and nurture those skills that will make them become effective representatives."* Well, he'd follow Arlo's advice when he met with the ones who'd agreed, which he hoped to do in the next two weeks. Arlo had emphasized how important it was for him to go to the company's training conference out in Schaumburg, which was coming up real soon—June 22. He'd have to be sure and attend, even though he didn't want to face the $695 price tag for the event, *plus* hotel room and meals. They didn't have much cushion in their bank account. But maybe he'd have sold some product by then and lined up some associates. Two weeks was two weeks.

Greg saw the Jaspers' white minivan bringing the whole family home about three that afternoon. Did their church really go that long? Maybe they went out to eat or something. But he didn't want to waste time waiting around. His stop at the boat show Friday evening had given him an idea. He'd use the boat show as his excuse for dropping in on the Jaspers, ask whether they'd attended or not, and if so, how they'd enjoyed the show. He could mention a few of the things he'd noticed when he'd dropped by. Then he could casually introduce SlowBurn. *"Oh, by the way . . ."*

Greg considered Jared a prime candidate for an associate, a real go-getter, always busy. As they say, if you want something done, ask a busy person. Besides, with three teens, certainly he'd welcome some additional income.

Greg waited a little longer to give everyone time to kick off their church shoes or whatever, and then he put a six-pack of the small cans in a brown paper bag and headed up the street.

"Singer!" Jared said when he opened the door. "Come on in."

There was no foyer in the Jasper home. The door opened right into the living room. "Hope I'm not bothering you folks. But I, uh, wanted to share something with you. You got a minute?"

"Sure." Jared waved him inside.

"I wanted to ask how you enjoyed the boat show. Did you get a chance to attend?" Greg asked.

"No. We've been so busy we didn't get down there. But here, have a seat and tell us how it was."

As Greg settled on the couch, Jared's son wandered through.

"I bet Destin would love to hear this. You remember my son, don't you?"

"Sure do." Greg reached out his hand and Destin stepped forward to shake it.

"How you doin', Mr. Singer?"

As Greg sat down, Destin stepped back and leaned casually in the doorway that led into the dining area. Greg told about some of the big yachts he'd noticed at the show, the ultralight airplane, and the flyboard demonstration, where the rider was lifted into the air on two jets of water streaming from reverse nozzles at the end of a giant hose.

"Awesome," Destin said. "Wish I'd seen it."

"Yeah, it was." Greg turned to Jared. "But there's something else I wanted to mention to you. I'm starting a new business and wanted to tell you about it." Greg was tempted to ask if Jasper's wife could join them, but Jared squirmed a little when he mentioned "business," so he pressed on while he had the man's attention.

He reached into the brown bag and pulled out a couple of cans of SlowBurn, tossing one to Jared and one to Destin. "Here, give it a try." Destin immediately popped the top and took a sip as Greg described the basics of SlowBurn and how it helped keep a person alert. "I imagine that's pretty important in a profession like yours, Jared—you're an air traffic controller, right?"

"Oh, yeah. But anything stronger than coffee could get a guy in trouble." Jared was shaking his head. "I rely on Dr. Pepper myself." And he set the can down on the floor beside his chair.

"That's the thing. SlowBurn really doesn't have that much caffeine in it. It's not like other energy drinks you might buy at the grocery store, because it relies on other ingredients."

Jared shrugged. "Well, that'd be a problem, getting anything else approved. No performance enhancers, no drugs, no nothing on the job. It's the law. In fact, even for prescription meds there's a whole list of what's approved. I mean, it's like a twenty-four-page circular. Anything new could take ten years of testing before it's approved. To be honest, I don't think ATCs would make very good customers for this SlowBurn of yours."

Greg was realizing he wasn't getting anywhere when Jared's wife came into the room. "Hi, Greg! I hope you'll excuse me for not coming out earlier." The attractive woman held out her hand. "I have an appointment downtown this evening. Someone is picking me up at five, and I needed to get ready. How are Nicole and the kids?"

Greg stood up to shake her hand. "They're fine, fine. Didn't mean to keep you folks. It's just such a wonderful opportunity, I wanted to let Jared, here, know about it on the ground floor."

Michelle Jasper just smiled, kissed her husband on the cheek, and breezed out the front door.

Jared stood up too. "I appreciate it. But I'm really not in a position to take on anything like that."

Greg was obviously being dismissed. They chatted a minute more at the door, but Greg was soon walking down the sidewalk toward his own home. Destin had accepted a sample can of SlowBurn and acknowledged it was good. But Jared hadn't even tasted it.

Chapter 17

Two of Greg's Monday appointments with people from church canceled when he called to confirm, and discouragement drifted over him like a dark cloud. He fought back. Obviously there'd be days like this before a new business took off.

Instead of calling Arlo for a pep talk, he began calling his old associates from Powersports. After all, it was the company's last day, and people would be eager for a new direction. Three of them expressed real interest. Unfortunately, none of the three would've been Greg's top picks for solid reps. One was Ethel Newhouse, Hastings' secretary, whom he planned to keep on after Powersports closed. Ethel was nervous and didn't know if the arrangement would last, so she was interested in alternatives, but she wasn't ready to get onboard just yet. "Chuck still has a mountain of things he needs me to do as he closes up. But I'll get back to you as soon as I can."

Tuesday, Greg worked his warm list of former business contacts. A couple of people said they might be interested, but he'd have to drive down to Indiana and up to Michigan to meet with them. He decided to wait until he could put together a trip before locking in a date.

By midafternoon, he was frustrated. "Nicole," he called down to the schoolroom, "I need a break. I'm going out to mow the lawn."

"Okay. I've gotta go to Dominick's for some groceries. Will you still be around to watch the kids? They're involved in an art project and don't want to go with me."

"No problem." He didn't expect the art project to last very long, but so what? He wasn't trying to work on the computer. The kids could just come outside.

Greg had about half of the front yard done when over the roar of the lawn mower he saw Destin Jasper, the young man from up the street, standing on the sidewalk, waving to get his attention.

He finished the swath and shut down the mower. "Destin. Imagine that, two times in the same week. What can I do for you?"

"Hello, Mr. Singer." Destin stepped up to him, hands deep in his pockets. "I really liked that drink you gave me the other day."

"Great. You want to order some for yourself?"

"Yeah, kinda. I drank both cans, the one you gave me and my dad's too." He shrugged with a nervous laugh. "He's kind of a Dr. Pepper fanatic, if you ask me. But what I really wanted to ask is if there's an age requirement for . . . for selling that drink."

"Age? No." Greg frowned. "I don't think so. No. I'm sure there isn't. It's not like alcohol or anything. Anybody can buy it, so pretty sure anyone can sell it. Why? You interested?" Might Destin become his second rep?

"Yeah. I need a job, especially because I'm doing a Five-Star Basketball Camp this summer that costs quite a bit, so I have to pay my folks back for the tuition."

This could be good. The kid was motivated. A smile tickled his mouth. Why not? Young people—young athletes, in particular—would make ideal customers.

"Well, Destin. I think we can talk. You heard me describe the company to your dad on Sunday, but that was just an overview. Let's go into the house. I've got a brochure that describes the business a little more, and I want to show you the website."

A few minutes later they were huddled before Greg's computer. "Everything's up on the web, but it's best to go through a sponsor, like me, where you have the support and encouragement to make this a real success."

Greg spent the next hour going over all the details with Destin. The kid grasped things quickly, and though he asked a lot of questions, they were the kind that let Greg know he really understood the company's objectives and business model.

"So how much do you owe your folks for this basketball camp?"

"They chipped in fifty bucks for the registration fee. But I borrowed another five hundred from them for the tuition. So, I gotta pay back that whole five hundred. Plus, I need money for clothes and other stuff. Do you think I can—"

"No problem, son. When SlowBurn gets rolling, you'll pay 'em off and put money in the bank. Now, we've got this starter kit for only forty-nine dollars." Greg opened the brochure that listed the options. "It includes twelve six-packs. The company presumes you'll give away a dozen cans as samples. The product sells itself."

"How much can I sell it for?"

"Whatever the market will bear. You set the price. Some people sell it for two dollars a can, or more."

"Hmm. That wouldn't go very far to pay for my camp." Destin scanned down the page of the brochure to the bottom. "What about these? Says *larger discounts*. What's that mean?"

"Well, the larger your order, the greater your discount. More profit, you know. There's the bronze, silver, gold, and even platinum orders. With each level you get an additional ten percent discount on your purchase, and there are bonuses too. But they're kind of expensive."

"How much is the platinum?"

"Well now, that'd be kind of steep for someone just starting out, nearly fourteen-hundred bucks." Of course, Greg had sprung for that amount. Maybe Destin could become his superstar and sell that much.

"Oh." Destin seemed sobered. "But I wouldn't have to pay nearly a dollar per can for it, right?"

"No. In fact, with the platinum, you're only paying about sixty cents per can."

"So, what would it be for the silver, eighty cents a can?"

"Right. For three hundred dollars"—could the kid afford that much?—"you'd get sixty-four six-packs for sale plus a bonus of six more the company estimates you'd need for samples. Of course, you could sell them, too, if you wanted. The order includes a total of seventy six-packs, or four hundred and twenty cans."

"Yeah, and if I sell it for the right price, I could pay for my basketball camp." Destin pursed his lips as if pondering his options, then nodded his head. "I think I'll take the silver."

"You sure? You know you could start off smaller and work up."

"But you just told me the profit is so much better with larger orders."

"Yeah, that's right." Greg smiled. He was recruiting a real go-getter!

"When can I get it?"

"Oh, I've got the product sitting in the garage right now. Soon as you pay me, it's yours."

"You mean I can't get it on . . . whadda they call it . . . consignment or something?"

Greg shook his head. "As much as I trust you, Destin, I can't do that. It's company policy." Arlo had explained it to him when he'd wanted to do the same: "It destroys the incentive, and the company's whole approach is to help each rep become the best salesman he or she can be."

Destin's face fell.

"Look, Destin, maybe you should begin with a starter kit. Do you have any money, any at all?"

"No way, sir. I'm broke. That's why my folks had to spring for my basketball camp."

Greg wanted to lighten the mood before he lost this rep. "So you have no money tucked up under your mattress or in a cookie jar?" He laughed. "Seriously, think. Any money in a bank account that's in your name, anything?"

Destin's face brightened. "Well, yeah. There's my college fund. I'd forgotten about that."

"Hmm. College fund. Not sure that's—"

"No. It's in my name. My grandparents set it up, but I've added to it whenever I could—ten, twenty dollars here and there that Mom made me put in. It's up to three or four thousand by now."

Greg shook his head. "I don't know if that's a good idea, Destin."

But the boy had brightened. "No, it's okay. It's my money. I got the passbook and everything."

"Well, you'd have to be committed to paying it all back, or your folks will be very upset."

"Oh, I would. No question about that. And like you said, this stuff should sell easy. I'll earn a lot, maybe even enough to grow my college fund. Right?"

Did Greg still believe it would sell easily? He did. And he'd jumped in just as deep, using money he'd otherwise designated to pay bills and live on. But the product was good. It was just a matter of getting it to the consumers. And that's where Destin and others like him came in. They were his key to success. He needed Destin. And if it could help this young man out with his future, all the better.

"Right." He nodded confidently. "It's really just an investment. You'll earn it back and lots more."

The teenager chewed on his lower lip. As confident as Greg felt, he hesitated to push Destin any more. Let him make his own decision. He'd already sold Destin on the idea of SlowBurn, and Destin had come up with a way to pay for it, so the best route was to let Destin's ambition make his decision for him. It was a test of how much he wanted it.

After a few moments, Destin sat back and blew out a huge breath as though he were bursting to the surface after a deep dive. "I'll do it. I'll go for the silver."

"You sure now? Well, that's great. When do you want the product?"

Destin grinned and bobbled his head. "When *can* I get it?"

"As soon as you bring me the money. I've got the product out in the garage, waiting for you right now."

Greg was in high spirits when Harry Bentley picked him up that evening to go to the men's Bible study. Two reps wasn't much, especially when one was an old lady. But who knew? Perhaps she would contact some eager relatives. As for Destin, Greg had high hopes for him. In fact, the more he thought about it, the boy's high school friends and sports buddies made for the perfect customer profile. Destin could end up selling a truckload of the product.

"So tell me about this dog you work with," he said, sliding into the passenger seat of Harry's Dodge Durango. He looked over his shoulder into the cage-like compartment in the back. "You part of some kind of a K-9 unit?"

"Yep, drug interdiction."

"No kiddin'. I guess dogs have a pretty good nose?" Greg's own nose caught a slight whiff of dog in the sturdy gray SUV.

"Oh definitely. They say a dog's sense of smell can be ten thousand times more sensitive than humans."

"Amazing. So I suppose you had to spend a lot of time training her."

"Yeah, we trained together some, but she was primarily trained at Lackland Air Force Base in Texas."

Greg let the conversation die as Harry darted through traffic. As interesting as Harry's K-9 partner sniffing out drugs on trains might be, he needed to focus on meeting the men at the Bible study. How much should he say about SlowBurn? It was probably *not* the place to actually sell product—and he hadn't brought any samples with him—but perhaps a lower-key approach would work best.

As Harry backed his car into a tight parking space in front of a brick three-flat, Greg asked, "Now who lives here?"

"This is Peter Douglass's place. He and his wife, Avis, are leaders in our church, but some of the guys in the study are from other churches too. You'll like 'em."

"You always meet here?"

"Usually, unless Peter's out of town."

They climbed to the third floor, and Harry tapped on the door that had been left ajar.

A growling voice said, "Get on in here, Bentley. You're late. We were beginning to think you were off on one of your cross-country trips."

"That's Ben Garfield," Harry murmured over the back of his hand as they entered the apartment. "He's got a voice like a bullhorn, but he's really an old teddy bear."

Greg followed Harry's example of slipping off his shoes and adding them to the pile near the door. The shiny hardwood floors set off the bright area rugs and the modern beige-and-black furniture as they entered the living room.

"All right now. Everybody behave." Harry swept his hand to indicate the whole group. "This is my neighbor, Greg Singer. And this motley crew is made up of Peter Douglass, who lets us hang out every week—or maybe it's his wife who's the tolerant one."

Douglass, a tall, smartly dressed African American, his white shirtsleeves rolled up a turn, extended his hand.

"The guy next to him is Ben Garfield, the loudmouth of the group."

"Hey, hey, that's no way to recommend me. What's he gonna think with an introduction like that?" Garfield was older, white, a little dumpy with gnarled hands and a reddish, bulbous nose.

"Denny Baxter and his son, Josh." Josh had a shock of light brown hair and appeared to be in his early twenties but wore a wedding ring. His dad's tan face and trim frame did not suggest a desk job. "Denny's the athletic director at West Rogers Park High," Harry offered while they shook hands.

Greg tucked that into the back of his mind. One more connection to young athletes.

"And this is Carl Hickman. He's the plant manager at Peter's company, Software Symphony." Carl was a wiry black man with what Greg thought were the lines of a hard life etched in his face.

"How ya doin'?" Carl kept his seat, gave a small wave.

Harry Bentley scanned the room again. "Looks like a couple of brothers are missin' tonight, but this is most of us. Why don't you have a seat over there on the sofa, Greg, and I'll take this chair."

"And," put in Peter, "looks like you're the one to open us up in prayer, Harry." He turned to Greg. "We've got this tradition where the last man in before we start has to pray. But you're exempt . . . at least for now."

After Harry's prayer—crisp and to the point—Peter asked the group to turn to First Corinthians and began reading chapter 16. He read aloud until he came to a natural break, and then another man read the same verses in a different translation, more of a paraphrase.

Greg's ears perked up as they discussed the second verse: "On the first day of every week, each one of you should set aside a sum of money in keeping with his income, saving it up, so that when I come no collections will have to be made."

"Does that mean we have to tithe?" asked Josh. "If so, what about the person who doesn't have enough to pay the rent? Some of the people in the building where I work literally spend every penny on rent, the electric bill, and food. And they're on food stamps too."

Carl spoke up. "Well, it's in the Bible. 'Will a man rob God? . . . Bring ye all the tithes into the storehouse.' I heard more'n one message on that in my day."

"I don't know 'bout that," argued Harry.

The debate went on until Ben Garfield held up both hands. "Hold it a minute." He waited until he had everyone's attention. "I'm not saying you're right. I'm not saying you're wrong. But this is why you *goyim* . . ." He turned to Greg. "Uh, that just means a non-Jew, so don't take offense."

Greg nodded. "None taken."

"Anyway, that's why you need me, an old Jew who knows a thing or two. It's not as simple as you make it out to be, you know. The Torah prescribes different kinds of tithes and offerings. So if you want to follow the Law, then you couldn't brag about merely contributing ten percent of your paycheck. And today Jews don't technically pay *tithes*. To whom would they pay them? There's no temple, so there's no ordained Levites or priests, who are the only ones authorized to receive the tithes. Instead, religious Jews pay an annual fee for membership in their synagogue—for building maintenance and salaries—and in addition, most contribute to charity. But for me"—he shrugged—"that was my old life. I think God looks at the heart."

That's my kind of man, thought Greg.

Harry jumped in. "But a lot of people use that as an excuse to contribute next to nothing to God's work. And they're not even regular."

"You're right there," said Peter. "You know, if you make fifty thousand a year and put a twenty in the offering every week, you might be feeling rather proud of yourself, but . . ." He paused and closed his eyes for a moment. "That's only about two percent."

"Yeah, and that still doesn't say anything about where your heart is."

When they ran out of time discussing the Bible passage, Peter invited prayer requests around the circle. When it was Greg's turn, he searched for how to say what was on his mind. "Well, I was stuck in a rut in my old job, but God's given me a great opportunity. I'm starting a new business. So I could use some prayer. And the prayer is, I need the right kind of associates: people who have ambition, people who aren't afraid to speak to other people about a good product, and people who need to make more money than they're making now. So, if you'd just pray that I'd find the right people, I'd be grateful."

Greg was moved that two or three of the group took his request seriously and prayed for him during the prayer time that followed.

After the group was over and the guys were just hanging around talking, Ben Garfield came up to Greg. "So what's this business you're starting?"

Ah. A spark of interest. "Well, it's multilevel marketing, direct sales with the highest rate of return I've ever seen."

"You don't say. I'm a retired Buick salesman, myself. Number one at the dealership year after year. I think they made me retire just to give someone else a chance." He chuckled. "Nah, just kidding. But I never would've retired if I'd known the wife was about to have twins—at her age, can you believe it? But because of those little rascals, I've gotta be flexible. Gotta help Ruth, ya know. So I couldn't go back to a nine-to-five—though it was usually ten-to-ten. How is it workin' for yourself?"

Greg clapped the man on the shoulder. "Well, maybe we should get together and talk. You got a phone number, Ben?"

Chapter 18

NICOLE HAD BEEN UP HALF THE NIGHT with Nathan. He had the flu—at least she hoped it wasn't anything worse. The poor kid had been erupting at both ends from midnight to 4 A.M. before the Pepto-Bismol finally slowed things down. He had a fever, too, as far as Nicole could tell by touching his sweaty forehead, but now that he was finally asleep, she didn't want to waken him to check it.

When the sun's rays broke into his room at half-past-five, she got up from the cushions on the floor by his bed and closed the blinds. The kids' bathroom was a testimony to the poor guy's battle and desperately needed cleaning. And it smelled as bad as it looked. Down on her hands and knees, she scrubbed the floor, the toilet, and the bathtub. She took all the towels and the throw rug down to the basement and started the laundry.

On her way back up to the first floor, Greg called from their bedroom. "Nicole? What's all the noise? Isn't it too early to be doing laundry? I was hoping to get another hour or two of sleep."

She stepped to the bedroom door. "Nate's sick."

"What? Sick? I'm sorry. Is it serious?"

She sighed. "Don't think so. Seems like the flu. I've been giving him Pepto-Bismol, and he finally fell asleep about twenty minutes ago."

"That's good. How 'bout you? You coming back to bed?"

"Just cleaning up the mess."

"Oh. Well, don't take too long." He flopped back down and mumbled groggily, "You need your sleep, too, honey."

Yes, she did, but Greg hadn't offered to take over, had he? Nicole climbed to the second floor as quietly as possible, put out clean towels in the kids' bathroom, and opened the window a few inches. The vent fan might make noise. She peeked in on Becky. *Thank God, she seems to be sleeping okay.*

Back downstairs, she curled up on the sofa and pulled the afghan over her. Maybe she could get a little more sleep, but at least she could hear Nathan from here if he needed her.

Greg's voice woke her from their bedroom. "Oh, no. It's nine-forty! Nicole, did you turn off the alarm? I've got an appointment with Ben Garfield in twenty minutes, and I'm not even showered. Could you make some coffee and toast for me?"

She hadn't turned off the alarm, but she hadn't set it either. Ever since Greg had stopped going in to Powersports, there'd been no need to get up with an alarm. She always awoke at about the same time and would give Greg a push when she got up to get him started on his day. Ten or fifteen minutes either way didn't make much difference. But of course, last night had messed with her internal clock.

Nicole staggered into the kitchen to start the coffee, then went upstairs to check on Nathan.

"Mommy, my head aches. I still don't feel good."

Nicole checked his forehead. "Hmm. I want to take your temperature. Maybe we can give you some Tylenol. How's your tummy?"

"It kinda feels glooky."

"Like you're gonna throw up again?"

"No, just glooky."

Greg's voice came from downstairs. "Nicole, did you make my toast?"

"Sorry. Came up here to check on Nate."

"Is he worse?"

"No. Better. Sorry about the toast. Can you make it yourself?"

"I don't have time, Nicole!" She heard the frustration in his voice.

"Then drink one of your energy drinks." She felt guilty the moment she said it, but good grief! The man wasn't helpless.

Greg didn't answer, but she could hear him grumbling and banging around in the kitchen. He was obviously worried about his appointment, but she couldn't be in two places at once even if she wasn't so tired.

When she came down fifteen minutes later, he was gone. They needed to have a talk. This business of him being around the house all the time without taking more responsibility for the kids—or himself—wasn't working. She'd sometimes thought the claustrophobia of being cooped up in the house all day would be eased if she just had another adult to talk to. She'd even called some other homeschool mothers to see if they wanted to combine their kids on some days just to have company. Nothing had worked out so far. But having Greg around wasn't solving anything either.

Greg was ten minutes late arriving at Ben Garfield's house.

Ben met him at the door. "Come in, Singer. Sit down. You're lucky. The twins are at school, and Ruth's at some birthday celebration at Manna House."

"Manna House?"

"Yeah, that's a shelter for homeless women where she and some of her Yada Yada sisters help out sometimes."

Greg decided not to ask what Yada Yada was. He was here on business, not to write a family diary. He took a seat on a well-worn sofa that sank as low as a pillow on the floor. The house had a faint smell of baking bread and black coffee. Greg felt hungry.

Ben listened patiently while Greg explained SlowBurn and sampled the energy drink without commenting one way or the other on its taste, but Greg noticed he didn't finish the whole can.

"So who d'ya think is going to buy this energy drink?"

"Anyone. Anyone who drinks tea, coffee, Coke, juice. It's better than any of those. We like to call it 'the Time-Release Energy Drink that won't let you down!'"

Ben threw out a bunch more questions in his gravelly voice, the obvious ones as well as questions that hadn't even crossed Greg's mind—like whether he needed to be registered with the state and if not, how they'd collect and pay state sales tax. "'Cause even if you're not incorporated and are operating as a sole proprietorship," Ben pointed out, "every retail business has to file a Form ST-1 and pay sales tax."

"Of course," Greg said hastily. Hopefully that sort of thing would be covered at the SlowBurn training in a couple of weeks. He still needed to get registered for that. "But you don't have to worry about that here on the front end while you get started."

Ben rubbed his chin and flipped the brochure over for the fifth time as if it would reveal new information when he did. "Tell you what I'll do. Give me a starter kit, and we'll see how it goes. Maybe we'll do more, maybe not."

Knowing the man was an experienced salesman, Greg gently tried to talk him up to the bronze or silver level, but the old man was resolute. "Nah. I'll know very quickly how people respond to this stuff. If it goes well, I can always move up, right? If not, I don't want to have more invested in it than I know I can get out."

"Starter kit it is, then." And they filled out the necessary forms.

Starter kits usually came in a special box, but Greg had loaded enough individual cases in the back of his Cherokee to fulfill a silver order. "Can I just give you enough individual six-packs to equal a starter kit? You don't need it in a special box, do you?"

Ben agreed, took his product, and they shook hands.

Greg arrived home eager to tell Nicole he'd recruited another rep. Didn't say one was an old lady with very little sales potential, one was young kid, and the third was an experienced older salesman too cautious to risk much, but he had three reps working for him. That ought to count for a lot. But Ben's caution had triggered a concern in the back of his own mind—*he* hadn't yet sold any product directly to consumers—but that would come. First, he'd needed the time to recruit his team.

"Nicole!" The back door slammed behind him as he came in through the kitchen and went to the top of the basement stairs. "Hey, Nicole, guess what."

"What?" came her feeble voice from the bedroom behind him.

He turned and peered through the doorway. "You okay? What're you doin' in there?"

Nicole raised herself up on her elbow in their bed. "I think I'm sick. Same thing as Nathan."

"You sure?" He started across the room toward her and then stopped. He couldn't risk getting sick too. "Oh, yeah. I can see from here you don't look too good. How's Nate?"

"A little better, I think. He's still upstairs."

"Becky? Does she have it too?"

"Don't think so. I let her go down and watch a video. You might check on her."

He nodded. "Okay, I will. Whadda you think it is?"

Her eyes drooped, almost closed. "Probably just the flu. I haven't thrown up yet, but . . . I've got chills, headache. Just feel rotten."

"Gee, I thought the flu season was past. You sure it wasn't something you ate?"

"Maybe, but we all had the same spaghetti and salad I made last night. Everything was fresh. You're feeling okay, aren't you?"

"Sure." But the moment he said it, a queasy feeling hinted at nausea and a wave of light-headedness came and went. Had to be the power of suggestion. He hadn't felt anything before. "I'll go down and check on Becky."

"Thanks. Can you go see how Nate's doing too? Make sure he's drinking. He lost a lot of liquid through the night."

Greg sighed as he left the room. Half the family sick? Not good. Not while he was trying to launch his new business. But with Nicole sick too . . .

Becky seemed to be totally content watching *Beauty and the Beast*, no flu symptoms, and happy not to be doing schoolwork. "When's lunch, Daddy?"

"I don't know, honey. You'll have to ask Mom." But as he headed back up the basement stairs, it dawned on him that Mom probably wouldn't be up for cooking.

Upstairs, Nathan was on his back in bed, staring at the ceiling. Greg approached cautiously as if the germs were ready to pounce on him. The boy looked pale, but when Greg peered into the large plastic bowl next to his bed, there were no signs it had been used.

He sat on the foot of his son's bed, just out of the boy's reach. "How you doin', buddy?"

"Pretty good. Where's Mom? I called her, but she didn't come up."

"I think she's sick too. She might've been sleeping when you called. You need something?"

"Guess not. Just wanted her to be here with me." He looked at his dad hopefully. "Can you stay?"

"Stay? Well, maybe for a little while." Greg sat on the end of the bed for several minutes and finally reached out to stroke his son's forehead. When Nathan drifted back to sleep, he slipped into the bathroom and thoroughly washed his hands, then scurried downstairs and quietly sat down at his computer to register Ben Garfield. Next he'd make some lunch for Becky and himself, but then he really needed to get out of the house and sell some SlowBurn.

Greg blew out a big breath, toying with a pen on the desk. He had to deal with this situation rationally. He felt badly that Nicole and Nate were sick, but how would they have managed if he'd been away at an office? This was just the flu, not an emergency that would've required him to stay home from work. All families had to cope with the flu from time to time, and they had to do it without disrupting the whole family's schedule.

The big issue right now was making sure he didn't get sick. As the breadwinner for this family, he needed to make getting his business off the ground a priority.

Getting up from his desk, Greg slipped quietly through the master bedroom to wash his hands again in their bathroom. When he came out, he tiptoed past the lump in their bed that was Nicole. But halfway down the hallway he heard her feeble voice. "Greg . . ." She sounded terrible. "Can you come back? I need you."

Chapter 19

By Friday, Nicole and Nathan were back on their feet, and so far, neither Becky nor Greg had caught the flu. But Greg felt uptight and frustrated over the amount of nursing he'd had to do. How could he start a business from home when so many domestic demands impinged on his time?

He felt guilty for resenting the help he'd given his family, but what was he supposed to do? Weren't these the kinds of obstacles God was supposed to clear out of the way so they could get his blessing? He was certainly doing his part.

Greg was in the middle of filling out his online registration for the SlowBurn training for the week after next, when Nicole came in and stood beside him. "Yeah?" he said without looking up from the screen.

"Just wanted to let you know, I need the car this afternoon to do the shopping that I missed the other day."

Greg remained focused on the computer. "You'll be taking the kids, won't you?"

"I'm still not a hundred percent, Greg, so I thought it'd be faster if I left them here, but I—"

"Nicole!" Greg lifted his hands off the keyboard like a pianist ready to pound out a major chord. "If they're around here, then I'll have to be dealing with them while I'm trying to work."

"No you won't. I've already arranged for Tabitha to come over."

"Tabitha?" He finally turned and looked up at her. "Who's Tabitha?"

"Tabby Jasper, the girl from down the street I had over for a mother's helper the other day."

"Oh . . . oh yeah. Okay. Thanks." He turned back to his computer. "Just tell them to stay out of my office and keep the noise down."

She started to leave, but then turned back. "So now it's *your* office, huh?"

"Come on, Nicole." He leaned back and rolled his eyes. "Yes, this is *our* living room, except when I'm working in here. Then it's my office. Okay? I'm trying to start a business here so . . . so we don't have to move to Florida or Canada or—"

"*Florida? Canada?* Why would we have to move there?"

"I don't know. Someplace where they manufacture more boats than they do in Chicago so I could get back into that business."

"Well, I don't want to move either." Nicole started out again. "Like I said, I've got it covered with Tabby, and I'll tell her to not let the kids bother you."

"Thanks."

Tabby arrived about three thirty, and Greg heard her apologize for being a little late in getting home from school. But as promised, Nicole carefully instructed her to not let the kids disturb him. "I'll take them outside," Tabby said.

Greg almost called out, "Appreciate it!" but then realized he wouldn't even be overhearing this conversation if he were in an office.

On the other hand, every office had its own conversations . . . and politics and meetings and time-wasting reports and other distractions. He really should be more grateful. The best of both worlds would be a real in-home office with a door and a space of his own. That's what he needed. When they got their new house, he'd make sure he had a large office with plenty of light, maybe on the second floor, situated where the noises of household life wouldn't disturb him. And there ought to be an access for clients, perhaps not a separate entrance but at least a way to bring them into his office without walking through the domestic clutter of a home with young children.

But they weren't there yet, and they weren't going to get there if he didn't get his SlowBurn "burning." So how could he make do with what they had? He began brainstorming. There was quite a bit of space upstairs, but no way to carve out another room, and at their age, both kids needed a separate bedroom. What if he took over the dining room and closed it off? No, Nicole would never go for that, and he didn't really want to do that either. The back porch might be an option. But that would involve enclosing it, winterizing it, and providing heat—several thousand dollars to do it right, and then it still would be kind of cramped. What about an office over the garage? It would be expensive to add another story and get heat and air conditioning installed, but that would be fantastic. What if—

The back doorbell rang. He glanced out the living room window. Tabby and the kids were out front playing hopscotch, so it wasn't one of them. He got up and went to the kitchen door.

"Destin, good to see you. You looking for your sister?"

"No, Mr. Singer. I brought my money." The teenager held out a check.

"Hey, that's great. Come on in." Greg took the check. It was a bank draft for the full three hundred dollars. "This is great. I hope you have some way to haul your cases down to your house, 'cause my wife's got my car, and we're talkin' over two hundred pounds of SlowBurn here."

"Uh, really?"

"Yeah. Seventy six-packs, 420 eight-ounce cans."

"Oh gee, I don't know where I'd put all of that. Is there any chance I can take what I need right now and leave the rest with you?"

Greg shrugged. "Don't see why not. Come on out to the garage."

They separated Destin's cases into one stack, while he took one case with him down the alley to his home.

"Good luck," Greg called after him. "You can pick up the rest anytime."

Just as he was heading back into the house, he heard the garage door to the alley go up. Nicole must be returning. Feeling encouraged that his third rep was launched, he waited to help his wife bring the groceries into the house.

"Thanks," she said when he showed up and reached for a couple of grocery bags. "I have about as much energy as a drained battery."

"You go on in and take a load off your feet, honey. I'll bring everything in." He watched as she stepped through the doorway and walked slowly toward the house. Yeah, he needed to be more sensitive to the toll this job transition was taking on his wife.

Sunday, supposedly a day of rest. But Greg felt anxious about taking a whole day off from building the clientele he needed for SlowBurn. Well, maybe when he got to church he could track down the two guys who'd canceled on him and reschedule a time to tell them about SlowBurn. And when he got home, he'd make a few other calls.

Pastor Hanson's message was on "Speaking Life into Our Dreams." Greg perked up the moment he heard the title. That's exactly what he needed. He had a dream and the blessing seemed so close. What did he need to do to speak life into it?

The pastor's primary text was Proverbs 18:21: "Death and life are in the power of the tongue, and those who love it will eat its fruit."

Pastor Hanson stepped around to the side of his clear plastic pulpit—a custom, Greg had noted, which preceded his identifying a false teaching. "Some people would say this proverb deals only with the hurtful words one could say to or about someone else. And that's a valid understanding as far as it goes. James, chapter three, for instance, reviews what a fire of evil the tongue can stir up. A malicious and false testimony can literally lead to someone's execution while the words of a faithful witness could save his life. However"—he allowed a pregnant pause—"the context for this verse suggests something more."

The polished preacher returned behind the pulpit and picked up his Bible. "The verse just before this morning's text says, 'A man's stomach shall be satisfied from the fruit of his mouth; from the produce of his lips he shall be filled.' In other words, what you say can bring fruit sufficient to fill your stomach, to fill all your godly desires. Do you want to be healthy? Luke nine-six says Jesus and his disciples 'went through the towns, preaching the gospel, and healing everywhere.' *Everywhere!* If you were there and sick, you would've been healed. But he also said, 'I am with you always, even unto the end of the world.' So Jesus is here now and that same healing is for you now."

Pastor Hanson's voice rose. "Which means this promise in Proverbs is also for us *now*. Just speak life! Do you need a new house? This same Jesus who went before you to heaven to prepare a mansion for you there, wants to see you living in a beautiful home *right now*, and He wants you to move in. Speak life into that dream, and the blessing will be yours!"

Greg glanced sideways at Nicole to see how she was responding. She moved her finger across the page of her Bible under the words of verse 20—once, twice, three times—as though she was trying to digest their meaning. He craned his neck to read them himself. "*Wise words satisfy like a good meal; the right words bring satisfaction.*" Not exactly what Pastor Hanson had read from the New King James.

"What version do you have today?" he whispered.

She flipped it over and pointed to the cover: *The New Living Translation.*

Hmm. No one could construe that translation into a promise for getting a mansion. So which was right? Greg sat up stiffly. He couldn't say Nicole had spoken death over their prosperity, but she'd been hesitant to embrace the pastor's teaching that promised financial success.

"And you'll notice," continued Pastor Hanson's booming voice, "the last portion of our text returns to the same, personally beneficial principle: 'And those who love it will eat its fruit.' You love life? Speak life and you will *eat its fruit*."

Greg wasn't sure whether the immediate question that popped into his mind was his own or what he imagined Nicole might ask. But how did that phrase break down grammatically if diagramed like he had to do in high school English class? If it meant those who loved life would eat the fruit of "speaking life," then the pastor's application seemed accurate. But what if the antecedent of "it" was the tongue? Then the meaning might simply be, those who love the power of the tongue would reap the consequences of using it, whether it was to build other people up or tear them down and reap the consequences to one's relationships. In that case, it might have very little to do with a principle about achieving personal prosperity or health.

He checked himself. What was he doing? Undermining his own faith in what the pastor was trying to teach?

He tuned back in as Pastor Hanson was pointing out how universal the principle of speaking life or death was. "You tell yourself that you'll never hit that fastball, and you won't. But if you speak life to yourself, if you tell yourself you can hit the ball, you'll hit it, perhaps not on the first swing or the second. But if you keep speaking life, you will hit it."

That sure made sense to Greg. Encouraging words build you up, whether you speak them to yourself or someone else speaks them to you. Discouraging words bring you down. There was no question about that, but did the passage mean more? Was it the key to everything he wanted?

As the family headed home after church, he didn't voice his thoughts to Nicole. He was afraid of what she'd say. And graciously, she spent nearly the whole trip asking the kids about Sunday school. They both gave their versions of the Bible stories they'd heard while Greg continued to wrestle with his thoughts.

The pastor had encouraged everyone to get up in the morning and look in the mirror and "speak life" into their situation by saying that you'll have favor wherever you go and in whatever you do. "Tell yourself that everything you attempt will come back gold, everything will succeed. Start declaring that you are healed, prosperous, blessed, and you will be. It's gonna turn around for you!" He'd said it louder. "It's gonna turn around for you!" And when he said it the third time, the whole congregation was on its feet, cheering and clapping.

It'd been a powerful message.

But a few questions still nibbled at the edges of his thoughts. What about all the apostles who'd suffered and died? Or the Christian martyrs through the ages . . . would they have been prosperous, happy, and enjoyed a life of ease if they'd only learned the principle of "speaking life" over their circumstances? What about Jesus himself? Greg had to admit that *his* life hadn't appeared prosperous, certainly not in the way Pastor Hanson described prosperity. And yet, here it was, over two thousand years later, and the church Jesus founded still thrived.

But Greg didn't know if he wanted that kind of prosperity.

He shook himself into the present as the Jeep Cherokee made its way up their alley, having made the trip home nearly on auto-pilot. He pressed the control button to open the garage door. He was just feeling discouraged because SlowBurn hadn't taking off as fast as he'd hoped. And because their bank account was going down while their credit card balance was going up.

But it would all turn around. Hadn't the pastor said so? Backed up by Scripture? He needed to hang on to that.

Chapter 20

THE RAIN TUESDAY AFTERNOON didn't dampen Greg's spirits as he drove out Touhy Avenue and turned north on River Road. Both SlowBurn appointments with the church members who'd canceled the week before were back on. He'd only had to twist their arms a little before guilt kicked in from having broken their earlier commitment and they agreed for Greg to drop by. First, he was going to meet Sam Ludlow in Des Plaines at five thirty and then come home, grab a bite to eat, and head up to Evanston at eight to meet with Jennifer Cooper, who oversaw the coffee bar in the lobby of the Victorious Living Center.

This second meeting meant Greg couldn't go with Harry Bentley again to the men's Bible study that night, but business was business, and if he could convince Jennifer to carry SlowBurn at the church coffee bar, he would make a killing and the church would benefit from its share of the profits.

As for the Bible study, he could catch up with the guys some other time. Besides, now that Ben Garfield was one of his reps, perhaps Ben would be more successful reaching the other guys. Greg wanted Ben to experience enough success for him to step up his participation to the next level.

The sheets of rain and dark skies made it hard for Greg to find the street signs where he was to turn into the development along the Des Plaines River where Sam and Louise Ludlow lived. But he finally found Berry Lane and followed it around until he spotted the rambling ranch Sam had described to him. He jumped out of the Cherokee with a sample six-pack and ran for the porch but got soaked by the time he made it under the eaves and rang the doorbell. There were lights on inside, but Greg saw no movement through the windows.

He rang the bell again, and finally Louise opened the door.

"I'm so sorry, Greg. Sam's out in the garage trying to start the generator. Come on through."

"That's okay. I don't want to bother him if he's busy, but what's the problem?" He slipped off his wet shoes and left the six-pack of SlowBurn on the floor before following Louise. "Looks like your whole neighborhood has lights."

"Oh, we've got lights . . . for now." She led him through the kitchen. "But Sam says he's learned his lesson to get that generator started early. Frankly, I think the only lesson to be learned is to move. We've been through this too many times."

She led him into the garage, where Greg found Sam Ludlow—perhaps sixty-five years old—on his knees tinkering with a home generator.

"Hey man, what's the problem? You want me to hold that light for you?"

Sam grunted as he turned to look up. "Oh, hi, Greg. Yeah, that'd be a big help."

Greg held the droplight closer while Sam fiddled with the carburetor.

"There!" Sam pushed himself up with several groans and stood there unsteadily. "These old knees don't bend so well anymore. Here, let me push the starter button and see if it'll kick in."

The starter ground and ground as the battery wore down. Just when Greg thought it was about to stop, the little engine backfired once, chugged a couple of times, and roared to life. Even though the exhaust was piped outside, Sam had to yell to be heard. "I'm going to leave it run for a while."

It continued to run, but Greg thought the governor wasn't working properly, because the engine roared and slowed and roared and slowed like a wheezing dragon. Sam leaned toward him. "I need to get a new one, a bigger one. But I can't afford it right now."

"This one looks pretty big as is."

Sam beckoned him back into the house. Even inside, the generator still seemed loud.

"I know Sam wants iced tea," Louise said, opening the refrigerator. "How about you, Greg? Iced tea, water, orange juice, Coke?"

"Hey, I brought along a drink I want you folks to try. Do you mind?" Greg went back to the entryway and retrieved the Slow-Burn before they could respond. When he returned, Sam was seated at the kitchen table, so he sat down across from him and gave his hosts samples, popping a can for himself.

"So why do you need a larger generator?"

"The river." Sam pointed out the kitchen window. "That's it right out there. You can see it if you stand up. Our backyard's right on the bank. Every time it rains hard like this, we're at risk if the power goes out. I've got five pumps installed around the yard, but if that river spills over, which it's done four times since we've been here, those pumps and a whole lot of sandbags are the only thing standing between us and a flooded home."

Greg was shocked. The place seemed too beautiful to cower under a perpetual threat. But no wonder Louise thought they should move. He shook his head. "Seems like every few years we hear about flooding along the Des Plaines or the Fox River, but somehow I never imagined it happening to homes like this. Can't the county or the Army Corps of Engineers do something?"

Sam laughed. "Well, there was a plan back in the 1980s that was supposed to stop the flooding, but only one of six projects has been completed. There are places up the road worth two or three million, and if those people don't have enough clout to get the projects done . . ." He shrugged helplessly.

They talked about the river while the generator continued to throb in the garage until, with a chug and a hiss, it suddenly died. Sam jumped up. "See what I mean? I need a new one." He started for the door from the kitchen to the garage.

"Sam, Sam!" his wife called after him. "Sit down. There's nothing you can do about it tonight."

"But what if the river—"

Louise held up her hands. "You know that the only real answer is for us to move."

"Well, we can't move tonight," Sam groused as he settled back into his chair. An awkward silence of the couple's unresolved dispute descended on the room.

Greg finally held up his can of SlowBurn. "So, what do you think about this drink?"

"Oh, it's good," they both said, seeming eager to change the subject.

Greg launched into his presentation, but he could tell Sam's mind was on larger issues. After thirty minutes, Greg broached the question of whether they wanted to sign on. "You could both be reps, you know. I'm sure you move in slightly different circles, have different friends. You could move more product that way."

"Not now," Sam said, a firm tone to his voice. "Even if we had the money, a new generator would have to come first. First things first, you know." He looked out the window where the rain still fell in the fading light. He stood up and extended his hand. "Thanks for stopping by, Greg, but I gotta get out to the garage and get that thing going again. No way of knowing when that rain will stop or whether we'll lose power."

A few minutes later, as Greg drove toward home, he wondered how Pastor Hanson's teachings applied to the Ludlows. They attended the same church. They'd heard the same messages. Why weren't they prospering? Were they just not "speaking life" over their situation?

Knowing he had to head up to Evanston in a short time, Greg parked the Cherokee in front of their house. The heavy rain had lightened up as Greg readied himself for a dash to the porch, but as soon as he opened the door of his vehicle, he heard someone calling his name.

Harry Bentley was standing on the porch of the Molanders' house across the street beckoning to him. He could see Mrs. Molander behind him, peeking around with both hands over her mouth.

Was the old man, Karl, having a heart attack? Or perhaps he'd already died. Greg ran across the street and up onto the Molanders' porch. Boxes and old suitcases and other dusty household items were piled all over the porch so that it looked like the Molanders were moving. "What's the matter? Is it Karl?"

"Nah, I think he's okay," said Bentley gruffly. "It's their sump pump." He continued talking as he led the way into the house, apparently presuming Greg would follow. "It went out, and with this much rain, the basement's flooding. I was on my way to Bible study when I noticed them piling stuff out there on their porch and came over to see what was going on." He paused momentarily as he passed the ashen-faced older man leaning back in his living room recliner. "You doin' okay, Karl?"

"Yeah." Molander's voice was weak and breathy. "I took a couple of nitro pills, and the pain's pretty much gone. I'll be okay."

"But you gotta go see your doctor again," said Eva Molander, who was following them. "Tomorrow. We need to call."

"But for right now, you stay in that chair, Mr. Molander," Harry said. "All right if we put your stuff out in your garage? I'm afraid if the wind picks up, the rain's gonna blow in on your porch."

"Not much room in the garage with the car and all."

"Well, where're your keys? We can park it out front."

"Oh, I never leave my car out. That's why it's in such good shape."

"Yeah? That's good. But tonight, we need the garage space. I'm sure that old Buick can hold off the rain for a while on its own. Now, where're your keys?"

Molander shrugged, then raised a gnarled hand and pointed toward the bedroom. "Show 'em, Eva."

As Greg made his way down the outside steps a few minutes later, he realized the basement was awash in a couple of inches of water. Not too bad compared to the five feet of water the Ludlows said they'd had in their basement before Sam installed all his pumps. At least there was no river near Beecham Street poised to overflow. And if the Molanders had stored everything up on blocks or shelves, they wouldn't be having this problem.

As Greg carried his first armload of boxed Christmas tree ornaments out to the garage, he wondered about his own basement. They'd never had anything other than a small bit of dampness in one corner during the heaviest of rains. But with everyone else having trouble, maybe he should've checked before coming over to help.

He checked his watch when he hustled down to the basement for another load. It was already too late for him to get any supper before driving up to Evanston, and the amount of stuff still in the basement—many of the boxes and items already wet on the bottom—would take a couple of hours for the two of them clear out. The water he sloshed through was mostly rainwater, but there was a slight smell of sewage. He'd definitely have to shower and change clothes before meeting with Jennifer Cooper.

"Hey Harry, anybody else we could get to help us clean this place out? It's going to take forever if there's just the two of us."

Bentley leaned an arm against the wall, arching his back as though all the lifting had caused it to ache. "Good point. Maybe we'll just have our Bible study down here. Love in action, you know. We just studied First Corinthians thirteen a couple weeks ago, so this would be good practice." He pulled out his phone. "*Hmm,* that's strange. Can't get a signal down here. I can get one just fine in my basement. Be back in a minute."

He headed up the inside stairs as Greg lugged another box out to the garage.

Greg made several trips before Harry reappeared. But the older man looked triumphant. "Reinforcements are on their way!"

"No kidding. All those guys are coming over here and help?"

"Yeah, except we disqualified Ben. He'd be up there in a recliner with Karl Molander if we let him tote too many things up the stairs. Josh Baxter said he'd bring his tools too. There's a good chance he can get that sump pump going again. He's real handy with stuff like that. Manages a six-flat for homeless single moms called the House of Hope. Great kid." Harry picked up a box fan in one hand and a suitcase in the other and started to leave, then turned back for a moment. "Hey, guess who else I snagged."

Greg looked up from rolling a small, soaked rug. "Who?"

"I went out on the porch to make the call just as Lincoln Paddock was coming up the street, so I waved him down. Said he'll be here as soon as he changes his clothes."

Greg stood up, watching Harry struggle up the back steps and head out to the garage. *Lincoln Paddock,* the playboy lawyer with the limos who'd been hitting on his wife? *He* was coming to help? Greg checked his watch: twenty minutes to eight. If he left right now . . .

But something stopped him. No, he couldn't do that. There'd be a big enough crew to finish off this job before it got too late tonight, but that'd still be a while. He couldn't leave Harry here alone to tackle all this. The man was assuming he'd do the neighborly thing and stick it out. What if it was his own basement? He needed to stay, even if it meant he had to cancel his appointment with Jennifer Cooper.

Which he better do now rather than later. He pulled out his own phone.

Chapter 21

"I don't really have any openings in my schedule for getting together in the next couple of weeks," Jennifer Cooper said the next day when Greg called again to reschedule their appointment. "But I have a few minutes right now. Can we talk about this on the phone? You said it's about a business opportunity you think I'd be interested in. What is it?"

"Oh. Can't really do it over the phone. I have some stuff I'd like to show you in person. But I could say you're doing a great job with the coffee bar at church. It's great. I know a huge number of people come through there each Sunday between services. Everybody loves it. But I do have a suggestion for something that might make it better. However, it's an idea much better shared in person."

"Well, then," her tone became abrupt, "why don't you see if you can catch me Sunday? Things usually slow down once second service gets underway."

Greg could tell he shouldn't push it any more at the moment. "Thanks, Jennifer. I'll do that."

He stared at his phone for a moment after they'd hung up. Maybe he should've excused himself last evening and gone to meet Jennifer. It was business, after all, and finally there'd been enough hands to empty the Molanders' basement before ten. He hadn't been that essential. He'd tried to call Jennifer and explain why he couldn't come, but he'd only gotten her voice mail. Now she wasn't interested in rescheduling a third appointment. Yeah, he'd broken his appointment, but so had she. Why not give him another chance?

Greg looked out his front window. Across the street a green van sat in front of the Molanders' house. Large yellow letters on the side announced: "Disaster Recovery. We clean up after fires, floods, and storms!" A man was carrying two commercial blowers that looked like huge green snails into the house. So, the Molanders were getting their basement dried out. Good! What else would they have to do? Probably open the basement walls to prevent mold. What a mess. But Greg had to admit it'd been fun working with the guys the night before. Josh Baxter had gotten the sump pump running, which drained the standing water in no time. Even Lincoln Paddock had worked just as hard as anyone else and without any overly familiar comments about "Nikki." In fact, he hadn't mentioned her at all or acted self-conscious around Greg. Maybe he'd been overreacting to the guy.

It crossed Greg's mind that Paddock's stretch limos had minibars in them and might be a good place to stock SlowBurn, but he wasn't ready to go that far. Let the guy be a good neighbor . . . *at the end of the block*. That was close enough.

By afternoon, the air had turned hot and muggy. Greg had made all the calls he could think of at the moment, so he offered to give Nicole a break and took Becky and Nathan out onto the front porch to build a LEGO city. He was personally LEGO-ed out, having lost interest a couple of years earlier, as soon as Nathan could build his own creations. But he was happy to sit on the front steps and keep the kids company while he brainstormed how to get SlowBurn into some commercial settings. This business of making a killing by selling it to individuals wasn't working for him. He hadn't even gone door to door around his own neighborhood. But he'd leave the low-hanging fruit to Destin as a way to encourage him.

Speaking of Destin, he saw the boy coming up the street on his bike right then.

"Hey, Destin!" Greg waved him over and then met him on the sidewalk. "How's it goin', man?"

"Okay."

They bumped fists. "I was just thinkin' about you. How are your sales going? Makin' a killing with your friends?"

Remaining astride his bike, Destin looked up the street. "Sold a couple of cans, but that's all. I don't know, Mr. Singer. Maybe I'm not cut out for this."

"Of course you are! Gotta think positive, Destin. Positive! Don't doubt yourself. You're gonna do great. Hey, I'm gonna give you a break. The only people on this street I've spoken to about SlowBurn are your family, the Bentleys"—he pointed across the street—"and Mrs. Krakowski, who lives below them. She actually became a rep. I don't have such high hopes for her as I do for you, but . . . What I'm saying is, I'm leaving the rest to you. They're part of your warm list, people you know personally. You know everybody on the block, don't you?"

"Uh, not really. Not everyone."

There were a few families Greg didn't know either. "Well, that doesn't matter. You can still tell them you're their neighbor. Should be easy sales."

Nodding his head at each house, Destin looked up and down the block. But the look on his face was like he'd just swallowed a spoonful of noxious medicine. "I'll try, Mr. Singer."

"That's the spirit. And what about your friends at school? You giving out samples?"

"Yeah. I've used up two six-packs so far. But it's costin' me more than I'm makin', lots more."

"You can't look at it like that. This is a business. You have to invest before you reap the rewards. How many more days of school do you have?"

"School's out Friday."

"Well, you've got to take advantage of that. If your school's anything like mine was, these last few days are pretty much blow-off days. Right?"

"Yeah. Tests are all done. I don't know why they make us attend."

"There you go. All these young people gathered together in one place so you can sell them SlowBurn. How 'bout that? That's why you have to attend. Our tax dollars at work for your benefit."

Destin grinned at Greg's humor, but then he shrugged. "It's just . . . I feel kinda awkward, like I'm taking advantage of our friendship or something."

"Now you can't let that stop you, Destin. You like to play video games, don'tcha?"

"Yeah."

"What's your favorite?"

"NBA 10."

"Never heard of it, but doesn't matter. You have a copy?"

"Yeah. It runs on PlayStation."

"How much did it cost?"

"I got a deal, $19.99. A friend told me about it."

"That's my point. If it's something you like, then you don't have any hard feelings toward your friend for telling you about it, do you? In fact, you're probably grateful. Right?"

Destin nodded.

"It's the same with SlowBurn. You know it's good. You know it gives you extra energy. And because of that your friends are going to be happy with you when you tell them about it. Get what I'm saying?"

"All right, Mr. Singer."

"You've got two more days of school. Make 'em count. Especially work on your basketball buddies. They'll trust you. They'll give it a try. And don't worry about giving out samples. That's the only way they're going to know. The returns will come. You'll do great. Selling's just like anything else. It's hard at first, but then it becomes second nature. Like riding a bike." He gave Destin a slap on the shoulder and sent him on up the street to his house.

Greg went back up to his porch, taking a few moments to admire the LEGO village his kids were building, then he lowered himself onto the top step. He hadn't said anything to Destin he didn't believe himself, but he had to admit, he hadn't been selling much of "the Time-Release Energy Drink that won't let you down" either. And the truth of the matter was, he also felt awkward trying to sell people on something they weren't asking for. It'd been so much different when he was working with Powersports Expos. All his clients were in the business. They were looking for ways to present their products to the public. And even if the recession prevented the public from buying their products, people were still interested in looking at the latest boats, four-wheelers, and snowmobiles. Everyone wanted to hear about what he had to offer.

But now, most people didn't care what he had to offer, so he had to make them care.

How was he supposed to do that?

"O God, in the name of Jesus, just give me my blessing!"

Nicole was late getting to her seat in church the following Sunday. There'd been some holdup in the line for checking Becky and Nathan into the children's program, and it had taken an extra twenty minutes. But Greg had gone on ahead to save their usual seats in the balcony of the Victorious Living Center.

The last praise song was just ending as she worked her way down the row of people before they sat down. Greg smiled and held out his hand to her. She was grateful that the tension that had been building between them since he lost his job seemed to have eased a little in the last few days. She smiled back and cuddled close to him as they took their seats.

Pastor Hanson stepped to the pulpit. His image appeared on the big screens and then faded to black as the lights in the auditorium dimmed. A video of the huge, distorted mouth of Mick Jagger began, and the sound came up to full blast.

You can't always get what you want
But if you try sometimes you just might find
You get what you need!

The refrain repeated again and again, and then faded to silence and black as the lights came up and Pastor Hanson's image again filled the screens.

"Brothers and sisters, that was Mick Jagger and the Rolling Stones. We know . . . we know they were not sent from heaven." Chuckles swept the auditorium. "Yet the world—and even many Christians—accept their words as if they were a message from God Himself. Do you?"

He paused for dramatic effect.

"Well, you shouldn't. That's worldly wisdom, and the Bible tells us . . ." The words of 1 Corinthians 3:19-20 replaced Pastor Hanson's image on the screen.

> For the wisdom of this world is foolishness with God. For it is written, *"He catches the wise in their own craftiness"*; and again, *"The Lord knows the thoughts of the wise, that they are futile."*

"So I won't even commend Mick Jagger's counsel as 'worldly wisdom.' It's just plain foolishness. Let me show you why. He begins by telling us, *You can't always get what you want*. Well, I'm here to tell you, you can! You can get what you want. But hold that promise, and I'll tell you how in a few minutes."

Nicole closed her eyes and took a deep breath. Why did every Sunday's message focus on *getting, getting, getting*? She glanced at Greg. He was leaning forward, elbows on knees, chin in hands, eating it all up. How were they going to avoid another big quarrel on the way home from church? Maybe she wouldn't say anything. Maybe if Greg asked her what she thought, it'd be better just to . . . well, not lie, but deflect—yes, deflect his question. She could tell him about the long line at children's church and how that had caused her to miss the worship so that her mind wasn't on what the pastor said.

But it was.

Pastor Hanson pointed up to one of the screens. "The second falsehood is that if you *try*—that is, if you try hard enough in your own strength—then sometimes, just sometimes, you *might* get what you need. Now who wants to live like that?"

The pastor waved his Bible. "But the Bible says, 'Not by might, nor by power, but by my spirit, saith the Lord of hosts.'"

The verse with the reference, Zechariah 4:6, appeared on the screen, and Nicole checked it in her translation. It was the same, and she felt confused. The principle seemed biblical. What we try to accomplish in our own strength is likely to fail, or, as the song said, had only a *sometimes* chance of success.

"But the heart of this . . . foolishness"—Nicole had expected him to say *heresy*—"is in the initial premise: *You can't always get what you want*. Because Jesus said in Mark eleven, twenty-four: 'Whatever things you ask when you pray, believe that you receive *them*, and you will have *them*.'

"Believe and receive. Believe and receive. So, I'm here to tell you, you *can* always get what you want. Say it with me, *You* can *always get what you want! You* can *always get what you want!* Yes you can!"

All over the auditorium, people were standing, and Greg joined them, lifting his hands high and repeating, "*You* can *always get what you want*!"

Nicole gripped the edge of her seat, a sense of horror gripping her heart. Something was wrong with this, something terribly wrong. It was so nearly right while being deathly wrong.

"Now . . ." Pastor Hanson stretched out his hands over the congregation. "Now brothers and sisters, everyone remain standing."

Nicole stood hesitantly, joined by many others across the auditorium who had not risen spontaneously earlier.

"Some of you may be wondering whether this is a new gospel I am preaching. It is not. It is the same gospel Jesus gave us, the same message the apostles preached, and the same promise the church has celebrated until only a few decades ago. If you doubt me, consider this old hymn of the faith. It's somber and slow—a little country, if you will—penned by Paul Rader nearly a hundred years ago. But we're going to sing it as we close. Meditate on the words, and you'll realize they say exactly what I've been telling you this morning."

Only believe, only believe;
All things are possible, only believe.
Only believe, only believe;
All things are possible, only believe.

The band led off with a very country version of a song Nicole recalled from her childhood. They sang it twice, and then Pastor Hanson held up his hands again to stop them while the band played softly in the background.

"Now I want you to turn to your neighbor and take your neighbor's hand. And we're going to sing it again, except this time, I want you to sing it *to* your neighbor. That's right, *to* your neighbor. Now don't get squeamish on me. Just do it. It's a simple chorus, and you're not auditioning for *American Idol*. You're just trying to help your brother or sister receive God's word for today."

Nicole took Greg's hand as the congregation began to sing, but she couldn't look at him while he sang to her. All she could do was cry. The tears came faster and harder, and her words turned into big sobs. What was wrong? Somewhere in the back of her mind, she felt the answer was in the verses of the hymn, and they weren't singing the verses. But she couldn't quite remember the words.

Chapter 22

GREG DIDN'T UNDERSTAND why Nicole had been crying during church, but the kids were giggling and whispering about something on the way home. So it didn't seem like the right time to ask questions. Besides, she kept her face turned toward the side window for most of the trip.

He parked the Cherokee in the garage and took a moment to clean some trash out of the car while the kids and Nicole went into the house. When he got to the house, both Becky and Nathan met him at the kitchen door, bouncing up and down like Jack-in-the-boxes.

"You've got to go to your room, Daddy," Becky said.

"Yeah, an' close the door," Nathan added.

"Hey, what's going on here? I haven't been a bad boy. Why do I have to go to my room?" He feigned mock injury, making them giggle.

"You'll see. You'll see." They began pushing him toward the bedroom.

"How 'bout my book? Can I get my book? It's just a thin book with a black and yellow cover by my computer."

"No," Nathan said. "You have to go straight to your bedroom, and no looking around." But Becky volunteered to get the book. It had come with a packet of information from SlowBurn as part of his registration for the training that was to begin on Tuesday. Greg was supposed to read it before he got there, but he hadn't taken time to even crack its cover.

Once Greg was sitting on his bed, book in hand, the kids left. But just before slamming the door, Nathan turned back, his eyes wide. "An' no coming out till we tell you." *Wham!*

Greg fell back on the pillows, a big smile on his face. His kids were something else. But with Nicole being so upset at church this morning, maybe he ought to offer to take everyone out for dinner. It'd been awhile, and even though money was getting short, he wasn't about to live as though *You can't always get what you want.* No. He could get it. They could get it.

"Nicole?" He got up and went to the door, but at the last moment left it shut in order to play along with the kids' game, whatever it was. "Nicole? Hey honey, you want to go out for dinner? It's Sunday and all."

He could hear his wife and kids murmuring to one another in the kitchen, but he couldn't make out the words.

"No. That's okay." Her voice was light. "Already got something started." Her response was followed by more murmuring and stifled squeals from the kids.

Well he'd asked. Greg drifted back to the bed and picked up the book. *Network Marketing: Overcoming Your Fears to Realizing Your Dreams*. But in spite of his good intentions to read the network marketing book, he soon drifted off to sleep.

He awakened fifty minutes later when Nathan and Becky flung open the door. "You can come out now. It's time for dinner."

"Ahh," Greg yawned. "I was just starting my nap. But if it's dinner, guess I'll come." Greg stood up and headed toward the door with an exaggerated stagger.

But as soon as he stepped out, both kids began chanting, "Happy Father's Day, Happy Father's Day," as they danced before him into the dining room.

The table was set, steaming dishes of food were ready, and red and yellow streamers hung from the chandelier to the corners of the room.

"What? Is this Father's Day?" He hadn't even remembered.

"Yes, it's Father's Day, and I made a card for you . . . all by myself." Nathan gave Greg a little push toward his chair.

Greg glanced toward Nicole. She gave him a sly smile. "Well, *we* didn't forget. Sit down before the food gets cold." Her distress of the morning seemed to have passed. She'd put on fresh makeup and looked great, though Greg could still see traces of red in the whites of her eyes. But it wasn't the time to bring up whatever had troubled her earlier.

"Read my card, Daddy." Becky thrust it toward him.

Greg sat down and read both kids' cards, as well as a beautiful card from Nicole. He didn't pay much attention to the printed verse, but she'd signed it, "With all my love, *your* Nikki." He looked at her as she took her seat at the other end of the table. Maybe his concerns about Lincoln Paddock were groundless. Today, he was a happy man.

He took a large helping of his favorite pasta dish: spaghetti with fresh tomatoes, basil, and garlic. The mix was laced with small cubes of extra-sharp white cheddar cheese and extra virgin olive oil. He topped it with coarsely ground black pepper, which Nicole had left off because it was too spicy for the kids. In addition, there were some strips of grilled flank steak and a helping of steaming broccoli.

"What a meal, Nicole. How'd you fix it so quick?"

"We started yesterday," Becky said.

"And"—Nathan's eyes grew big—"we made cupcakes for you."

"For everybody," Little Miss Sweet Tooth corrected. "Besides, Nathan, that was supposed to be a surprise."

Greg reached over and tickled her nose. "And it all is a surprise too. I'd completely forgotten this was Father's Day."

As he enjoyed the scrumptious meal and all the appreciation from his family, it crossed Greg's mind that Pastor Hanson hadn't said one word about this being Father's Day. That seemed strange, especially for someone who often spoke about the importance of husbands being the heads of the families and for the wives to submit in all things. The pastor must've forgotten.

Greg knew how easy that was. He'd forgotten Mother's Day just as completely. A twinge of regret stabbed him. The contrast between this thoughtful celebration and his lame effort a few weeks ago to make up for his oversight by taking Nicole and her mom to that restaurant in Andersonville was painfully obvious.

"Maybe this afternoon you should call your dad," Nicole suggested.

"Yeah. Good idea. I'll do it, right after we have those scrumptious homemade cupcakes you kids made." But Nicole's reminder was another stab. He hadn't given his own dad a single thought—not early enough to send a card and not even this afternoon while his whole family was talking about Father's Day and honoring him.

Maybe . . . maybe he and Pastor Hanson were just two peas in a pod—focused on more important concerns.

Nicole felt bad about the hard time she'd had with Pastor Hanson's message on Sunday. She knew it had meant a lot to Greg, and she wanted to support him. He'd seemed so encouraged by their Father's Day celebration that she didn't want to bring him down by discussing her reservations about Pastor Hanson's teaching. But she couldn't get the closing song out of her mind: *Only believe, only believe; all things are possible, only believe.*

Songs weren't necessarily authoritative, like Scripture, but if this old song—one she recalled from her youth—actually meant all you had to do to get what you wanted was to believe, then maybe she'd been wrong all these years.

Once she had the kids settled doing their reading Monday morning—something she'd insisted continue even though it was summer break now—she switched on the basement computer and did a search for the song's lyrics. When she finally tracked down the hymn, it was as old as Pastor Hanson had said, having been penned by Paul Rader in 1923. She hummed the tune quietly as she read the words, but realized as she went along that it did *not* promise people could get all the riches and blessings they wanted if they "only believed." In fact, the final verse clarified the message the songwriter intended.

> *Fear not, little flock, whatever your lot,*
> *He enters all rooms, "the doors being shut,"*
> *He never forsakes; He never is gone,*
> *So count on His presence in darkness and dawn.*
>
> *Only believe, only believe;*
> *All things are possible, only believe*
> *Only believe, only believe;*
> *All things are possible, only believe.*

Nicole sat back in the desk chair and blew out a breath. The songwriter wasn't singing about "believing" for a new car or even recovery from sickness and tragedy. That was *not* the promise. The song called God's people to believe that Jesus would be with them and never forsake them no matter how bright or dark their circumstances . . . *"whatever your lot."*

"Mommy, what does m-u-s-t-a-n-g spell?"

"What?" Nicole pulled her attention away from the words on the computer.

"M-u-s-t-a-n-g, what's it spell?"

"Mustang. It's a kind of a horse, Nate."

"What kind of horse?"

"Uh, uh . . . a wild horse, out west."

She turned back to the song on her computer screen.

Her jaw tightened. How *could* Pastor Hanson use this song to tell people they could get everything on their wish list, do everything on their bucket list, and have a pain-free, worry-free life if only they believed? What a cruel distortion of the truth. Yes, she knew the Bible made some extraordinary promises, but the greatest was Jesus' promise just before He returned to heaven, "Lo, I am with you always, to the very end of the age."

But Greg had swallowed everything Pastor Hanson said—hook, line, and sinker. Why? Why was he so eager to believe it completely and so impatient when she questioned it? Sometimes he'd talked about a bigger house or a new car, but she hadn't known him to be driven by raw greed. Perhaps he was more worried about this job change than she realized. Maybe he was just scared and grasping something to hold on to.

She wanted to help, not make things harder for him. But what could she do? Greg had been out of work for over a month now, and as far as she knew, he hadn't made any big sales with his new SlowBurn business. He handled all the money for the family, so she didn't know where they stood financially, but things must be getting tight.

Greg was going to be gone the next few days at the SlowBurn conference. What if . . .

Nicole glanced at the extension phone hanging on the wall above the computer. Greg was upstairs in the living room working and never used the home line for business. She dug through her purse until she found Lincoln Paddock's business card, then went to the bottom of the stairs and listened. She could hear Greg talking on his cell. Good. Picking up the receiver to the house phone, she dialed Lincoln Paddock's work number.

She was surprised when the call went straight through to him. "Uh, Mr. Paddock? This is Nicole Singer, your neighbor from down the street."

"Oh yes. Hi, Nikki. What can I do for you?"

So friendly! "Hi . . . I was, I was just wondering whether you might be needing some clerical help in the next few days. You'd mentioned—"

"You're kidding! What great timing you have. We just got in a truckload of work, and I had no idea how we were going to finish it in time. When can you start?"

"Well, maybe I could help out tomorrow for a while if I can arrange childcare for the kids, but—"

"That's great. When can I pick you up?"

"Uh . . . I'm not sure. Can I call you back on that?"

"Sure. Just let me know, and if the morning doesn't work for you, I'll send the car whenever you can make it."

Nicole hung up and sat down slowly, almost gingerly, in front of the computer, her heart pounding and her head swirling as if she'd been spinning on a tire swing. What had she just done? She wanted to run upstairs and tell Greg, but what if it didn't work out? What if she couldn't do the work? And then there was the big question of what to do with the kids.

She reached for the phone again and called the Jaspers. After all, this possibility had been in the back of her mind when she'd tried Tabby out as a mother's helper. It would've been best to test how she did on her own for shorter periods. But necessity had a way of altering the best-laid plans.

A sullen voice mumbled, "Hello?"

For a moment Nicole thought she'd dialed the wrong number. "Is this the Jaspers? This is Nicole Singer."

"Oh, yeah. Hi, Mrs. Singer." The voice brightened. "This is Destin. How you doin'?"

"Fine. Is your mom there?"

"No. She's workin'."

Of course. "Any chance you could give me her work number?"

"I can give you her cell. Will that do?"

"Yes. If you would."

To Nicole's great relief, Michelle answered her cell on the third ring. "Thanks for taking my call, Michelle. Sorry to bother you at work, but I was wondering whether Tabby would be available to babysit for the next few days, starting tomorrow. I figured I should ask you first before I talked to her." Given Tabby's young age, it seemed right to Nicole to ask Michelle first rather than speak directly to the girl.

"Oh, I'm sure she'd love to, but Tabby's down in Indiana at cheerleading camp this week. Won't be home till Saturday evening. Maybe next week, though. She's said how much she enjoys watching your young ones."

All the excitement drained out of Nicole. "Thanks, Michelle. Yes, next week might work. I'll get back to you."

She sat there discouraged after they hung up, but then she got another idea and dialed her mother.

"Hi, Mom. You busy tomorrow?"

"Not at all, honey. You wanna go shopping together?"

"No. Can't do shopping. Would you be able to watch the kids for me for the next few days? I've got a temporary job offer, and Greg's going to be away at a training conference. The easiest would be if you could come up here and stay over. Does that seem possible?"

There was a brief silence. "Well, you know I love my grandchildren, but I don't know if I can keep up with them for several days. They're quite a handful sometimes."

Nicole tried to keep her voice upbeat. "Oh, you can do it, Mom. All you've gotta do is set firm boundaries. You sure knew how to do that for me." She laughed.

"I know, honey, but I was younger then. And you may not realize how much it takes out of a person."

Nicole did know. In fact, she'd started to realize it was part of the long-term exhaustion that dragged her down—kids all day every day, being teacher, wife, housekeeper, and now she had to run interference to make sure the kids didn't disturb Greg while he worked. Whatever made her wish he could spend more time at home?

Her mother finally broke the silence. "Well, all right, dear. I'll give it a try for a few days, just to see how it goes."

"Oh, Mom, thanks so much. And it'll only be for this week. I think I've got someone else who can do it next week, if the job lasts that long."

"Oh, but you've got to be careful who you let care for your children, sweetheart. I know you wouldn't let a stranger watch them"—though the way her mom said it, she was probably afraid Nicole had called a babysitting service—"but there're little things like letting them get away with backtalk or . . . or not obeying when spoken to. Kids are so sassy these days."

"I know, Mom." Her mom had *always* been hard on sass, too hard. "This is someone I know personally and she's watched the kids before under my supervision. It'll be okay. Could I pick you up about seven-thirty tomorrow?"

Chapter 23

GREG SHRUGGED INTO HIS SPORT COAT, slicked his dark hair back on the sides once more, and checked his appearance in the full-length bedroom mirror. Light gray shirt open at the collar, dark gray sport coat, light gray slacks. Face still nicely tanned from his last Powersports boat show. Good. Casual but businesslike. He wanted to make a good impression when he arrived at the Hyatt Regency for the SlowBurn training sessions today.

He needed to get an early start. He couldn't leave Nicole without a car for four days, but hiring a taxi to take the twenty-five-mile trip out to Schaumburg would be pretty pricey, and he was becoming more and more conscious of their dwindling finances. But arriving at the Hyatt on a public bus would look pretty shabby. So he'd come up with a plan.

Greg grinned to himself as he made for the kitchen and poured a cup of coffee. All he had to do was take the 'L' on the Red line down to the Loop and the Blue Line out to O'Hare. Then he could catch the Hyatt Regency shuttle from the airport to the hotel in Schaumburg. It might take him a couple of hours, but if anyone saw him arrive, it would look like he'd flown in for the conference.

He glanced at his watch. If he left in the next fifteen minutes, he'd easily be there in time for the SlowBurn training since it didn't start until noon.

"Greg! The hot water ran out again," Nicole yelled from their bathroom.

Oh, no! Not this morning. He didn't have time to mess with the water heater. But he couldn't leave the family without hot water. He took another swallow of coffee and called to his wife, "I'll take care of it!"

On his knees in the laundry room downstairs, he opened the little door at the base of the water heater and bent down. Sure enough, the pilot was out again, so of course the burner hadn't come on. He'd relit the thing several times in the past few weeks. At some point he needed to figure out why it kept going out. Was it set too low? Was there an adjustment? He didn't know.

He shined a flashlight around the interior of the firebox. The burner was heavily scaled with rust, and the area around the small orifice for the pilot light glistened with . . . water? Sliding his hand underneath the water tank, he felt a small puddle, no larger than a jar lid, but it was definitely wet. Water must be dripping on the pilot and putting it out. He'd have to find where the leak was coming from, tighten a fitting or close a valve or something.

But he didn't have time to track that down this morning.

He went through the relight sequence and reached the propane lighter in until the pilot caught, waited sixty seconds, turned the valve to On, and the burner roared to life.

Whew! Fifteen minutes wasted, and he should probably clean up a little, but if he still hurried . . .

He arrived late, and the standard room he'd reserved turned out to cost him $149 per night even with the conference discount. As the receptionist at the front desk took his card, he almost stopped her to ask if anyone from the conference was interested in sharing a business-class room to save a little money. But of course the hotel people wouldn't know that, and he didn't wanted to look cheap, so he let her swipe his card.

Handing five bucks to a bellhop to take his bag up to his room, he asked the concierge where SlowBurn was meeting.

"They're in the Copper Room." The man pointed. "Past the stairs, third door on your right."

Forty or so women and men had already gathered, a light lunch buffet along one wall of the conference room, when Greg slipped in and found a seat at a table in the back. Arlo was up front making announcements. He paused momentarily and nodded his recognition of Greg. That felt good. At least someone knew him and was glad he was there.

Each place along the long narrow tables held a leather-covered tablet, a pen, and two cans of chilled SlowBurn. Greg gratefully opened one of his cans and took a swig. Ahh. Refreshing. Should be easy to sell the stuff. But Greg hadn't yet figured out how.

The afternoon proceeded with one of the SlowBurn executives from New York reviewing the history of the company and the development of the secret formula for the drink—stuff Greg had already read online. Then a middle-aged African American couple from Florida told how SlowBurn had revolutionized their lives and how they were now living the high life in a waterside villa with a private boat slip in which they'd parked their new forty-eight-foot yacht. They both had BMWs and were on their way to Alaska for a three-week vacation.

"We just wanted to stop over here in Chicago and wish y'all the best from your SlowBurn family in Key West. You're welcome to drop in and see us any ol' time, ya hear? And please forgive us for duckin' out, but we have a plane to catch."

Greg watched them go. Really? Lucky stiffs.

That evening at the awards banquet, Greg sat at a table with seven other Chicago area reps. All of them seemed gung ho and doing well. He tried to match their enthusiasm, but his claims felt like dust in his mouth. Could the others tell?

At the banquet that evening, Arlo was again the emcee, which gave Greg a point of connection, but Arlo hadn't done anything more to recognize him during the day other than shake his hand and say he was glad Greg had made it.

"And now," Arlo said, "it's time to recognize all the hard work you've been doing recently."

Yeah, yeah, yeah, thought Greg as he took another bite of his chicken cordon bleu. The conference was supposed to encourage and train the reps, but so far Greg hadn't learned anything new that would turn his business around. In fact, in comparison to all the other success stories, he was beginning to feel downright discouraged. Maybe SlowBurn wasn't his ticket to success after all.

Arlo's words broke through his gloom. "Greg Singer, come on up here. Greg's our rookie salesman of the cycle with three, no it's four reps working for you now, isn't it, Greg? And he's only been on the job for two weeks. So, everybody, put your hands together for Greg Singer!"

Greg could feel the heat rising up his neck, turning his face red as he slid his chair back and walked toward the front. He never expected this . . . and wait a minute, he didn't have four reps working for him. He had Mattie Krakowski, Ben Garfield, and Destin Jasper—an elderly lady, a dumpy-looking retiree, and a teenager. As far as he knew, not one of them had sold more than one or two cans of SlowBurn. And there was no fourth rep. But he was already walking toward the platform.

At the front, rather than take Arlo's proffered hand, Greg leaned forward and whispered, "I only have three reps, not four."

"Ha, ha, ha!" Arlo's voice boomed through the microphone to the whole group. "Greg's trying to tell me he only has three reps." He threw his arms wide. "How can that be?" And then he slapped Greg on the back. "It's because the man's so modest, he forgot to count himself. Here, this is for you." He stuffed an envelope into Greg's left hand and shook his right hand. "So let's give it up for Greg Singer, rookie rep of the cycle."

Greg's face was burning up. He acknowledged the group's applause with a nod and small wave and hurried back to his seat.

"Believe me, ladies and gentlemen"—Arlo's voice followed Greg—"in this business there's no room for modesty, because we're all winners. Isn't that right? Greg's a new winner, and some of the rest of us are old winners, but we're all winners, so we don't need to apologize for anything."

Greg took his seat and scanned the big smiles from others around his table.

"Congratulations, Greg. You're doing great," said the older man to his right.

Greg nodded and turned his attention to the next award recipient—the first rep from Rockford, Illinois, was celebrating his one-year anniversary. But while he listened to Arlo describe the woman's accomplishments, Greg looked down and opened the envelope between his legs. It held a beautifully printed certificate with his name on it and a crisp hundred-dollar bill.

What?

Greg glanced from side to side to see whether those sitting next to him had noticed. No one was paying any attention.

Wow! When Arlo had first described the SlowBurn business to him, he'd emphasized the many rewards a person could earn with increased sales, but he'd never mentioned this little perk. A hundred dollars wasn't much, but it certainly lifted his spirit.

The award ceremony continued for another forty-five minutes until it seemed half the people in the room had been recognized for one thing or another. As Greg watched, he noticed other people pull a bill out of their envelope too. A few waved theirs at those around them, but no one seemed surprised to have received it.

There were no scheduled events after the award presentations, but for the first time, people began to reach out to Greg, congratulating him, calling him by name—even though he'd been wearing a nametag all day—welcoming him, and asking what part of the city he was from. Everyone seemed so friendly as the group moved like an amoeba out of the Copper Room, down the hall, and into the bar where they began ordering drinks.

Greg didn't drink alcohol, but he wanted to remain sociable, so he had a Coke and schmoozed with the others. He soon saw that the tradition was to buy drinks for all those standing around you with your hundred-dollar bill. His Cokes were three bucks, but some of the mixed drinks others ordered on his round were three or four times that much.

An hour later he slipped up to his room with only twenty-three dollars of his award money remaining in his pocket.

When the conference was over on Friday, Greg headed home congratulating himself that he hadn't succumbed to the pressure to take advantage of the full financial management program SlowBurn was offering. Greg had always handled their own money at home and was sure he could do the same for his new business.

He had, however, agreed to the company's tax package. The SlowBurn executive said it would help him decide whether it would be most beneficial for him to operate as a sole proprietorship or incorporate as an S-Corp. "Taxes can be a real headache. There are monthly taxes, quarterly taxes, and annual taxes. And you don't want to get behind or mess up any of them because you don't want to attract an audit from the IRS. I can help you get it set up right, and later, if you want, you could do it yourself."

But the tax assistance package for the first year was fifteen hundred dollars. Greg signed up but hadn't paid any money. "This'll just reserve you a spot in my schedule," the executive said. "If you don't want to follow through, you can always cancel later."

The guy sitting across from him on the shuttle from the Hyatt to O'Hare left his newspaper when he got off, and Greg picked it up and took it with him.

Once seated on the 'L' on his way into the city, he opened it to catch up on the news of the last few days. He flipped from page to page until one headline caught his attention: "Unemployment Benefits Extension Nixed for Nearly 1 Million."

Greg frowned as he read. It didn't say unemployment benefits would be eliminated. It just said they wouldn't be extended for people who were already receiving them.

Was he one of the unemployed? He'd never thought of himself that way, but at least until he started making some money, it would seem he could qualify. Maybe he should find out. He'd certainly had enough unemployment tax deducted from his checks over the years to qualify for something. But the idea of admitting that he'd lost his job, was unemployed, and didn't yet have a source of income was really hard to face. It felt like admitting defeat.

Still, an unemployment check would bring in a little money, more than he'd made so far. But he'd heard that to receive unemployment benefits, you had to actively search for work. Was he willing to do that while SlowBurn was still a possibility? Did he even have any viable leads? The idea made him feel defeated.

So much for coming home from a rah-rah conference that was supposed to fire up all the SlowBurn reps. He felt flat, like a glass of ginger ale left out overnight.

In the Loop, he transferred from the Blue Line to the Red Line and headed north toward home. It was the middle of rush hour, and he had to remain standing until the train got to Ravenswood before a seat opened up. He couldn't let Nicole see him this way, nor the kids either, though they probably wouldn't understand.

The thought of his family cheered him up, especially remembering the Father's Day surprises they'd had arranged for him. They really did love him.

Nicole met him at the front door with a breezy kiss on the cheek. "Welcome home, honey. Sorry to run out. I was just ready to take Mom home. Go say hi to the kids. They're down in the basement." She called over her shoulder, "Mom, you ready? We gotta go."

Frida Lillquist came out of the master bedroom and down the hall to the foyer pulling a small, rolling suitcase. She smiled when she saw him. "Oh, there you are, Greg. We were going to take the kids along, but they didn't want to leave their show. Now that you're here, they can finish it."

"Hi, Mom. Good to see you." Greg reached for her case. "Here, let me take that. You have a sleepover?"

Nicole's mother chuckled. "Hmm, something like that."

"Hey, I can take that. It's light." His wife grabbed the luggage from Greg as though they'd been running a relay with it. "Go on down and greet the kids. I'll be back in a half hour or so. Supper won't take long when I get back. I bet you're tired."

Greg watched them go. Well sure, it made sense for Nicole to invite her mom to stay over while he was gone. Maybe she'd been lonely. Strange that she hadn't mentioned it when they spoke on the phone the other night though.

Chapter 24

TRUE TO HER WORD, Nicole had supper on the table within thirty minutes after getting back with the car. Spaghetti with Nicole's homemade sauce. Not exactly a "welcome home" meal, but plenty of it and Greg was hungry. "Did you kids have a good time with Grammy?" he asked.

"Uh-huh." Becky pursed her lips and slurped in a long strand of spaghetti, earning a frown from her mother.

"Who cooked this meal?" Nate looked around the table as if a chefs' competition was in progress.

"I did, silly." Nicole pinched him playfully.

"You're a good cook, Mom."

Greg smiled at the little ritual Nathan had adapted from his mother's positive reinforcement techniques when the kids did a chore without being reminded or otherwise did something noteworthy. But he was curious about Mom Lillquist's visit, which puzzled him because Nicole hadn't mentioned it on the phone. "How long was your mom here?"

"She came over on Tuesday, and she was so helpful. I'll have to tell you all about it—but later, okay?"

Greg got the *later* message and let it rest. In fact, he forgot about it until after the kids were in bed. "Oh, hon, look at that sunset," Nicole said as she came into the living room where Greg was on the computer.

Greg turned toward the front window. Deep reds and burnt purples outlined the dark clouds in the west.

His wife rubbed his shoulders. "Let's go sit on the front steps. I want to hear about your conference."

Greg looked back at the computer screen where he'd been studying the members-only page describing the financial management assistance SlowBurn offered its reps—for a very steep fee. He saw nothing new on the page he hadn't heard at the conference. He clicked out of it, glad he hadn't put down any money.

"Sure, why not." He got up and followed Nicole out the front door. A tree had once inhabited the parkway right in front of their bungalow, but it had died and the city had removed it several years ago. Sometimes Greg groused that they hadn't yet replaced it, but the gap in Beecham's tree-lined canopy allowed the Singers to view sunsets over the roof of their Hispanic neighbors across the street.

They sat on the steps in silence, taking in the gnarly sky as its last embers died.

Nicole reached out and touched Greg's arm. "I wanted to tell you why Mom was here. Remember how I had Tabby—Tabitha Jasper—come down to be a mother's helper for me a couple of times?"

"Yeah. You were thinking of doing some work for that lawyer guy, right?"

"Yeah." Her voice brightened at his recollection. "Well, when I called to see if Tabby could come over this week, I found out she was away at a cheerleading camp in Indiana. But Mr. Paddock had some paralegal work for me, so I called Mom, and she seemed happy to come over."

"Did he call you?" He knew his question carried a sharp challenge in his voice, but he couldn't help it. He had no problem with Mom Lillquist caring for the kids, but . . . he'd already suspected this guy was hitting on his wife.

"No, I called him. Why?" Her hand dropped away from his arm.

"But why? Why would you call him?"

"Because . . . because you were going to be gone this week, and I thought it would be a great opportunity to test picking up a little work. I'm sure we can use the money until . . . while SlowBurn gets going."

She had him there, but money wasn't the issue right now. Still, it stopped him for a moment. "So what did you do? He drop off some typing for you or something?" At least Nicole's mom would've been home when the man came by.

"No. I went down to his law office, fifty-first floor of the AON Center. He's with Watkins, Ellis, and Katz."

Greg chewed on what Nicole had just told him. "AON? So he's in a real firm, not a back room in his limo company's garage?"

"Of course not." Nicole said it with eye-rolling tolerance. "It's a big firm, Greg, over eight hundred attorneys plus hundreds more support staff. It's legit, big. Turns out Lincoln's a junior partner, which makes him pretty important in a firm that size. Know what I mean?"

"Yeah." Greg thought about it some more. "So what did he have you do? You go to court?"

"No. I spent all week preparing a bunch of boring contracts. But at least I was back in my field."

"Contracts about what?"

"Greg, client/attorney privilege!" She punched his shoulder. "You know if I told you, I'd have to kill you."

"All right, all right." The tension was broken.

"Here." She handed him a folded slip of paper. "This is the good part."

He opened it and by the light coming through the screen door saw it was a check from Watkins, Ellis, and Katz for $1,152. "Wow! How much were they paying you per hour?"

"They paid me thirty-six an hour, but on a fee-for-service basis. I had to sign a waver with HR stating that I had not been hired and am responsible for all my own taxes, etc. But if I continue, Lincoln said they'll put me on the payroll."

"*If you continue*? Uh, Nikki, I appreciate you doing this, but you've got the kids and all. I can't let you start supporting us—"

"Well, is SlowBurn paying the bills yet? You don't tell me anything, but I haven't heard you crowing about any big sales. And I'm sure you would if they were coming in like you said they would."

Ouch, that hurt. "Not yet. It takes time to establish a business. You just don't understand these things."

She stood up. "Is that right?" She turned on her heels and slammed her way through the screen door, calling back, "I may understand a lot more than you think."

Greg sat in the dark, the neighborhood now illumined only by the peach-colored streetlights and the glow from the windows of other homes along Beecham Street. There, he'd gone and done it again. But she was so sensitive . . . too sensitive. He didn't like feeling as if he had to walk on eggshells around her.

Still, he knew she'd been trying to help. He nervously flicked the check in his hand. If she only realized . . . wait. Greg looked at the amount again: $1,152. That nearly met the cost of his training conference—$695 for the seminar and three nights at the Hyatt Regency at $149 per night, plus tax, minus the $23 he'd saved from his reward. He calculated it all in his head. Not exact, but almost.

A hot breathlessness settled over him. Was this a gift from God?

Maybe . . . maybe not. But one thing was certain: It was a gift from Nicole.

He got up and strode into the house.

"Nicole! Nikki? Where are you?"

He went into the bedroom. The door to the master bath was closed, but light came from below it and he could hear water running.

"Nicole? Hey, honey, I'm sorry. You did a great thing, and I was being a jerk. Can you forgive me? Nikki?" He waited a moment and then tapped lightly on the door. "Nikki, please open the door."

Nicole recognized that Greg's advance was his way of wanting to make up, but she just wasn't ready for it yet. After several minutes, she opened the bathroom door. He was still standing at the door, but wordlessly she slipped passed him. She could feel her husband's eyes on her as she got ready for bed, but after several long, silent moments he left the bedroom. Crawling between the sheets—earlier than usual—she turned out her bedside light and faced away from his side of the bed.

She could hear him being none too quiet as he shut down his computer, locked the doors, and shut off the lights. A few minutes later, she heard the TV go on downstairs.

Her chest tightened. Maybe they should get some marriage counseling. Seemed like every time one or the other of them did something, it was the wrong thing. Didn't seem to matter what she did, no good deed went unpunished. Like trying to earn a little extra money to help out in this time of need. She reviewed the last four days working with Lincoln. Everything had gone so smoothly. Even when she didn't know what to do or did something wrong, he'd been so understanding and patient, always appreciative of her efforts.

She'd even identified someone she thought had been one of the two girls standing up in the back of one of Lincoln's limos as it sped down Beecham Street. The woman worked in HR and had been the one to explain the form Nicole signed. In the office, everything seemed all business, no flirting between anyone. Maybe she'd misjudged Lincoln. Maybe he wasn't a playboy.

Her thoughts drifted back to the zoo trip. Their time together had been so pleasant, like in the office, but on a far more personal level. What kind of a man was he, really? Why wasn't he married?

She drifted into a dream where she was sitting in the back of a gondola, leaning into the gentle arms of Lincoln Paddock. Instead of propelling them through the Venetian canals, the gondolier was giving them a private tour on the Chicago River, pointing out all the dramatic buildings, describing their history or builder in a most intriguing manner. As they bobbed gently along, a much larger tour boat passed, filled with people. The bullhorn voice of its guide was also describing the city's architectural wonders. Nicole choked as she caught a whiff of the boat's diesel exhaust just as she recognized Greg sitting in the back of the tour boat—just as he had years ago when they'd taken the same tour, only this time he was alone, head down.

Why had she ever thought that trip was romantic? This was real romance.

A large wake from the tour boat rocked the little gondola, threatening to capsize it . . . and Nicole woke up.

But it was just Greg getting into bed.

Her heart pounded as she broke out in a heavy sweat. She remained facing away from her husband, wondering if he knew, fearing she might've said something in her sleep. But she hadn't been talking in her dream, so what could she have said to give herself away? She'd just been enjoying the ride.

It was only a dream. You can't control what you dream about, can you?

But the thrill of it clung to her, and she welcomed it like a warm blanket on a chilly day. It was only a dream, but Lincoln's arms had been so comforting.

Once her heart slowed until she could no longer feel it thumping in her chest, she willed herself back to sleep . . . perhaps to dream again.

Chapter 25

"NICOLE, WE NEED TO TALK." Greg shuffled barefoot into the kitchen, rubbing his eyes from a restless night.

His wife turned from the stove, her mouth open, and the color seemed to drain from her face.

"I mean, *I* need to talk about what I said yesterday. I'm sorry."

She took a deep breath, and color slowly returned to her face, but she said nothing, just turned back to flipping the pancakes on the griddle.

"Look, I'm trying to apologize here. Can you at least say something?"

"Sorry. My mind was someplace else. You're apologizing for what exactly?"

Grrr! She was going to make him retrace every detail. He took a deep breath and dove in. "For jumping all over you about taking that job. I should've been more grateful, but—" No, he shouldn't add a *but*. "I'm just grateful. Period. Hey, you probably didn't realize it, but the amount of your check almost covers my exact expenses at the training seminar. I think it was God's provision. Don't you?"

She didn't answer for a moment. "Your four days cost eleven hundred dollars?"

"Yeah. Things like that aren't cheap, but God provided by giving you that temp job. So it didn't set us back at all. Isn't that great?"

Nicole turned to face him, arms crossed, spatula in hand. "I guess. But Greg, you've been so private about this whole Slow-Burn thing I have no idea how it's going. I mean, you're busy every day, but is it getting us anywhere? And what's our money situation? You never tell me about that. I'm totally in the dark. Do you think I can't understand, or I can't add and subtract?"

"No, no, honey. It's not that. It's just that I'm tryin' to take care of you and the kids, make the money, and, you know, keep the car and the house in good repair so you'll be safe and comfortable. You know, my responsibility as your husband to provide and protect. It's a division of labor. I mean, you work hard taking care of the kids and the house. I don't want to burden you with the financial end of things—"

"Argh!" Nicole threw her hands up and waved her spatula like a fly swatter. "Greg, that's so . . . so last century, so *Father Knows Best*."

"What d'you mean? We weren't even born then."

"But our parents were, and I've seen some of those old reruns."

Greg leaned back against a kitchen counter, shaking his head. How did they get to this place in the conversation in so few minutes? He'd come in here to apologize, sincerely, but they ended up fighting again. "Look, you may call it last century, but Pastor Hanson says I'm supposed to be the head of my family, and that's what I'm trying to do. But it's a little hard with a wife who won't submit to her husband like the Bible says."

Nicole stared at him, and then her lips tightened into a hard line. She turned back to the griddle where the last six pancakes had burned on the bottoms. She scooped them off and threw them in the trash with a vengeance. "All right. You handle the money, and I'll run the house . . . with your *permission*. But I told Mr. Paddock I'd be back next week to finish the big project he had me on. And I've already arranged for Tabby to watch the kids next week. So you don't have to worry about that. Is that okay?"

"Of course. Of course." Finally, a way out of the rat's nest. "In fact, that's what I came in here to tell you, honey. I'm grateful for what you did. In fact, if that's something you want to keep doing, it's okay by me." Oops, had he gone too far? "I mean, for a while, on a part-time basis. Right? But can you keep it to half days?" He didn't really want her to be working for Paddock at all, but at this point he wasn't about to explain why. She'd just call it groundless jealousy.

✧ ✧ ✧ ✧

Pastor Hanson was gone on Sunday, leading the summer five-star Holy Land tour. The Victorious Living Center sponsored three Holy Land tours each year—one during the Christmas season with special attention to Bethlehem and a retired astronomer who talked about what the Wise Men may have seen in the Middle Eastern sky, one during Easter week that focused on Jerusalem and the events of Holy Week, and a summer tour with more time spent in the Galilean countryside where Jesus focused so much of his ministry. Greg really wanted to go on one of those tours, but such an expense would have to wait until SlowBurn got on its feet. He'd found some other tours online for half the price, but they didn't include Pastor Hanson as guide and expositor.

The pastor's absence on Sunday was a mixed blessing. An assistant minister gave the message on Psalm 23, which didn't raise any of the challenging issues Greg and Nicole seemed to end up disagreeing over. On the other hand, Greg had hoped Pastor Hanson would give a definitive teaching on family roles that would help Nicole understand the responsibility he was trying to shoulder in their home. The pastor often made side comments like, "Of course, as heads of your family, you men need to lead the way into prosperity. Don't leave it to your wife to do. That's not her responsibility." But what Greg wanted him to do was preach a complete message on the issue that would put it all into perspective. Maybe that would convince Nicole.

Nevertheless, on the upside, the trip home and Sunday dinner were a peaceful and welcome relief from Sundays' usually tense conversations.

They were just getting up from the table when Greg glanced out the front window and noticed Destin Jasper walking by. He dropped his napkin onto his plate and hurried to the front door.

"Hey, Destin. Got a minute?"

Destin turned. "Oh, hi, Mr. Singer." The boy came sauntering back, and Greg went down the steps to meet him.

"So how'd it go this last week? You get around to all the houses on the block?"

Destin looked down at the sidewalk. "I got to most of 'em, but . . . not everyone."

"What's that mean? Who'd you miss?"

"I didn't talk to the houses on either side of you. I rang the doorbell for the two-flat"—he pointed to the red brick building just north of Greg's place—"but the woman who came to the door couldn't speak English, so I just nodded and said, '*Hasta luego.*' I've had two years of Spanish in school, but that's all I could think of."

Greg nodded. He'd never really been able to connect with those neighbors either, but Destin's lack of initiative was getting to him. "And the family on the corner?"

"Never got there."

"And how much did you sell at the other places?"

"Two six-packs, but I gave out eight samples." He said it as if that'd been a great accomplishment.

"You gave out eight cans and sold twelve. You think that's big business, Destin? You think you're gonna make your five hundred bucks or whatever you're shootin' for like that?"

"No." Destin's head hung lower.

"Me either. You better get your butt in gear, young man. And pull your pants up while you're at it. You tryin' to look like some kinda gangbanger or hip-hopper?"

"No sir."

When Destin did hitch his pants up, Greg realized they hadn't been that low, just a little loose in the seat. Instinctively, he pulled his own pants up.

He calmed his voice. "Look, I don't want to be all over you about this sales thing, but I'm gonna have to let you go if you don't start selling."

Destin looked away. Greg had no idea whether he could fire someone. He hadn't really hired anyone. They weren't technically his employees, just recruits to sell SlowBurn. And just because Destin hadn't sold much yet, didn't mean he wouldn't find his groove in time. Besides, Greg reminded himself, Destin had already paid for the SlowBurn he was trying to sell.

"You think you can do any better this next week?"

"I don't know, Mr. Singer. I got basketball camp startin' Wednesday, so I'll be going down to—"

"Hey, there's your opportunity." Greg laid his hand on the kid's shoulder like a coach. "That's your chance. I've said it all along, your main asset is that you are a young athlete, and that's gotta be the biggest market around."

"I don't know, Mr. Singer. I've studied the schedule. They keep us busy just about every minute we're not sleepin'. I don't think there'll be much time for sellin' anything."

"Ah, you can find the time. How long does it take to tell a teammate SlowBurn's the best energy drink in the world? They see how it lights your fire, keeps you goin' when they're draggin', and they'll be begging you for a can. Heck, they'll wanna buy a case."

Destin laughed nervously and grinned, as if regaining some of his confidence. "I know I won't be able to take whole cases with me, but maybe I can write up orders and deliver them later."

"*Now* you're thinkin' like the businessman I know you can be." Greg slapped Destin on the back to send him on his way. "To be effective, you have to turn over every stone. And if you need any help, just let me know. I'm always here for you."

Greg stood there looking after Destin as he walked up the street, a bit more of a bounce in his step. Would the kid break through? Had he given the boy the right balance between reprimand and encouragement? Who knew? Greg shook his head. He hated to admit it, but as a boss, he was expecting his team to do what he hadn't yet been able to do—sell SlowBurn. But like he'd just told Destin, to be effective, he had to turn over every stone.

Looking past Destin, he noticed the shiny black Town Car parked in Paddock's drive, and a thought struck him. *Every stone!* That was one stone he'd passed up earlier, but maybe it was time to see what might crawl out.

"Hey Destin, hold on a minute." He jogged up the street to join him. "When you were going house to house, did you talk to Lincoln Paddock, the guy who lives there?" Greg pointed to the McMansion.

Destin looked worried, like he feared another chewing-out. "Well . . . I didn't actually speak to him, but I talked to the woman who works in his house. I think she's his maid or cook or somethin'. She said she does all his shopping, and she's certain he wouldn't want any."

"Didn't want any, huh? But you didn't speak to Mr. Paddock himself?"

"No. Don't think he was home."

"That's okay. Don't worry about it. I think I'm gonna go talk to him right now."

When Greg came back, Nicole thought her husband seemed particularly lighthearted. He ran in and out of the house a couple of times during the afternoon, obviously busy with something. Then he sat down and worked on the computer.

Sunday evening supper at the Singer house was usually root beer floats and popcorn in front of a video—though ever since Greg lost his job at Powersports, he'd been too busy to join her and the kids. But to her surprise, he shut off the computer and came down to the basement family room to watch *Finding Nemo,* laughing with the kids at all the right places in a movie they were enjoying for the umpteenth time.

Nicole followed him in amazement when he helped pick up the popcorn bowls and empty glasses and headed up to the kitchen.

"Hey, honey," he said as he put them into the dishwasher, "you want me to put the kids to bed this evening? You've probably got things you need to do to get ready for tomorrow."

"Well, sure, but *tomorrow*? What do you mean?" She always had things to get ready for the next day.

"You know, getting ready to go to work a bit earlier. Sorry. Should have mentioned it sooner. I was talking to Paddock this afternoon, and he said he had to go out to the Skokie courthouse tomorrow morning to represent a client. He asked if he should send a car for you, but I told him you could take the 'L.' I figured it was generous enough for him to offer you some work without becoming obligated to him for a ride."

Nicole felt her breath catch. "You were talking to Lincoln Paddock?"

"Yeah. Business stuff." Greg grinned. "He took two cases of SlowBurn!"

She breathed again. "He bought two whole cases?"

"Well, not exactly. He took them on consignment to stock the mini-bars in his limos. He'll charge two-fifty a can, and we'll split the profits. Not bad, huh?"

"Well, sure. That's great." Maybe Greg had a point. She sure didn't want to be Lincoln's charity case. Her memory of their day at the zoo would certainly lose its glow if he'd only done it because he felt sorry for her. "Uh, but I thought you said reps had to pay cash for their product."

"Well, they're supposed to, at least that's what Arlo says. But it's not a law. I can run my own business however I want. Besides, Paddock's not a rep. He's just letting me use his limos as an outlet—to see how it goes. I'm gonna make up some little cards, like business cards, that he'll keep in his cars so if people like SlowBurn, they'll have a number to call to order it from me. I think this might be the way to go."

"What do you mean?"

"Getting it into outlets—offices, waiting rooms, maybe even vending machines—rather than trying to sell it face-to-face or through reps."

"Hmm. Maybe so." She put the last of the dishes into the dishwasher and turned it on, then started scrubbing on an encrusted baking pan that'd been soaking since the noon meal. "He's quite an entrepreneur, isn't he?"

"No-o-o. That was all *my* idea."

"Oh, of course. I just meant, it's amazing how he has his hand in so many different things." She shrugged. "And now something of yours."

"Yeah, I've noticed." His carefree tone had changed, his comment almost a sneer. "By the way, I talked to Paddock about one other thing. Said I appreciated that he'd found work for you to do during my job transition, but it'd work better for our family if you could work from home."

She turned to face him. "You *what*?"

"I said, if he has work for you to do, he could drop it by the house, and you could do it here."

"Greg! That would . . . that would cut out all kinds of projects I might do. I mean, even last week, I was just working on contracts, but I had to use the firm's contract templates and database and look things up in their files—all kinds of things I couldn't do from home."

"Well, he said he'd see what he could do."

Nicole was livid. Turning her back, she scrubbed harder on the already-clean pan in the sink. All it needed was rinsing, but the water ran cold. Where did Greg get off micromanaging her life? She didn't trust herself to speak for several moments. When she finally found her voice, she kept her back turned. "Yeah, I'd appreciate it if you put the kids to bed—and I can't get any hot water again. I wish you'd fix that blasted water heater once and for all!"

Throwing the scrub brush into the sink, she left the room and slipped out the front door. The neighborhood was dark, but she needed a walk—a long walk.

Chapter 26

When Harry Bentley called on Tuesday to see if Greg wanted to go to Bible study that evening, Greg said yes. It'd be a way to casually check on how Ben Garfield was doing selling SlowBurn. And he needed to talk to the guy who was a coach or something. What was his name? Dennis, no Denny—Denny something. Oh, yeah, his son was Josh Baxter. Yes, he needed to talk to Denny Baxter because he still believed that young people, especially young athletes, were a goldmine market . . . if only he could convince Destin of that fact.

He also was eager to get out of the house for the evening. Sunday's calm had only come before "the great summer freeze." Nicole hadn't said one word to him since Sunday evening that wasn't absolutely necessary. Seemed like they couldn't talk about Lincoln Paddock without her getting touchy, which confirmed his suspicions of that guy. And now he had a business connection with him.

At the Bible study, the same guys who'd been there the first time Greg attended— and showed up to help carry stuff out of the Molanders' basement—gathered again at Peter Douglass's, as well as one other man—fifty-something, short and stocky, gray around the temples. Harry introduced him. "Greg, this is Pastor Joe Cobbs. Sometimes he can't make it because of his responsibilities at SouledOut Community Church over in the Howard Street shopping center. But we like having him whenever he can drop by."

Greg's eyebrows went up as he shook the man's hand. "There's a church in that shopping center by the Howard 'L' station?"

"Sure is, southeast corner. Though you're not the first person to miss it." The pastor turned and spoke across the room. "Say, Deacon Douglass, do you think we could come up with some better signage for SouledOut? This young man has never noticed the church."

Douglass chuckled. "I'm sure we could do something, Pastor. I'll look into it. All right, brothers, let's take our seats and get into the Word."

Greg glanced around as the men sat down, Bibles in hand. He felt stupid. He'd been so eager to get out of the house that he'd come to a Bible study without his Bible. He glanced at Harry Bentley and gratefully realized he wasn't alone. Harry didn't have one either. "Excuse me, Peter, do you have extra Bibles? Harry and I forgot ours."

"Oh, no. I'm good." Harry whipped out his cell phone and held it up. "I got mine right here. Estelle thinks I'm a pagan for reading the Bible on my iPhone, but I just tell her, it goes with me everywhere with over a dozen translations. Can't beat that. I can search out anything a lot easier than in my paper Bible."

The guys laughed as Peter pulled a Bible from the bookshelf behind his chair and passed it across to Greg. "I think we're in Second Corinthians chapter six this evening. Sound right to everyone?" There were quiet murmurs of agreement. "Josh, since you were the last one to arrive, would you open us up with prayer?"

As the young Josh Baxter prayed, Greg began to feel an unusual peace. No one had even blinked at him forgetting his Bible, and Baxter's prayer was simple, just asking that God would be with the guys who couldn't make it and open the hearts of each of them who had. "Amen."

Man, these guys were so down-to-earth. Greg remembered Harry Bentley saying, "We're just a group of guys seeking the truth in God's Word, tryin' to get it right."

What could be more basic than that? Greg recalled reading somewhere in the Bible about the Bereans, who were commended because when the apostle Paul taught them something new, they checked it out in the Scriptures to see if it was true. Greg had already spent an evening with these guys batting around a passage from the Bible, and he'd worked with them dragging soggy boxes and damp rugs out of the Molanders' basement. They were just regular guys, and that made him feel comfortable . . . somehow different than the high-powered expectations of the Victorious Living Center.

Peter Douglass asked for a volunteer to start their reading. Carl Hickman laughed self-consciously. "Ya'll know I don't read so well, but if you'll hang in there with me, I'll kick it off." Greg was only half listening until Carl got down to verse four:

> ". . . as servants of God we commend ourselves in every way: in great endurance; in troubles, hardships and distresses; in beatings, imprisonments and riots; in hard work, sleepless nights and hunger; in purity, understanding, patience and kindness; in the Holy Spirit and in sincere love; in truthful speech and in the power of God; with weapons of righteousness in the right hand and in the left; through glory and dishonor, bad report and good report; genuine, yet regarded as impostors; known, yet regarded as unknown; dying, and yet we live on; beaten, and yet not killed; sorrowful, yet always rejoicing; poor, yet making many rich; having nothing, and yet possessing everything."

"Okay," Peter Douglass broke in. "Let's stop right there and see what God has for us in this passage."

"Ha, ha, ha. One thing I know," barked Ben Garfield. "God's got a big surprise waitin' for some of them TV preachers."

"And good news for us too," Josh added.

Harry frowned. "What are you guys getting' at?"

Ben snorted. "Huh. Those TV preachers are always sayin' God wants you to get rich quick—usually if you send them a big fat check first. It stinks, I tell ya."

Most of the men laughed. Greg squirmed. He had to admit, Pastor Hanson usually said something about proving your faith through giving more. But was that what he really meant?

"Oh, yeah," Ben grumbled. "Everything's suppose'ta work out fine if I believe hard enough. Rich I'm gonna get, troubles won't find me, and health problems are what the other guy'll have. But," Ben pointed to his silvery hair, "see this? I've lived long enough to know life's not like that. And I've *never* heard one of 'em preach on a passage like this. What was wrong with the apostle Paul's faith that all this suffering came on him if it's God's will for everyone's life to be *easy peasy*?"

The room was silent for a few moments. "And I'll tell you another thing." Ben wagged a finger in the air. "Man is born to die, and death doesn't knock on the door. It'll come to every one of them preachers."

"Unless Jesus comes back first," Josh added.

"Right. Unless Jesus comes back first. But from what I've seen, death usually ain't pretty or easy. Even Jesus died . . . in pain, and from what you guys tell me, he had perfect faith."

Silence again replaced Ben Garfield's gravelly voice as Greg waited for someone to challenge the old guy.

Finally, Peter prompted, "So, what's the good news for us you see in this passage, Josh?"

"Well, not everything in the passage is negative. Paul was just rehearsing what he'd been through. In addition to getting beaten, thrown in prison, going hungry, and living in poverty . . ." Josh looked down at his Bible and traced the words with his finger. ". . . Paul points out that he received purity, understanding, patience, kindness, and sincere love. He had the power of God and weapons of righteousness, and sometimes he experienced glory and good reports so that he lived on, was able to rejoice, made many rich—though I'm not sure he's talking about money-rich—and possessed everything."

Josh's father nodded. "All right now. I see that."

"And I see something more," added Pastor Cobbs. "Back in verse two Paul quoted God as saying, 'In the time of my favor I heard you, and in the day of salvation I helped you.' Through everything Paul experienced—both good and bad—God was always with him, always helped him. That promise echoes again and again throughout the whole Bible. To the patriarchs, God promised, 'I'll never leave you or forsake you.' And Jesus promised to send the Holy Spirit, who would be with us forever. Before he returned to heaven, Jesus said, 'Surely I am with you always, to the very end of the age.' It's the most important promise in the Bible, because it helps us through the hard times as well as the easy times."

"Yeah, yeah" . . . "Amen" . . . "Ain't that the truth," several men murmured.

Greg stared at the Bible in his hand, trying to sort it all out.

"You guys probably heard this before," Harry said, "but I had to learn that lesson the hard way. You remember when I lost the sight in my left eye and how scared I was that I might end up blind in both eyes? Well, when I was goin' through that, I thought there was nothin' more important to me than gettin' my sight back. I prayed for a miracle, I believed for a miracle. I'm sure I felt as desperate as Paul when he was beaten and left for dead."

"All right, now," put in Carl. "You were goin' through it. No doubt about it."

"Oh, believe me, brother, I wanted a miracle in the worst way. I would've gladly mortgaged my future to put ten grand in the pocket of one of those TV preachers if he could've slapped me upside my head and healed my eye. I was that desperate, don'tcha know—'

"Now you're preachin'!" interjected Carl.

Harry sighed and quieted himself. "But it didn't happen that way. In fact, every time I went to the doctor, somethin' else was wrong, and it seemed like I needed another operation."

Greg looked hard at Harry's left eye. Could he see out of it now? Seemed like he could.

"I got to the point," Bentley continued, "where I began doubting God's very existence because he wasn't doing for me what I'd asked him to do. And that thought exploded in me like a bomb! If God wasn't there, then nothin' in life had any meaning. Suddenly, somethin' became a lot more important to me than being able to see. Was God real? Did he really care? Recovering of my eyesight seemed like nothin' compared to me needing to be aware of Jesus' presence. Was he really with me, or not? I had to know!"

Greg nodded. Sometimes lately he'd started to wonder the same thing. Where was God in what he was trying to do?

Harry chuckled. "And then my miracle happened. My eye wasn't instantly healed. Oh, no, I had to go through several more procedures before I got my sight back. But when I realized how desperate I was to know that God was there, I realized he'd taught me something. He'd taught me that his presence was more important to me than my eyesight. That, brothers, proved God was with me."

"What?" Greg couldn't contain his consternation. "How did that prove God exists?"

"Oh, it was proof all right. Just think about it: A nonexistent being can't teach you anything. But the fact that he'd made the effort to teach me something proved not only that he existed, but it proved he was with me and cared about me."

The room again fell silent for several moments.

Peter Douglass closed his Bible with a thump. "Well, I think we got our lesson for this evening from the Word, brothers. We've got a miracle-working God, but he's God all by himself. We don't tell him what to do. We don't schedule his miracles. He has his own purposes and his own times, and he hasn't promised us a rose garden. But he has promised to be with us through the good times and the bad. As that second verse in the chapter says . . ." He fumbled with the pages as he reopened his Bible. "Here it is. 'In the time of my favor I heard you, and in the day of salvation I helped you.' " He looked around at the men in his living room. "That's a promise, brothers, so let's gather up the prayer requests, lay them before the Lord, and call it a night."

On the ride home, Greg appreciated that Harry let him wrestle with his own thoughts. At some point he might need to talk, but first he had to sort out what his questions were.

He suddenly snapped his fingers.

Harry jumped. "What?"

"Oh, nothin'. I needed to talk to Ben Garfield about something this evening and completely forgot. I'll give him a call tomorrow."

Chapter 27

Just because Greg objected to accepting any favors that might obligate them to Lincoln Paddock, Nicole had to take the 'L' all week downtown to the AON building. She saw Lincoln only a couple of times in the office. He smiled and gave a friendly wave as he hurried to some meeting while she did the jobs assigned to her from various attorneys. However, after she picked up her check Friday afternoon and headed for the elevator, she saw him coming from the other direction, briefcase in hand. They met at the elevator, and he pressed the down button with his free hand.

"Hey there, beautiful, how's it goin'?"

"Good. Everything's good." Nicole blushed as the elevator dinged and they both stepped in, pivoted the obligatory 180 degrees, and waited until the doors enfolded them into the already full car.

Lincoln leaned sideways. "You ever wonder why we all get on and face the same way, even if there's nothing to look at but blank stainless steel doors? Why not turn toward one another"—which he did—"and have a meaningful conversation as we descend from the lofty heights of Watkins, Ellis, and Katz?"

She laughed. "Probably because"—she paused, facing him with an impish smile on her face—"you can't start a meaningful conversation with someone when you don't know where the person intends to get off."

"Today you're in luck. There's plenty of time because I'm headed all the way down to the parking garage. You want a ride home?"

The door opened on the forty-third floor, and six more people forced their way in, pressing Nicole and Lincoln into a close dance. "Or, uh, maybe this is why everyone faces the doors," he said, rolling his eyes. "What if I'd been talking to Ms. Krenshaw? I wouldn't be able to breathe."

Nicole stifled a laugh. Delores Krenshaw was the section manager—Nicole's de facto boss this past week while Lincoln was busy in court and having meetings with clients. Delores was huge, smelled of cheap perfume, and had refused retirement over the last six years every time the firm offered it to her.

"Seriously, can I give you a lift home? Your husband told me you could take the 'L' when I offered to arrange a car, but today's hot, and . . . where do you get off, at Jarvis? That's gotta be over a mile walk from home, right?"

"Yes, about that, but it's okay."

"No, today you're going to ride home with me."

They filled their rush-hour ride up Lakeshore Drive with work-related chitchat. Had HR put her on staff yet? No, she was hoping to mostly work at home as her husband had requested . . . did he think that was possible? No problem, he'd meant to speak to HR about it but had forgotten. Sorry. He'd be sure to take care of it Tuesday, right after the holiday. Were they going to take the kids to the fireworks Saturday night? No, she said, probably Sunday night, the actual Fourth. They usually went up to Evanston where the crowds weren't so bad.

Lincoln was so easy to talk to. She felt none of the tension that always seemed to develop with Greg. Before she knew it, the smooth-riding Town Car pulled to a stop in front of her house. She studied the front window. Was Greg watching? She didn't think so but jumped slightly and turned when Lincoln touched her on the arm.

"I just want you to know," he said, his hand still on her arm, "how much I appreciate you, Nikki. Even if Ms. Krenshaw's telling you what to do, you're really working for me, and that means a lot."

Nicole felt goose bumps rising on her arm and for some strange reason, her eyes began watering. "Thanks. It's been good for me too." She opened the door and started to step out, determined to escape before her voice failed her.

"Oh, Nikki, one more thing. I actually have a project right now you could do from home. It's in my briefcase." He reached into the backseat for his briefcase and rifled through it. "Oh, no. I only have part of it here. But tell you what, I can log into the office server from home and get the database to go with this." He handed her a thick folder. "I'll copy it onto a thumb drive and bring it down to you. That okay?"

Nicole glanced at the house, thinking of Greg's discomfort with Lincoln. She held up her hand, rejecting the folder. "Why don't you just call me when the whole thing's ready? I'll come up to your place to pick it up. It'd be easier for you to show me what you want me to do without the kids underfoot. Okay?"

"No problem. I'll give you a call."

She closed the door and watched the Town Car cruise quietly up the street to the cul-de-sac. Did she really need to be away from the kids to get instructions for the project . . . or had there been another reason she suggested going to his house? Heading up the walk toward her own front door, she relived the tingle of Lincoln's touch on her arm.

"Arlo," Greg said, "can you hold on a minute? I've got a bunch of noise here."

"No problem, *mon*," Arlo said, like he'd just come back from Jamaica.

Greg got up and went to the archway into the front hallway. "Oh, hi, Nicole. I didn't realize you were home." He hollered toward the kitchen. "Hey, Tabby! What's going on? I'm on a business call here and can't hear a thing. Can you keep the kids quiet back there?"

"Don't worry," Nicole said. "I'll take care of it." She headed for the kitchen and used her look-out-kids voice. "Nathan! Rebecca!"

Greg went back into the living room and sat down in front of his computer, putting the phone to his ear. "Sorry about that. Wife just got home and the kids . . . don't know *what* was going on. Where were we?"

"You were asking about getting SlowBurn into vending machines. And my answer is, do it if you can. It would be a real coup. But the big beverage companies have those franchises sewn up so tight we haven't broken in anywhere. Still, give it a try. Who knows?"

Greg's call with Arlo was over within a few minutes, and he let out a big sigh. Nothing seemed to work out as easily as he first envisioned it. He got up and wandered into the kitchen, where Nicole was paying Tabby while the kids bounced around her like Ping-Pong balls.

"Please, please, Mom. Can we have a push-up? Tabby said we had to wait until you got home."

"Oka-a-ay. Becky, you get them out of the freezer. Nate, you get first pick of the flavor."

"That's not fair! I don't get nothin' out of that."

"Rebecca, you're not going to get *anything*—the word is *anything*—out of it, either, if you don't stop complaining."

"Oh, all right."

Greg waited his turn, having endured the whole day—no, the whole week—without her help mediating such squabbles. Usually, he just ignored them, which seemed to work surprisingly well.

Once the kids ran out the back door, he gave Nicole a peck on the cheek. "You're home early."

"That I am, and . . ." She picked up her purse from the counter and opened it. "I brought home the bacon." She held up her check between two fingers, barely pinching the corner as though it were newly printed money she didn't want to smudge.

Greg reached out and took it. The amount read $1,440. "Wow. Did you work a full week?"

"Yep. I stayed a little late a couple of nights, and they're still not withholding anything."

"That's good." It *was* good. He had a stack of bills to pay and the checking account was getting uncomfortably low. And for the first time all week, Nicole's attitude had perked up.

"And I don't have to go in next week, at least not at first."

"I should hope not. Monday's a holiday."

"That's not it. Mr. Paddock's got a project I can do from home. I don't know how long it'll last, but at least that's what I'll start with."

"That's good." So Paddock had taken his request about Nicole working at home seriously. And Nicole seemed to be accepting it. "You'd still use Tabby, though, right?"

"Of course—or neither of us would get any work done. Mr. Paddock's going to call me a little later when he has the project gathered together. I'll get it then."

Greg nodded. If she was going to work for that guy, doing it at home was definitely better. "Hey," he said, pulling his thoughts back to the present, "should we go out to eat? You know, payday and all that."

A pained look flitted across Nicole's face as she shook her head. "Only you can answer that, but I don't have any problem making supper at home."

It was an hour and a half later before the meal was on the table, partially because it had taken Nicole at least forty minutes to walk up the street to get her assignment from Lincoln Paddock. Greg wondered whether she could include that time on her time slip, but he kept his mouth shut, knowing that was a stupid question. Besides, by that time, the kids were cranky enough he didn't want to add any more fuss to the mix. Hard as it was to accept that he wasn't supporting his family right now, he needed to be grateful for Nicole's help.

That night when he crawled into bed, Nicole was turned away from him again, but he wasn't going to allow that to deter him. He reached out and touched her shoulder, allowing his hand to slide down her arm in a gentle stroke that he repeated again and again.

After a while, she flopped over to face him, and for a moment he thought he'd done something terribly wrong, but she reached out and threw her arms around his neck, pulling him to her fiercely, kissing his face and mouth as wild and awkwardly as a teenager. And she didn't stop. They hadn't experienced anything like it since their honeymoon. Only better—a honeymoon's pent-up passion but the confidence and skill of experience.

It was out of this world!

However, later, when it was all over, and he was lying on his back in the dreamy afterglow, he realized Nicole had turned away again. He listened and thought he heard a sob and a few moments later, another one.

"Nikki, you okay?"

"Yeah." Her voice sounded hoarse.

He reached out and laid his hand on her shoulder, but she shook him off.

"I'm fine, Greg. Just . . . go to sleep."

Chapter 28

When Greg awoke the next morning, Nicole's side of the bed was already empty. He rolled over and squinted at the digital clock: 6:24. Why was she up so early on a Saturday morning? They usually tried to sleep in a little on the weekends. He stretched and tried to go back to sleep, but reruns of their lovemaking the night before danced through his mind, chasing away any chance of more sleep.

He padded to the bathroom, dashed some cold water on his face, and then wandered out to the kitchen in search of Nicole. He found her in the living room, sitting in her rocker, reading her Bible. The table lamp beside her was still on, suggesting she might have gotten up while it was still dark.

"Hey, hon," he said, slipping up beside her and massaging the back of her neck. "Last night was somethin' else, huh?"

"Hmm." Her tone sounded noncommittal.

"We shouldn't wait so long."

No response.

Greg retrieved the newspaper from the front porch and came back in to sit on the couch. He stretched out using the full width of the couch like a chaise lounge, but a movement from Nicole caught his attention. Had she just wiped a tear from her eye? Maybe she was just brushing away a sleepy.

"Whatcha readin'?"

"A psalm."

After last night, Greg expected everything to be smooth between them. But her short responses suggested a chill still lingered. He knew there were still issues—probably having to do with money. Maybe she was still questioning Pastor Hanson's teaching on prosperity, and she was probably upset that she wasn't up to speed on their financial situation. But did that have to create a barrier? He didn't mind her knowing what they had in the bank. He'd just prefer to wait until the bottom line looked a little better before trying to walk her through it. And the fact was, he didn't know how they were going to make it if his business didn't take off pretty soon.

Still, it wasn't his fault they were close to the bottom of the barrel. He wished Nicole could understand that. Chuck Hastings was the one who shut down Powersports. If Chuck hadn't pulled the plug, they'd be doing fine! Greg never would've taken that way out. He'd have found some way to make it work.

He watched Nicole for a few more moments. Maybe he was reading too much into her mood. Could be PMS, or just groggy from waking up too early. He opened the *Sun Times* and read an article about the Deepwater Horizon/BP oil spill. "According to the National Oceanic and Atmospheric Administration, there is a 61-80 percent probability prevailing winds and ocean currents will deposit significant amounts of oil on Florida beaches and the Keys . . ." Blah, blah, blah. That was someone else's problem.

The rest of the day passed without any disagreements flaring up between him and Nicole. And the next morning, the same assistant minister preached again because Pastor Hanson was still on his Holy Land tour. It was a patriotic message for the July Fourth Weekend based on Romans 13, which started: "Everyone must submit himself to the governing authorities, for there is no authority except that which God has established. The authorities that exist have been established by God. Consequently, he who rebels against the authority is rebelling against what God has instituted . . ."

Greg frowned. *I'm supposed to be the authority established by God in my own house. Why can't I make it work?*

The minister's main emphasis was on honoring and respecting the government and being thankful for the freedoms they enjoyed in this country. But he did acknowledge that there were times when Christians "must obey God rather than men," as the early disciples had told the authorities when they were arrested for preaching. "God forbid that we will ever face that in this country, but with the way some things are going, we need to be prepared."

The young pastor noted that Victorious Living Center supported missionaries and believers in other countries who faced that very test.

Greg could see that. If someone was told he couldn't worship Jesus or preach about him, he should definitely "obey God rather than man" and do it anyway. But did that exemption extend beyond preaching or witnessing? In the Bible, young Daniel had resisted eating the king's rich food. And what about doctors and nurses who refused to perform abortions today?

For some reason, Greg's mind drifted to the brothers in Harry Bentley's Bible study. As far as he knew, they were all patriotic Americans, but about half were African Americans and Ben was ethnically Jewish. What had "submitting to the authorities" meant for their ancestors? Would they have been right to resist evil authorities?

Down on the platform, the minister was now praising the founders of our country for the freedoms they'd established. That was good. Greg felt a lump in his throat thinking about all that this Independence Day meant. But . . . hadn't those revered American revolutionaries been resisting the very authorities the preacher had just said were established by God? Why was he now praising them for doing that?

He glanced sideways at Nicole. And then there was the undercurrent of resistance Greg felt in his own home. What was his wife thinking as the minister preached about "submitting to the authorities"? Was she making any connection to their domestic situation? Was she thinking of herself as duty-bound to submit? Or was she thinking she was exempt—like the disciples, like Daniel, like the American revolutionaries?

It was confusing, and something definitely was going on with Nicole, something he didn't understand. But he wasn't going to get into a debate with her about the morning's message. They'd just have to work out their issues on a case-by-case basis.

Greg shut down his computer and looked at his watch. Five o'clock already? "Hey, Nikki! We better get ready if we're going up to Evanston to see the fireworks."

He wandered into the dining room where she was working on a photo album. "I'll go out and put folding chairs and blankets in the car. You want me to bring the cooler in here so you can pack our picnic? Anything else you need from the garage?"

Nicole sighed deeply. "You know what? I really don't feel like dealing with the crowds or listening to those things boom and bang all evening. They give me a headache. Would you mind taking the kids without me?"

Greg looked at her dumbfounded. She was the one who always wanted to spend more time together as a family. What was going on? But as he stared at her, she averted her eyes.

"Please, Greg? I just don't want to go. Okay?"

"Well, maybe we should all stay home and play games or something, have our regular popcorn and ice cream floats."

Becky, who'd been digging in the coat closet to find the cap she'd gotten the year before, the one with stars and buttons and sparkling whirligigs, overheard him. "No, no. I don't wanna stay home. We gotta go to the fireworks! You promised, Daddy! We go every year."

Nathan picked up the cry. "Yeah! You promised! I wanna go."

"Okay, okay. Calm down. We'll go." Greg turned his palms up in a helpless gesture to Nicole.

She slowly shook her head. "Look, I'll pack the picnic for you. I've got some cold chicken, and I picked up a tub of potato salad, but I just don't want to go myself. Okay?"

Greg shrugged. "If that's your choice. I just thought . . ." He clamped his mouth shut. Fine. What was the use arguing about it? If she didn't want to go, he'd take the kids himself.

Nicole sighed deeply once Greg and the kids headed out the door. She leaned against the kitchen counter, her arms crossed. It was true, she really didn't want to go, but she also needed to check with Lincoln Paddock about the job he'd asked her to do this week. Earlier when they'd met, he'd gone over all the details and then handed her a small black thumb drive. "Here, I downloaded the database you'll need to use on this. Just pop it into your computer's USB port and you'll be good to go."

But when she'd gotten home and tried it, her computer could read the thumb drive well enough, but there were three database files on it, and she couldn't tell which was the one she needed for Lincoln's project.

She went out onto the front porch where she could look up the street to see if Lincoln's Town Car was still in his driveway. It was. That didn't guarantee he was home, but it was worth a try. She ran back in and down to the basement where she pulled the thumb drive from her computer. Back upstairs, she stopped briefly in the bathroom to freshen her makeup before heading out the door.

As Nicole walked up the street, she rehearsed to herself why she needed to see Lincoln right now. The words in her head were the defense she'd give if Greg challenged her. *I had to see Mr. Paddock because he's the only one who could tell me which database to use, and if I waited, he might be gone tomorrow or in meetings or in court all day Tuesday.*

But why didn't you just phone him?

Because, he'd need to see the actual file to be sure which one I should use. Legal work is too important to leave any chance for error. What if we sent out the wrong stuff to the wrong person?

Then why did you stop in the bathroom to freshen your makeup?

Nicole stopped herself. What a stupid conversation. She wasn't defending herself in court. She wasn't even arguing with Greg. Besides . . . a girl didn't have to justify checking how she looked. She should always look as good as possible. Didn't mean a thing.

Stop it, Nicole!

Why was she fixated on justifying herself as though she were guilty of arranging a secret rendezvous with Lincoln? That's not what she was doing. No one was accusing her of anything. No one knew what had gone on in her head last night. Besides, what difference did it make? Greg had a great time. He even said so and without a flicker of suspicion.

Walking up the sidewalk and around the cul-de-sac to the big house, she pressed the doorbell and heard the Westminster Chimes play inside the grand house. She waited . . . and pushed the bell again. He must not be home . . . but then the door opened, and a big smile spread across Lincoln Paddock's face.

"N-i-i-i-kki. Hey, didn't expect to see you today. Wassup? As the kids say."

"Oh, not much really." She pulled the thumb drive out of her pocket and held it up. "I was just having some trouble with this. I plugged it in and—"

"Here, come on in. Where are my manners, leaving you standing on the steps." He swung the door wide and stepped back.

She followed him through the two-story high foyer, marveling again at the huge crystal chandelier until they stopped at the bottom of the sweeping curved staircase. "Do we need the computer, or do you want . . .?"

She glanced up the stairs. Had he gestured that way with his head? Better take it a bit slower. "Probably the computer." She handed him the small flash drive. "It's just that there are three databases on the thumb drive, and I wasn't certain which one you wanted me to use."

"Oh, no problem. Come on." He beckoned her down the hall to his office with its sweeping mahogany desk, shelves of books, and iMac with its twenty-seven-inch flat screen. "Here, sit down here"—he swiveled his high-back leather chair for her—"and I'll pop in this thumb drive."

He rested his hand on her shoulder, and it felt so hot, Nicole could hardly concentrate.

"Open Finder . . . there, click on WEK-23. That's the thumb drive. There, it's that file right there. See? It's got the most recent date."

"Okay. Sure. Guess I could've seen that." She reached up and put her hand on top of his.

"Easy to miss. There, click on the drive again to eject it."

A woman's voice yelled from somewhere else in the house, perhaps upstairs. "Lincoln, where are the clean towels?"

Nicole jumped and pulled her hand away, clasping her other hand in her lap.

"Ha, ha!" Lincoln laughed nervously. "My holiday guest. Sometimes she can't find her own toothbrush when it's in her mouth." Lincoln leaned over to pull out the thumb drive, and then stepped to the door. "Towels are in the closet to the left of the bathroom, just like always, Karen," he yelled back.

Nicole stood up, rolling the desk chair back so fast it bumped into Lincoln. "Well, I better go. I . . . I need to get home." She felt herself blushing and wondered if he could see blotches on her cheeks like often happened when her color rose. She took the thumb drive without looking him in the eye and headed for the door.

"How are the kids doin'? You guys go to the city fireworks last night?"

"No. Greg took 'em this evening, up to Evanston."

"Oh, that's great." He followed her down the hallway toward the front door. "Hey, why didn't you go with them? I don't want you to get so busy with this work thing that you don't have any time for your family."

She reached for the latch on the front door. "Oh, it's not that. I just didn't want to listen to all those booms. Thanks for the help. I'll get right on this job."

She was out the door and heading down the steps when he called after her. "Not tomorrow, though. Tomorrow's a holiday, and if you're working for me, you have to take it off because I don't want to pay double time." He laughed awkwardly. "See ya, Nikki."

She forced herself to turn back toward him briefly. "I won't. Thanks for the help."

"Should've offered you some coffee or something."

"No, that's okay." She turned and headed home, her face burning.

What in the world had she done? Made a total fool of herself, that's what.

Chapter 29

"UNLESS THE LORD BUILDS THE HOUSE, *its builders labor in vain . . ."*

The words in his mind woke Greg. He knew they came from the Bible and their truth was thundering down on him. Without God's blessing, his business was failing!

Nicole was already up and busy elsewhere in the house as Greg swung his legs onto the floor and sat on the edge of the bed, elbows on knees, chin in his hands. "Come on, God, don't make a fool of me here," he moaned. "Pastor Hanson said all I needed was to put my faith into action. Well, I've been 'acting,' but I'm beginning to feel like Noah trying to build an ark in the desert. Where's the rain? Where's the blessing?"

He sighed. Today was supposed to be a holiday—Monday following the Fourth of July—but should he take the time off? It would express confidence in his business, maybe even faith in God. But he felt desperate.

He stood up, stuffing his fears. He would take a break! Besides, what could he do that would make a difference? And his "honey-do list" of projects around the house was getting longer, not that Nicole was adding much to it lately. In fact, she'd been cutting him some slack in that department while he launched SlowBurn. He should thank her. Still, the water heater needed replacing. The gutters were so clogged the last heavy rain had cascaded down the side of the house like Buckingham Fountain. And there were half a dozen other projects that needed attention.

He'd start with the gutters. Then maybe he'd go to Home Depot and order a new water heater—if it was open on the holiday. And depending on how much it'd cost. He might have to just keep relighting it till they got back on their feet.

After breakfast, Greg set up the ladder near the front corner of the house and was halfway up when he noticed Destin Jasper walking past on the sidewalk. He scrambled down and called, "Hey, Destin. Hold up a minute." He'd just check on—no, encourage him a little.

Destin waited for him to catch up. "How you doin', Mr. Singer?"

"I'm good, but how're you doin'?" Greg noticed Destin didn't seem able to look him in the eye. Maybe he should say something about that to the young man. You can't be good at sales if people don't trust you, and people don't trust someone who looks away or down or gives the impression they'd rather be anywhere else than with you. "How was that basketball camp you went to last week?"

Destin cleared his throat. "Oh, the camp was good. Got some good instruction." He smiled and finally looked at Greg. "Got an award for Best Post-Up Moves."

"Get out!" Greg said playfully and bumped knuckles with the kid. "Does that mean you got recruited to one of the Big Ten?"

Destin chuckled self-consciously and looked down again. "Not really, but . . . a couple of scouts did take the time to talk to me."

"That's great. Absolutely on schedule for getting you a scholarship." Now that he'd given the kid a little encouragement, it was time to check up on business. "I bet after gettin' an award and all, the guys were wondering what you were chuggin' that gave you all those hot moves, right? You sell a lot of SlowBurn to the other guys?"

Destin looked off down the street with a thousand-yard stare. "Wasn't able to do that."

"What do you mean? How much did you sell?"

Destin looked back at him, a defiant glint in his eye. "Mr. Singer, I didn't make a penny. When the coaches saw me tryin' to sell those cans of SlowBurn, they confiscated every one of 'em on the spot like I was tryin' to peddle drugs and told me one more infraction of the rules and I'd be outta there. I never saw any rule about that. Believe me, Mr. Singer. I wasn't meanin' to break any rules, but . . . it just didn't work out."

Destin shrugged and started on down the sidewalk in the direction he'd been going.

"Hey, don't worry about it." Greg caught up with him. "We all have these little setbacks, but we can't let them get us down."

"I hear ya, Mr. Singer, but I don't have much time left. I got a lotta money to pay back—to my folks and my college account. I'm gettin' worried."

Greg put his arm around the boy's solid shoulder and walked along with him. "I know what you feel like, but we're in this together. We *gotta* make it work, and there's only one way to do that: Find someplace else to sell the SlowBurn. Find some new kids who'll love it. I'm sure they're out there."

"Maybe so, Mr. Singer, but I don't know where to look."

Greg couldn't let on how familiar that feeling was to him. He had to help Destin make it work. "Maybe you gotta look for a new location. Know what I mean? Kids hang out together all the time, and they usually have a can of something in their hand, or they're just coming out of a 7-Eleven with a Big Gulp. There's your market! SlowBurn's definitely better than that stuff."

Destin was nodding his head by the time they got to the corner of Chase Avenue, and it was time to let him go. He'd given the kid his best pep talk. He slapped him on the back and peeled away. "Go get 'em, tiger. You can do it."

Destin glance at him sideways and gave him a skeptical smile and a wave as he turned the corner on Chase.

Back home, Greg did not climb the ladder again to work on the gutters. Instead, he went into the house and flipped on his computer. He didn't know what he was looking for or what he could do, but having just pumped up Destin, it didn't seem right to take the day off himself.

His email downloaded—some spam, a few messages from friends, but nothing related to launching his business. And then a notice flashed on his screen: "Internet Connection Lost." *Rats.* Seemed to be happening more often lately. Each time he'd called his Internet Service Provider, he'd gotten a recorded message that the company was aware of the problem in his area and was working to restore full service as soon as possible.

Sometimes it took only a matter of minutes, sometimes hours, but it always came back on, and he'd never been able to do anything to speed them up. In fact, it was almost impossible to reach a real person by phone. Greg pushed his chair back. It was futile to call again. But he ought to do something. Maybe he should call Arlo. Arlo might give him a pep talk, get him going again, but what could Arlo say that he himself hadn't just said to Destin?

Tuesday morning—another workday he couldn't pass off as a holiday. The Internet was back up, but as Greg sat at his desk, he let his head sink. The truth was, he wasn't who he thought he was. He wasn't an entrepreneur. He wasn't a great salesman. He had no idea how to start a new business, not really. And he wasn't sure people wanted to drink SlowBurn even if he could figure out how to introduce it to them.

It. Just. Isn't. Working.

He'd been unemployed now for five weeks. Might as well admit it. He was unemployed! Maybe it was time to pull the plug on SlowBurn and look for something else . . . No! He'd just been scoffing at Chuck Hastings for closing Powersports prematurely, bragging that he'd never have done that himself.

Greg closed his eyes, took a deep breath, and gritted his teeth. He might not be who he thought he was, but he was not a quitter!

More reps—that's what he needed. And he'd almost forgotten about the old lady, Mattie Krakowski, who'd bought a forty-nine-dollar starter kit of SlowBurn to sell at her family reunion. He should check to see how people liked it and if there was any chance to recruit some of her relatives to sell it.

He went across the street and rang her doorbell. It seemed like two minutes passed before she opened the door a narrow crack, secured with a safety chain.

"How're you doing today, Mrs. Krakowski?" He noticed she was still in her housecoat. "I hope this isn't too early. Could we talk a few minutes?"

She shook her head vigorously. "Not interested. Don't wanna become a Mormon or Jehovah's Witness or whatever, so don't come back again!"

The door started to close, but Greg put his toe in the crack, realizing as he did so that he was behaving worse than the Mormons or Jehovah's Witnesses. "But Mrs. Krakowski, wait. I'm your neighbor from across the street. Greg Singer. Remember?"

She squinted her eyes and pulled the top of her housecoat tight around her neck.

"Remember? I sold you those cans of energy drink that you took to your family reunion. I think it was for your son's birthday. Do you remember now? You did take them, didn't you?"

"Oh. Yes, yes, I took 'em, and we had a great time too. Wonderful picnic."

"Glad to hear it. Uh, do you think you could open the door and let me come in for a minute?"

The old woman hesitated, then finally relented and removed the chain.

Inside, the only chair not piled high with papers and books and stuff was the old lady's rocker, so Greg stood. The TV was blaring too loudly to talk easily, but Greg persisted in asking his question.

"Well now, far as I recall, everybody liked the drink. In fact, I intended to bring a can home for myself, but I think I gave every single one of 'em away."

"You *gave* them all away?"

"As I recall, yes. It was a large picnic, you know, and kinda hot that day."

"Did anyone want more?"

"I don't know. If they did, I didn't hear about it, because I didn't have any more, you see. It was all gone by then."

Greg tried to keep impatience out of his voice. "Did you tell anyone they could become salespeople for SlowBurn?"

"*SlowBurn*? What's that?"

"The name of the drink."

"Oh, yes. No, no . . . nobody asked to sell it."

Greg sighed deeply. This was hopeless. "Uh, thank you very much, Mrs. Krakowski." He headed toward the door and then turned back. "One more thing. Do you have your son's name and phone number? I'd like to call him if I could."

"Sure." She shuffled down the hall and came back a few moments later with a ragged-edge scrap of paper torn off a brown paper bag and handed it to Greg.

He studied the numbers scribbled on it and repeated them to her. "Is that your son's number?"

"Yes. That's Donald's number, though sometimes he doesn't answer. He's very busy, you know."

Greg felt a knot tighten in his gut as he trudged home, his hope of finding another rep fading.

It wasn't working.

He made a fist and shook it. He should go down to the Illinois Department of Employment today and apply for unemployment benefits. Should've done that the first thing when Powersports closed.

Back at his desk, he checked his email—two spam messages. What'd he expect? He scanned the news headlines: "Retailers Devise Stimulus Plans to Revive Sales," "China Fears Consumer Growth Flagging," "Pakistan Army Finds Taliban Tough—"

"Dad! Dad, hurry! You gotta come down here right now!"

Greg could hear his son thundering up the stairs from the basement. "What's up?"

"A flood! There's water all over the laundry room floor, and it's coming down the hall to the family room!"

Chapter 30

GREG TOOK ONE LOOK AT THE WATER spreading across the basement floor and swore under his breath. So much for his plan to apply for unemployment that day.

The flood in the basement was coming from the water heater. It was no longer a tiny drip that occasionally doused the pilot light—more like a torrent. Greg quickly shut off the water main to the house, and the stream slowed, but there were still forty gallons of water in the tank spreading across the floor, soaking the old rug in the family room and anything else in its advance toward the sump pump.

"Why did they put the sump pump in *that* corner?" Greg yelled, as if there was someone around to answer him. Running out to the backyard, he brought in the garden hose, connected one end to the outlet spigot near the bottom of the tank, and put the other end down into the sump pump. Then he opened the valve on the tank and let it drain. That slowed the leak even more and within a half hour emptied the tank.

Greg stood in the middle of the mess and shook his head. He should've found out where that leak was coming from weeks ago. Now it was obvious the rusty old tank had blown out a hole in the bottom. Couldn't have happened at a worse time.

Nicole was out doing errands, and he had no way to call her to come home since she didn't have a cell phone. The kids tried to help, sloshing around in the basement, getting things up off the floor, but when Becky started crying, Greg realized his own frustration and frantic efforts were putting too much pressure on the children.

He called them over to a dry corner and enwrapped them both in his arms. "*Shh, shh.* It's okay, Becky. You didn't cause this flood and neither did Nathan. The water tank just rusted out. Couldn't be helped, so don't worry about it."

But it could've been helped if I'd dealt with it at the first symptom.

Well, it was what it was. Greg took a deep breath and gave the kids another hug. "Tell you what, why don't you go on up to your rooms and get something dry on your feet? Maybe you can read for a bit while I clean up down here. Okay? When Mom gets home she'll fix us all some lunch."

It was almost noon when Nicole got home. She took one look at the mess in the basement and looked as if she might cry.

"Honey, don't worry. I'll finish cleaning up down here. You just see about some lunch, okay?"

In a few minutes she called downstairs, "How am I supposed to cook with no water?" And two seconds later, he heard Becky yelling from the second floor. "Dad! Dad, the toilet won't flush, and it really smells bad!"

Greg closed his eyes as if to make the whole scene disappear and then trudged up the basement steps, his legs already feeling like lead. At the bottom of the stairs leading to the second floor he called, "Sorry about the toilet! I had to shut off the water to the whole house. You'll just have to make do, okay?" When Becky didn't respond, he added, "A little smell isn't going to hurt anyone."

He poked his head into the kitchen. "Can't you make sandwiches or something that doesn't require water? It's just lunch."

"I was going to make deviled egg sandwiches. But don't worry about it. We'll have peanut butter and jelly."

"Make mine cheese," he growled. "You know I hate peanut butter and jelly."

Greg trudged back downstairs, feeling as if he were being banished to a dungeon. But then he looked around. Maybe it wasn't so bad. Other than the family room rug, which was now out in the backyard, a few boxes with wet bottoms, and a damp basement floor, the damage had been stemmed. He should be thankful. It was nothing like the several inches of water that had flooded the Molanders' basement, but it still took him most of the afternoon to clean it up. Finally setting up a couple of box fans to help dry things out, he examined the water heater.

Hmm. Certainly couldn't be that hard to replace one of those things. He wasn't particularly mechanical, but he was no dummy.

All he needed to do was disconnect the two water pipes . . . and the gas line—gas could be dicey—and the exhaust pipe. Remove the old tank. Slide in the new one, and reconnect everything. Light the pilot—at least he knew how to do that—and they'd be back in business.

But how soon could he get a replacement? Cleaning his hands on some old rags, he went upstairs to his computer. The Home Depot website showed a forty-gallon tank for $328 plus a $40 delivery charge. Looked just like the old one, and it was in stock at the store up in Evanston. If he got up there and paid for it tonight, they could get it here by noon tomorrow.

It took forty minutes to disconnect the old tank before he could tip it over. Uhhh. Hot water tanks weren't light, even when empty. He rolled and dragged it to the bottom of the outside basement steps . . . and stopped. No way he was going to get the bulky thing up the steps alone. And he certainly wasn't going to ask his wife to help. That wouldn't be right.

He sat on the bottom step, breathing the already moldy-smelling basement air. It was five o'clock. Who could he ask to help? Maybe Harry Bentley. He laughed at the memory of the older man taking charge of rescuing the Molanders from their basement flood. Bentley wasn't young, but he was strong and the only help Greg could think of at the moment.

"Sure thing," Harry said when Greg dropped by the two-flat to ask for help. "And let me give Josh Baxter a call."

The kid from Harry's Bible study? Why him? "Don't think we need three of us just to get that thing outta there."

Harry shrugged. "Just thought he could give you some tips about installin' a new one. He does building maintenance. Knows about this kind of stuff, ya know."

With the two of them huffing and puffing, it didn't take long to get the old tank out to the alley. "Hey, man. Thanks so much. It would've taken a block and tackle to get it up those steps by myself."

"No problem. Glad I could help."

Greg was reaching to shake hands when Nathan called from the second floor window. "Hey, Dad, when can we use the bathroom? There's still no water up here."

"I know. Just go ahead and use it." Greg shrugged helplessly at Harry.

"You cut the water off to the whole house?"

"Yeah. Had to stop the leak somehow. I'll look for a plug when I go to Home Depot."

"Humph! Let's go back down and have a look."

It took Harry only a minute to find a valve in the cold water feed to the tank. "Here. We can close that, and you should be able to turn the water back on for the rest of the house."

Once it was done, Harry pulled out his iPhone. "Now I'm sure you need Josh Baxter." Before Greg could object, Harry hit the Call button. "Hey, Josh, any chance you got a few minutes to come by? You remember Greg Singer from the Bible study group? His water heater's gone out, and he's getting a new one. Thought you might give him some tips about installing it."

Harry listened. "Sure . . . Sure, I understand. . . . Okay. I'll tell him." He ended the call. "Josh is busy right now, but he'll drop by tomorrow about noon."

Chagrinned, Greg said, "Appreciate that."

"Hey, you want a ride to Bible study this evening?"

Greg sighed. "Think I'll take a pass tonight. I'm whipped. And I need to get up to Home Depot and buy the new tank. But I appreciate you asking."

Nicole could tell Greg was uptight. He didn't even finish his dinner before pushing back from the table and announcing he had to go to Home Depot. "They've got the water heater I want in stock right now, but there's no guarantee they'll have it tomorrow. The way things have been going lately, it'd be just my luck for someone else to buy it out from under me."

Nicole watched him head out the door.

What else could go wrong? Seemed like everything was falling apart—and not just the water heater either. They needed help. They needed prayer. They needed . . . *wait*. Earlier in the day, Estelle Bentley had seen her out front and invited her to drop by Grace Meredith's house at seven that evening. "We've been prayin' with a couple of the neighborhood sisters on Tuesday nights. Why don't you join us?" Nicole had dismissed it at the time, but . . .

Would they mind if she brought Becky and Nathan? She could take a couple of books and some study pages for them to do. Wouldn't hurt them to have a little "homework" even if it was summer. If it seemed awkward, she could just excuse herself and meet with them some other time.

But Greg certainly needed some prayer, and . . . and so did she.

After hurrying the kids to finish supper, she collected some things for them to do and left Greg a note: *"Just down the street at a friend's. Be home about eight."*

Nicole and the kids were turning into Grace Meredith's walk when she heard Lincoln call from the end of the block. "Hey Nikki, how's it going? Is that project coming along okay?"

She pretended she hadn't heard him. "Hurry up, kids. Let's go on in. We don't want to keep them waiting."

There were only three other women there: Estelle, Grace, and a young girl named Ramona who was staying with Grace. She'd expected Michelle Jasper to be there, but she wasn't. Grace was glad to set the kids up at her kitchen table and gave them both a glass of juice.

Nicole sank onto the couch. Even though she didn't know any of the women very well, they seemed glad she'd come, and no one pushed her for details when she said it was being really hard for Greg to get his business going. "I'm really grateful Harry could stop by this afternoon and help with that hot water tank. He got the water back on for us too."

But no way could she bring up her confused feelings about Lincoln Paddock. After all, he was their neighbor too. What would they think if she confessed what happened the other night? It may not have been anything more than a daydream, but . . .

Home Depot still had the tank Greg wanted, but delivery was another matter. Somehow the computer had been wrong. The delivery guys were booked for the whole day Wednesday.

"Oh, man, what am I gonna do now?"

"Suppose you could rent one of our trucks and take it yourself," suggested the sales associate.

"This evening?"

"No. We don't let out trucks this late, but if you're here first thing in the morning, it should work. We'd be glad to help you load the water heater."

Greg bought the water heater and was back the next morning by eight o'clock. An hour later he stopped the truck in the alley behind his house. Scavengers had already carried off his old tank, so he knew he'd better not leave the new one out there lest someone think he was throwing it away. Instead, he wrestled it off the truck and "walked" the thing into his garage on the wood frame that enclosed it. He stared at it, already bushed. Well, he'd return the truck and then figure out how to slide the tank down into the basement.

It seemed to take forever to finish with the truck's paperwork and get back home . . . just as an old beater of a car pulled up to the curb in front of the house. Josh Baxter.

"Hey, Greg, I made it a little earlier than I thought." Josh climbed out of the car with his hand outstretched. "Hear you lost your water heater."

"Yeah, quite a mess last night, but I got a new one." Funny that Josh showed up at just that moment. "Uh, it's still sitting out in the garage. Any chance you could help me slide it down the steps?"

Turned out the job took more than Josh just helping him move the tank down into the basement. Even though the new water heater was the same size and height as the old one, the inlet and outlet pipes were in different positions, and Josh ended up adding a couple of elbows in order to align the connections.

"How'd you learn how to do all this stuff?" Greg asked, watching him work. Josh grunted. "Had to. I'm the property manager for the House of Hope—it's connected to the Manna House shelter for women, except it's for single moms and their kids." He laughed. "Ha. This is nothin' compared to the stuff that breaks down in an old six-flat." He finally stood up. "There, that oughta do it. Let's turn on the water."

Though Greg assured him he knew how to light the tank, Josh still hung around until the burner roared to life and the water was actually heating. Greg offered to pay him for his time, but Josh brushed him off with a wave. "Gotta run. Glad I could help."

After cleaning up a few things, Greg went back upstairs and announced, "It's done, honey. Should have hot water in an hour or so." Finally he could get back to work.

"That's good. Okay for me to take the car now?" Nicole was already gathering her purse. "Mom's sick, and I want to check in on her."

"She's sick? She never gets sick."

"Well, she's sick today. Sounded terrible on the phone. Hopefully just a summer cold."

"Yeah, go ahead." Greg turned on the computer and called up email. "Seems like it never rains but it pours around here," he muttered.

"What's that supposed to mean?"

"Oh, you know. The business isn't coming along like I'd like, and then the water heater burned out, and now your Mom's sick."

"My going to see Mom shouldn't make anything worse . . ." Then Nicole sighed. "If you want, I'll take the kids, though I was hoping not to expose them to whatever she has."

Greg waved his hand at his wife. "Go ahead, leave 'em here. Makes sense. Just don't stay too long, okay?"

Nicole had only been gone five minutes when Nathan appeared in the archway between the living room and the hallway. "Can I watch TV?"

Tempting. That would keep them entertained. But . . . "It's still damp down there, Nate. Why don't you play up in your room today?"

"There's nothin' to do in my room. I don't care if the floor's damp. It's not flooding anymore, is it?"

Greg frowned. He was trying to write an email to Ethel Newhouse, his boss's old secretary, to get contact information for the last of the former Powersports' employees he hadn't yet tracked down about repping for SlowBurn.

"Dad . . .?" Nate still stood there. "Can I?"

"Can you, what? Can't you see that I'm busy here?" His voice was getting louder without him even trying. "How am I supposed to support this family if I can't even get a decent day's work done? Go on! Go on, get outta here. Do whatever you want. Just let me work."

Out of the corner of his eye, he saw his son slink away. Greg sighed. He'd probably been too harsh, but if he was going to work at home, the kids had to show some respect for his time.

He'd typed only one more sentence when the house phone jangled from the kitchen. He doggedly let it ring until the answering machine kicked in with Nicole's instructions to leave a message. It was a little hard to hear from the other room, but the voice that recorded the message suddenly got his full attention.

"Nikki, how's it goin'?" Lincoln Paddock. "Hey, I just wanted to call about the other day when you came over. After you left, I realized it must've seemed kinda strange to you to find a woman in my house. But it wasn't what it looked like. Karen's my kid sister. She's headed to graduate school at the University of Michigan and had a bunch of things to do here in Chicago. She's been so busy lately, I hardly get to see her anymore. But I should have introduced you. Uh . . ."

There was a long pause as though the man didn't know what to else say but didn't want to end the call. Greg rose and crept toward the kitchen, holding his breath so as not to miss any words. Finally, Paddock continued. "I wouldn't want you to get the wrong idea. Okay, give me a call when you can."

Greg breathed again and looked around the kitchen as if he needed someone to confirm what he'd just heard. The red light blinked on the answering machine. He pressed the button and played the message again.

What was the guy saying? Why should he care what Nicole thought of him? Did they have some kind of an affair going on? Was he trying to reassure her that she was the only one?

His jaws hurt from clinching his teeth so tight. He played the message one more time.

Halfway through, it was interrupted by a piercing scream from Nathan, the clatter of his aluminum ladder against the side of the house, and then a sickening thud.

Greg tore outside and around to the side of the house. His son was lying on the narrow strip of grass between the side walkway and a row of bushes.

He was not moving.

Chapter 31

"O God, no! No! No! No! Don't let this be happening!"

Greg knelt down beside his son. "Nate . . . Nate?" The boy gasped and his chest gave a heave. "Are you okay? No, no . . . don't move! Just stay still."

Nathan slowly rolled over and sat up, which Greg was relieved to see even though he'd told him not to move. "Are you okay? Did you hit your head on the sidewalk? Did everything go black?"

"Uh-uh. I don't think so." The boy took a deep breath, and then started to sob. "I . . . I j-just c-couldn't breathe."

"But did everything go black when you hit the ground?"

"N-no." More sobs. "I heard you coming, an' . . . an' then you were here, an' I knew everything was gonna be okay." Nate started to get up.

Greg put a restraining hand on his shoulder. "You better stay right there for a minute." He moved the aluminum ladder out of the way, which was lying at a rakish angle across the bushes. *O God . . . what if Nathan had hit the sidewalk?* He knelt down again beside his son. "Feel your head and see if there're any sore places."

As Nathan felt his head with his right hand, Greg looked for blood but didn't see any.

"It's okay," the boy said, but then began rubbing his upper left arm. "It's just my arm. It hurts. I think I broke it." He whimpered quietly.

"Can you move it?"

Nate raised his left arm, making a grimace and grabbing it again as he did so.

"I don't think it's broken if you can lift it that far. Hopefully you just bruised it." Greg steadied his son as he helped the boy stand up. "You okay? You dizzy or anything?"

Nate shook his head, gulping air and trying to hold back the tears.

Greg heard a noise behind him. Turning around, he saw Becky standing on the walkway, her eyes bugging in horror. "Don't worry, honey. He just had a fall. He's going to be okay." But was he? Out of caution, Greg picked Nate up in his arms. "Go up on the porch, Becky, and hold the front door open for us."

As Greg carried his son into the house, waves of shock rolled over him at the thought of his son falling from the ladder—the ladder he'd left out there for two days. "What were you doing up on that ladder anyway?"

"I . . . I . . ." The sobs broke through. "I was trying to clean the gutters for you."

"What?" Greg turned sideways to get through the door and laid the boy on the sofa in the living room. "What do you mean, you were trying to clean the gutters for me? You didn't need to do that!"

"But you were so mad at me. You . . ." Tears flooded out. "You couldn't get your work done 'cause I was interrupting you, so . . . so I thought I'd help you."

The boy's words felt like a sucker punch. "Ah, Nate, buddy. I didn't mean . . . I wasn't mad at you." He knelt on the floor by the sofa and embraced his boy. "I mean, it's not you. It's other things like the water heater and . . . and—" And now his family was suffering.

"That's why I was trying to help you."

Greg glanced over his shoulder. Becky was standing only a few feet away, taking it all in. "Well, I appreciate your trying to help, but climbing a ladder is dangerous. I don't want either of you kids climbing that ladder again. Understand? Next time you get an idea about helping me, ask first. Okay?"

Nate nodded, curtailing his sobs with a frown so big it turned his mouth upside down.

"Now you just rest here for a while. I'm going to make an ice pack for your arm. Either of you want something to drink? How about juice boxes?"

Nate sniffed. "Grape." But Becky didn't say a word.

After he got Nate settled with an ice pack and a juice box—Becky took hers upstairs—Greg went outside and returned the ladder to the garage. He shouldn't have left it leaning up against the house. It was his fault . . . but why did everything seem to be happening to him right now? He'd gone through a time like this once before, when he was in college. He'd wrecked his little Toyota and then gotten sick with the flu, which made his Western Civ term paper late. In the hubbub, he'd forgotten to pay his tuition bill on time, incurring a seventy-five-dollar late fee—big bucks for a poor undergraduate. And then his girlfriend dumped him . . . all within one week. "Hell week," he'd called it, and it had nothing to do with pledging a fraternity.

Felt like the same thing was happening now. It was enough to make a person superstitious, like, *just stay in bed until the cosmic disturbance passes over*. But he knew that wasn't true.

Greg came back in the house and checked on Nate. Should he go back to work, or call Nicole to let her know about Nathan's fall? Huh. If she'd been here, it probably wouldn't have happened. The thought no sooner passed through his mind than he chided himself. He had no cause to blame her. The only person with any real responsibility was himself for leaving the ladder up—and dumping his work frustrations on his son.

No, he'd better call Nicole now, or she'd be plenty upset if he waited.

She came straight home, arrived in twenty minutes, and as soon as she saw Nathan on the sofa with an ice pack on his arm, she insisted they take him to the hospital. "It could be broken, Greg. There's no way for us to tell."

"But kids fall down all the time."

"Not off ladders. What if he—"

Greg stopped her with an upheld hand. "Emergency room visits and X-rays aren't cheap, and we're not covered." He'd realized this was true for the last couple of weeks and had intended to do something about it, but . . .

"What do you mean, *we're not covered*? Didn't you sign up for COBRA? It's supposed to allow you to continue your coverage for eighteen months after you leave a job, right?"

"Yeah, but you still have to pay, so I haven't done it yet. Besides"—he shrugged nervously—"we might not qualify. Powersports was a pretty small company, and . . . and it went out of business. I think that makes a difference."

Nicole's eyes flashed. "I don't care! I'm taking my son to the hospital to get him checked out. You think you're the big provider, well here's your chance. I don't care how long it takes you to pay off the bill, or . . . or I'll pay it off working for Lincoln Paddock, but my son gets checked out!"

"Now hold on a minute, and speaking of Lincoln Paddock—"

"Oh, shut up, Greg, and carry Nate out to the car!"

Their normal suppertime had long passed by the time they got back from the hospital. Nate checked out fine except for a badly bruised arm. The doctor said to continue intermittent ice packs for the next twenty-four hours and give him Tylenol as needed.

But Greg and Nicole weren't talking.

She set out some leftovers on the counter, fixed a plate for Nathan, and took him up to his room.

Greg and Becky ate in the breakfast nook. The atmosphere was so tense in the house, he couldn't think of anything to say to his own daughter.

Finally, she broke the silence. "Are you going to go back to work someday, Daddy?"

Greg rolled his eyes. Out of the mouths of eight-year-olds. "Well, I have been working, honey. It's just that my work is here at home now. I'm starting this new business, you know."

"Yeah, but you seemed a lot happier when you used to go down to the Loop. Why don't you do that again?"

"That's when I worked for Powersports, honey. You know, setting up shows for those sports vehicles and boats. I took you to one, remember?"

She vigorously nodded her head, eyes big. "That was fun."

"I know. I liked that job too. But that company ended, and now I'm starting my own company."

"But it doesn't make you very happy, Daddy."

Greg's tongue lay like a wad of cotton in his mouth. It was true, he wasn't happy right now . . . but it was all circumstantial. If things were going better, he'd be in the money, and that would make him happy. That thought begged the question, however. Did he really like what he was doing—trying to sell an energy drink, recruiting reps to work for him, using his friendships and relationships to pressure people into helping him make money? No, he didn't like those parts of his business. But what job didn't have *some* unpleasant aspects?

The problem was, except for the money—which hadn't yet materialized—he wasn't sure he really liked any other aspect of SlowBurn. In fact, he didn't even drink the stuff that often. It was okay and it did give him a lift, but he'd just as soon have a Coke.

Greg sighed. "I guess you're kinda right, Becky. When I worked for Powersports, there were a lot of things I liked doing. I liked planning those big conventions. I liked the travel. I liked meeting people, and I sure liked the boats and the four-wheelers and the jet skis. Got to ride them sometimes too. So, yeah. That was a more fun job."

"Then why don't you do it again?"

"Because Powersports doesn't exist anymore."

"But aren't there other companies like that? Why don't you work for one of them?"

He grimaced and shook his head. "There aren't any other ones around here, Becky. I've looked."

"But isn't there something you'd like to do, Daddy? There's gotta be something."

Greg stared at his daughter. Yeah, there ought to be something he liked, too, but he wasn't sure he'd found it yet.

Chapter 32

NICOLE DUMPED NATHAN'S EMPTY CEREAL BOWL into the sink and sighed as she sank down at the breakfast nook with a second cup of coffee. Thursday morning already and she'd barely looked at the project Lincoln Paddock had given her. She had no way of estimating how long it would take to finish it, but she was sure he'd want it back soon.

She glanced at the clock. Almost eight. Was it too early to call the Jaspers to see if Tabby could babysit today so she could get some work done? No way was she going to ask Greg. Frankly, she still didn't want to talk to him.

Taking a chance, she dialed the Jaspers' number. To her relief the girl answered, even seemed eager to help out with the kids. "Might as well. Destin has to take Tavis to his basketball camp, so everybody'll be gone anyway."

"Great. Uh, actually, I could probably use you tomorrow too. Do you want to check with your mom?"

"Mom's already gone to work, but I'm sure it's okay. I can probably help Saturday too if you need me."

"I just might. Thank you so much, Tabby. Uh, just to let you know, Nate fell off the ladder and hurt his arm yesterday. I had to leave for a few hours to check on my mom, and, uh, Mr. Singer was busy, and it . . . just happened. But I don't want to leave the kids unsupervised again. You're a real lifesaver, Tabby. See you when you get here."

Nicole no sooner got off the phone with Tabby than it rang. Her mother. "How is Nathan? Is he okay?"

"He hurt his arm, but it's not broken. Mostly a bruise. The doctor said he'll be fine, but this morning he's having fun with a sling I made for him out of a dishtowel."

"My gracious, is it that bad?"

"Not really. You know how kids are, enjoying the attention. How are you today, Mom?"

"Oh, fine, fine. Much better than yesterday, thank you."

Her mother always said she was "fine," so that didn't mean much, but her voice definitely sounded better. "I'm glad, Mom. I've got a lot to do today, but if you need me, you call, okay?"

As soon as she was off the phone, Nathan wandered into the kitchen. "Do I have to wear this thing all day? I can't do anything with it on."

"Of course not, but I thought you wanted to wear it. You said your arm still hurt."

"It does . . . a little, but not that bad."

She helped Nate take off the dishtowel sling and examined his arm. "*Hmm*. Well, you're getting a black and blue mark there, but it should go away in a few days."

With his arm free, Nathan ran out into the backyard just as Greg strolled into the kitchen. Nicole tensed. They still hadn't made up for the spat they'd had over Nathan's fall, and she was feeling a little defensive that Greg had been right—nothing broken. But she still blamed him for the fall, and now they were facing some big medical bills with no insurance.

But he had the look on his face that telegraphed a challenge was coming. "I heard the phone ring, which reminds me, you got a call yesterday from Lincoln Paddock. I was busy, so it went to the answering machine."

Nicole glanced at the phone. "Light's not blinking."

"That's because I listened to it, but I'm telling you, he called." He pointed at the machine. "Go ahead." He leaned against the doorway, arms folded across his chest.

Nicole looked at him a moment, feeling defensive before she even knew what it was about. She had to level the playing field. "You should've told me." She went over and pushed the Play button.

> *"Nikki, how's it goin'? Hey, I just wanted to call about the other day when you came over. After you left, I realized it must've seemed kinda strange to you to find a woman in my house. But it wasn't what it looked like. Karen's my kid sister. She's headed*

to graduate school at University of Michigan and had a bunch of things to do here in Chicago. She's been so busy lately, I hardly get to see her anymore. But I should have introduced you. Uh . . . I wouldn't want you to get the wrong idea. Okay, give me a call when you can."

The recording ended with a beep, and Nicole saw Greg's eyes narrow. She bobbled her head and opened her eyes extra wide. "Thanks a lot for telling me. He's probably wondering why I haven't called back."

"And why would that be?"

"Didn't you hear? He said, *Give me a call when you can*. He probably wants to know when my project's gonna be done. But with everything going on around here, I've barely begun."

"Yeah." Sarcasm bathed Greg's tone. "And that explains why he needed to reassure you about the woman in his house. What's going on, Nicole?"

"What do you mean? Nothing's going on. The man gave me some work to do. At home. Like you wanted. Good grief! Get a grip, Greg!" She spun around and busied herself at the sink.

"What I mean is . . ." His voice lowered and became husky. "Are you having an affair with that man?"

"A *what*?" Her response came out loud and panicky, but she resisted turning back to look at him. Of course she wasn't having an affair, but would her eyes betray her fantasies? She gritted her teeth. What if her eyes did betray her? Nothing had happened, and besides, what did Greg expect after acting like such a jerk lately. Oh, yeah, her husband was still a hunk, and anyone would think she'd made a good catch. But after more than ten years of marriage, she knew romance took more than looks. Now Lincoln had good looks *and* he was attentive, considerate, and not preoccupied with starting an impossible business.

She turned around, leaned her back against the sink, and glared at her husband. "No, Greg, I am not having an affair, but if I was, you wouldn't notice unless you got a phone call telling you so. You're so preoccupied with . . . with your SlowBurn fixation. So just chill out. Okay?"

He pushed himself away from the doorframe and stood up straight, a threatening glint in his eye. "What's that supposed to mean?"

"You figure it out."

They stared at each other a few moments, then he *humphed,* turned away, and left.

Greg returned to his desk, blood pounding in his ears. How did she manage to enrage him so? He had to let it go or he was going to give himself a stroke. Yeah, a stroke at age thirty-six! How would that be? Trying to shake off his foul mood, he checked his email then clicked on the CNN news feed: a 5.4-magnitude earthquake in California, two people still missing from the tourist boat that overturned in the Delaware River, and a Texas woman who'd won the million-dollar lottery—for the fourth time.

Man! Why couldn't he have a little luck like that? Maybe he oughta play the lottery—

No! If God was going to bless him, it'd be through his business. But the tension in his house was so high he couldn't concentrate. "God, you gotta help me break out of this mess!" he hissed through gritted teeth.

Pushing back his chair, Greg got up and strode through the kitchen and out the back door without acknowledging Nicole. He needed to bleed off some of his steam.

As he descended the steps, his son came trotting across the yard. "Hey, Dad, where you goin'?"

Greg sighed. "Nowhere. I was just . . ." He put out his hand like a traffic cop. "Sorry. Can't play right now, buddy." He turned toward the side of the house.

"But Dad—"

"Not this time, son," he called over his shoulder, heading up the walk. "I'll catch you later."

Emerging in front of the house, he stopped. Instead of going for a walk as he'd intended, he sank down on the front steps. Elbows on knees, head in hands. What was he going to do? For five minutes, maybe ten, he just sat there until he heard someone call his name.

"Hey, Singer!"

Greg looked up. Harry Bentley was coming across the street toward him, his black dog trotting at his side.

"Ah, man. Am I glad to see you." The older man took out a big handkerchief and wiped the sweat off his face. "You got a few minutes? I don't know what happened, but for some reason the fans in Corky's transport kennel were running all night, and it wore down the battery in my SUV. Can't get the engine started, and I've gotta get to work. Need to catch the Texas Eagle down to St. Louis at one-forty-five. Could you give me a jump?"

Greg pushed himself up and came down the steps. "Sure, no problem." It was a relief to have something to do that he could actually *do*.

"If Estelle was home, I could jump it off our RAV-4, but she's at Manna House."

"Let me get the Cherokee. Where're you parked?"

"Around back, in my garage. I'll open the alley door. Just pull in. Should be able to get close enough."

Ten minutes later, Harry's car was running and they were rolling up the jumper cables and closing the engine hoods. "Thanks so much, man. You're a real Godsend."

"Glad to help."

"Hey, shut off your engine and come on up for a cup of coffee. It's the least I can do. Or . . . do you only drink that energy stuff you're sellin'?"

"No, I like coffee. But aren't you in a hurry?"

"I'm good. Got a few minutes now that my battery's charging. I was just worried that I'd have to call a tow truck or somethin'. No tellin' how long it'd take for them to get here. But thanks to you, it's all copacetic." Harry chuckled as he closed the overhead door to the alley, leaving the side door to the yard open since his car was running.

Seated around the kitchen table a few minutes later with steaming cups of coffee in their hands, Harry shook his head. "Wow! Must've been the Lord movin' my feet. Can't even recall why I went out to the garage, but as soon as I opened the car door, I noticed the dome light didn't come on, knew something was wrong."

Greg sipped his coffee in silence as Harry made small talk for a few minutes. Harry seemed to give God credit for every little thing. Didn't feel like he had that much to be thankful for himself—

"So how's it goin' for you, Greg? Your business takin' off?"

Harry's question pulled him back to the Bentley kitchen. "Ah, not really." Greg was surprised at himself. Why had he admitted that? He usually put on a good face, projected success for success, and all that. But somehow the tone of sincerity in Harry's question had taken him off guard. "What I mean, is, you know, working at home . . ." Greg clinched his fists in front of his chest and moved them from side to side like a tug of war. "A little tension with the missus. But it'll pass."

Harry nodded thoughtfully, staring at him with a calm gaze. "Sorry to hear that." Greg felt as though the man could see right through him, but there was no judgment there.

Still, he wasn't ready to go into his suspicions about Nicole and Lincoln Paddock. "Oh, say, good thing you asked Josh Baxter to come over and help me with the new water heater. He made some modifications to get the pipes connected. Would've taken me twice the time, even if I could've figured it out by myself."

"Yeah, he's a good kid." Harry glanced down at his watch. "Uh-oh. Now I do have to go. Sorry 'bout that." He stood up, and Corky jumped up, too, wagging her tail eagerly.

"Yeah, I gotta get back to work myself." Greg followed Harry and the dog down the outside back stairs and started around the house toward the street when Harry called him back.

"Hey, where you goin' so fast? Your car's still in my garage!" Harry laughed as Greg sheepishly came back. "Thought I had myself a new Jeep there. Besides, man, I want to say one more thing . . ." He laid a hand on Greg's shoulder. "I was out of work for a long time, too, and I know it's tough. But it's gotta be just as tough on your wife. Be sure you pray together about the frustrations you're feeling and decisions you gotta make. Know what I'm sayin'?"

Greg nodded politely as he got into the Cherokee and backed out of the Bentleys' garage. But . . . pray together? He and Nicole weren't even speaking right now.

✧ ✧ ✧ ✧

To Greg's relief, Nicole was holed up in the basement working on Paddock's project when he got back, and the kids were out with Tabby at the park or somewhere. Greg didn't try to keep up with their whereabouts. Right now, his domestic concerns involved his wife and Paddock, but he didn't know what to do. He had no proof of anything actually wrong happening, just a feeling in his gut. He either needed proof or he needed to put aside his suspicions.

But by Friday, nothing had changed with SlowBurn, and he felt frozen. Didn't know how to move forward. Didn't know whether to throw in the towel. And not knowing what to do, he realized he'd been frittering more and more of his time away on the computer, running down rabbit trails that had nothing to do with his business. Already, he'd whiled away most of the morning.

This was becoming a crisis!

Crisis . . . the last time he'd thought of his life in those terms had been after being released—*fired*—from Powersports. That was when Pastor Hanson's teaching had brought him hope: The two Chinese characters making up the word for "crisis" meant *danger* and *opportunity*. Well, he was there again. But what could he do about it?

His mind looped back to Nicole, and he typed "Watkins, Ellis, and Katz" into Google search and came up with the firm's familiar website. Maybe this time he would learn something new. It certainly was a big firm, and Paddock was named as a junior partner. He clicked on the tab describing the firm's services.

A refined descriptive page came up, and then a gaudy popup ad. How did that happen? He had his popup blocker turned on, but he knew an ad sometimes got through anyway. He clicked on the X to delete it, but it popped right back up. Who was doing this?

Couldn't miss the bold, golden words on a black background for the Big Returns website: "Make up to 81 percent on your investment in less than 60 seconds by trading binary options."

What? He'd never heard of binary options. Eighty-one percent? Unbelievable. But he kept staring at the words. Were they *danger* and *opportunity* or just a scam?

Almost without realizing he was doing it, he clicked on *Learn More.*

Chapter 33

DANGER AND *OPPORTUNITY . . .*

The *Learn More* link took him to the Big Returns' website. It looked like a casino, and he nearly clicked out of it, except for the box titled, "A No-Risk Way to Earn Big Returns." He leaned closer to read the smaller print, which explained that anyone could participate in trading binary options without special training, licensing, or experience . . . and there were no fees. "You're in total control of how much you invest or how long you participate. You can withdraw any time."

Greg frowned at the screen. But what exactly was binary trading? He'd never heard of it. Apparently, other people were just as unfamiliar, because the website offered an answer at the top of the page: "A binary option is simply making a prediction on the direction a stock, commodity, index, or foreign currency will move within a designated period of time, from as little as 60 seconds to 24 hours." Below was a trading simulator, inviting anyone to try it out without investing a single cent.

Greg murmured, "Thanks," when Nicole put a plate with a sandwich and an apple on the edge of his desk along with a tall glass of iced tea, but he was relieved when she left without trying to claim any more of his attention. Should he try the trading simulator? Why not? Just as a matter of curiosity. He might learn something.

When he clicked, the simulator asked him to enter his first name. Greg hesitated . . . but then it was only his first name. The instructions explained that the simulator offered options on the US dollar against the euro. In the next sixty seconds, did "Greg"—ah, that's why they wanted his first name, to make it more personal—think the dollar would increase or decrease in comparison to the euro? A real-time chart was displayed showing how the dollar had moved over the last few hours. So far that Friday morning, it had increased in a saw-tooth incline, but the repeated down jags showed that during many sixty-second periods, it had lost value even though the overall trend was up. The challenge was, what would it do in the time period Greg chose?

It looked like a gamble, but so what, he didn't have to risk anything to try the simulator. He selected one hundred dollars as his pretend investment, and clicked the up button. He watched the graph, and just after the value had clicked down for a few seconds, he hit start, presuming it would soon reverse its loss and continue increasing in value. The hand of the onscreen stopwatch swept around while the dollar value continued declining. At 20 seconds, its graph line was still headed down. Nearly halfway through the time period, Greg saw a momentary blip upward, but it didn't survive. More loss continued until 38 seconds into the minute when the line finally began a steady climb. But would it be enough? Greg held his breath. And then just as the bell sounded, the border of the graph flashed green, indicating that the final value of the US dollar had ticked fractionally above Greg's starting point.

He slapped his hands together. "I won!" he shouted.

A moment later the screen flashed in large print. *"Congratulations! Your payout would have been $170."*

A hundred and seventy bucks? His initial $100 plus $70 more? Wow! That was huge! An astounding 70 percent profit in one minute was more than he'd ever dreamed of earning doing anything.

Greg pushed back from his computer. Could it be true? Was there really a legal way to earn such a high percentage so quickly? He slowly rolled his chair forward, as if creeping up on his computer, and typed in a Google search for "binary options." Up came over a million hits. He clicked on the first few top links and discovered dozens of companies offering online binary trading options. Some looked like casinos—similar to the Big Returns site he'd been on—but others were more refined, projecting an image as staid as a Wall Street bank. Unlike the glitzy sites, Greg noticed these more dignified companies carefully referred to their activity as "trading," not "playing." Money was called "earnings," not "winnings." Participants were "investors," not "players." Obviously, they didn't want the public to think of their enterprise as gambling. Okay, he could see that. He wasn't a gambler himself and wouldn't want to be involved in anything suspect.

But with so many prominent sites, it seemed like the concept had to be legitimate even if a few companies played fast and loose, otherwise the Securities and Exchange Commission or some such federal agency would shut them down. Right?

He visited site after site, and while the tone was different, the concept and the way one participated was basically the same. A few online articles warned about the risks of losing a lot of money with binary trading, but even these "negative" sites didn't say it was illegal or necessarily a scam. Participants just had to be wise and not get in over their heads. Which was true of any high-risk venture.

But then, 'nothing ventured, nothing gained.' Right? And Greg definitely needed to gain a lot right now.

Should he try it?

After a couple of hours of research, Greg selected TopOps as the site he felt most comfortable with. It wasn't as stuffy as a gray granite bank, but it didn't feel like cheap thrills either. Just a straightforward presentation of the company's operation and how he could participate. The introductory video for TopOps clearly explained how wins and losses were calculated. When he won on a 60-second trade, he would earn 70 percent on the money he invested. If he lost, he would only lose 85 percent.

Gulp! That was a lot, but it wasn't like risking *all* of his capital. He'd still have 15 percent to move forward. After all, a loss was a loss. He understood that.

Taking a deep breath, Greg clicked on the link to *Open a new account.* He'd try it and pull out immediately if anything seemed fishy. But his hands shook as he entered his credit card information. That felt more risky than providing such information when ordering a product online, but of course TopOps needed some way to receive his investment, and a credit card was so much simpler than making a bank transfer. Besides, if anything backfired, his credit card company was supposed to provide some degree of protection. Besides, the card was nearly maxed out anyway, so they couldn't get too much from him.

Within ten minutes he was ready to make his first actual investment.

The house phone rang . . . and rang . . . and rang. "Nicole, can you get that?"

No answer from the basement. Where was she anyway? He heard the answering machine click on, but rather than leaving a message, the caller hung up. A few moments later, the phone began ringing again.

"Nicole!"

This time the caller recorded a message—a male voice, definitely not Lincoln Paddock, so Greg didn't pay any attention until he heard the words, ". . . have her come home immediately. There's been a family emergency."

What? Who was calling?

He jumped up and ran into the kitchen, catching the last few words of what he finally recognized as Jared Jasper's desperate voice asking them to have Tabby come home. He yelled down the stairs to the basement. "Nicole, you down there?"

"What?"

"Where have you been? Didn't you hear the phone ringing?"

"Sorry. I had earphones on listening to music. What's wrong?"

"It's Jared Jasper. There's been some kind of emergency, and he wants Tabby to come home immediately. Where are the kids?"

"Tabby took them across the street to play with the Horowitz children."

"Well, can you go get her? He sounded urgent."

"Uh . . . okay. Just give me a sec."

Greg didn't notice when Nicole left the house or when she and the kids returned, but some time later, they were just there, making noise and running up and down the stairs.

By then he was too deep into TopOps to ask Nicole why Tabby had to go home early. When he finished reviewing all the steps to making a trade—it was actually rather simple—he invested one hundred dollars on a sixty-second option on the euro/US dollar platform, and clicked *Down* and then *Start*. The dollar had been going up so steadily for the last several minutes, so he was sure it was time for a dip. But as he watched with his heart pounding, it wasn't happening. And then in the last fifteen seconds, the value plummeted, and when the bell rang, his payout was $170, just like the simulation. Only this time, he had actually earned $70.

He gleefully slammed his fist into the palm of his other hand. Even though the introductory videos and articles and simulator had told him it was possible, he'd expected to be disappointed and feel like a fool. But he'd won!

No, he shouldn't use that term. He'd *earned* the money with a shrewd trade. Maybe he had a gift for this kind of thing.

He immediately made another trade and earned another $70. He did it a third time with success. Then doubled his investment to $200 and was right when he predicted the dollar would rise.

He looked at his watch. Within five minutes, he'd made $350.

Wow!

Greg got up and paced around the room for a few moments, feeling so lightheaded he thought he might pass out. This was not like some sweepstakes where the chance of winning was one in a million. No. He sat back down and thought through the odds. Even if you only flipped a coin, didn't every bid have a 50/50 chance of being correct—up or down, just two possibilities? But certainly, if you used your head, you could do a little better than flipping a coin. You could make an informed guess . . . no, an informed *bid*, couldn't you? He'd just done it four times in a row.

This was what he was looking for!

Greg was ecstatic. He wanted to support his family so badly. He was ready to do anything for them, but all his efforts so far had been fruitless since he'd lost his job. Finally—finally!—God was answering his prayer. Had to admit he hadn't been praying that hard, but God must be showering mercy on him, pouring out that fantastic blessing Pastor Hanson had promised, prosperity beyond all imagination.

He felt like laughing. All the wealth the SlowBurn people had offered—new car, bigger house, boat, whatever—it was coming through another avenue.

For the next hour, Greg kept going, bid after bid. His enthusiasm was tempered a little when he lost, three times in a row at one point, and with larger bids on the block. But when the market closed that afternoon, Greg was—as the TopOps site described it, "in the money," with $120 more than when he started.

That cooled his jets. He'd made more than that in a day back when he worked for Powersports. But the potential was still there with TopOps, and very alluring. Maybe it wasn't going to be $350 every five minutes, but big earnings were still possible.

Even though the market had closed for the day—for the weekend, actually, since it was Friday—Greg wanted to learn more. Trading on international currencies wasn't the only way to bid on binary options. Stocks, commodities, and various indexes could also be traded. He needed to explore them all.

When he finally shut down his computer and stood up, the tension of the day had so sapped his strength that his knees felt shaky. But he was happy. He should take Nicole and the kids out to dinner to celebrate. So far, he hadn't even told Nicole about his breakthrough, just dismissed her when she came into the room while he stared, white-knuckled at the progress of his latest bid.

As soon as he walked into the kitchen, Nate and Becky ran up to him, hands covered with flour. "Daddy, Daddy, Daddy, we're baking bread. We're gonna have hot bread for dinner tonight."

"Hot bread?" He looked down at the white handprints on his jeans. "That sounds great." He leaned down and scooped them up. "I can't wait." Maybe this was better than going out. His whole family together, everyone excited, the perfect time to tell them the good news.

Nicole got up early Saturday to make a special breakfast—eggs in a nest, plus bacon, the kids' favorite, especially when she sprinkled grated cheese on the eggs. She wasn't really celebrating Greg's "breakthrough," which frankly sounded more like gambling than a solid business plan. But whatever it was, it had sounded too complicated to discuss at the table with the kids present. And then as soon as dinner was over, the kids had begged to go out for ice cream, which Greg agreed to do while she cleaned up the kitchen and went back to work on the last section in Lincoln's project. He'd even offered to read to the kids and put them to bed.

By the time she'd staggered up to bed—still not finished—he was already asleep.

Asleep but happy. Well, that was something. She'd ask him more about this new binary trading today before trying to finish up her work project. She should give Greg a chance. Maybe it would be a good thing.

She stepped out of the kitchen and peeked into the master bedroom. "Greg, you up? Time to eat." Then she circled around and called up the stairs. "Time for breakfast! Becky, Nathan, I made eggs in a nest!"

That got the kids tumbling down the stairs and seated at the table, and Greg showed up a few minutes later. Serving up the last slice of grilled toast with eggs nestled in a hole cut in the middle, she turned off the griddle and started to sit down, when the phone rang. "Let me get that first. Then you can pray for us, Nate."

Nicole picked up the receiver. "Hello, Singer residence." The voice on the other end was speaking so fast, she could barely understand her, but she finally realized it was Tabby Jasper. "Slow down, girl. You say you can't watch the kids this morning? You have to go where?" She listened more carefully. "What? Both of them?" She clasped her hand to her mouth. "Wait, Tabby, don't hang up—"

Then, as if in a trance, Nicole slowly hung up the phone and turned toward the curious faces staring at her from the breakfast nook.

"Tabby can't come. She and her mom are heading for the hospital." She swallowed. "Both Jasper boys were shot yesterday."

Chapter 34

GREG STARED AT NICOLE. *Shot?* Both boys? How in the world had *that* happened?

"We need to pray for them." Nicole grabbed hands around the table, her voice rising and falling as she prayed protection and healing for Destin and Tabby's twin brother. Greg's mind spun as she prayed. Wounded apparently, not killed, thank God. Were they in a gang or something? Hard to believe. The Jaspers seemed like a nice family. Boys seemed like such great kids too.

He had no idea how seriously the boys had been hurt, but one thing seemed certain—if Destin was in the hospital, he'd be out of commission for a while. Maybe it was because the kid was young and in need of cash, or maybe it was because he'd been someone Greg imagined he could motivate to break into a youthful market, but he realized he'd been counting on Destin to provide the breakthrough he needed to make SlowBurn work.

Greg stared at the unfinished breakfast on his plate and sighed. At least God had guided him to an alternative in time. What was it Pastor Hanson always said? *One door never closes but God opens another. So just keep knocking!* Well, that's what he'd been doing, and it had paid off with TopOps.

Still, it was really tragic about Destin.

"You think we should do something?"

Nicole's question broke into his reverie. "Uh, yeah, sure, but what? We don't know how serious it is or even what hospital they're in."

"Yes, but they're our neighbors, and you hired Destin."

"I know, I know. I'm just as concerned as you are, but until we know what's needed, it's hard to know how to respond."

"Well, I'm gonna check with Estelle Bentley as soon as we're done with breakfast. She ought to know."

Greg nodded. "Sounds good, and I agree. If there's anything we can do, we should."

While supervising the kids as they cleared the table when Nicole ran across the street to see Estelle Bentley, Greg's phone rang. He stepped into the dining room to take the call away from the squabbling between Becky and Nate. "Hello. This is Greg."

"Hey Greg, wasn't sure I could catch you on a weekend. Is this your personal number? I was afraid all I had was your Powersports number."

"Not Powersports." He should know that voice, but he couldn't quite place it. "Powersports closed. So what can I do for you?"

"Well, last time we talked—back in May or early June, I think it was—you were interested in joining Potawatomi's sales staff . . ." Greg snapped his fingers—it was Roger Wilmington from Potawatomi Watercraft. "But at the time, we couldn't afford someone at your salary level, and I didn't want to try to talk you down. Hope you don't have any hard feelings over that."

"I understand, Roger. Business is business." Though Greg recalled Roger had taken several days to get back to him, and then only by email. That had seemed like a rebuff, but he wasn't the kind of guy to hold grudges.

"Right. But now I'm coming back to you. Turns out we lost another man, which leaves us shorthanded. Problem is, business hasn't picked up that much, so we can't offer you much more, and I'm not sure what you're doin' now, but thought I'd just reach out and see if you were interested."

Greg waited a few moments, knowing silence was often the best question, but when Roger didn't offer more, he finally said, "Well, I've started a new business, and that's kept me pretty busy. But what are we talking about here?"

"To begin with, there'd be a base salary, same as all our sales staff, and a commission on top of that. We can't budge on the salary even though I know you're living down there in the city where it's more expensive, but I got you a couple of extra percentage points on your commission to sweeten the offer. If things go well for Potawatomi, they'll go *very* well for you."

"And those numbers would be . . .?"

"Like I said, the salary's locked in relative to seniority at forty-two grand to start, but I was able to bump you up to a whopping 38 percent on the commission. And of course, we offer medical and dental on top of that."

Greg's heart sped up a little. *Thirty-eight percent?* But he needed to stay cool. "And what's the commission on? Just new boats, or is it on everything—trailers, accessories, storage contracts?"

"Anything connected with a new boat sale."

"Hmm . . ." He'd been making sixty-two thousand plus benefits at Powersports. If sales were decent, he might match that with a job like this, but it wasn't guaranteed, and it sure wouldn't be the "prosperity" he'd been anticipating. "I don't know, Roger. I really appreciate you thinking of me. Could I get back to you early next week with an answer? I need to weigh some issues . . . the commute for one, and like I said, I've just started my own business, and it's got a lot of potential. But I'll give your offer some serious thought if you can give me a little time."

"No problem, man. I'll look forward to hearing from you. You got my number, don't you?"

"Yep, right here in my phone. See ya."

Greg walked into the living room and stared out the front window. There'd certainly be some relief in having a steady income again, like a bird in the hand. But he was so close to catching two in the bush . . . no, more like a half-dozen in the bush. And it sounded like Potawatomi was running a little lean. What if the commissions weren't even enough to match his former salary? Then Nicole would need to go back to work. Humph. She might agree if it was for Lincoln Paddock, but he wasn't going to stand for that.

He watched out the window as she returned from across the street. It looked like she'd lost a little weight. The bounce was back in her step and her blonde hair ruffled in the morning breeze like waves in a wheat field. Hmm, nope. Going back to work was out of the question if it would be for Paddock!

He turned as she came in the front door. "Find out anything?"

Nicole nodded. "Estelle said Michelle phoned last night to ask for prayer. Said Destin was hit in the leg. Tore it up pretty badly, but the bullet missed the bone. The younger one's a little more serious. Tabby's twin was hit in the stomach. But he's supposed to recover."

"Man! How'd all this happen?"

"Estelle didn't know. Shooting took place somewhere down near Hamlin Park, she thinks."

"Anything we can do?"

"Estelle said she was going to provide meals, and I said I'd be glad to help, but I don't know what else."

Greg shook his head. How did a nice kid like Destin get caught up in a shooting? Shootings happened all the time in Chicago, but usually they were gang related. Greg hadn't seen any sign that Destin was involved with a gang, but what did he know? Maybe the kids were just at the wrong place at the wrong time.

The next morning, Nicole did the usual hurry-scurry to get the kids and herself ready for church, but to be honest, she didn't feel much like going. The messages had been easier to swallow while Pastor Hanson was away on his Holy Land tour the last couple of Sundays, but the Victorious Living Center still seemed so far removed from the church she'd grown up in . . . though she had to admit, her greatest complaint as a teenager had been that it was boring.

Greg went on ahead to their regular seating area in the balcony while she checked Nate and Becky into the children's program. It took longer than usual, and when she finally hustled up the stairs, someone had already taken their usual seats. Looking around, she finally saw Greg waving to her from the next section over.

The congregation of nearly four thousand was on its feet while the full, hundred-voice choir and praise band belted out a thunderous new song. Laser beams swept through the auditorium, colorful spots throbbed with the music, and fog from machines snaked across the platform, spilling down into the front rows of the congregation. She knew all the hoopla was because Pastor Hanson was returning, but she was glad she wasn't down there on the main floor.

The house lights dimmed while the giant overhead screens showed video clips of the Holy Land tour—Pastor Hanson baptizing people in the Jordan River, praying at the Western Wall, riding a camel, teaching on the Mount of Olives, preaching from a small fishing boat in the Sea of Galilee, silhouetted on the brow of a hill with his arms outstretched as though he were a cross, serving communion at the Garden Tomb, and then boarding a private jet at the Tel Aviv airport.

The next scene was of a silver Cadillac Escalade stopping in front of the church, followed by a black Tahoe with darkened windows. Four men in matching black suits and wraparound shades got out of it, looking like Secret Service agents with coiled earphone leads curling over their ears and into their coat collars. Two stood stiff-legged, facing the church, while the camera followed the other two to the silver luxury vehicle, its smoked windows hiding whoever was inside. But when they opened the back doors, Pastor Hanson emerged, followed by First Lady Sheila in a slinky, black-sequined gown.

Oh, brother!

On the screen, the pair walked briskly toward the church entrance, led by the first two "agents" and followed by the other two. The camera stayed ahead of them, wobbling a little as they came through the main doors, into the church vestibule, and finally down the center aisle to the screams of the congregation.

It was then that Nicole realized the video presentation had transitioned seamlessly from the Holy Land report to live views of Pastor Hanson's grand entry into the Victorious Living Center. Over the edge of the balcony she could see him now as he stepped through the stage smoke and climbed the four riser steps onto the platform and made his way around behind the massive pulpit. The four men in black—wraparound shades and all—positioned themselves across the front, standing at parade rest, facing the congregation.

"Amen, amen, amen!" Pastor Hanson called above the music and cheering. "It's so good to be home." He waved with his arms for the music to subside until it was quiet except for background riffs from the Hammond organ. "Thank you so much for such a joyous welcome. You know I love you all, each and every one of you. And I want to thank you for that generous gift of my new Escalade. Did you all see that silver ride I came up in?" A rousing trill from the organ. "And how about my new armor bearers?" He gestured to the men in black. "You know, I met with some security experts in Israel, and there's nobody in the world who knows more about security than the Israelis. And they gave me some important advice. How many of you know, when you're leading a ministry as powerful and important as the Victorious Living Center, the enemy doesn't like it. He'll bring every weapon against you. But the Bible says, 'No weapon formed against you shall prosper,' and so, in spite of the threats—oh, yes, there have been real threats against me and my family—" He gestured toward his wife, sitting in the front row. "We are not afraid. But we are also 'wise as serpents.' So when you see these brothers around, don't mess with 'em, or you might not find them to be so *brotherly*, if you know what I mean."

He laughed, a wide grin spreading across his tanned face as he clapped his hands. That broke the tension that had come over the congregation, and everyone, it seemed to Nicole, applauded him. But she didn't clap. What was going on here? A welcome like a rock star, an entourage like a king, guards, and talk of threats? Were those men *armed* . . . right here in church?

She sat down, and a few minutes later everyone calmed down and took their seats as well.

"My text this morning is brief but powerful. It comes from Jeremiah twenty-nine, eleven." The words appeared on the big screens.

> "For I know the plans I have for you," declares the Lord, "plans to prosper you and not to harm you, plans to give you hope and a future" (Jeremiah 29:11, NIV).

"Hear that, people? Plans to *prosper* you . . ."

Nicole knew that the pastor had quoted that verse in other sermons to support his emphasis on prosperity, but she didn't recall him using it as his primary text. She flipped in her Bible to the reference to see if her New Living Translation said the same thing. Instead of "plans to prosper you and not to harm you" it said, "plans for good and not for disaster." Hmm. In one sense it meant the same thing: God had a good plan for us. But her version certainly didn't suggest that plan primarily involved financial wealth.

She glanced back up at the screen, but the verse was gone, replaced by a close-up live feed of Pastor Hanson, his blue eyes glinting with enthusiasm. She leaned over to Greg. "Let me borrow your Bible a moment." His was a New King James Version, the one the pastor usually used. She found the verse in it, and it said that the Lord had "thoughts of peace and not of evil." Hmm. Again, basically the same sentiment of goodwill toward us, but without a promise of wealth.

"*Psst,* Greg. What translation was that verse the pastor put up on the screen?"

He shrugged and put a finger to his lips.

No help there.

Nicole frowned. Could it be that only one version used the word *prosper* in translating this verse? If you weren't thinking just about money, the word prosper was in general agreement with the other ways of translating the concept. God *does* have our welfare at heart, good plans that won't lead to our harm but will give us a future and a hope. But by pulling out that one word from one translation, Pastor Hanson seemed to be making his case for living large.

She tuned in to what he was saying again. He was really getting into it.

"You see my Escalade, and you want my accolades. You see my glory, but you don't follow my story!" The man wiped his glistening brow with a white hand towel. "You know, when you get to be my age, you ask, why not have a little fun? Well, my story is, you can. You can have it all! All you've got to do is seed into God's ministry, and he will reward you twenty, thirty, a hundredfold!"

Much of the congregation was on its feet, cheering and clapping, but Nicole looked down at Greg's Bible. She turned back to the preceding chapter. Maybe she should read straight through to get the context.

What she discovered shocked her.

In chapter 28, a prophet named Hananiah had showed up promising that within two years God would break the yoke of Nebuchadnezzar and return all the exiles in Babylon to their beloved city, Jerusalem. He would restore everything that had been stolen from them, including the throne, upon which Jehoiachin would be crowned as king of Judah.

But Jeremiah had responded in effect, "Great, I hope it happens, but you're a liar, a false prophet. Things are going to get much worse, and before the year is out, you, Hananiah, will die." In the seventh month of that year, he did die.

Then Jeremiah sent a letter to the exiles in Babylon telling them to settle down and make the best of their captivity because it was going to last for seventy years. Only when that time was up would God restore them to their homeland.

Nicole hardly noticed that Greg and most of the congregation had taken their seats again as she came to Pastor Hanson's text in chapter 29 and read beyond it:

> For I know the thoughts that I think toward you, says the Lord, thoughts of peace and not of evil, to give you a future and a hope. Then you will call upon Me and go and pray to Me, and I will listen to you. And you will seek Me and find Me, when you search for Me with all your heart. I will be found by you, says the Lord, and I will bring you back from your captivity; I will gather you from all the nations and from all the places where I have driven you, says the Lord, and I will bring you to the place from which I caused you to be carried away captive.

Nicole blew out a breath and sat back, staring straight ahead without seeing the big screens or hearing what Pastor Hanson was saying. In context, the Scripture was clear: God loved his people and had not abandoned them. He would listen to them when they called upon him, and they'd find him when they got serious about seeking him. But the promise of restoration wouldn't be fulfilled to the individuals who received the letter. They would all die in captivity. The "future hope" in which they could take comfort was that their grandchildren would return to Jerusalem.

Her mind raced as the story sank in. God had been implementing a larger, long-range plan. If the people to whom the prophecy was directly addressed couldn't cash it in for their personal "prosperity," what right did Pastor Hanson have using it as a get-rich-quick scheme for today?

As her eyes finally focused on the pastor's video image on the screens, a wave of heat rose up her neck and enveloped her head with sudden dizziness. Were his days as numbered as those of the false prophet Hananiah?

She had to get away, get the kids out of this building before something tragic happened. Nicole swallowed down her panic, knowing she couldn't explain it all to Greg. But the service was almost over. No one would notice if she left a little early. She handed Greg's Bible back to him and whispered in his ear. "I'm going to pick up Becky and Nate. I'll meet you at the car."

Chapter 35

GREG FOUND HIS FAMILY SITTING in the Cherokee waiting for him when he came out of church. The windows were down, and from two cars away he could hear Nate whining as Becky teased him about something.

"Hey, hey, hey, what's going on?" He opened the door and slid into the driver's seat.

"She said my picture of Peter walking on the water looked like a LEGO Ninja in the desert."

"Yeah, that's because the water should be blue."

"Water can be brown."

"No it can't."

"Yes it can. Besides, somebody else had the blue crayon."

"Kids! That's enough." Greg put the key in the ignition. "Nicole, you here with us? You look like you're a thousand miles away."

She blinked and turned toward him, eyes wide. "What? What's the matter?"

"The kids! They're going bananas, and you're just sitting there."

"Oh. Sorry."

"I can't believe—" He stopped himself. He was sure the service this morning had upset her. Probably why she left early. Even he had to admit the drama of Pastor Hanson's "triumphal entry" had been a little over the top. But Nicole looked like it'd put her into a catatonic stupor.

Whatever! He put the car in gear and joined the stream of cars pouring out of the parking lot after the second service so there would be room for third-service people. But he was learning how futile it was to argue with Nicole about Pastor Hanson. He always felt inspired by the pastor's sermons. She was always upset. He gritted his teeth. They couldn't go on this way! But trying to resolve their differences while driving home from church hadn't worked either. What he really needed was some prosperity in his own life. *That* would show her it worked. And he knew she would appreciate the rewards. As they say, nothing succeeds like success.

And he was pretty sure it was beginning to happen with TopOps.

He said nothing, and that afternoon he walked up to the Jaspers to ask about Destin and his brother. It would help to know how seriously Destin was hurt—the kid still had cases of SlowBurn sitting in the Singers' garage. Greg rang the doorbell several times, but no one seemed to be home.

Well, at least he'd tried. Hopefully Nicole would give him some credit for that.

Nicole kept to herself most of the afternoon. She still felt shaken by the sense of fear that had overcome her during church that morning, fear of God's righteous anger at false prophets. Weren't there a lot of references in the Bible that mentioned the "fear of the Lord"? Even the times when God's messengers had to assure people, "Don't be afraid!" underlined how important it was not to provoke the God of the universe.

God has our good in mind, she reminded herself as she absently loaded the dishwasher after lunch. *Otherwise he wouldn't have embarked on a plan to save us. But you don't trifle with God.*

Kinda like that old vintage lamp beside her bed when she was a teenager, she mused, glancing out the window in the back door to check on the kids in the backyard. She'd rescued the thing from a garage sale, but it had a short, and twice she'd gotten a jolt before her dad made her throw it away. "You don't mess with electricity," he'd warned her. At the time she didn't think it was such a big deal. But one day she'd gone with her mom to take her dad's lunchbox to him where he was working with a Commonwealth Edison crew on a junction box at a small electrical substation. Signs on the high fence surrounding the substation warned, "Danger, High Voltage!" but the box the men were working on got more specific: "7,200 volts." The men stood several feet back as they opened some kind of a switch using a long wooden pole. Enormous gloves like huge oven mitts covered their hands and arms. Everybody wore helmets and shields over their faces.

That was power, Nicole thought, remembering the fear she'd felt for her father. Electricity wasn't malicious, but you didn't mess with it! *Maybe God is a little like that.* She shuddered. She didn't want to be anywhere near Pastor Hanson if the sparks began to fly.

She heard the front door open and close. Greg must be going up the street to see the Jaspers—he'd said he would that afternoon. She was glad he hadn't asked her to go with him. Her mind was still spinning. Dishes done, she sank onto the living room couch, hugging a throw pillow. She'd seen through Pastor Hanson's misuse of Jeremiah's prophecy, and trite as her electricity analogy might be, she congratulated herself on recognizing the importance of a healthy "fear of the Lord"—something the pastor seemed to ignore.

"But what about you?" The words filled her ears as if God had spoken them aloud.

Me? The question bounced around her mind like a pinball, ringing up points as it *ka-chinged* off the good things she did all the time—loving her kids, homeschooling them, managing a household, putting up with an unemployed husband in this trying time, visiting her lonely mother. There were lots of points up on the board, but then the pinball disappeared into a hole labeled "Lincoln Paddock."

That didn't count. She'd just been earning a little extra money to help with the family finances . . . to help her husband. Besides, she argued with herself, one doesn't earn salvation by ringing up points for good deeds.

But she also knew this wasn't about her salvation. It was about the fear of the Lord. She felt the heat rise up her neck again, and a slight wave of dizziness caused her to put her hand to her head. Was she catching a virus? A summer cold? The images of Lincoln Paddock she'd savored while making love to Greg filled her mind unbidden. She tried to shake them away, but they lingered a moment more. Sweet and rich . . .

Rich and *private*! She could never tell Greg! He'd be so angry. He was already jealous of Lincoln when he had no right to be. After all, she hadn't *done* anything. It had just been a harmless fantasy and hadn't hurt anyone. In fact, hadn't she given Greg a good time that night? So why not have a little fun?

"Why not have a little fun?" . . . wait. She'd heard someone else say the same thing recently.

Out of the corner of her eye Nicole saw Greg coming back up the walk toward the house, and she scurried down the hall to the bedroom. Shutting the door and leaning against it, her breath came in short gasps as she remembered.

Pastor Hanson had said the same thing in his sermon that morning.

Greg hit the TopOps trading site with enthusiasm Monday morning, and it began to pay off. Of course, he didn't win every bid, but his balance climbed steadily throughout the day until by closing time that afternoon, he was over a thousand dollars ahead.

He blew out a breath of satisfaction. This was the time to explain what he was doing to Nicole. He transferred five hundred from his TopOps account to his credit card account, bringing down the balance owed on their credit card. She'd be happy about that.

He strolled into the kitchen. "Hey, Nikki, what's for supper?"

She just kept cutting up sweet red peppers. "A pasta dish with chicken and veggies. Should be ready in about thirty minutes."

"Mmm. Sounds good." Should he tell her now? No, he'd wait till she wasn't busy. "Hey, mind if I drop in on the Jaspers for a few minutes? They weren't home yesterday. Still need to find out how the boys are."

Nicole shrugged. "Just be back in time for supper."

Greg stared at her back a few moments before leaving. She was hard to read these days. Oh well, he'd keep doing what he could, and maybe it'd finally melt the ice.

He waited several minutes after ringing the Jaspers' doorbell, but this time Michelle opened the door. She looked pretty tired.

"Hey, Mrs. Jasper. We, uh, heard about the boys. Nicole and I are so sorry. I wanted to check in and see how they're doing."

The boys' mother didn't open the door any wider than was necessary to talk. "I just got home with Destin, Mr. Singer. Tavis is still in the hospital, but he seems to be doing fairly well." She paused for a moment. "Jared's at the hospital with him, but we're going to switch a little later. If you come by about eight, I think he'd be here by then."

"Oh, sure. That'd be great. I'll do that. Maybe I can see Destin then."

She hesitated. "Well . . . maybe, if he's not asleep by then. He needs his rest."

"Of course. I understand. I'll try to drop by later when Jared's here."

Michelle closed the door slowly without saying anything more. Greg knew it had to be a stressful time for them, but he got a funny feeling something else was going on. Or maybe Destin needed her. He walked back down their porch steps. At least he wouldn't be late for dinner.

The pasta dish was too large for the kids to pass, so after Greg said a blessing, Nicole served everyone. Handing Greg's plate to him she said, "You seemed to have your nose in the computer again all day. Is that new thing you're trying working?"

"As a matter of fact, it is." Nicole asking the question would make it so much easier to explain. "Today . . ." He grinned proudly at his kids. "I won a thousand dollars!"

Nate's eyes got big. "Wow, Daddy, you're rich!"

"Not yet, but we're gonna be." He checked to see how Nicole responded. "In fact, you'll be glad to know, honey, that I transferred five hundred of it into our credit card account to reduce our balance." He didn't mention that was where he got the money to invest in TopOps in the first place.

Nicole toyed with her pasta. "I still don't quite understand what it is you're doing. How do you *win* a thousand dollars in one day? It sounds like gambling."

"Ah, I shouldn't have used the word *win*. It's earnings. It's based on the markets. It can be the stock market, commodities, or international currency. That's what I've stuck with until I get more skilled. You see, the value of the dollar is always fluctuating relative to other currencies."

She stared at him. "You mean you're betting that the dollar will lose value? That sounds un-American."

"Well, it's not." Greg threw up his hands. "Why do you always presume the worst about anything I do?"

"I'm sorry. I didn't mean that. It's just . . ."

He closed his eyes a moment. "What I do doesn't have any effect on the value of the dollar. I just analyze what the trend has been, and then predict what will happen in the next . . . minute. You can do it longer, but that's what I've been doing."

"And if you win—I mean, if you're right—who pays you? Where does that money come from?"

"From the exchange. The company I'm working with."

"And they get their money from . . .?"

"Other players, I mean, other investors who predicted the opposite."

"Can we be excused?" Becky piped up. "I'm done, and this is boring."

"After you finish your plate."

"But you gave me too much," Becky whined.

"Me too," Nate echoed.

Nicole sighed. "All right. Just take your dishes into the kitchen and put them on the counter."

Greg managed to get a few bites of his pasta as the kids did as they were told and then scurried downstairs to the family room. But his wife picked up the subject again.

"Look, I get the stock market. Like a pharmaceutical company wants to develop a new drug, but it's going to cost a lot of money to develop and test. So investors buy stock in the company, essentially loaning them the money. If it's successful—a cure for arthritis, say—the company makes millions, and the investors get a share. But it doesn't sound like this binary thing produces anything for anyone."

"Sure it does. It produces a profit, and it can be a pretty sweet one too." But as soon as Greg said it, his words sounded hollow. He knew she was right.

"I don't know." Nicole shook her head and stood up, gathering dishes to take to the kitchen.

"Well, a thousand bucks is a thousand bucks, and that's pretty good pay for one day, I'd say. We need the money. Don't know why you're complaining."

"I'm not complaining, Greg. I just want whatever you end up doing to . . . to work in the long term. But this sounds like gambling."

Greg stood up fast enough to almost knock his chair over backwards. He threw his napkin on his plate and stomped out of the room, out the front door, and stood on the top step of the porch staring at a cutthroat sunset bleeding through a dark overcast that stretched like a Frank Lloyd Wright cantilever toward the western horizon.

He blew out his bottled frustration. He should probably go back inside and try to bring the conversation to a better conclusion, but he didn't want to. Not now. The argument wasn't his fault. He thought she'd be happy he'd made some money.

He checked his watch—eight fifteen. Maybe Jared Jasper was home by now. Hands deep in his pockets and shoulders hunched, he went down the steps and headed up the street to the Jaspers.

"Oh. Singer. Michelle said you might drop by." Jared looked back over his shoulder. "Uh . . . maybe we should talk out here. You mind?" The man stepped out onto the porch.

"No problem. Just wanted to stop by and see how Destin was doing."

"He's getting around, but he's on his way to bed right now."

"Just wanted to say how sorry we are. I was so shocked to hear about his accident."

Jared pulled the door closed behind him. He stared eye to eye at Greg. "No accident, Singer. These weren't stray bullets. My boys were the targets."

"What? Oh, man. That's terrible." Thoughts swirled through Greg's mind of gang paybacks. "How could they be caught up in something like that?"

Jasper's eyes narrowed and his expression hardened. "Like what?"

"Oh, I didn't meaning anything by that," Greg said hastily. "I'd just always seen them as, you know, really wholesome kids. Not the kind who'd end up as targets." Oh, man, he should shut up. He was getting himself in deeper with every word.

"You really don't know, do you?" Jared's jaw clenched, his eyes still narrowed.

"Know what?"

"They were shot selling your . . . your stupid energy drink." Jared spat out the words.

"What?"

"That's right. Your energy drink. That SlowBurn junk you got him involved in."

"Now wait a minute. You're not suggesting—"

"No, *you* wait a minute, and answer me this. Did you tell my boy he needed to find a new location, some place where kids hang out?"

"No! I mean, he wasn't getting anywhere trying to sell it to his sports friends, so maybe I suggested he look for a new market or something, but I never—"

"You know where he found it—this 'new market,' as you call it—and took his younger brother with him?"

Greg just shook his head.

"A street corner near Hamlin Park. They were lookin' for a place where kids hung out, and they found 'em. Only problem was, some gangbangers saw them passing out stuff from their backpacks and thought it was drugs, thought my boys were trying to jump their territory. That's why they got shot! Now do you understand?"

Greg didn't know what to say to the man who was getting right up in his face. "I . . . I'm sorry. But I didn't tell Destin to go down there. I don't even know anything about that neighborhood."

Jared tapped an angry finger on Greg's chest. "It's obvious you don't know *anything*, but you're the one who got my boy so deep in debt with all those cans you sold him that he was desperate to unload 'em, even in a place that wasn't safe. And my baby boy got pulled into it too. Do you realize, *they both could've been killed?!*"

Greg threw up his hands. "Look, Jasper, Destin came to me because he needed a job to earn money for a basketball camp you wouldn't spring for. So you can't put it all on me."

The muscles on the sides of Jared's jaws were pulsing as he stared at Greg. Suddenly, he turned, went into the house, and slammed the door behind him.

Greg stood rooted for a moment, his own anger flaring. What just happened? He'd come here out of kindness to see how Destin was doing. Hadn't expected to be verbally attacked and blamed for the shooting.

Going slowly down the steps, he turned toward home, his thoughts churning. Jasper hadn't said anything about the shooting taking place near a 7-Eleven, but Destin had obviously found a corner where guys hung out, just like he'd suggested.

He heard the Jaspers' door open again behind him. "Hey, Singer! My kid used his college money to buy that junk from you. The least you could do is buy it back, ya know!"

Greg waved his hand without looking back and kept on walking.

Chapter 36

Greg's bidding on TopOps went well Tuesday morning, increasing the available funds in his online account. But he couldn't escape the feeling that he was being attacked on all sides. Jared Jasper's accusations from the night before nagged at him, along with Nicole's conclusion that binary trading was just gambling—not to mention that he hadn't yet hit it big on TopOps. He didn't even want to think about SlowBurn anymore.

Wasn't anyone on his side? All he needed was that breakthrough!

He kept rehearsing arguments against Nicole's opinions . . . while catching himself referring to his money as "winnings." If he was going to convince her, he'd have to revise his terminology. Still, he knew his "investments" didn't buy stock in TopOps or in any company that produced a product or service. When it came down to it, binary options involved a zero-sum game where no real wealth was created. When he won, TopOps lost. When he lost, they won. And simple logic told him that since there were so many binary companies out there, it had to be profitable for the owners, which meant that the players—*oops,* "investors"—lost often enough for the companies to stay in business. He gritted his teeth. Was Nicole right? Was he just gambling against the "house"?

But he'd been gaining . . . with a potential for even bigger gains as he increased the size of his bids. He'd started with hundred-dollar bids, but now he'd increased them to two hundred dollars, which meant $140 in profit every time he won. And he distinctly felt he was getting the knack for when to "call" and when to "put." It might be time to go to the next level, perhaps three hundred per bid.

By noon, he again had a thousand dollars in his online account. If the trend continued, he could withdraw double what he'd taken out on Monday and still have sufficient seed money for Wednesday . . . or perhaps he'd leave it all in and go for really big returns.

Then he hit a losing streak. By three o'clock he'd drained his balance. Slapping the desk with his hand, he got up and paced around the living room. "*Argh!* I hate losing even more than I hate not winning!" Had he said that aloud? He stopped pacing a moment and listened. Neither Nicole nor the kids were on the first floor. Good. He didn't want them knowing about the losses. He stood at the front window, hands jammed in his pockets. The words he'd muttered seemed illogical . . . but as he thought about it, he realized when he was on an upswing, he could handle some losses. But when he was going into the hole, he began to feel desperate—desperate enough to do anything, take any risk, to win back what he considered to be "his."

That's where he was right now. He had to do something. Anything. Press through, get beyond this losing streak. Okay. He'd go back to his credit card and withdraw the five hundred he'd deposited the day before. It'd only be temporary, right? He'd told himself he wouldn't do it just to make larger bids, but he couldn't end the day with a loss.

Going back to his computer, he made the transfer. With a new infusion of money, his first two bids won . . . but then the losing streak returned. Fighting panic, he called on his credit card for another three hundred and got a message: *"Card not acknowledged. Contact bank."*

What? How could that be? He'd just used it not thirty minutes before. He dug out his wallet to find the card and call the number on the back. Wait . . . why not check his balance online, so when he called he could talk specific numbers. It took him a few minutes to log in, and then he saw the problem: He was within $238 of his maximum.

Rats! He hadn't known they were that close to their $5,000 limit. He stared at the screen a few moments. Should he quit? But if he did . . . he hated to think of how much he'd lost. He couldn't accept that. All he needed was one more chance!

And there was still one way to get it . . .

Back on TopOps, he charged two hundred bucks against his credit card, and it went through. With a sigh of relief, he set up his next bid. Only twenty minutes before the site closed. Could he recoup his losses in so little time? He bid all two hundred—and won . . . and won . . . then won again. All right! That put him up by $420, and there was still time for one more bid. If he put the whole $620 that was in his account on the next bid and won, he'd end the day with $1,054—certainly nowhere near his morning high, but at least he'd be able to sleep that night, not having gone in the hole for the day.

He watched the trend of the ticker. It had been declining over the last hour, but now it was just bobbing up and down. He set up his bid as a "put"—predicting the US dollar would go down—with all $620 on the line for a one-minute run. At three minutes before closing, he clicked and waited, watching the second hand go around and the value frame change from green to red to green. His heart was pounding as the seconds counted down . . . and when the bell sounded, it was red. The value of the US dollar had slightly declined against the euro.

He'd won.

"All right!" He leaped from his chair and jumped around the living room.

"What happened, Daddy? Why are you yelling?" Becky and Nate came thundering down the stairs like a pair of wildebeests.

Laughing, Greg went down on one knee and held his arms wide to embrace his kids as they ran into the living room. "Oh, nothing. Daddy just . . . just earned a little money at a very important time. It wasn't that much, but it was exciting." He gave them another squeeze. "I love you both."

Standing up, Greg wiped his forehead with the back of his arm. "Where's Mom?" He didn't really want to tell her how desperate he'd gotten or how excited he'd become at climbing out of the hole he'd gotten himself in that day. "Is she downstairs?"

"No. She said she was going over to talk to Mrs. Bentley."

"Oh. Okay. Well, you guys can run back up and play some more."

"Can't we watch TV?" Nate stuck out his lip. "I'm bored."

"Have you watched any yet today?"

"Only a little, not my full time."

"I don't want to watch TV," Becky said. "I'm going back upstairs." And she darted out of the room.

"Please, Daddy."

"Well, all right. But when Mom gets home, if she says stop, that means stop. Agreed?"

"O-o-ka-a-y." Nate left for the basement, head down, as if Greg had given him a punishment rather than a privilege.

Greg returned to his computer. Without sitting down, he noted his balance with TopOps had indeed returned to $1,054. What a relief. He exited the site and shut down his computer. It was, indeed, time to quit, and he felt wasted.

But the thought of Nicole talking to Estelle Bentley reminded him that this was Tuesday night, and Harry would probably be asking if he wanted to attend his men's Bible study. He didn't really feel like going. If Harry called, he'd come up with some kind of excuse.

Greg was still feeling good when Nicole called them to the dinner table. As he reached for Nate's hand on one side of him and Becky's on the other before blessing the food, Nicole spoke up. "As we thank God for our food, I think we should pray for Tabby's brothers. Okay?"

"Sounds good to me." Greg said, and he added Destin and Tavis to his usual mealtime prayer.

"An' help them get better so Tabby can come babysit us s'more," Nate added before Greg said his "Amen."

Greg and Nicole exchanged glances as the kids dived into the individual pizzas they'd helped their mom make. Nicole cleared her throat. "Estelle told me some more about what happened to the Jasper boys."

The way she said it made Greg tense. "Oh, yeah?" He tried to keep his voice casual as he reached for the salad dressing. "What'd she say?"

"Turns out the boys weren't selling drugs. Have to admit that's what I thought at first. But police said they were clean, and the only thing in Destin's backpack was that energy drink of yours and some homework. But apparently, there's a turf war going on in that area between rival gangs. One of the gangs probably thought Destin and Tavis were trying to take over their corner, and that's why they got shot."

That energy drink of yours . . . Greg frowned.

Becky—always the one with the big ears—spoke up. "But if they weren't selling drugs, why did the gangbangers shoot them?"

"Well, maybe they just *thought* the Jasper boys were selling drugs." Nicole kept her eyes on Greg. "I suppose if they were selling SlowBurn on a corner like that, it'd be pretty easy for someone to mistake that for peddling drugs. You know, if it looks like a duck and quacks like a duck, somebody's going to think it's a duck."

Greg frowned. It was the same argument Jared had used the night before. "You're making it sound like SlowBurn was at fault." He knew his voice sounded testy. "But I never told those boys to take over some drug dealer's spot. And I'm sure Destin wasn't trying to do that either. It was an accident. Wrong place at the wrong time, is all."

Nicole suddenly looked flustered. "Oh, Greg, I'm not suggesting it was your fault. Like you said, *wrong place at the wrong time.* That's all." Her voice trailed off as she pushed back her chair and headed for the kitchen. "Uh, there are a couple more little pizzas. Who's ready for more?"

"Me!" Nate yelled, his mouth still full of his first one.

But Greg pushed his plate away. He suddenly didn't feel very hungry.

Greg ignored the ringing of his phone the next day when he didn't recognize the number. He needed to focus on his next bid. Things were still up and down in terms of his profits, and at the moment he was down again. Just as he won the next bid, the phone rang again—same number. He answered.

"Greg, what's going on?" Nicole's angry voice yelled through the phone. "Our card's been denied! What's happening? Why won't it go through?"

"What do you mean? Where are you?"

"I'm at the grocery store, calling on the pay phone. And it's really embarrassing. When I tried to pay, it comes back, 'Card not acknowledged.' The clerk said that probably means it's maxed out. Do you know anything about this?"

Instantly, Greg realized exactly what was going on. He hadn't put money back on the card since last night. And there'd only been thirty-eight bucks left before they hit their limit.

"Uh, don't worry about it, honey. It's just a mistake. I'll get it cleared up right away. You still at the store?"

"Of course. I had to put all my groceries back in the cart and find a phone. This is so embarrassing, Greg. What's wrong, and how are you going to fix it?"

"Like I said, it's just a mistake. How much do you need?"

There was a big sigh on the other end. "I owe $93.76."

Greg knew he had thirty dollars in his wallet. That plus the thirty-eight still available on the card came to $68. "You got any cash on you?"

"Not that much."

"I know, but I've got some in my pocket. If you'd come get it—"

"Come home? What am I supposed to do with my cart?"

"I'm sure they wouldn't mind you leaving it there for a while, but you . . ." He paused, knowing this would upset her even more. "*Um,* you might have to put some of it back."

"What are you talking about?" Her voice was getting louder. "I'm not putting anything back. I only bought what we need, and we need it all. Besides, that's not fixing it. You said you'd fix it. What's wrong with our card, anyway?"

"Just calm down and give me a second, would you?" An alternative was coming to him. He checked his balance on TopOps. His rough morning left him with only $180 in his account. If he transferred a hundred back into the credit account, the card should work. But how long would it take to go through—a minute? an hour? He didn't know, but it seemed like the only option. "Look, Nikki, give me a few minutes to work out something with the bank. Then you should be able to pay for the whole cartload. Okay?"

"And what am I supposed to do in the meantime? I've got two hungry kids with me."

"Can't you give them an energy bar or an apple or something?"

"Greg, what's happening? I don't know if I'm coming or going. People are getting mad, telling me to get out of the way." Amid background noise, her yelling was turning into hysterical crying. "I don't know if I'm actually going to be able to pay for these groceries, and I don't even know if there's enough gas to get home on, and you want me to just wait here by the phone."

"What's this about gas? You didn't mention gas before."

"The empty light's on, and I was going to fill up on the way home."

"Then just . . . just use whatever cash you've got on you."

"All right." Her crying changed to gasping sobs. "But you still haven't told me what the problem is. I want to know the whole story, Greg."

"Sure, sure. When you get home." Greg got up and paced around the living room, still holding the phone to his ear. "Look, for now just wait there, and I'll call you back as soon as I know the funds are in the account so you can use the card. Okay?"

As soon as the phone connection ended, he realized he hadn't asked her for the number of the pay phone.

Chapter 37

GREG HAD A MOMENT OF PANIC. How was he supposed to call Nicole back without the number to the pay phone? Wait . . . it had to be in his caller ID. He checked, just to be sure, then took a deep breath. Okay. His first priority was to transfer money from his TopOps account to his credit card so Nicole could pay for her groceries.

He sent one hundred dollars over.

Now what? Greg knew it wasn't like waiting for a paper check to clear, but just how long would the bank's computers take to register the transfer? He logged on to his credit card account. It still showed only $38.20. He got up and paced around the room, imagining Nicole and the kids waiting at the Jewel. This really was a mess, but all he could do was wait.

Heading for the kitchen, he opened the refrigerator and pulled out a baggie with half of a personal pizza from the night before. Cold pizza for lunch, *ugh.* But with his first bite he felt guilty. His kids were stuck at the Jewel, hungry and wanting lunch.

When he returned to the living room, he refreshed his computer screen.

"Finally!" He pumped his fist.

Grabbing the phone, he hit Redial. Nicole answered on the first ring.

"Nicole, the money's there. Card should work now."

"You're sure? I'm not going through that humiliation again."

"Yes, it's there. Just checked. But when you stop for gas on the way home, don't use the card. Just put in however much cash you have."

"But why can't I fill it?"

"Just do what I said." He didn't want to explain that the cost of a full tank might max out the card again.

"I don't understand. I thought you said you got the card fixed! Greg, what's going on here? Something's not right. I . . . I can't take this anymore."

"I know, I know, honey. Just get the groceries. We can talk about it when you get home."

A half hour later he heard the back door slam as the kids came in. Greg got up from his computer and went out to help Nicole bring in the groceries. No small talk. Just *looks* as they passed each other on the walk bringing in the shopping bags.

He set the last bag on the counter. "Uh, I already ate. Had the leftover pizza. You guys go ahead with lunch." He headed back into the living room. Before she'd arrived home, he'd won one bid that increased his remaining $80 to $136. But then he'd lost $85. Should he try again? Greg sat there staring at the screen, confidence drained and unable to make his move.

From the direction of the kitchen he heard Nicole hurrying the kids to finish their lunch, then she was on the phone making arrangements to send Nate and Becky across the street to play with the Horowitz children. He looked up as she came in and stood in the archway into the living room. Her eyes were still red from the morning's ordeal.

Minimizing the TopOps screen, he got up and gestured toward the couch. "You wanted to talk." He sat on the edge of the recliner as she sat down, dreading trying to explain their situation to Nicole. Finally, he took a deep breath. "I'm really sorry about that money screwup. Won't happen again."

"It already did." Her voice was tight.

"What do you mean?"

She rolled her eyes. "Well, the card worked at the Jewel, so I tried to use it for gas. But I got another 'Card not acknowledged' notice."

Greg gritted his teeth. "But I told you—"

"Don't put this back on me, Greg Singer!" She spat the words out. "I only had eight dollars and some change with me. I'd end up having to go back for more gas within a couple of days. I shouldn't have to put up with any of this garbage!" She glared at him. "I want you to tell me what's going on!"

"All right, all right." He raised both hands in surrender. "Look, the card was maxed out. I'm sorry. It won't happen again."

"Maxed out? How can that be? We have a $5,000 limit. Haven't you been paying our bill?"

"Of course I have. We haven't missed any payments. But it's been a little tight since . . . since I lost my job. So I've only paid the minimum. And we were already carrying a pretty heavy balance, you know, for a lot of stuff you bought over the last few months. It's not just me. Anyway, we just hit the ceiling. But like I said, I'm gonna get it fixed."

Nicole eyed him suspiciously. "You said that on the phone. But it was barely enough to get the groceries. I didn't think we were *that* close to our maximum. And if we are, how were you able to activate it again so quickly?"

"Well . . ." Greg took a deep breath, not knowing how she would respond. "My TopOps account is tied to the credit card, so I just transferred over a hundred."

She gaped at him. "It's connected electronically? You mean, you're using our *credit card* to finance this trading you've been doing?"

"No . . . well, I guess, yes. But it's not the way you make it sound. It's just a convenience. Like today, I was able to quickly transfer that money. That was good, right?" He was an experienced salesman, so why was he having so much trouble selling his wife on this?

"But you're saying"—she narrowed her eyes again—"our credit card is where you got the money to invest in the first place. Right? How much?"

He felt like she was busting him. "Hey, it's not just what I invested. I've earned quite a bit too. Look, in business, you can't make money without spending money. I told you the other day that I put five hundred bucks back into our credit card account to bring down the balance. Remember?"

"Yeah, but now we're maxed out, so what happened? Did you withdraw it all again, plus . . . plus more?"

Greg felt as he was being backed into a corner. "Well, I had to . . . but it's just temporary." He leaned forward, trying to regain control of the conversation. "The thing is, Nicole, you need to understand business. Any business requires startup capital. I mean, a half million wouldn't be unusual to launch a small business. But I'm trying to get up and running with our own money rather than take out some big business loan. You don't seem to appreciate that."

Nicole folded her hands in her lap and looked down at them for several moments as though she'd been duly chastised. Maybe he was making some headway after all . . . but then he saw her head begin to slowly turn from side to side. "Greg, I don't know what's going on, but . . . I can't live like this. I've tried to support you, and I've even tried to do part-time work at home like you asked. But I can't take the tension. I need a break." She stood up. "I'm going to take the kids and go over to Mom's for a while . . . until you get this thing fully straightened out."

"What? But I did straighten it out. It was just a glitch, my mistake. Won't happen again, I promise."

"It's not straightened out. There wasn't even enough money for gas. Do what you need to do, but I still need a break."

Greg followed her out of the living room and down the hall. "Nicole, you can't leave. We're married—for better or worse, remember? It's not Christian."

She turned and glared at him, hand on hip. "It's not like I'm not divorcing you, Greg." Though the way she said it, it hit him as if it might actually come to that. "I just need some space. Look, you want to do the macho thing and run the whole show? Okay, do it. Maybe you've got a great plan that's going to make you rich like you want, but maybe you don't. All I'm saying is I can't stay in the middle of this chaos. When it's over, let me know."

Turning on her heel, she left him standing alone in the hallway.

Greg didn't really believe she'd leave, but for the next hour he heard Nicole rustling around in their bedroom and then going upstairs, packing bags for herself and the kids. When Nate and Becky came home just before 4 p.m.—just as the trading on TopOps closed—he heard her tell them they were going over to Grandma's for a sleepover.

A short while later Nicole stood once more in the archway into the living room. Her face was puffy and blotchy, mascara smeared a little under one eye. "There's some lasagna from last week in the freezer and leftover chicken soup in the fridge. Since I shopped this morning, most things are stocked up." She stopped, and then in a husky voice added, "I'll call."

"Nicole!" he said as she headed for the back door. "Wait!"

She came back around the corner, but the look on her face told him she wasn't going to change her mind. Still, he had to try. "You don't need to do this, you know. We can work it out."

"Yeah, maybe, but not right now. I'm taking the car." And then she was gone.

He wanted to run after her. Instead, he paced around the living room trying to resist the anger that surged within him. The old Kenny Rogers song started playing in his mind: *"You picked a fine time to leave me, Lucille . . ."* He rewound the refrain a couple of times, inserting Nicole's name. It fit. Was that what was really happening? Was his wife making her move for that playboy, that Lincoln Paddock, just setting it up so it seemed like his fault?

Greg wasn't much of a country-music fan, but that song said it all and left him thoroughly intoxicated with self-pity. Refreshing his computer screen, he searched the Web until he found the lyrics so he could sing all the words. But the end of the third verse stopped him. The man "Lucille" was trying to pick up in the bar walked away from the affair rather than break up a family.

Were there men with a conscience? Did Lincoln Paddock have one?

Greg wasn't about to beg, but he wasn't going to let Paddock have his wife without a fight. Maybe he should go down to that McMansion right now and say . . . something! Going out onto the front porch, he looked down the block to the dead-end where Paddock's big house sat. No cars out front. Probably not home.

But for the next hour, he cast around in his mind for what he might say that could make a difference. No . . . what he really needed to do was win his wife back. He had to make himself more attractive than Paddock. And given how upset Nicole had gotten about the maxed-out credit card and the financial stress, he figured the first thing he needed to do was make her feel more secure.

And to Greg's way of thinking, that meant success . . . money!

Settling down at the computer once more, he called up his credit card account on the Web, but was shocked to see the notice: "Overdrawn, insufficient funds. Call your bank immediately." What? His balance showed that he owed $5,046.96. How could that be? After adding a hundred, there should have been about $138 available, and Nicole said her groceries were $93 something.

He quickly calculated the numbers in his head. There should still be about $40 left. So why was he overdrawn? He could understand why Nicole wasn't approved at the gas pump. They probably anticipated a full tank costing fifty or sixty bucks. But where did these extra charges come from that put them past their limit?

Greg looked more closely at the activity on his card. Today was the billing cycle, which meant the bank had added $56.20 of interest to the total he owed. That put him over the $5,000 limit—and for that infraction, they'd also charged an additional fee of $35, a penalty that would be added again and again, a notice said, for every day he remained over his limit.

"Argh!" he screamed and grabbed his head.

Okay, okay, he needed to think. Fast. He checked the time. Five-thirty. Was the bank still open? He called the number on the screen. It rang and rang until finally someone answered, "One moment please. Can I put you on hold?" which she did before Greg had a chance to protest.

Finally, after ten minutes of scratchy elevator music, the woman came on the line asking him how she could help. He had to go through a whole process of confirming his identity—password, mother's maiden name, etc.—before he could explain the situation and ask his question. "What can I do?"

"Mr. Singer, you're going to have to pay off your credit card before we can release it for use again."

"I understand. But we've got some money in our checking account. Can you transfer that over by phone to free this up?"

"We'll need a check for that, and I'd suggest you come in tomorrow morning rather than mail it so you don't continue to incur those daily fees until it arrives."

"Okay, I can do that." Except it suddenly hit Greg that Nicole had the car. "But just to be sure, if I get there before ten, how much would I need? I mean, by what time tomorrow would another fee kick in?" Greg knew the checking account was low, but he thought there'd be enough to bring the balance down and give him a little margin with which to work TopOps.

"Well, if you got here right away, I think I could get special approval to wave tomorrow's fee. So, let me check . . ." She was quiet for a moment. "That would be $5,046.96."

"What? No, no, that's the whole amount I owe. I understand, but I'm just asking how much I need to release the card."

"That *is* the amount. You see, Mr. Singer, once you've gone over your limit, the bank doesn't want to risk that continuing to happen. So the policy is, you need to clear the entire balance on the card. It was all there in your credit card agreement when you signed up."

Greg was choking on air. He'd never read the fine print, and every few months they changed it anyway, sending out some amendment. But she couldn't be right. It didn't make any sense. "I've never heard of a policy like that! What's the point of it?"

"I admit it catches some people by surprise, but ever since the recession, banks have instituted a number of new policies designed to help people avoid getting overwhelmed by debt. It's for the good of the customers. This is just one of those changes that's really in your own best interest, Mr. Singer."

"But I . . . I can't pay the whole thing off just like that. And until I do, you're going to keep hitting me with these daily penalties. That's not fair!"

"Oh, you misunderstood. As soon as you bring it down below your $5,000 limit, the daily fees stop. But the card can't be activated for new charges until it's fully paid off."

"All right!" Greg managed, then slammed down the phone. He couldn't talk to the woman any more. He felt as if his life was snowballing. He could've dealt with any problem by itself, but it was one thing on top of another, each compounding the other.

What was he going to do? He didn't have that kind of money. And he didn't know anyone he could borrow it from either—not his parents, certainly not Nicole's mother. And the only asset they had was the Cherokee—they'd be lucky to get that much for it. Besides, they had to have a car. And of course the house, but you can't sell a house overnight—

He stopped midthought. Wait just a minute. They had a preapproved home equity line of credit. In fact, it had come with a checkbook.

That was it! That's all he needed to do!

Chapter 38

NICOLE WOKE UP IN HER CHILDHOOD BED. Her mom hadn't preserved the room like some shrine, but it still had her old single bed, bookcase, desk, and posters of Sting and Michael Jackson. She was amazed her mother left them up. She'd never approved of either singer and probably wasn't even aware of Michael's death. She'd been right: They hadn't made very good role models. Nicole took them down before Becky and Nate started asking who they were.

Sticking her toes into her slippers, she slipped down to the basement where the kids were "camping out" with sleeping bags on air mattresses in the old family room—at least that's what they used to call it when Nicole was growing up. Now it was mostly used for storage, except the old orange shag carpet still covered the floor and the familiar olive green rocker gathered dust in the corner. The kids had left the purple lava lamp on all night, giving the place a 1970s feel—even before Nicole's time. But the kids always liked to play down there when they came over to Grandma's house.

Nicole smiled at the lumps inside the sleeping bags and decided not to wake them.

"There's fresh coffee in the pot," her mother said when Nicole came back upstairs. Frida Lillquist broke an egg into the blueberry muffin batter she was mixing. "Whatever gave you the idea of having a sleepover? I think it's delightful. You know, as much as I love us living so close, that's one thing I miss. Whenever we get together it's usually for such short periods of time. I'm tempted to keep you here for a week! There are so many things we could do with the kids."

"Well, you might get the chance." Nicole shrugged, as though her coming or staying was nothing more than a whim.

"Remember when we drove to Boston to see my folks when you were nine or ten? That was such a great vacation. We stayed two weeks."

"Yeah, that was fun." Nicole stirred cream and sugar into her coffee, then leaned against the counter where her mother was working. "Say, Mom, is that old computer Greg set up for you still working?"

"Ha, I have no idea. Oh my, I think the last time I used it was last year before Christmas. Never could stand that awful squeal every time I tried to connect it to the telephone—that modem thingy. And it didn't make any sense to me. If I want to talk to someone, I can always call them. If I want to write someone, my mailman still comes around every day except Sunday. I couldn't see the use of the thing. Though I know the younger generation loves them."

"Mmm, right. Well, you wouldn't mind if I tried using it, would you?"

"Of course not. It's still in that back storage closet, right where Greg set it up. But you'll have to move the coats. I hung them back up in there."

Nicole sighed with relief. The large storage closet, converted to an office cubicle, had nothing but a small table as a computer desk and a straight-backed chair. A bare bulb hung down from above, and she'd have to leave the door open in order to pull the chair out and sit in it. But it would work. Nicole had brought the thumb drive with the project on it she'd been doing for Lincoln. She was almost finished. And as soon as she could turn it in, she could get paid. It was obvious she couldn't depend on Greg for cash at this point.

"There," her mother said, sliding the muffin tin into the oven. "Should be ready in about thirty minutes. Are the kids awake yet?"

It took half an hour to get Becky and Nate up, dressed, and to the table, but after breakfast, her mother got the kids to help clean up the kitchen—why were they so much more cooperative at Grandma's house than at home?—while Nicole turned on the old computer. It booted up as expected, and there was one USB port in the back for her thumb drive. But she couldn't get the computer to open the files on it. She spent an hour fiddling with it and finally gave up. By then her mother and the kids were playing a board game, so she used her mom's phone to call the law office.

When she finally got through to Lincoln Paddock, she apologized for bothering him. "But I was wondering if I could come into the office this afternoon. I'm almost finished with the project you gave me. I think I could finish it up in a few hours, but I'm not able to use my computer right now."

"No problem. Do you need me to send a ride for you?"

"No, no. I'm actually at my mother's house right now, and it's easy to catch the 'L' from here."

"Sure. See you when you get here then."

Nicole arrived at the offices of Watkins, Ellis, and Katz about eleven thirty, and after checking in with Lincoln, she got to work at the desk Delores Krenshaw assigned her to. Shortly after noon, she heard a knock on the edge of her cubicle and turned to see Lincoln leaning casually against the opening, arms folded, a broad grin on his face.

"Hey, neighbor, time for lunch. Let's go down to Sopraffina's. It's on me."

She tried to keep her voice nonchalant. "What's Sopraffina?"

"Just a little Italian café on street level of this building. We might still beat the rush."

She felt herself blush as she shook her head, aware of her blonde hair swinging. "I don't know. Just got here. Better get some work done first."

"Don't worry about it. Besides there's something I need to talk to you about, and I have meetings all afternoon. Come on."

Nicole grabbed her purse and followed him.

Five minutes later they were seated at a table for two in a back corner. After they'd ordered the minestrone soup and two of their gourmet sandwiches, he smiled at her. "I hope it's worked out for you doing this legal work, but—okay, I'm a little embarrassed to ask you, but I really need some help at my limo company. Is there any chance you could come in for the next few days? It's mostly just clerical and accounting stuff, but my usual staff person is on sick leave, and it would be such a big help."

Nicole didn't even blink before saying yes. She went home that afternoon with a check from the law firm that would pay for necessities for the next few days plus a card from Lincoln's limo service with the number she was to call for a ride the next day. Lincoln had insisted. "There's no good place to park around there, and you'd have to take the 'L' and two busses. I'll just send a car. Call when you're ready in the morning, and someone will pick you up in thirty minutes."

How considerate! What would it be like working at his limo offices? Would he be there during the day? As rough as things had become with Greg, it was more than a comfort to know she had other options . . . in fact, tantalizing that someone else, someone as attractive as Lincoln Paddock, valued her.

Greg got up early Thursday, showered, shaved, and ate a light breakfast, ready for the day. He wasn't going to let Nicole's absence get him down. Even though she hadn't phoned yesterday like she'd promised. Wait . . . she said she'd call, but she hadn't actually said when. Maybe he should call her.

No! That would just be a distraction. He had to focus. If he wanted to win back his wife, the key was to get his business on solid footing and straighten out their money. That's what he should concentrate on today and nothing else. In fact, it might be good to not go chasing after her. He didn't want her to think he didn't care, but she had some responsibility in this whole thing, and a little time to cool her heels might help her see it—as long as Lincoln Paddock wasn't part of the picture.

Greg went out on the porch again and looked up the street. The man had a big garage, but it seemed like he always parked one of those Lincoln Town Cars out front. No Town Car this morning though.

Coming back inside, he sat down at his desk and started digging through the file box that had all their mortgage papers in it. He pulled out the folder labeled Home Equity Loan and began reading—the fine print this time.

Two cups of coffee and an hour and a half later, he leaned back in his chair. As far as he could tell, the money was there for his taking, and the interest rates were really great. In 2007, when banks were still encouraging everyone to borrow more money, they'd offered Greg and Nicole this home equity loan. The bank covered the appraisal, and at the time, based on their equity, issued a revolving loan of $28,000 at 4.25 percent interest, one point above prime.

With the recession, Greg had suspected that their little bungalow might have declined below their original purchase price of $350,000. Everyone was saying real estate values had taken a dive. But the bank hadn't retracted the home equity amount. It had sat there unused for three years, and all he had to do was use it.

But he wanted to do his homework. He spent the next hour reviewing all their liabilities. He'd told Nicole that he'd paid all their credit card bills on time—true—but he was behind on three car loan payments, and there was a mortgage payment due, plus two department store credit cards, and some utility bills. All together, to clear the credit card and pay off all their bills, he needed about eight thousand to cover everything. It'd be good to put a couple thousand in the checking account, too, so Nicole would feel secure. Keeping it at round numbers, he figured ten thousand would put them in the clear for everything.

But he wouldn't have any working capital for TopOps unless he started dipping into the credit card again. It sure would be nice to tell Nicole he wasn't doing that any more.

Greg stared out the front window. What if he withdrew all $28,000 and used eighteen of it to launch his business the right way? After all, he'd told Nicole it wasn't uncommon for a business to require half a million to get started. That might be true, though he didn't actually know anyone who'd received that kind of money. And business loans required close scrutiny by the lending agency before they were approved. However, the home equity loan was his money to use as he pleased. If he believed it was a good deal, he was the decision maker.

It felt kind of heady to be stepping into this opportunity in such a serious way. But he was a serious guy. And this move could put everything on solid footing.

Pastor Hanson would be proud of him taking this bold step, thinking positive, thinking big. But maybe he should pray about it too. Greg scrunched his eyes. "Jesus, I'm going to step out in faith, knowing that you desire to prosper me just like you promised to do. I believe it! I claim the blessing, and I'm . . ."

His mind drifted to how he was going to get the money from his bank to TopOps. The online introduction to TopOps website had said you could use a credit card or a wire transfer.

A wire transfer . . . that's what he would do.

On the TopOps website, he found the wire transfer instructions again and jotted down the routing numbers he needed before heading out the back door. *Rats!* Nicole had the Cherokee. Okay . . . Plan B. The bank was less than a mile away. The day was a little muggy and hot, but the cloud cover would help. He could walk and still be there in twenty minutes.

Chapter 39

THE AFRICAN AMERICAN DRIVER of the sleek Town Car looked slightly familiar to Nicole as she slipped into the leather backseat. She glanced up and caught him staring at her in his rearview mirror. He looked away, checking the traffic to the side and then back at her. "I thought you lived up on Beecham Street."

"I do," Nicole said nervously. "I'm just staying down here with my mom for a few days."

"Hmm," the driver said as he pulled away from the curb. "My dad lives on Beecham in that graystone. Harry Bentley. You know him?"

"Really?" That was a coincidence. "A little. He and his wife, Estelle, have been real friendly since they moved into the neighborhood. Estelle especially."

The driver chuckled. "You can say that again. She's my stepmom. I stayed with them for a couple of months in the spring until I got a place of my own."

"I thought I recognized you." She smiled at him, but his eyes were on his driving. "Guess it's a small world, huh?"

"Got that right. You'd be surprised at the people I meet in this job. Of course, my boss lives at the north end of Beecham. That's how I got this job. You been working for him long?"

Nicole didn't really want to talk about Lincoln. "What was your name again?"

"Didn't say, but I'm Rodney, Rodney Bentley." He made a left turn and accelerated down a narrow street.

"Good to meet you, Rodney. I'm Nicole Singer." Then feeling she needed to provide some explanation for being driven to a rendezvous with Rodney's boss, she added, "I've been doing some legal work for Mr. Paddock at his law firm, but it seems he needs some help with his limo business."

"Oh, yeah. Hazel's been out for a week. Surgery, I think, but the office is a mess."

The headquarters for Lincoln Limo proved to be a small warehouse that served as the garage for half a dozen cars, two of them fancy stretch jobs. Rodney pulled in, got out quickly, and politely opened the door for Nicole. He guided her toward the back of the building, zigzagging around other parked cars and three men Nicole took to be drivers who were cleaning and servicing them. The whole place smelled of car polish, oil, tires, and gasoline. Nicole was inclined to hold her breath.

"That's the restroom." Rodney pointed to a door under a set of stairs up to a mezzanine level. "We oughta have a sign on the door, but nobody uses it 'cept the folks who work here. Just lock it when you go in."

Nicole imagined porta-potty quality and smells and determined to avoid it as much as possible.

He pointed to a couple other closed doors. "Those are storerooms for parts and stuff, and that's Joe, our dispatcher."

The open dispatch office under the mezzanine was separated from the rest of the garage by a counter, covered with notebooks and in/out boxes. Inside, under a greenish florescent light, a fat, balding man sat at a desk with three phones and a pedestal microphone. He glanced momentarily away from his small-screen TV at Nicole without registering that he saw her.

"Up here's the business offices," Rodney said as he led her up the steps. "With Hazel gone, I don't think anybody's up here since I didn't see Mr. Paddock's car." He opened a door and flipped the lights.

Though tucked up under the rafters of the warehouse, the suite of offices looked orderly and pleasant, and Nicole noticed they either smelled better or she was becoming used to "garage" odor.

"This is Hazel's office. I'm sure you can use her desk. Through that door"—ajar, but still dark—"is Mr. Paddock's office. He said for you to give him a call when you got here, and he'd tell you what to do. So . . . think you'll be okay?"

Nicole looked at Rodney wide-eyed. How could she know whether she'd be okay?

Apparently Rodney took her look as a yes, because he backed out of the door. "If you need anything, just call. I don't have another fare till three this afternoon, and after that any of the other guys can help you." Turning, he headed down the steps.

Nicole stood in the middle of the office, wondering what she'd gotten herself into. Stepping over to a window along one wall of Hazel's office that looked out over the garage, she watched Rodney walk to his car, speaking casually to some of the other men in the garage.

Since the door between Hazel's office and Lincoln's was partially open, she walked over and tentatively looked inside, flipping on the light. The office was spacious with a large oak desk, a leather executive chair, a couple other nice chairs in front of his desk, and a matching leather sofa along one wall. There was what looked like a functioning gas fireplace, and the two large art prints on the paneled walls were not originals but numbered, nonetheless. Vertical blinds over his window looking out into the garage were turned closed.

"Nice," Nicole mused as she backed out and shut off the light.

But she was here to work. Picking up the phone on Hazel's desk, she dialed Lincoln's number.

"Ah, you're there. Did everything go okay, picking you up and all?"

"No problem. Thanks for the ride." She paused a moment. "So what is it you'd like me to do?"

"Oh, yes. On my desk are two piles of papers . . ." She listened as he outlined what he wanted her to do, grabbing a notepad as he gave her the password to his personal computer. He promised he'd be there within the hour to answer any questions she might have and set her up with the other work that needed doing.

After they hung up, Nicole frowned. Did he mean for her to work in *his* office? Why not at Hazel's desk? She tried the password on Hazel's computer, but nothing happened. Oka-ay. But she felt awkward working in Lincoln's office and on his computer. She was careful not to open programs or files that did not specifically relate to the assignment he'd given her, but she could've gotten into them. He'd given her access to the very heart of his business. If there was anything private or confidential, it was open to her.

Did he trust her that much? What did that say about their relationship?

It was a relief when she heard Lincoln coming up the steps, shouting some encouraging instructions to some of the men down on the floor. Nicole instinctively got up from Lincoln's desk chair and stood awkwardly beside it.

"Ah, there you are." He burst into the office with a flurry. "Here, have a coffee. I just stopped by Starbucks, so they should be hot." He held out the cardboard tray to her. "Cream, sugar?"

"Yes, please. Thank you." She busied herself fixing her coffee, then remained standing as she started to explain what she'd been doing.

"No, no. You sit down." Paddock indicated his executive chair. "You're the one who's working here." He came around the desk and leaned over her as she talked, affirming what she'd been doing, asking a question now and then about some detail. She could smell his aftershave . . . subtle, manly.

"That's great," he said finally, walking around to the front of the desk and sitting down in one of the "visitor" chairs. He leaned back and rested one ankle on the other knee, staring at her a few moments. "Rodney said he picked you up someplace in Andersonville."

It was an obvious question. Nicole looked down at her hands a moment. "Yeah. The kids and I are staying at my mom's for a while." He'd been so trusting of her, opening his computer and business, she wanted to respond with similar trust and tell him what was really going on between her and Greg. "I . . . well, we—Greg and I—are at a bit of a difficult point. I just needed a little space."

Deep lines scored Lincoln's forehead as he stroked his chin. "I'm sorry to hear that."

His sensitivity made her want to tell him everything, but would he think less of her? Still, she really did need to talk to somebody, and before she knew it, she was blurting out the situation. She did her best to not badmouth Greg, but . . . "I know it's not all his fault, but something's got to change. The stress is getting to me. I can't go on this way." Staring into Lincoln's concerned eyes, she imagined him coming around the desk and putting a comforting arm around her shoulders.

When he planted his feet on the floor and leaned forward, she thought for a moment he was going to get up, but all he did was rest his elbows on his knees and steeple his hands to support his chin. "I don't know quite how to express this to you, Nikki, but . . ." He paused, looking down at the floor while she held her breath, anticipating what he might say—what she wanted? what she feared?

When he looked at her again, his eyes glistened. "I had a family like yours once, a beautiful wife and three-year-old son. You and your kids remind me of them, make me long for what I once had."

Nicole's mind raced. What was he saying? Was he hoping to recreate his idyllic family with her? She reigned in her imagination. He hadn't said that. She was foolish to go there.

"Then I made the worst mistake of my life." A cloud passed over his face. "We were having problems. Big ones, little ones, who knows?" He shrugged. "There's no way to compare them to what you and Greg are facing. All I know is they seemed insurmountable at the time. And so, when Annie said she wanted to leave, I just let her go . . . without an objection, really. Guess I thought that's what she deserved or maybe that's what I wanted too." He stopped and turned away, staring blankly at the office wall. "Nothing has brought me more sorrow. And nothing"—his hands made a sweeping gesture of the room around him—"nothing I've accomplished since has replaced it."

Nicole could hardly breathe. Why was he telling her this? She suddenly felt sorry for him, wanted to reach out to him and make it better. Maybe they could be for each other what they both were missing, maybe—

"I would do anything to win her back," Lincoln continued. "But Annie hooked up with some other guy and moved to Atlanta. Now I seldom see my son at all. He's eleven, the very years a boy most needs his dad." He paused and looked seriously at Nicole. "Don't make the same mistake I did."

What? "But I thought . . . since you . . ."

He gave a hollow laugh. "You thought since I partied all the time, I didn't care about family?"

"No, I—I was thinking that maybe we . . ." What was she saying? Had she really thought she and Lincoln could create the family of her fantasies?

Lincoln seemed a bit taken aback. "Oh, Nicole . . . Look, I've admired you and your kids from the first time I saw you. Guess I idealized you, the family I didn't have. Made me want to spend time with your kids—you know, the zoo and stuff. And then when you said you could use some work . . . But, oh man, I'm sorry if I gave you the wrong impression. I mean, I would never want to come between you and your husband. I know what pain that can bring and would never wish it on you or him." He leaned back in his chair as if suddenly spent. "No, no, there's no 'we' in either of our futures."

Nicole turned her face away and bit her lip to keep it from trembling. What a fool she'd made of herself! How could she have done so? She felt naked—not naked beautiful, just naked, exposed, humiliated. How could she have created all those fantasies?

She heard him blow out a breath. "Look, Nicole. I'm sure this is very awkward. All I ever intended was to provide you with some work. I knew Greg was starting his new business, and that's always a rough venture. I just thought . . . And then when you came into the law office, you had the very skills we needed. It was no charity gig. Everyone at the firm thought your work was superb, even old Krenshaw with her cheap perfume."

His little joke gave Nicole the courage to look at him through tears that made the whole room swim.

He cleared his throat. "Hey, I understand. If all this has made our working relationship too awkward, I can pay you for today, and I can find someone else to help me out until Hazel gets back."

Nicole sat silently for a long minute, and then swallowed, hoping her voice wouldn't crack. "I don't want to leave you in a lurch here, but . . . maybe it'd be best for now. Perhaps later, if you're open to it, we could talk if there's an opening at the firm. Maybe in a larger setting like that . . ." She stood up and started to gather her things.

Paddock stood up quickly too. "Yeah, that sounds good." He walked her to the outer door of Hazel's office. "Huh. Guess I've been baching it too long, not really thinking how my actions would affect you. So how about we make it a rule: no lunches alone, no rides alone. Would that help?"

Nicole couldn't talk. She just nodded.

"But let me see if Bentley's free—he could take you back to your mom's."

Nicole took a deep breath and shook her head. "Thanks, but . . . no. I can get myself home." She didn't want to talk to Rodney Bentley or Lincoln Paddock or anyone else right now.

Except maybe God. If he was still around and listening.

Chapter 40

Greg sat down with a personal banker that afternoon. He'd put on a shirt and tie, wanting to look professional. The name-plate on the desk said Mike Walker. Glancing at the desk calendar beside it, he noted the date: *Thursday, July 15.* The day all his troubles were going to get squared away. Especially if it was true that accessing his home equity money would be as easy as writing a check.

After entering the account number, the banker clicked a few computer keys, and then looked across his desk at Greg. "You haven't used your home equity before, right?"

"No, we've never had occasion to do so." Greg felt a twinge of resentment at the question. The personal banker looked still in his twenties. What did he know about the complexities of family finance?

"Well, everything looks in order. Do you still have those initial blank checks?"

"Yes, but I actually want to do a couple other things. First of all, I want to pay off our credit card."

"Good idea, especially if you have a large balance and high interest."

It took only a few minutes to complete that transaction before Walker assured Greg the card was now good to go.

Okay. Here goes . . . "The next thing I need is a wire transfer for $18,000."

The banker's eyebrows went up and his head moved back a bit. "That's a piece of change. You know, Mr. Singer, if you're doing a remodeling job on your house, contractors sometimes ask for a 10 to 15 percent deposit, but if the one you're scheduling is asking for the full price upfront, you might get some competitive bids."

Obviously Walker thought the money was going into the house. But Greg had just read the fine print on his home equity contract and hadn't seen any requirement that the money be spent on home improvements. In fact, he'd seen no restrictions at all. But would the bank find some way to tie up the money if Walker knew it was going to TopOps? Greg couldn't think of a quick solution other than to proceed as though this was an entirely normal transaction. "It's not a remodeling job. You can send it here." He passed over a slip of paper with the company's name, address, phone number, bank routing number and account number.

"Hmm, Key West, Florida. So you're not getting a new bathroom." The young man glanced up with a friendly grin. "What's up? You leasing a waterfront villa down there for the winter?"

"Ha, ha, I wish." Greg decided not to say any more.

The banker didn't even flinch, just typed in the information Greg had given him, explained there would be a $30 service fee, printed out a page Greg had to sign, and then handed him a receipt of the transaction.

"How long will it take for that to be transferred?"

Walker glanced up at his clock. "It's not yet three . . . shouldn't take more than thirty minutes to reach the bank. Somebody there waiting for it?"

Greg shrugged. "Oh, one more thing. Could you transfer the remaining amount of our home equity line to our checking account?"

The banker frowned. "And you want to do that because . . ."

"We just have a number of bills we want to clear up. We're reorganizing our finances, and it would simplify everything if we had a single payment rather than several small ones."

"I understand, but that doesn't leave you any margin for an emergency."

Greg bit back a sharp response. This young man really didn't have authority to quiz him on what he planned to do with the money, or a more formal declaration would have already been required. He took a breath and tried to relax. Obviously, Walker thought he had Greg's best interests at heart. "You're right, having an emergency cushion would be nice, but right now this consolidation has higher priority. Know what I'm saying?"

"Of course. Consolidation can be good." The banker did some more work on the computer, had Greg sign another form, and then they shook hands.

It was done!

Greg kept up a good pace on the walk home, hoping to arrive in time to make some serious money that afternoon before trading closed. But his TopOps account still showed a balance of just $51. Almost four o'clock . . . it'd been nearly an hour since he'd sent the transfer. A cold fear gripped him. What if the whole thing was a scam, stringing victims along until they made a large investment, and then stealing their money? No, that couldn't be. The TopOps site hadn't disappeared, and his account was still open showing *he* hadn't been erased. But if the banker was right, the money should be there by now. What was the problem?

Wait . . . the banker had asked if someone would be there waiting for the money. Maybe that was it. Maybe he needed to notify TopOps. He clicked on the *Contact Us* link on the website—and did a double take. TopOps headquarters was in Italy! What? They were located overseas? He swallowed nervously. Wasn't the Mafia in Southern Italy and Sicily? What if the Mafia was running this thing? Somewhere he'd read that they were expanding into Internet fraud.

Okay, calm down, he told himself. After all, the bank he'd sent the money to was located in the U.S. That ought to provide him some protection. Could he get his money back? How many months or years would that take? Greg clicked his way through the screens to the page with the instructions for wire transfers to check that he'd copied the address correctly. And then he noticed an asterisk by the words *Domestic wire transfers.* He scrolled down to the bottom of the page to find the note: *"Bank transfers within the United States will be posted to personal accounts by the next business day after they are received in the respective TopOps bank."*

He read it again, processing the information. So even if his money had safely arrived at the Key West bank, it wouldn't show up in his TopOps account until tomorrow.

Whew! If that was true, he was still okay. But the scare had been so strong it took him half an hour of reassuring himself in order to calm down. Even then, he kept checking his balance.

Walking into the kitchen, he made some fresh coffee. Sliding into the breakfast nook, he took several sips of the strong hot liquid. Time wise, not what he'd hoped for. He'd wanted to call Nicole that evening and tell her everything was cleared up, she could come home now. But maybe he should wait, call her tomorrow when he had even better news.

Greg didn't like these kinds of emotional roller coasters. Maybe he should just walk away from the whole thing.

But he couldn't. He was too far in to quit now.

The bedroom was still dark when Greg woke up the next morning. Something was wrong . . . and then he remembered. The other side of the bed was empty. The whole house was empty. His wife and kids were at her mother's, had been for two nights.

But maybe by this weekend they'd be home. As soon as Nicole knew the credit card had been paid off, that there was money in the checking account, and he was bringing in a healthy income, surely she'd return.

He flopped over, telling himself he should go back to sleep for a couple more hours. But he felt wide awake, his mind racing. Should he get up? Go to work? No . . . Even if the money was there, he couldn't do any trading yet. He tossed and turned, still haunted by the possibility that TopOps was a huge scam. He tried to calm himself down with the notice he'd found on their website that his wire transfer wasn't even scheduled to show up until today.

He needed to think positively. Yes, plan now how he would invest his money wisely. He wouldn't risk investing it all at once. He'd play the market, perhaps with $2,500 bids, at least until he was sure he had the pulse of how the currencies were responding today. And then, once he was sure he had its pulse, he'd make his big move . . . or would it be best to continue with small, measured increments?

Finally, he got up and turned on his computer . . . just to see.

Still only $51 in his account.

Greg took a shower, shaved, and made himself some breakfast. But his stomach was too jittery to handle something even as supposedly soothing as a small bowl of farina, and his reheated coffee from yesterday was bitter in his mouth.

He forced himself to stay away from the computer, but at eight o'clock he figured the Key West bank might be open since its time zone was one hour earlier than Chicago. His hand was shaking when he sat down in front of his computer and clicked the key to refresh the screen that was already logged into his TopOps account.

$18,051.00! It was there, all of it.

Leaning back in the chair, he closed his eyes. "Thank you Jesus! Thank you, thank you, thank you."

Now it was time to get to work!

His stomach still upset from the recent tension, Greg watched the euro/dollar currency graph for several minutes. He needed to be very careful here. This was the day he graduated from dabbler to market player—no not a player but an investor, a shrewd businessman. He would follow his plan with limited bids.

At 8:36 he placed his first $2,500 "Put," predicting that in the next minute the dollar would decline relative to the euro. The seconds ticked by with more tension than he'd felt on any previous bid. But when the timer dinged, the dollar had indeed dropped, and Greg was in the money.

Carefully he recorded his success on a notepad—the time of day, the amount the dollar declined, the value of the euro, and how much he'd won, a cool $1,750 for just one minute of breath-holding tension. Not bad!

He was certain God was with him this morning, but it wouldn't hurt to pray. Greg stopped and thanked God for his success and asked for guidance in his next bid. In that moment, he decided he was going to proceed by faith, not by sight. Wasn't that in the Bible? He scrolled the page up so his balance—now at $19,801—was off the screen where he couldn't see it. He'd record the details of each individual transaction, but let God handle the final results and reward his faith with buckets of prosperity.

This time he placed a $2,500 "Call" on the dollar to increase in value over the euro. Even though the day was already warm for the middle of July, Greg's hands were cold. He wrung them together as he watched the currencies jockey for values. And . . . he won again. And again, he was careful to record the details of his bid and thank God with a brief, heartfelt prayer.

His next bid lost, but Greg took it in stride. He was a seasoned trader by now and knew disappointments came with the territory. He had faith, and—though he didn't look at his balance—he knew he was still in the money. After recording the details, he also prayed again.

After a couple more rounds following this exact routine, Greg chuckled to himself as he took a quick break to make some fresh coffee. He was becoming like those baseball players who followed a precise routine or wore their "winning" pair of socks to increase their luck. Of course, he didn't consider prayer superstition, but what could it hurt to do everything the exact same way? Maybe he did have God's attention.

Fresh coffee in hand, again and again he bid $2,500, recording the results and thanking God whether he won or lost.

Once he reached twenty bids, he checked the time. Two thirty already! Where had the time gone? He stretched, deciding that to remain disciplined, he should treat this like a job, stop and go get some lunch. He'd keep it short, but a lunch break would be important.

Returning fifteen minutes later with a grilled cheese sandwich, a dill pickle spear, and a can of SlowBurn, he decided this would be the right time to check his progress. Watching his balance with every bid might not be exercising his faith, but occasional checks would be wise.

He scrolled down the screen. Wait . . . his balance was down, down to $13,301. How could that be? He thought he'd been winning most of the time—and yet if his balance was correct, he'd been losing. He went over his notes, counting his wins and losses. Exactly ten wins and ten losses. Each win had earned him $1,750, but each loss had cost him $2,125.

This was terrible! Hadn't he prayed each time? Thanked God, win or lose? Where was God? He could have done as well by flipping a coin!

Shoving his chair back, Greg paced around the room, his sandwich forgotten. After a few minutes, he fell to his knees beside the living room couch. "O God, what are you doing to me? I trusted you to prosper me, and now you're destroying me! Why? Why? Maybe you didn't realize it, but I was going to tithe all my earnings. You know I've been doing that faithfully, so why haven't you rewarded me? This isn't fair! And it's not just me. My family is counting on this too. And you know, God, I'll do anything for my family."

Greg stopped. What would be a proof of his faith?

He rolled back on his heels, looking over the top of the couch and out the living room window. Was it faith to back out at the first setback? No, he should go forward, no matter what. Getting up, he returned to his seat at the computer.

Slowly, and very deliberately, he placed one more bid for $2,500 . . . and won!

A smile spread over his face. "Not bad. Thank you, Jesus," he murmured. "And I will definitely give you all the praise and glory. I'll call Pastor Hanson this afternoon and tell him it works." Tears trickled down his cheeks. "Hallelujah! I can feel it, and I believe it! I can feel the presence of the Lord right now! And I'm gonna get my blessing. This is it. This is it. No more waiting!"

Greg's balance was at $15,051. TopOps allowed bids as high as twenty grand. Time to go for it. Greg entered $15,000 for his next bid. But which way—up or down? Call or Put? He watched the ticker as it nudged up and then down and then up again. Overall, it'd been rising all day, but would it do so over the sixty seconds of his next bid? Taking a deep breath, he selected Put for the dollar to fall and waited a moment, his finger above the key that would determine his family's whole fortune.

"O God, here goes!" And he clicked.

The instant his finger hit the key, a blue rectangle flashed on the screen with the warning: *"Your Internet connection has been lost."*

"What? No, no, no!" he yelled. "This can't be happening!"

Chapter 41

Trying to stem his panic, Greg clicked around on his computer screen without anything changing. He tried refreshing his screen, but the blue rectangular notice remained. *O God,* he groaned. Why, when he'd just made a go-for-broke bid? By now, the sixty seconds of his bid had passed. He'd either won or lost—won an additional $10,500 or lost another $12,750!

He tried to console himself with the fact that if he lost, he wouldn't lose everything. But he couldn't afford to lose 85 percent. Having started the day with over $18,000, he'd be down to a mere twenty-three hundred. The reality of all eighteen thousand being borrowed money struck him like a California earthquake. Whether he'd won or lost, he had to know. And he had to know NOW!

He called his Internet service provider, and after entering his ID, a recording informed him they were aware of problems in his area. "Our technicians are doing everything possible to restore your service as soon as possible. Please be patient."

Patient? How could anyone be patient with so much on the line?

Greg paced back and forth in the living room, shoulders hunched, hands jammed in his pockets. He was glad he hadn't told Nicole yet about the money. Maybe she wouldn't have to know . . . and then it struck him. He'd been telling himself the home equity money was his to do with as he pleased, but actually it wasn't. It was borrowed money, a home equity *loan,* secured by his family's home. If he couldn't pay it back, they could actually end up losing their house.

He groaned again. Could this get any worse?

"Get a grip, Greg," he muttered to himself. After all, he still had a 50-50 chance that he'd won the bid.

Every few minutes, he checked his Internet connection or called his ISP, but got the same recorded message . . . until an hour later when the message changed to say they expected the service to be restored within twenty-four hours.

Oh great! Just great! Twenty-four hours of not knowing. He threw his phone across the room and marched through the kitchen, slamming the back door and heading for the alley to walk off his frustration. He gave each garbage can he passed a violent kick and sometimes stopped to pound so hard on their plastic tops with his fists that his hands ached. But just as he got to the end of the alley and was ready to turn the corner that went behind Paddock's oversized house, he heard someone call his name. He looked back.

Harry Bentley was coming up the alley behind him with his black dog. Greg felt mortified. His neighbor was far enough along through the alley that he'd obviously seen several of Greg's tantrums, and now that they'd made eye contact—Harry was giving him a wave—there was no chance to pretend he hadn't seen the man and slip around the corner. Stuffing his trembling hands deep in his pockets, he strolled slowly back toward the older man, resigned to face whatever music his neighbor chose to play.

"Hey, how you doin,' Singer?"

"Uh, okay, I guess. How 'bout you? You off work today?"

"Had a late run last night, so I get comp time today." Harry looked Greg up and down. "But you don't look so happy."

"Oh, I'm good. I'm good."

"No kiddin'?" Harry gestured toward his black Lab who was sniffing each garbage can. "Even Corky knows that's a crock." As if on cue, Corky trotted over, tail wagging, and gave Greg a sniff. "Be straight with me, man. What's up, anyway?"

"Ah, it ain't nothing."

"Of course not. That's why—being such a little thing—you can tell me all of it. Now bleed!"

Greg choked out a laugh, feeling like if he said one more word, he'd end up blubbering like a schoolboy.

"Come on, now." Harry put a hand on Greg's shoulder. "We're just a couple of brothers with different mothers. You can talk to me."

That broke Greg. The idea that a black man would count him as a brother, that their relationship in Christ was greater than history, broke down all his efforts to hide. "I . . . I'm afraid I really screwed up."

"Yeah, we all got a tendency to do that from time to time."

"Ha, not like this, I hope."

"Oh yeah? What?

Greg blurted out a sketchy summary of how he'd worked so hard to make a killing with his bidding, how his wife had walked out on him, and how he just might've dug himself into an impossible pit of debt. Harry listened as the two men slowly strolled around behind Paddock's place, and down the other alley to Bentley's two-flat.

"So you have no idea whether you won or lost, huh?"

Greg shook his head.

"Well, doesn't sound like there's anything you can do about it at the moment. Why don't you come on up for a cup of coffee?"

"Ah nah, I gotta get back, and—"

"And what? You said the Internet's down. Your wife and kids aren't home. Ain't nothin' you can do but pray, and we can do that together—you know, 'where two or three are gathered together'? Besides I got the air on, and it's too hot to stand out here."

Upstairs, sitting at Bentley's kitchen table with a cup of coffee that had turned bitter from sitting in the pot too long, Greg began to shake his head. "I just don't understand it. Don't understand where God is in all this."

"Oh, I reckon he's around, but what'd you have in mind?"

Greg found himself telling Harry how inspiring Pastor Hanson's Sunday messages had been over the last few months, especially since he'd lost his job with Powersports Expos. They'd convinced him a crisis was just an opportunity for God to bless him financially, not just to meet his needs, but to give him an abundance. He recounted several examples Pastor Hanson had offered, including the pastor's own luxurious lifestyle. "If others can end up so outrageously rich, I don't know why I can't make it work for me. But now . . ." Greg's shoulders slumped. Recounting the story aloud to another person made him realize that everything he'd tried since Powersports had been an utter failure.

"Humph!" Harry muttered. "When I was comin' up, they used to say those kind of preachers were fleecin' the flock."

"Oh, I don't know about that." Harry's comment riled Greg. "There are some very wealthy people in that congregation who testify that their prosperity came by applying the very methods the pastor preaches."

Harry shrugged. "And yet, look what it's done for you. You think there might be other people in your same fix?" He leaned forward. "Look, I'm not against wealth honestly earned. God gives each of us different gifts. But it's also possible to manipulate a group of people, even a congregation of poor people, to make a preacher wealthy."

They sat silently for a while. Greg had an uneasy feeling Harry might be right. Sometimes even he'd chaffed under Pastor Hanson's arm-twisting for people to give more and more to the ministry. But he'd always dismissed it because of the promise that God would pay him back many times over. But it hadn't happened.

He finally shrugged and held his hands out, palms up. "So what'd I miss? What'd I do wrong?"

For a long moment, Harry still didn't say anything. Then the older man straightened himself up in his chair. "I want you to know that I do believe in a miracle-working God. He can move mountains or calm storms or make the blind see. That's actually a very personal one for me since I lost my sight awhile back—but that's a story for another day." He waved a dismissive hand. "And because he's a miracle-working God, I know he can take care of you. I've never been to your church, but from the way you describe what your pastor's been teaching, I've seen some of those preachers on TV. And they're right about *some* things. God's a big God. Nothing's too hard for him. He loves us and wants the very best for us. He has a perfect plan for our lives. Also, they're right in saying we can't outgive God. God will provide our every need for the work He's called us to do. But—"

Harry suddenly stood up, frowning at the cup in his hand. "This coffee's terrible. Here, let me throw yours out. We'll make some new."

As Harry went over to the sink and began making fresh coffee, Greg said, "So why won't it work for me?"

"Ah, now there you go. Remember that question, because I think it's a very important question."

While the coffee brewed, Harry returned to his chair and rested his elbows on the table. "You remember when you wanted me to sell that energy drink for you?"

"Yeah, SlowBurn. I'm still a distributor. I could cut you in."

"No. And my reason's the same today as I told you then. If I took up something like that just so I could get rich, I'd be penny wise and pound foolish."

"What do you mean? I didn't understand you then, and I don't now."

Harry chuckled. "My mama used to say that to me. 'Boy, don't you be penny wise an' pound foolish!' What she meant was, when you focus on the small things—the pennies—you can easily overlook the big things to your detriment." Harry raised his eyebrows and nodded toward Greg as if to say, *"Whaddaya think of that?"*

Greg snorted. "Believe me, Harry, I haven't been pinching pennies, and I *have* been focusing on making the big bucks. That's the point. I've been trying to go all out for the prosperity God's supposed to have for me, but I haven't received any of it."

"Uh-huh." Harry got up and went for the coffee. "You mean you haven't been bugging your wife about whether she saved fifty cents on the latest sale?"

"Not at all, never." But she'd still left him. The thought of it stabbed his heart.

"I believe you, because I'm sure you've been focusing on what seems like big things—stuff like a new house, fancy car, nice boat, maybe a couple of cruises every year, and all the bling you can wear. Right?"

Greg shrugged. "I don't go in much for bling, but yeah, I want *real* prosperity. I want to be the head and not the tail, the lender and not the borrower. I want to be on top. That's where I've kept my focus, on the big things."

Harry handed him a mug. "Here's your coffee. I forgot to ask, you take anything in it?"

"A little milk, if you have it."

When Harry returned with the milk and sat down, he repeated Greg's comment. "'Head and not the tail . . . lender and not the borrower.' I seem to remember that's from the Bible, but wasn't that a promise to Israel if they would obey God's commands? But then I'm no theologian, which is why I focus a lot on what Jesus taught, because he was pretty clear when he said, 'Seek first the kingdom of God and His righteousness, and all these things shall be added to you.' That's what I meant about penny wise and pound foolish. All the necessities of life—where you'll live, what you'll eat, the clothes you'll wear—those aren't the pounds. They're actually just the pennies. If you focus on them, you might miss the pounds, the really big stuff."

Greg just sat there bewildered. The things he'd been reaching for certainly didn't seem like pennies. He'd been imagining big-ticket items, things like Pastor Hanson's Escalade or a condo in Florida. But what was Harry saying—that Escalades, thousand-dollar suits, and personal bodyguards shrank to mere "pennies" when compared to the kingdom of God? He had to admit, Jesus clearly placed the kingdom of God and his righteousness at the top—though if asked to define the kingdom of God, he wasn't sure he could do it. Pastor Hanson made it sound like the kingdom of God was kinda like Disneyland with all its riches and glory. But maybe that's not what Jesus meant.

Harry leaned back. "Does any of that make any sense to you?"

Greg sighed. "Yeah, when you put it that way, I guess. But I've still got fifteen grand hanging out there, and if I lose it . . . well, it might seem like small stuff to you, but to me—"

"No, no, no. I know it's not small to you, and it wouldn't be small to me, but it's small to God. Remember, he's a big God. He would have no trouble taking care of you, even if this situation threw you into bankruptcy. Hear what I'm sayin'?"

Greg snorted and shook his head. "Bankruptcy!" He hadn't even thought of that. Was that where he was headed? "I still don't want to go through it."

"None of us would. But remember a few minutes ago when I told you to remember your question, *Why won't it work for me?*"

"Yeah."

"What were you expecting to work?"

"Oh, I don't know. God, prayer, believing in faith—all the stuff Pastor Hanson talks about."

"That's what I thought. But seeking God and his kingdom isn't a program you can *work* like a politician shaking hands to get votes. There may be a connection between faithful and generous giving and God's blessing on our lives, but he's no ATM machine where you can key in a prayer with your 'faith believing' ID and out comes the money. That'd be like me saying, 'I talk with my wife so she'll cook me a good meal.' *Huh*. If she thought that was the only reason I talked to her, she'd let me starve."

Greg laughed, releasing a little nervous tension.

Harry grinned too. "I'm not sayin' God's gonna let you starve. But the reason I talk with my wife is because we have a relationship, and we both want it to grow and deepen. I don't do it to *get* something, even though I know she's gonna take care me because she loves me. Same thing with God. We can't *work* him like a genie. The question, *Why won't it work?* presupposes some kind of a formula or system you can *work*. God's not like that."

Greg heaved a sigh. "Yeah, I hear ya." The truth of what Harry had been saying was sinking in. "But, man, I still don't know what to do. I'm in a pretty big mess right now. Even if I agree that trying to twist God's arm so I could live large wasn't right, I still gotta think about my family and how to keep from losing my house. I don't have a source of income right now, you know."

Harry shook his head. "Can't offer you any easy way out on that. This whole idea that the Christian life is supposed to be Easy Street forgets that some of the people in the Bible who were the most qualified to receive such supposed benefits didn't receive them, at least not in this life. Jesus lived a perfect life of faith, yet he died on a cross. And from what I've read, all his disciples except John were martyred. Fact is, a lot of faithful Christians have suffered down through the ages. No, it's not about ease and luxury. But God did promise to be with us. And he did promise to take care of all those 'penny' things we might need to do his work."

Greg grasped onto Harry's last words. "So you think he's still going to take care of me, even though I've made such a mess of things?"

"Yep, but I don't know how or what that'll mean."

Greg leaned over the table, head in his hands. "I still don't know what to do."

"Well, if Estelle was here, she'd tell us the first thing to do is pray. You okay with that?"

Greg nodded and closed his eyes as he felt Harry's hand on his shoulder. His voice shaking, Greg told God he was sorry he'd made such a mess and asked him to show him what to do to get his family back. Then Harry prayed, asking God to make his presence known to Greg in a powerful way, and especially to restore the relationship between Greg and his wife.

As they got up from the table, Greg said, "Thanks, man. I really appreciate it."

Corky got up from where she'd been lying under the table and walked with them as the two men headed slowly toward the front door. At the top of the stairs leading to the lower level, Harry stopped. "Greg, you keep sayin' that you don't know what to do. I hear ya. That's a man thing. We always feel we gotta do something. But right now, what's done is done, right? As far as you know, no way to undo that bid?"

Greg nodded his head.

"Okay, then here's my suggestion. Don't do anything on your computer until Monday morning—"

"Monday morning!"

"Right. Don't check to see if you lost money or won it. Don't even turn it on. Instead, spend the next three days seeking God and learning to trust him. If you're like me, you'll find a ditch on both sides of that path. Your mind will tend to spin out into fear that you've lost it all. And at other times you'll swerve off the path into hope—an unfounded hope, really—that you're gonna come out of this rich. But I tell ya, man. Resist both. They're just tempting distractions. Just seek God and the confidence that he'll be with you no matter what."

Greg stared at the floor, trying to imagine how he could do that. The man was right about those ditches. Even as he thought about it, Greg vacillated between fear he'd lost it all and euphoria that he'd be on his way to prosperity.

"Look"—Harry interrupted his thoughts—"that was just a suggestion. You go on home and pray about it. Do whatever God tells you to do."

Chapter 42

GREG TRUDGED UP HIS PORCH STEPS and tried the front door. Locked. And he'd gone out without his keys. Which meant he'd left the back door unlocked. Good grief. That was stupid. But as he went around to the back and came in, everything seemed the same as he'd left it—including his computer, which was still running in the living room, the screen saver swirling rainbow colors across the screen.

Harry had said don't even turn the thing on, but . . . it was already on. A touch of the mouse would bring up the TopOps page and perhaps the answer of whether he'd won or lost . . . if the Internet was back up, that was. He reached out . . .

Should he do it?

Greg hesitated. Harry had called his instructions "just a suggestion," not a big word from the Lord, not some law found in Scripture.

He reached out again but stopped. He could just switch the computer off. People lost power to their computers all the time from a storm or tripped breaker switch. It wasn't the way you were supposed to shut down a computer, and you'd lose any unsaved documents. But he didn't have a half-finished document sitting in the computer's memory, nothing to lose. Switching it off would merely mean it'd take a little longer to clean itself up the next time he turned it on.

Why would he do that? Harry said it'd be a chance to seek God and the confidence that God would be with him no matter what. But so what? He could seek God any time. What difference did it make if he knew whether he'd won or lost?

Greg had been trying to exercise faith—faith that God would prosper him big time, and it'd taken a lot of faith. He'd really believed God was going to make him prosperous! But somewhere on the edge of his consciousness, he began to realize that it took a lot of faith to trust God for what he *didn't* know. What was that verse from the book of Hebrews he'd memorized years ago? *"Faith is the substance of things hoped for, the evidence of things not seen."* Wouldn't that apply as equally to his hope for prosperity as it did to the hope that God would walk with him through this crisis?

But suddenly, he saw the difference. One was material wealth—things that would bring pleasure for a time but would ultimately disappear, the kind of treasure Jesus said would rust, be eaten by moths, or get stolen. The other involved a relationship with God, something that could last for eternity.

He could almost hear the voice in his head: *"So Greg, which is more valuable?"*

That's what Harry must've meant when he said all those enticements Pastor Hanson dangled before his listeners—no matter how big they seemed—were mere "pennies" in comparison to the "pounds" of the kingdom of God. One could be seen all around him, tangible, physical, noticeable . . . while the other would remain unseen, a relationship, a confidence in his heart.

Greg walked over to the front window and parted the sheer curtains, looking across the street and up a few houses toward the graystone two-flat he'd left not fifteen minutes before, Harry's words still tumbling around in his head. His neighbor hadn't been downgrading *faith,* hadn't been telling him to "face reality" as though the supernatural was a fantasy. He'd been calling Greg to a higher faith.

Could he do that? Did he believe it? Was it really possible to have the kind of relationship with God that was greater than all Pastor Hanson's promises of cars and boats and big houses?

Greg reached out again, not to the mouse but to the power strip, and switched off the computer.

Friday night was the pits. Greg didn't know what to do with himself. He tried to call Nicole at her mother's, but it went right to an answering machine. "Honey, please give me a call. I'd like to talk to the kids. Are you coming home soon? Just . . . give me a call so we can talk." But both the house phone and his cell remained silent.

What did they usually do Friday nights? Nicole sometimes wanted to get a babysitter and go out, but Greg couldn't remember the last time they'd done that. Not since he'd lost his job at Powersports anyway. Sunday nights they usually had popcorn and root beer floats, and he'd watch a DVD with the kids while Nicole had some personal time. *Man!* He'd even watch *Home Alone* or *The Incredibles* again if the kids were home.

But as it was, he ended up zoning out in front of the tube watching two straight hours of cop shows and reality TV, and then the ten o'clock news before heading for bed. But when Greg woke the next morning, he felt as if he'd been tossing and turning all night. He sat on the edge of the bed, holding his head.

The house was quiet. Too quiet.

Forcing himself to get up, he headed for the kitchen to make coffee. Still in his pajama trousers and T-shirt, he took a mug out onto the back porch. Sipping his coffee, he tried to get a handle on the feelings tugging at his gut. Harry had been right about the temptations he'd face on either side of the path toward simply trusting God to be with him. One moment he had to fight with fear of a devastating financial loss . . . and five minutes later he was still having fantasies of God making him rich—especially if his bid had been right. But the fear had his gut in knots. After all, he'd been the one who got himself into such a desperate financial mess, so perhaps it was his feeling of guilt over such recklessness that pitched him most often into the fear ditch.

The neighborhood was quiet. Saturday morning. People sleeping in. Peaceful . . . But might as well be full of roaring engines and shouts and lawn mowers, for all the turmoil in his head.

Greg pitched the last of his coffee into the yard. He wasn't well acquainted with fear. As he went back into the house to take a shower and get dressed, he tried to remember times in his life when he'd been afraid. There'd been a few—like the bully he finally stood up to in the seventh grade, the tornado that crossed I-55 forcing him to take refuge under an overpass, a knee injury playing football, getting lost while deer hunting in Michigan's Upper Peninsula. Those times usually involved an external threat he could fight.

But this time the fear was rising from within over things he'd caused and now couldn't control, and he didn't know how to ride it through. Its tentacles gripped his heart—not just the possibility he was facing financial ruin, but that he might lose his wife and kids too.

At first he spent much of his energy resisting it, but that seemed to merely feed it, causing it to grow into waves of panic. Every time he went into the living room, he looked at the computer. Certainly by now his Internet was back up, and he could find out what had happened. Even if it was still down, he could go to the Chicago Public Library branch down on Clark Street and do the same thing.

But he resisted. Something was happening inside him by following Harry's plan. Not knowing what else to do, Greg got out his Bible and read a lot of scriptures about fear, about God promising to "never leave or forsake" his people, and about the Holy Spirit whom God sent to be the Comforter.

As the hours passed, he was slowly gaining confidence that maybe God's presence was still with him.

The doorbell rang Saturday afternoon. For a nanosecond Greg's heart leaped. Nicole and the kids? But she wouldn't ring the bell. He opened the door. "Hey." Harry Bentley stood on the porch. "Dropped by to see how you're doing."

The two men sat in the living room and talked. Greg was a little surprised Harry didn't ask whether he'd checked his computer, though it was probably obvious—either he'd be euphoric over a win or devastated by a loss. Instead, Harry started talking about how hard *he'd* found it to be unemployed from the Chicago Police Department, especially when his wife was still working.

"Huh," Greg said, "some people would've considered early retirement a dream option."

"Yeah, I know, but that wasn't me. I was just old enough—startin' to feel my age, you know—that sittin' around even with a pension made me feel useless. Estelle was still working, but who was I? Did anybody need me?" He shrugged. "I volunteered at Manna House, that shelter for women, and that helped some. But when we bought the two-flat and needed a little more income, I took this job with Amtrak—and frankly, Estelle's just as glad I'm not mopin' around the house. Just sayin' I can understand how hard it's been for you since your job ended, and you didn't even have a pension, so of course you need an income. Don't want you to get the idea I disrespect your efforts to launch a business on your own."

"Thanks. Appreciate it." Greg heaved a sigh. "But I'm in so deep, I can't even imagine how I'm gonna dig myself out. You think"—he hated to even say the words—"you think I'll have to declare bankruptcy?"

Harry shrugged. "You don't know how deep you are, do you? Have you looked?"

"No, no, I haven't looked. I'm just talkin' about the bigger question of how I'm gonna support my family."

"You're right about that." Harry nodded thoughtfully. "Can I ask, where was your wife in all this? Did she think this binary options thing was a good idea?"

Ouch! The man didn't mess around. "Never asked her, but I'm sure she didn't. Have to admit she's been skeptical of Pastor Hanson's prosperity teachings all along."

"There you go." Harry slapped his knee. "You have any idea how many jams Estelle's kept me out of? I mean, there's a reason God gave me a helpmate. And there's been a few I've guided her out of too."

"Yeah, but . . . you're still the head of the family, aren't you?"

Harry looked thoughtful for a few moments. "Yeah, though back in the day I used to think that just meant I'm the boss. But since I married Estelle, I see it more as a unique responsibility for the well-being of my family. But that doesn't always mean 'Father Knows Best,' cause I don't. And that's a fact. Take money: Some men know how to handle it. Some women know even better. But usually it takes both."

"I don't get what you're saying."

"Well, take your current situation. Maybe you're usually good with money and business decisions, but for some reason that prosperity teaching distorted your vision on this one. That's why God gave you a wife, to bring some balance."

"But I thought she was wrong, so how was I supposed to be the head if I let her call the shots?"

"That's what I'm tryin' to say, man. Being the head ain't about calling the shots! It's about taking responsibility to act together in unity. Only in the most extreme emergency would it be necessary for you to press ahead against your wife's counsel." Harry leaned forward. "Look, after your job with Powersports ended, how many hours did the two of you sit down and explore what direction you should take next?"

After a few moments of silence, Greg realized Harry's question wasn't rhetorical. He wanted an answer. "None, I guess."

"Uh-huh. Thought so. I'm tellin' you, man, when you really work together for a while, you'll start listening to each other until you come to unity, and you'll begin to defer to one another in certain areas. She'll realize you've got the best wisdom in some areas, and vice versa. When you get to that point, one of you will probably take the lead on certain things while the other acts more as a check to make sure all the angles have been considered. It's still a shared thing. But if you want to be the head, my brother, you need to take responsibility for helping the process to work well."

Greg's head was spinning. He almost wanted to ask Harry to give him some examples about how that worked in his own marriage, but the man was glancing at his watch. "Uh-oh. Didn't mean to stay this long." Harry stood up, stretching a kink out of his back and pulling a tattered, plaid flat cap onto his shaved head. "Um, don't usually have to work on Sundays, but tomorrow I gotta make a special run down to St. Louis and back. I've got Monday morning off though. You, uh, want me to come by when you get ready to fire up your computer and see where you sit?"

"Oh, you don't need to do that," Greg said hastily. He wasn't sure he wanted a witness to his downfall.

"I know, but I'm willing."

Greg hesitated, then nodded his head slowly. "Well, yeah . . . yeah. I'd appreciate that. About nine?"

"I'll be here."

✧ ✧ ✧ ✧

The emptiness of the house descended upon Greg once again after Harry left. He wanted to call Nicole again, but it was a nice day . . . she and the kids might be out. He waited until after supper, then dialed the house number. Her mother answered, and after going to get Nicole, she came back on the line to say Nicole was busy getting the kids ready for bed.

"Could you have her call me when she's done?"

"Of course. You doing okay all alone there? Sorry to monopolize the kids, but we're having such a good time."

"Glad you're having a good time." Didn't sound like Mom Lillquist was aware of the tension between Nicole and him. "Well, just have her call me."

It was nine thirty before his phone rang.

"Hello, Greg. Mom said you wanted me to call."

Gosh, it was good to hear her voice. "Yeah, thanks, honey. Just checking in. You and the kids doing okay?"

"We're fine." But her voice was flat.

"Good." He hesitated. "Listen, Nicole, we've got a lot of things to talk about. I . . . I've made some pretty big mistakes that I need to tell you about. When are you coming back?"

"I'm not sure Greg. What is it you're wanting to say?"

"I'd rather do it in person." He paused, but she didn't respond. "You going to church tomorrow?"

"Yeah, with Mom. How about you?"

"Ha! You got the car, remember? But it doesn't matter. I think I need to take a break from the Victorious Living Center."

"Really?" For the first time he heard some interest in her voice.

"Yeah, that's part of what I want to talk to you about. So when can we get together?"

"I . . . I'm not sure. Tomorrow's not good. We've got plans all day. Maybe Monday afternoon."

Monday. Felt like a long time to wait, but he'd know the lay of the land by then. "Okay. I'll be in touch."

To his surprise, Greg slept well that night and got up late Sunday morning. The waves of panic had become less frequent and had mostly flattened into ripples of anticipating the hard work he knew lay ahead of him—the work of resolving things with Nicole and the work of straightening out their money situation. And Harry was right—it was time to begin thinking of it as *their* money, not just *his* money. But he realized she might think it was a cop-out. He'd created a mess, and oh sure, *now* he was willing to include her in the cleanup.

No, he wanted to learn how to work with her more mutually, wanted to include her in the decisions from the outset. If only she'd give him a chance.

Greg toasted a bagel, buttered it, and then took the bagel, a mug of coffee, and his Bible out on the front porch to take advantage of the mild upper-seventies before the temperature hiked up into the nineties that afternoon. Yesterday when he'd been looking up those verses about fear, he came across one in Romans 8 that he wanted to think about some more. He read it over again several times: "Those who are led by the Spirit of God are sons of God. For you did not receive a spirit that makes you a slave again to fear . . . The Spirit himself testifies with our spirit that we are God's children."

The Spirit himself testifies with our spirit that we are God's children . . .

That was what was happening to him. Something new, something different—something important—was happening within his own spirit. He was experiencing a sense of God's presence with him in a way he'd never known before.

How strange that it was within the storm that he was finding the most peace.

Greg wasn't sure how long he sat out on the porch, his thoughts sometimes resembling brief prayers—if he could call them that. More like just talking to God in his head. But the midday heat eventually drove him back into his air-conditioned house. He hesitated at the arched doorway into the living room. The computer sat in the corner . . .

No. He'd promised Bentley he wasn't going to look at TopOps until they did it together on Monday morning. He needed something else to keep him busy. Maybe he should do some organizing in the garage. The place barely had room for the Cherokee ever since he'd stored all those cases of SlowBurn in there, and he couldn't even get to his tools.

But good grief! It was already nearly two! He should get something to eat.

Half an hour later Greg lugged a box fan out to the garage, plugged it in, and then stood in the middle of the floor, scratching his head. Where to start? That stack of cases in front of his tool chest, good as any. But as he grabbed the first one he noticed something he'd scrawled on it with a black marker . . . a name.

"Destin." On that box and on the whole stack.

A pang shot through his gut. He'd been so focused on trying to make a killing on TopOps, he hadn't even thought about Destin Jasper all week. How was he doing? Had the younger one even come home from the hospital yet?

But it wasn't like he could call and ask. His face flushed as he remembered Jared Jasper's finger in his face, practically accusing him of getting his boys shot for trying to sell SlowBurn on that rough corner.

Jasper's last words flashed through his mind. *"My kid used his college money to buy that junk from you. The least you could do is buy it back, ya know!"*

Greg swallowed. That was exactly what he needed to do. And if he was going to "clean house," Jared and Destin were a couple of people he needed to speak to. He headed for the side door. No time like the present. Better do it before he talked himself out of it.

As he came around the side of the house to the front walk, he noticed the Jaspers' white minivan pulling into a parking space in front of their house, probably returning the family from church. He headed up the street. "Hey Jared," he called, just as his neighbor started up his steps. "You got a minute? You too, Destin."

Destin, who was navigating the walk on his crutches, swiveled to look at him. Jared paused on the steps and looked up at his wife who was entering the house. She glanced back at him and shook her head as if in warning.

Greg approached, but stopped a few feet from father and son. "I . . . I owe you both an apology for having pressured you to sell more of that SlowBurn, Destin. That wasn't right. In fact, when you said you were using your college money to buy inventory, I should have stopped you right there."

Jared had come back down the steps and stood beside his son, his face unreadable. Destin shrugged. "That's okay, Mr. Singer. I shouldn't have done that without talking to my folks."

Greg wondered if Jared was going to tell him to bug off. "I had no idea where you'd be going to try and sell it, but I certainly was pushing you. So . . ." He swallowed. "I bear some of the responsibility for you getting shot, and I'm real sorry."

"Aw, no, Mr. Singer. I shoulda known that was a rough corner."

Jared finally spoke. "Appreciate what you're saying, Singer." The father laid a hand on his son's shoulder. "Truth is, I should've been more on top of things myself. I've been too busy, but that's changing."

Wasn't what Greg had expected to hear. "Uh, still . . . about all that inventory you still have in my garage, Destin. I'm willing to buy it back. In reality, you're not likely to sell it"—he waved a hand at the boy's crutches and laughed nervously—"and it's too much for any one person to drink."

"We'd appreciate that, Singer." Jared extended his hand. "I'm sorry for going off on you the other day."

They shook hands. Destin untangled his hand from his crutch and shook Greg's hand as well.

Greg headed home with a lighter step. Couldn't believe he'd offered to buy back Destin's cases of SlowBurn when he still didn't know if he'd gone in the hole big time at TopOps. Still, it was the right thing to do. He'd find a way to do it somehow. *Seeking first the kingdom . . .*

He glanced across the street at the graystone two-flat where the Bentleys and Mrs. Krakowski lived. The old woman had given away the case of SlowBurn she'd taken so there wasn't anything to buy back. But he should at least apologize to her for trying to drag her into his get-rich scheme the next time he saw her.

Chapter 43

WHATEVER MADE HIM AGREE TO WAIT until nine o'clock on Monday to check his TopOps account? That'd be ten on the East Coast. But Greg guessed it didn't matter. The whole weekend had been a lesson in patience. Waiting on the Lord . . .

The doorbell rang at a quarter to nine. "Hope you don't mind me being a little early," Harry said when Greg opened the door. "Thought we oughta start with some prayer. And coffee. You got any?"

Greg grinned wryly. "Just made a fresh pot."

"Good."

After Greg poured coffee—Harry took his black—they settled on either side of the kitchen nook table. "How you doin'?" Harry asked.

"Pretty good. I'm feeling nervous, but I think I've gotten over the fear. Mostly just anxious to find out what's next." Greg paused for a moment. "You know, you were right about me needing to find a peaceful place with the Lord. I can already tell that knowing God's gonna be with us, knowing he's gonna see us through no matter what happens is more important than how things turn out with TopOps."

Harry nodded. "Yeah, I think that's part of seeking first the kingdom. You wanna pray?"

Greg felt a bit awkward praying aloud—almost like having to learn a new prayer language—but he thanked God for giving him a new focus, for revealing the presence of his Spirit, and bringing him peace. Harry then asked God's blessing on Greg and his family no matter what happened with the money. The older man looked up after the *amen*. "Ready to go face the music?"

"Yeah, let's do it."

The computer seemed to take unusually long to boot up and connect to the Internet, but when they got to the TopOps site, Greg entered his ID and password, and then looked sideways at Harry before hitting the return key. "Here goes!"

Harry nodded.

Greg stared at the top of his account page. The balance showed $15,051.

"What? How can that be? That's what I had before my last bid!" He refreshed the page again just to make sure it wasn't showing old information from his computer's cache memory. Still said $15,051. Plus, the top of the page showed today's date and time: 10:13 A.M., Eastern Daylight Time. It was a live page.

Greg threw out his hands. "It's all there! I don't understand. According to this, I didn't lose anything . . . didn't win anything either. Nothing happened!" He turned to Harry, eyes wide and mouth agape. "I can't believe it. You think . . . you think God saved me?"

Harry chuckled. "Yeah, I think he did, Singer. I think he saved your butt."

"But how . . . wait, the connection must've broken an instant before I hit the 'Start Bid' button. But I sure thought I submitted it. I'm positive . . ."

"I think the finger of God was a little faster than yours."

Greg blew out a long breath. "Incredible. That's awesome." His eye caught the notepad on which he'd been keeping detailed records of his bids. "Hey, I wonder . . ." He picked it up.

"What're you doing?"

"I took notes on the exact time when I submitted every bid, even the one that crashed. See this graph on the screen? I can scroll it back to that exact time three days ago and see whether I would have won or lost—"

"Wait a minute, Greg. Are you sure you want to do that? God *saved* you. Isn't that enough? Don't you think the information you'd find by looking back might be one of those ditches we talked about on either side of the path? If he saved you from a loss, you might be elated. But if you would've won, how you gonna feel then? You gonna think God cheated you? Either way, man, you might be chasing pennies."

Greg leaned back in his chair and studied the computer screen. Bentley had a point. He tapped his balance on the screen. "You're right. This is a miracle. But it's not the biggest miracle."

Harry raised an eyebrow.

"I think . . . I think God did this to show me he hasn't forsaken me, that he's right here with me, taking care of us. That's where I need to keep my focus—on the pounds, like you said. The important things."

Harry slapped his knee. "That's what I'm sayin', brother. God is good, all the time!"

Awe held them in silence for several minutes, and then Harry said, "So you're done with the bidding stuff, right?"

"Oh yeah, no more of that for me. I'm through."

"But you did lose some money, didn't you? How do you feel about that?"

"I don't know. Let me see." Greg did some quick math on his notepad. "Looks like I lost about $3,600 to TopOps, plus I got charged a bank fee of $35 for going over on my credit card limit, and it cost me $30 to wire our home equity money to TopOps. Probably'll cost the same to get it back. Altogether, looks like I'm almost thirty-seven hundred bucks in the hole, plus I'll be paying interest on that home equity money until I get it paid off."

"But at least you can put the fifteen grand back, right?"

"Yeah. But . . ." Greg tossed his pencil. "I still feel terrible. Here I am out of a job, and I just blew a wad, a real wad, plus the weeks I've spent trying to make SlowBurn work."

Harry nodded. "Okay, that's bad—but not nearly as bad as it might've been. Might take a while, but you can dig yourself out of thirty-seven hundred dollars of debt. Gotta admit, I'm not much of a money manager myself, but Peter Douglass is a pretty sharp businessman. I bet he'd be willing to help you and Nicole put a plan together, make a real budget."

"Ha, ha. I notice you included Nicole. Yeah, I'll do that, and include her too."

"Of course, to make any plan work, you'll need a job. Got any ideas?"

"Nah. I scoured the Chicago area before I got into SlowBurn, even looked out of state. Didn't find anything . . . wait a minute!"

Greg felt like he'd just been slapped upside the head. How could he forget? "A guy I know at Potawatomi Watercraft called me a week ago. Said they had an opening up on the Chain o' Lakes. I never called him back because the salary wasn't what I was making at Powersports, and I was so high on the TopOps thing. But it wasn't a bad offer."

Harry threw up his hands. "There you go! Let's send up a prayer that the position's still available—and then you make that call."

Nicole was so nervous about talking to Greg that she didn't even bring the kids with her when she came back to the house to see him Monday afternoon. What was he so desperate to talk to her about? And what should she say to him?

The scene in Lincoln Paddock's limo office had been more than embarrassing. It left her feeling guilty, like maybe she needed to confess something to Greg. But that'd leave her in a weak position, more vulnerable that ever if Greg ended up bowling her over with some new scheme for getting rich. She couldn't take any more of that, especially if meant him continuing to isolate himself in his own little world with no consideration for her and her needs.

At least Lincoln cared about her.

Or did he? She'd imagined his kindness meant he was attracted to her, but then he'd rejected her not-so-subtle advances, blaming it on his "moral standards" because she was married. Huh. What a claim for a playboy. It had to be her. She felt more insecure than ever. How had she ever let herself get to the point of even thinking about leaving her husband? It's not what she believed. It's not what she thought she'd ever do. But there she'd been, seriously on the brink!

And it'd been Greg who nearly pushed her over the edge. Yet when he called the other night, he said he'd made some big mistakes. Well, that was new! And he'd said he was taking a break from Victorious Living Center. Perhaps there was some hope.

Only the screen door was closed when she stepped onto the porch. This was her home, but after being gone for five days, she felt so much like a visitor that she almost pushed the doorbell.

"Greg?" she called as she opened the screen door and stepped in.

"Hey, hon, back here." His voice came from the kitchen. She peeked into the living room before heading for the back of the house, surprised to see that the computer was off.

He grinned at her as she came into the kitchen. "I made some iced tea. Want some?"

"Sure. Is it sweet?"

"A little. Just the way you like it, I think." He handed her a frosty glass. "Uh, you mind if we go out back and sit in the lawn chairs under the tree? At least it's not too hot today. Weatherman even said it might rain a little at some point."

Nicole followed her husband into the yard wondering what all his solicitude was about. Was he buttering her up for something? He had a notebook under his arm.

Nicole sipped her tea as they sat in the shade, avoiding his eyes . . . though she could see him looking down at his hands, his tea forgotten, as though he was the one who was nervous. Finally he blew out a big breath. "I don't know how to tell you this, Nikki, but I—I've made some pretty big mistakes lately . . . and the biggest one has been shutting you out of my life. I didn't mean to, but I was feeling desperate after losing my job, and I bought into some wrong ideas about getting rich quick. I knew you were skeptical, so I started cutting you out and doing everything by myself. Wanted to show you I knew what I was doing. But . . . that led to some pretty big mistakes."

Nicole frowned. She knew SlowBurn hadn't been making much money, otherwise Greg would've bragged about it more. Then the TopOps venture had come up recently, and he'd been so enthusiastic.

She heard his voice get husky and glanced at him. With tears in his eyes, Greg explained that he'd drained their home equity line of credit, and had nearly lost it all.

"*What?*" Nicole couldn't believe her ears. "You drained our home equity line of credit? For that . . . that online gambling you've been doing?"

She wanted to scream. She didn't want to hear any more. No wonder he was confessing. He'd better confess! He'd ruined them!

"Nicole, please listen . . ."

It took her several moments after he explained how God had protected him from losing it all before the implications sank in. She finally found her voice. "So we didn't lose it all, but you risked it all . . . is that what you're telling me?"

He nodded soberly. "Yes. That's what I did, and if God hadn't pulled my butt out of the fire, I'd be nothing but a burnt-out cinder right now."

Nicole buried her face in her hands, unable to trust herself to speak. She wanted to give full vent to the rage she felt toward Greg right then . . . but at the same time, she recognized God's obvious mercy in the midst of his stupidity—to him, to her, to their family. *Well, let God be merciful. I'll give him the outrage and anger he deserves.*

But one little thing restrained her wrath. She deserved some wrath too.

"I do have some good news," Greg said, interrupting her imagined tirade. "I got a job offer."

She looked at him, rolling her eyes. Now what? Another crazy scheme?

"No, no. It's a real job with an actual salary." Greg described the offer from Potawatomi Watercraft and how he'd just called back to confirm that it was still open. "I could begin tomorrow, but I told Roger I needed to talk it over with you first."

She raised an eyebrow at him.

"I'm serious, Nicole. I—I've been talking to Harry Bentley across the street. He's a real down-to-earth guy. He helped me see I've been making a mess by acting like the Lone Ranger. I was ignoring your discomfort with Pastor Hanson's prosperity messages and didn't include you in any of the decisions I was making. Harry told me how he and Estelle try to work together as a team. That's . . . that's what I want too." Her husband reached out and touched her on the arm. "I need you, Nikki. I need your perspective. Probably wouldn't be in this mess if I'd included you in in the first place. Guess I'm asking if you'll forgive me and give me another chance."

Nicole hardly knew how to respond. Even though she knew Greg loved her and the kids, he'd always prided himself on being "head of the family," basically making most decisions on his own.

But what if he was serious? She asked some pointed questions, and he admitted he didn't have many answers. "I know we need some help, Nikki. Financially and otherwise. Harry said there's a guy in his men's group who might be able to help us set up a budget so we can dig our way out of this debt. But I want us to do it together."

Together. Wasn't that what she'd always wanted?

A breeze ruffled the leaves of the tree over their heads as they started listing what they already knew were their fixed expenses and what Greg *reasonably* believed he could earn at Potawatomi, given the fact that part would be commission. "I was also thinking," he added, "if that doesn't cut it, maybe you could go back to work—for a while, at least, if that's something you'd want to do. You said there might be a more permanent position at Lincoln Paddock's law firm."

Nicole suddenly felt slightly dizzy as Greg chattered on about realizing she might need a break from homeschooling, and maybe they could set up a plan with her mom or Tabby Jasper to watch the kids after school every day. "Guess I've been selfish expecting you to stay home full time when you're trained as a paralegal," he said.

Finally, Nicole found her voice. "I—I don't think working for Lincoln Paddock would be such a wise thing."

"You don't? But I thought—"

"Because . . ." How could she say it? It was almost too much. "Because you had some concerns about me working for him, and . . . and you weren't completely off base."

Greg's face suddenly clouded. "What? Did he hit on you?" He rose from his chair and stomped around for a moment. "I'm gonna rearrange that . . . that jerk's face! I knew he was a cad."

Nicole held up her hand. "No, no. He's not a cad. You don't have to worry about him. In fact, he was the one who suggested that we not have any lunches alone, no rides in his limos."

Greg stopped and stared at her. "What do you mean? Has something happened already?"

"Honey, please sit down." Nicole had no idea how much to tell Greg. She didn't want to destroy the miracle in their relationship that had been happening in the last hour—but would it be just as destructive to live with secrets? She sucked in a deep breath and let it out. "Greg, remember before we got married, when we talked to the pastor at my mom's church?"

He made a face. "You mean that one-shot counseling session?"

"Yeah. He hardly even named the challenges we had to deal with in our first year of marriage. But he did ask one useful question. He asked whether either of us had been sexually involved with anyone else. He said we didn't need to name names or share details but that neither of us should be surprised if something ever came up in the future."

"Yeah, I remember. I told you about that one spring break in college with the girl I was going with for a while. We never took our clothes off, but it wasn't good. You seemed able to handle that, and I have to admit, I was glad I told you." But Greg still looked wary.

Nicole nodded. "I'd like to do the same thing here. Mr. Paddock has not made a pass at me. There's been no touching, no words of endearment. But I . . . I was feeling lonely, and he was so kind to me and the kids, I began thinking the grass might be greener on the other side of the fence." She swallowed. "Is that enough?"

Greg stared into his glass of iced tea as if digesting what she was saying. "Just thinkin'? No touching? No secret rendezvous? And he wasn't hitting on you?"

"No. Just my fantasies, and I'm not very proud of them."

Greg was silent for several long moments. Then . . . "Guess I can handle that. I appreciate you telling me." He stared into his glass some more. "Sounds like I bear responsibility for not being the kind of husband you needed me to be." Greg reached for her hand. "I'm sorry, Nikki. Really sorry about that. Guess we may need some help to build up our relationship—but I don't think I'm going to ask Pastor Hanson. Maybe the Bentleys can recommend someone. I'm willing to do that."

Nicole stared at their hands, bridging the space between them. "Me too," she whispered. "I'd really like that. And maybe I can find a job someplace else."

They sat silently for a while, just holding hands, the warm breeze caressing them gently. Nicole felt too full to say anything.

But finally she realized it was getting late. "Guess I better go rescue Mom." She started to get up.

Greg gripped her hand and held her back. "Honey, let's both go rescue your mom and pick up the kids. Together."

Nicole smiled and nodded, no longer hiding the tears that were slipping down her cheeks. It was time to come home.

THE END

Book Club Discussion Questions for *Pound Foolish*

1. If you were walking in the rain with your children, what things would influence whether you accepted a ride from someone you knew lived on your block? What does that say about how well you know your neighbors?

2. What was happening in Greg and Nicole's relationship that caused Nicole to feel disconnected and unappreciated? Has that ever occurred to someone you know? Why didn't Greg's attempt to take the family on a vacation "restore some peace to the ol' *hacienda*" as he hoped it would?

3. Pastor Hanson continually used scripture in his messages. In fact, he bolstered his authority by quoting scripture for nearly every point he made. Why then was Nicole uncomfortable with his views? Describe a time when someone's use of scripture has caused you to be uncomfortable.

4. When Chuck Hastings told Greg he was going to close down Powersports Expos, he said, "All I ask is that you not mention this news, and I mean not to *anyone*." Greg felt betrayed and thought his boss hadn't done everything he could have done to keep the business going. Why did Greg want to speak to his clients before his boss did? How would you have handled the situation?

5. Why did Greg conclude that getting laid off by Powersports might actually be an opportunity for a more prosperous future? How did that view influence how he proceeded?

6. Describe a time when you or someone close to you got laid off and how you responded to that situation. How might a more realistic view of your situation have changed what you did next?

7. Greg told Nicole they needed to look at their situation right, "You know, with faith. . . . Our faith will bring God's blessing, just like it did to Abraham." What is the role of faith in a situation like this? Why wasn't Nicole encouraged by Greg's faith?

8. When Greg expressed suspicion and jealousy over Lincoln Paddock's attention to Nicole and the kids, she bristled. What would have been a better response, first by Greg and then by Nicole?

9. Greg looked hard for a new job before jumping on SlowBurn. One might say it was the only thing he could find. But what might have told him it still wasn't a good idea?

10. With SlowBurn not bringing in any income, why did Greg consider an even riskier venture with TopOps?

11. Do you agree with how Harry Bentley applied the adage, "penny wise and pound foolish," to Jesus' words, "Seek first the kingdom of God and His righteousness, and all these things shall be added to you."? How have you found that to be true in your life?

12. God saved Greg from his foolishness, though his actions were not without consequences. Describe a time in your life when you or someone you know experienced something similar. How were you able to learn from that?

Acknowledgements

Special thanks to **John Loeks**, our son's father-in-law, whose company sponsors numerous boat and sport shows and gave me insight into that industry.

Many thanks to **Jennifer Stair**, who has edited many of the novels that make up the "Yada Yada world" and remembers details about our characters that we've forgotten! Thanks, Jen, for dropping everything to edit *Pound Foolish* in spite of your busy schedule.

Thanks, too, to **Janelle Schneider** (fellow author and friend), **Michelle Redding, Lelia Austin**, and **Krista Johnson** for your willingness to proofread the edited manuscript on a tight deadline, as well as offering many helpful questions and comments. Add another star to your crowns!

SlowBurn is modeled after actual multi-level marketing companies that continually recruit representatives looking to live the "high life," and **TopOps** accurately reflects binary options trading that can entrap anyone on the web. As for the theological promises of **Pastor Hanson**, all too many TV preachers get rich off of people they seduce to "seed" into their ministries.

Neta and Dave

Excerpt from *Snowmageddon*
Book 5 of Windy City Neighbors series

Chapter 1

Bzzzzzzzz!!

Estelle Bentley's head jerked up. Wha ... what? She must've dozed off. Was someone at the door? Lands sake, what time was it? She glanced at her watch. Three-fifteen . . . too early for DaShawn to be home from school. Besides, the boy had his own house key. Who could it be? Maybe the postal carrier. Whoever. Umph. Guess she better go see who it was.

Hefting herself out of the overstuffed chair in the living room, Estelle padded in her house slippers down the stairs of the two-flat she and Harry owned, past their tenant Mattie Krakowski's door on the right, and pulled open the outside door.

The front stoop was empty.

She peered into the mailbox marked "Bentley." Nothing there either.

Hmph. Whoever it was didn't even give a body time to get to the door.

Annoyed at having to reclimb the stairs for no good reason, Estelle muttered all the way into the kitchen at the back of their second floor apartment. DaShawn would be home soon anyway, might as well fix him a snack. He'd be wanting something sweet, especially if he smelled the—

Estelle's eyes flew wide open! Her cake! In the oven! That buzzer hadn't been the front door. It was the oven timer, set to go off at . . . oh, good Lord! Don't let Michelle Jasper's birthday cake be burned!

Grabbing two potholders, Estelle pulled open the oven door and hauled out the Bundt pan holding the lemon pudding cake she'd put in an hour ago. She eyed it critically. Golden brown on top ... slightly pulled away from the sides ... hmm. So far so good. A few more minutes in the oven hadn't seemed to hurt it after all.

The round Bundt cake had cooled and was sitting regally in the center of the kitchen table, a lemon-sugar sauce dripping prettily down its sides, when she heard her step-grandson pounding up the front stairs. "Hey Gram!" Thirteen-year-old DaShawn Bentley came breezing into the kitchen, tossed his backpack into a kitchen chair, and pulled open the refrigerator door. "We got any milk? Oh, see it." The slender black teenager pulled out the plastic jug, got himself a glass from the cupboard, filled it, and chugged down the milk in one long draught. "Ah, that's good."

Estelle, meanwhile, stood with one hand on her hip and one hand leaning on the back of a kitchen chair. "Well, hello to you too, young man. Where's my sugar?"

DaShawn grinned as he wiped his milk moustache off with the back of his hand. "Oh, sorry. I was just so thirsty." He gave his step-grandmother an awkward hug and plopped into a kitchen chair—and then spied the cake. "Oh, man. Lemon cake! Can I have a piece?" He reached out a finger as if to take a taste then and there but pulled it back when Estelle slapped his hand.

"You let that cake be, DaShawn Bentley, if you want any food to eat in this house before the sun comes up tomorrow." Estelle snatched the cake plate off the table and whisked it into a far corner of the kitchen counter. "It's Sister Michelle Jasper's birthday today—Miz Jasper to you, don't you forget—an' I'm takin' this cake over to help 'em celebrate."

"Can I come? When you gonna go over? Miz Jasper is Tavis and Tabby's mama anyway. I know they'd want me to come too."

Estelle hid a smile. She'd planned for all of them to go across the street to the Jaspers with the cake—her and Harry and DaShawn. Had even told Michelle's husband she wanted to make a cake since he was working all day out at the airport, and he'd said, "Only if you and Harry and DaShawn come along to help us eat it."

But all she said now was, "Hmph. We'll see 'bout that if you eat your supper."

DaShawn settled for an apple from the fridge, then headed for the back door with his basketball.

"Where you goin'?" she asked, thinking the boy's "short Afro" was in need of a trim. Hadn't they agreed on two inches, no longer?

"Just gonna shoot some hoops. Tavis said he's comin' over."

Estelle frowned. "Wait just a minute. His mama told me the doctor said Tavis isn't supposed to play sports this fall, and school just started three days ago. Don't you go helpin' that child break doctor's orders. Lord, Lord, that boy's still not a hundred percent after gettin' himself shot this summer."

DaShawn rolled his eyes. "Oh, Gram. Shootin' some hoops in the alley ain't gonna hurt Tavis. He's pretty much healed up. Says the doc just didn't want him runnin' himself all ragged up an' down the gym—that kinda thing."

Estelle folded her arms across her ample chest and tapped her foot. "Well ... you hold off long enough for me to check with his mama. If she say okay, then okay."

DaShawn rolled his eyes again, but plopped down in a chair while Estelle used the kitchen phone to call Michelle Jasper's work number at Bridges Family Services. It was tempting to say, "Happy birthday!" when her neighbor answered, but since the cake was a surprise, she kept her query to whether Tavis was allowed to shoot baskets behind the Bentley garage.

"All right." Estelle hung up the phone. "His mama says he can play for about twenty minutes. Just shootin' though. No runnin' around, you hear me?"

DaShawn grabbed his ball. "Thanks, Gram." And he was out the back door and down the outside stairs. A few minutes later she could hear the thump thump thump of the ball on the alley pavement and the indistinct voices of the two boys.

"Thank you, Jesus, that boy gonna be okay," she breathed. It'd been nothing short of heart-stopping when the two Jasper boys—Destin and Tavis—got shot back in July by some gangbangers who mistook them for drug-sellin' wannabees, when all they were doing was trying to make some money selling an energy drink.

Well. Harry and Corky would be home soon. She better get supper on so they could eat right away and have time to skedaddle over to the Jaspers with dessert—'specially if Harry wanted to take Corky for her evening constitutional before they went over. Couldn't blame the dog. Working security at the Amtrak station downtown wasn't the best place to let a dog trained to sniff out drugs do some free sniffing and running around.

Estelle pulled out a frying pan, and then eyed her lemon creation on the counter. Might be a good thing to hide that cake or she'd be slapping Harry's hands from taking a slice too.

Sign up at
www.daveneta.com
to receive an announcement of the release of
Snowmageddon.

CPSIA information can be obtained at www.ICGtesting.com
Printed in the USA
LVOW11s1600040815

448798LV00001B/147/P